se

'Two days too long,' said Harry, then, to her astonishment, leaned forward, slipped an arm about her waist and kissed her.

'There!' he said. 'I've been dyin' to do that since I first saw you. You don't know what torments I've gone through, darlin', thinkin' you might have passed out of my life without knowing' how much you've touched me.'

'Touched you?' Clare said. 'I never laid a finger – '

'In the heart, in the heart,' Harry said, with a hint of irritation that Clare failed to detect. 'You're the loveliest girl I've ever seen . . .'

'I'm not lovely,' Clare said. 'I'm not – '

He touched her lips with a forefinger that tasted of tobacco. 'Hush,' he said, 'or I'll have to kiss you again just to prove my point.'

Her lips were moist, her throat dry. She felt as if she had stepped out of the privy into a dream.

Harry Fairfield was by no means the first man to flatter her but he was the first who had ever kissed her as if he meant it.

Also by Jessica Stirling

The Spoiled Earth
The Hiring Fair
The Dark Pasture

The Deep Well at Noon
The Blue Evening Gone
The Gates of Midnight

Treasures on Earth
Creature Comforts
Hearts of Gold

The Good Provider
The Asking Price

The Penny Wedding
The Marrying Kind

The Island Wife
The Wind from the Hills
The Strawberry Season

The Workhouse Girl

Prized Possessions
Sisters Three
Wives at War

The Piper's Tune
Shamrock Green
The Captive Heart

One True Love
The Haldanes (*as Caroline Crosby*)

About the Author

Born in Glasgow, Jessica Stirling is the author of more than twenty heartwarming novels, many with Scottish backgrounds.

JESSICA STIRLING

Blessings in Disguise

HODDER

First published in Great Britain in 2006 by Hodder & Stoughton
A division of Hodder Headline

A Hodder paperback

1

All characters in this publication are fictitious and any resemblance
to real persons, living or dead, is purely coincidental.

A CIP catalogue record for this title is available from the British Library.

ISBN 978 0 340 83491 6
ISBN 0 340 83491 9

Typeset in Plantin by Hewer Text UK Ltd, Edinburgh
Printed and bound in the UK by CPI Mackays, Chatham ME5 8TD

Hodder Headline's policy is to use papers that are natural, renewable
and recyclable products and made from wood grown in sustainable forests.
The logging and manufacturing processes are expected to conform
to the environmental regulations of the country of origin.

Hodder & Stoughton Ltd
A division of Hodder Headline
338 Euston Road
London NW1 3BH

CONTENTS

PART ONE

New Beginnings

I

As a rule Mrs Cissie Cassidy had no truck with the Irish, particularly those reprobates who occupied the crumbling tenements north of Riverside Road. In fact, the widow Cassidy had a 'down' on most immigrant sons of Erin and the reason for her prejudice was not hard to find.

If you ventured the length of Salamanca Street past Paddy Maizie's pub to the drab little burial ground behind St Kentigern's you would discover there a grave marked not by marble or granite but by a slab of indeterminate mineral that may, or may not, have been slate; a stone smeared with pigeon droppings and so stained by a decade of fogs, frosts and sour Scottish rains that it resembled the tomb of an ancient warrior and not the last resting place of Eamon O'Connor Cassidy, who had died in the spring of 1864.

They said it was his heart, that wide-open Irish heart, big as all Killarney, that had burst with the strain of the digging, but it was drink not digging that had done for him and even now, ten years on, Cissie was still mad at herself for having run off to Glasgow with a useless Irish charmer, still fizzing at Eamon for boozing himself into an early grave and leaving her childless, penniless and teetering on the verge of fifty.

One windy evening in early March Mrs Cassidy came scuttling up Salamanca Street from Kennedy's bakery where she worked in the kitchen behind the shop. She had learned to cook at her mother's knee and, one way or another, had been at it ever since.

The high point in her culinary career had been half a year of service in the Royal Restaurant, but the stifling heat in the Royal's kitchens had undermined her health and one night, while helping to prepare a wedding dinner, she had fainted dead away and had shed what had existed of little Cassidy number four, just as she had shed his predecessors, after which she had been fit for nothing but staying at home and looking after Eamon.

Soon after Eamon's death, however, Mr Belfer had found her a job at the bakery and now, in Kennedy's airy kitchen, she bored her workmates stiff with tales of high life in Glasgow's posh West End. But of all the little Cassidys or, rather, their absence, she said nothing, for her failure to carry a child to full term was nobody's business but her own.

March then, in the evening: the wind plastered her skirts to her calves and tugged mischievously at her bonnet, while little Mrs Cassidy clung to the large cardboard box within which nestled three meat pies.

When she rounded the corner into Salamanca Street a particularly boisterous gust of wind whipped off her bonnet and before she could recover her balance an unfamiliar voice said, 'Allow me, missus,' and a hand as big as a soup tureen placed the bonnet back on her head.

The stranger was young, a great giant of a man with shoulders as broad as a roof beam, an open face, all chin and brow, and smiling brown eyes. He wore a short-jacket suit and a chequered cap, but no muffler. His bare throat rose from his collar as thick and smooth as a marble column.

'Where did you spring from?' Cissie asked.

'From the deck o' the *Rose o' Tralee*,' the young man told her. 'Sprung as quick as me legs would carry me, for I was mighty glad to set foot on dry land after a perilous voyage on the bosom o' the deep.'

'You're Irish,' Cissie said.

'That I am. Nolan McKenna at your service.'

'An Irishman an' – I'll stake my life on it – a digger.'

'A digger for sure,' Nolan McKenna said, 'or about to be so.'

It was on the tip of Cissie's tongue to inform him that she had once been married to a digger but, in spite of the stranger's size and easy air, he was Irish and she'd had enough of handsome Irishmen to last a lifetime.

He leaned towards her, and said, 'What is that lovely smell? By Gar, what *have* you got in that box?'

'My supper.'

'We could be doin' with a bite o' supper,' Nolan McKenna admitted. 'Fact is, we ha'n't had much since yesterday, a crust o' bread bein' the best o' it. Maybe you could be directin' us to where we could find a cheap bit o' tuck, since us poor travellers ain't got our bearin's yet.'

'*Us* poor travellers?' Cissie said. 'Have you brought the family with you?'

'Aye, all the family God has spared me.' He jerked his thumb at two girls who huddled, shivering, against the weeping brick wall. 'Me sisters – for what they're worth. Come on, girls, say "How Do" to the pretty lady.'

The streets of Glasgow were littered with dirty little waifs, some as sharp as carpet tacks, others as dumb as oxen. The McKenna sisters appeared clean, however, and, Mrs Cassidy noted, had shoes with buckles, and trimmed shawls.

The smaller one even had a big straw bonnet decorated with silk ribbons and paper flowers that she held by her side as if she was embarrassed to be attached to such a frippery.

She advanced towards Cissie with quick, mincing steps and so resembled an elf or a fairy that when the wind gusted again Cissie was tempted to drop the box and grab the child just to stop her being swirled off into the sky.

'This is Evie,' Nolan McKenna said. 'The other 'un is Clare.'

'Well, well,' said Mrs Cassidy, quite nonplussed. 'Well, well, well.'

They weren't children after all, Cissie realised, but might even be as old as seventeen or eighteen. Crouching over her bundle, the one called Clare nodded a sulky sort of greeting.

'This kind lady will be tellin' us where we can find our supper.' Nolan McKenna paused. 'Before we start searchin' for Eamon again.'

Cissie Cassidy's heart leaped into her throat and a sharp little pain trickled down the length of her breastbone.

'Eamon?' she said.

'Our uncle Eamon,' Evie informed her.

'Lots of Irishmen called Eamon in these parts.' Cissie Cassidy just managed to keep the squeak out of her voice. 'Did – does this particular Eamon have another name?'

'Cassidy,' Evie said. 'Eamon O'Connor Cassidy. He's me mam's long-lost brother who shipped to Glasgow many years ago an' has not been heard of since. Mam's last words, whispered with her dyin' breath, were, "Find Uncle Eamon; he'll see you right." '

'Are you from Killarney?'

'Aye, Killarney.' Evie's blue eyes filled with tears. 'I'm wishin' I was back there now with Mam still alive, the stew pot bubblin' on the fire like it was before the blight took off the tatie crop an' we lost the tithe.'

Sniffing and wiping her nose on her cuff, she fought back tears. Her sister shuffled up behind her and patted her on the shoulder, saying, in a curiously flat voice, 'There, there, Evie, when we find Uncle Eamon, he'll look after us till we get back on our feet.'

The pies were growing colder by the minute. Mr Belfer would boil a pan of water to heat his up and Mr Macpherson would give his a minute or two on a tin plate on the hob. Why was she fretting about pies when Eamon's nephew and nieces were standing before her? Killarney, though? She had never heard of a sister in Killarney. Eamon had steadfastly refused to discuss what lay behind him in Ireland, except to brag about an older brother who'd been hanged in Dublin for killing a man in a dispute over wages.

'If you haven't heard from your uncle in umpteen years,' she said, 'why have you come to Glasgow to look for him?'

'Had a letter,' said Evie promptly.

'Who had – you?'

'Me mam.'

'Where is it then?' said Cissie Cassidy. 'Let me see this letter.'

'Can't,' said Evie.

'Why not?'

'It went.'

'Went? Went where?' said Cissie.

'Up in smoke,' said Evie.

'An' what did this letter what went up in smoke say?'

'Said he was wed to lovely woman an' had a house in the Riverside.'

'When was the letter sent?'

'Years ago, long years ago,' said Evie.

'Ten years or more,' said Clare.

'Sure an' I was no more than six years old at the time,' Evie went on, 'but I remember the gladness it brought me mam.'

'The wife,' Cissie said, 'did he mention his wife's name?'

'No name,' said Nolan.

'Or if there was, we've forgot.' Clare glanced at her brother. 'I told you, Nolly, it's a needle in a haystack. He could be gone, our man, shifted on somewhere else for all we know.'

'Aye, a miracle it will be,' said Evie, 'if ever we find him.'

'Supper an' a dry bed for the night will be miracle enough for me.' Nolan McKenna sighed. 'Well, lady, you've listened patient to our story an' it's none o' your blame we're lost, so we'll be goin' on our way. Come on, girls, hoist up your bundles. There's nothin' to keep us here.'

And against her better judgement, Cissie Cassidy said, 'Wait.'

They followed the woman across Salamanca Street to a tall smoke-blackened tenement separated from its neighbours by a broad lane.

Father Fingle, at the Catholic Mission, had told them that most of the old properties in the Riverside ward were owned by the Blackstock brothers and that rooms were rented out by the week or month, complete with bedding and a few sticks of furniture.

'Wait here,' Mrs Cassidy said.

'Can we not be comin' in?' said Evie.

'Not till I have spoke with Mr Belfer,' the woman said.

'Mr Belfer? Who's Mr Belfer?'

'He collects our rents an' takes care o' us in a general way.'

'His word is law, is it?' said Evie.

'It is,' Mrs Cassidy said.

'Is there a privy inside?' Clare asked.

'There's a closet on the bottom landing,' said Mrs Cassidy, adding, proudly, 'kept so clean in our buildin' you could eat your dinner off the floor.'

'Well, I've no dinner to eat,' said Evie, 'but I do need to pee.'

'You'll just have to hold it in,' the widow said. 'Mr Belfer doesn't like strangers usin' our facilities.'

Evie might have put up more of an argument if Nolan hadn't prodded her with his elbow, warning her to keep a clamp on her tongue. She was just weary enough to obey. Cork to Greenock at one shilling a head and all the bread you could eat, so the handbill promised. The bread had turned out to be mouldy and she had heaved most of it over the side before the voyage was half over. She felt now as if she had been travelling forever, forever hungry.

'Go an' speak to your man,' Evie said. 'We'll wait here.'

'I'll be quick as I can,' the woman promised and, reaching up, pinched Evie's cheek reassuringly, then vanished into the close.

'Do you think she swallowed it?' Nolan asked.

'O' course she did,' said Evie.

'Hook, line and sinker,' said Clare.

Mr Benjamin Belfer held the tin box by a string and dipped it into a simmering saucepan on top of the coal stove, which, in Cissie's opinion, was no way to treat a fine meat pie.

'There,' he said, 'the matter of my dinner is took care of, or almost so. What's here?' From a shelf above the stove he plucked a little clock and peered at the dial. 'Four minutes should do it nicely. Now' – he rubbed his hands – 'now, my dear Mrs Cassidy, what's all this about long-lost Irish cousins turnin' up on our doorstep?'

'They aren't cousins,' Cissie said, 'and I don't know if they *are* long-lost, leastways not *my* long-lost, nor Eamon's neither.'

'Did Eamon ever mention a sister in Killarney?'

'Never.'

'It was a long time ago.'

'It was,' Cissie agreed. 'He says he's a digger.'

'Who does?'

'The young man. Says he's come to Glasgow in search of work.'

'Oh, they all say that,' said Mr Belfer. 'Question is, what are you goin' to do with them?'

'If they are Eamon's kin it would be cruel to turn them away.'

'It was a long time ago,' said Mr Belfer again, adding, 'whichever side of the Irish Sea you hale from. I recommend caution.'

'I can't leave them out in the street.'

'Well, you can't bring them in here.' Mr Belfer held up both hands as if to ward off uncharitable thoughts. 'Even if I had space, which I haven't, there's precious stuff in my apartment an' they might not be honest.'

'It's the young girls I'm worried about.'

'Young girls?' Mr Belfer scrutinised the clock. 'Aye, well, I suppose it's different when unfledged females are involved. How young?'

'Sixteen or seventeen, thereabouts.'

'Hmm,' said Mr Belfer thoughtfully.

'Now Mr Coker's gone an' you don't have another tenant waitin' for his room, I wondered if you might not . . .'

'Rent them Coker's room, with poor Mr Coker hardly cold in his grave? That's a great deal to ask of me, Mrs Cassidy.'

'It's only till I find out if they are who they say they are.'

'How do you propose to do that?'

'I don't know,' Cissie admitted.

Dusk enclosed the tenement like wet flannel.

The drizzle had thickened into rain and the eaves high overhead had already begun to overflow. Across the lane Mr McLean would be grooming the cart-horses and old Mrs McLean, in the garret above the stables, would be counting her cats to make sure they were all safe and sound.

Cissie said, '*I'll* pay for the room.'

'You?' Mr Belfer said. 'Why would you do that?'

'If,' said Mrs Cassidy, 'they *are* Eamon's family, they're my family too.'

'It strikes me, my dear Mrs Cassidy, that you've rubbed along without family thus far an' you might find it less troublesome to rub along without them for a considerable while longer.'

'How much is the rent?'

'For the night?' Mr Belfer shrugged. 'One shillin'.'

'Fuel for the fire?'

'There's coal in the bucket.'

'Lamp oil?'

'The room's furnished well enough for homeless Irish,' said Mr Belfer testily. 'I got bills posted, you know, so if some respectable gent turns up in search o' lodgings out the Irish go, rain or no rain, females or no females.'

'One shillin',' said Cissie, 'is awful expensive.'

She had hoped for more help from Mr Belfer who had been her friend, almost her only friend, for the past ten years. He took his responsibilities as Mr Blackstock's collection agent very seriously, though, and would do nothing, not even in the name of friendship, to jeopardise his position.

'Take it or leave it, Mrs Cassidy. If they aren't happy let them slope up town an' see if they can find a charity bed in a hostel.' He consulted the clock, lifted the pan and set it on the table. 'It's my dinner time – past it – so if you want to fetch them in, do it now for I'll require to give them scrutiny before I rent them one o' my rooms even for a single night. Understood?'

'Understood,' said Cissie Cassidy meekly.

The moment Evie clapped eyes on Benjamin Belfer she knew he was the sort of man who liked to have everything his own way.

He stood in the doorway, arms folded. His ruddy cheeks, portly belly and striped waistcoat made him look more like a squire than a caretaker. His legs were short and somewhat bowed but he was a potent enough creature for a man of his years, his years, she reckoned, being in the region of forty.

The room was stuffed with furniture. There was linoleum on the floor, a half-sized dresser glinting with china, a table with a cloth on it, and a coal-fired stove. The mantelshelf was laden with a variety of trinkets of the sort that only a man would keep.

If there was a wife she had made no mark upon Mr Belfer's apartment which, in Evie's opinion, had 'bachelor' written all over it. She primped her hair and wondered if it would be better to simper or sob.

'Now then,' Mr Belfer began, 'Mrs Cassidy informs me you think you've a claim on her hospitality.' He spoke in a deliberate manner as if he assumed that, being Irish, they wouldn't understand Queen's English. 'It is incumbent upon me,' he continued, 'to ensure that you are what you say you are an' aren't pullin' the wool over this dear lady's eyes.'

'We have no business with this lady, sir,' said Evie. 'Our business is with Eamon Cassidy – an' he's provin' uncommon hard to find.'

The widow was clearly intimidated by the caretaker and more than willing to let him make the running.

'For your information,' Mr Belfer said, 'Eamon Cassidy is no more.'

'No more?' said Nolan. 'Sure an' what does that mean?'

'Means dead,' said Mr Belfer.

'Dead!' Clare exclaimed. 'Poor Uncle Eamon's dead!'

'May his soul rest in peace,' said Nolan, and crossed himself.

Evie let her lip tremble and her eyes water but Benjamin Belfer had already turned his attention to her sister.

'You, lass,' he said, 'what's your name?'

'Clare, sir.'

'Clare what, sir?'

'Clare McKenna.'

'Step out where I can see you better.'

Clare stepped into the lamplight.

'Where do you come from?' Mr Belfer said.

'Killarney, sir,' said Clare. 'In Ireland.'

Mr Belfer apparently took her to be an object of truth as well as beauty, a part Clare played to perfection. He said, 'Do you know what happens to young ladies who tell lies?'

'They burn in hell, sir.'

'Well, I wouldn't say hell.' Mr Belfer stepped back. 'No, not hell exactly since the concept of hell is out o' favour these days.' He drew in breath and released it slowly. 'I mean, young ladies who lie are always found out. Do you hear me, Clare McKenna, they are found out and punished. Tell me the truth now, are you really the niece of Eamon Cassidy, late of the town of Killarney?'

'Not the town of Killarney, sir,' said Clare. 'We come from a place on the Lakes on the flank of Bull Mountains. Me mam's family too, since we were all together, Cassidys and McKennas, tendin' those same scant acres.'

Benjamin Belfer might resemble a country squire, Evie thought, but he surely knew nothing of country matters or of the geography of Ireland.

'Tell them, Mr Belfer,' Mrs Cassidy said. 'Do tell them.'

Mr Belfer thrust a hand into his trouser pocket, his knuckles bulging inside the cloth. He was almost convinced, Evie realised, almost there.

He said, 'This was Eamon Cassidy's last place of residence. You can't find the man, for the man has gone to his Maker, but this kind lady, who has already took you to her bosom, is his widow; in a word, your aunt.'

'Oh!' Clare clasped her hands together. 'Our aunt, our dear, dead uncle's wife. Oh what a happy chance that is, sure is it not now?'

Then in a gesture that seemed entirely spontaneous, she sank to her knees and hugged the bewildered little widow who, like it or not, was about to inherit a brand-new family and all the trouble that went with it.

2

The old adage 'No smoke without fire' did not apply to the handful of dross that Evie had scraped from the bucket in the late Mr Coker's room.

On the hob were a blackened kettle, a frying pan and a toasting fork, but the bread had already been devoured and cooking on a candle flame was beyond Clare's capabilities. There was no oil in the lamp, no curtain on the window. The bed, hardly more than a cot, had been stripped to a mattress.

Evie crouched bare-legged in front of the grate. She was disappointed in 'Aunt Cissie'. After all the effort they had put into picking Eamon Cassidy's name from a gravestone and tracing his widow, she had expected a better reward. Three eggs, a quarter loaf and a cup of dripping wasn't her idea of generosity, though, to be fair, the woman had forked out for the room.

'Sure an' it's not goin' to spark up now, Evie,' Nolan told her. 'We'll be tryin' again in the mornin' when I've scrounged some kindlin'.'

Nolan had spread his travelling blanket and wrapped his boots in his jacket to make a pillow. He lay on the mattress contemplating the ceiling.

Stripped to her petticoat and bodice, Clare sat on the edge of the sink by the window, combing her long hair.

If the factor could see her sister now, Evie thought, he would be even more smitten than he was already. She had had her share of smitten parties, men who were willing to do anything to please her, this side of marriage. It was she, not Clare, who had tackled the priest in Cork and laid out the sorry story that had got them enough scratch to reach Glasgow.

'Spread out an' get some sleep,' Nolan said. 'It'll be another long day for us tomorrow, I'm thinkin'.'

'You will go lookin' for work, won't you?' Clare said.

'I will that,' said Nolan.

'Where will you start?' said Evie.

'I'll go down to the wall at the far end o' Salamanca Street an' see what's doin' there,' Nolan said, 'like the feller told me to do.'

'What feller?' said Clare.

'What wall?' said Evie.

'The wall the feller on the boat told me about, where they hire diggers for the new dock.'

'Who does the hirin', Nolly?' Evie asked.

'The contracuators,' Nolan told her.

Evie could see little of her brother in the flickering candlelight, just his big hummocky knees and his feet in dirty stockings.

'What if they're not hirin' tomorrow?' she said. 'We'll need money soon, since the widow woman ain't ready to take us at our word just yet.'

'She found us a room, did she not?' said Nolan.

'Aye, an' she's just as like to throw us out,' Clare said, 'if the man, the factotum, draws the line.'

'You can get round him, can't you?' Nolan said.

'Me?' Clare said. 'I'm not the one for that job.'

'You'll be doin' what you have to,' Nolan said, 'like we all will.'

Clare gave a little nod and tugged the comb from her hair. She drew the ball of her thumb across the teeth once, then again. She stroked her thumb across the comb the way you might strike a safety match, then, sucking blood from her thumb, said, 'I won't be lettin' him poke me.'

'He won't poke you,' Evie said. 'He's a gentleman.'

'There's none o' them gentlemen,' said Clare.

'Well, he might *want* to poke you, an' who can blame him for that,' Evie said, 'but he won't give in to the temptation.'

'How can you be so bloody sure?' said Clare.

Evie sat up. 'He has a Bible in his room.'

'Aye,' said Clare. 'So had Father Garbett.'

'Anyroads,' Nolan rumbled, 'that unfortunate event purchased us three tickets to Glasgow, did it not now?'

Clare attacked her left thumb with the same determination as she had attacked her right. She would not be happy, Evie guessed, until both thumbs were dripping blood.

She was beginning to suspect that her sister's reason had been affected by the incident with the priest, piled on top of the strain of watching Mam die, all yellow and bony, and having the peelers charge through the door before the three of them were hardly back from the funeral, with Father Garbett backing the peelers, and Mr Rogers there to speak for Lord Wring.

None of it would have happened, of course, if the sickening white down hadn't descended on the potato crop again and the oats hadn't fallen short of the haul that Lord Wring demanded in tithe.

She got to her feet and wrapped the shawl about her. 'I'm not waitin' for mornin',' she said. 'I'm off right now.'

Nolan sat up. 'Off where?'

'On the scrounge.'

'Beggin'?' said Clare. 'No, Evie, you mustn't beg. We promised Mam we'd never stoop to beggin'.'

'Mam's dead an' gone,' said Evie. 'Anyroads, there's a difference between scroungin' an' beggin'.'

'What? What difference?' Clare said.

'You tell her, Nolan,' Evie said, 'while I go explorin'.'

'Put on some clothes first,' Nolan said.

'No clothes necessary,' Evie said. 'All I'll be needin' is me hat.'

On nights when the wind blew hard the smoke in Jock Macpherson's third-floor room swirled about like ectoplasm. Indeed, so thick and choking did it become there were times when he wondered if the bones of a climbing-boy were stuck above the flue and if the sound he heard when he lay in bed was not just the wail of the wind but the forlorn cry of some ghastly orphan who had perished up there half a century ago.

Being a practical man, not usually given to fancies, he had tried poking about with a broom handle and had even fashioned a great long rod out of wire and bamboo, but the rod had brought down nothing but a deluge of soot, and the smoke remained prodigious when the wind was from the west.

He had arrived home later than usual that evening and had stumbled on some minor stramash in the hallway. Mrs Cassidy had thrust the pie at him as if the argument were all his fault and he had only glimpsed the strangers in Mr Belfer's room – a giant of a man and a sullen-looking girl in a shawl – before he'd hastened upstairs.

The wind howled about the chimneypots and another cloud of smoke puffed from the flue. The draught was good, though, so there were flames in the grate and the appetising aroma of gravy in the air as, clad in trousers and an undervest, Jock groped his way into the lobby to answer the knocking. He assumed it would be Mr Belfer or possibly Betty Fowler come to complain about the smoke but on opening the door he was confronted by a girl he had never seen before, a girl with sharp, pointed features and bright blue eyes, dressed in little else, it seemed, but a shawl and a flowery hat.

'By Gar!' she said. 'Is it an ox you're roastin' in there?'

Jock peered down at her. 'Are you one o' the Fowlers?'

'No, sir, there's nothin' foul about me.'

'You're not one o' the Fowlers?'

'I'm one o' the McKennas.'

Smoke billowed out on to the landing and collected in the cold air above the stairs like a huge grey fist.

'From where?' said Jock.

'From downstairs.'

'Are you new tenants?'

'Aye, we're new, but we might not be tenants for long.'

Jock pinched the collar of his vest and tugged it over his chest. He had a bushy beard and eyebrows but not much by way of hair on his head, which Betty Fowler had told him was very fetching; the rest of him was anything but fetching, unless you had a partiality for bears or very large dogs.

'If you've come to complain about the smoke . . .' he began.

'I haven't come to complain about the smoke,' the girl said. 'I've come to borrow a pickle o' coal an' any spare scoff you might have in your larder to fill the hole in me stomach.'

'How many?' Jock said. 'How many holes in how many stomachs?'

'Three,' the girl said. 'Me sister, me brother – an', well, me.'

'Come inside.'

'Is there a wife inside?'

'No wife,' Jock said.

'In that case, I'll be waitin' out here,' the girl said.

'For why?'

'For modesty,' she said, then, leaning to the left, peered past him into the room. 'Is that mutton on the hob?'

'Steak,' Jock answered. 'Mrs Cassidy sells us pies.'

'How much?'

'Tuppence.'

'Too much.'

'They're fourpence over the counter.'

'Far too much,' the girl said. 'Is it a big pie?'

'Big enough for two,' Jock said, 'not four.'

'What else have you got for a person to eat?'

Jock noticed Mrs Fowler peeking from the doorway across the landing and had no wish to be reported to Mr Belfer, who was adamantly opposed to 'private congress' between his tenants. He took the girl by the arm and drew her into the lobby.

'If it's your intention to talk me out o' half my supper, lass,' he said, 'you'd best come in an' make a proper job of it.'

'I'm not decent,' the girl said.

'Well, I'm not exactly robed for a night at the Gaiety.' Jock ushered her into the kitchen. 'Sit there at the table an' we'll pretend we know each other well enough to share a bite o' supper.'

Obediently, the girl seated herself.

Jock tugged a cloth from a hook, wrapped it around his fists, plucked the pie from the hob and placed it before her. He handed her a fork and a spoon. She gripped the fork in one hand and the spoon in the other and bathed her face in savoury steam for a moment; then she sat back, frowning.

'I can't eat it,' she said.

'What's wrong with it?'

'Nothin', but I can't go stealin' your supper.'

'Half my supper,' Jock said. 'That's not the reason, is it?'

'No.'

'It's your sister downstairs, is it not?'

'An' me brother,' the girl admitted. 'They're starvin'.'

She raised her hand and dabbed a corner of her mouth. She had fine fingers, Jock noted, and when the shawl slipped from her shoulder he glimpsed the strap of a bodice trimmed with lace.

'Aye,' Jock said. 'I see your predicament.'

He opened a cupboard, brought out a tin-plated meat safe and set it on the floor. Kneeling, he flicked the bolt on the safe and extracted a quarter loaf, a wedge of cheese and a slap of butter wrapped in newspaper. He put the food on the table, locked the metal safe and returned it to the cupboard.

'Why do you do that, with the tin thing?' the girl asked.

'To keep out the mice,' Jock answered.

'Mice?' said Evie.

'This place has its fair share o' them,' Jock said. 'The buildin's near fifty year old, after all. We're lucky, though. Some of Blackstock's tenements are no better than rat pits, hardly fit for beasts to live in. At least we're clean here, or fairly much so. We've a sink in every room, though when the pressure falls the taps don't work an' you have to go down to the old pump in the back court and lug the water up in pails. There's gas, too, but only on the ground floor.'

'Why is that?' said Evie.

'Because the Police Acts demand gaslight an' runnin' water in every home but the regulations are bent so out o' shape the health inspectors can't keep up.' He squinted down at Evie, frowning. 'No doubt, bein' as you're Irish, you'd also like tea?'

'Tea would be grand, sir, aye.'

'An' fuel for your fire?'

'You're a charitable man, sir, a very charitable man. Sure, you'll get your reward in heaven,' the girl told him and, looking up from the pie, gave him a wink and a dazzling smile.

Clare occupied one chair, Evie the other. Licking crumbs from the stubble on his upper lip, Nolan sat on the floor, cross-legged like a leprechaun.

'He'll be expectin' his reward long before he reaches heaven,' Clare said.

'He's not that sort o' feller,' Evie said.

'Give them half a chance an' they're all that sort o' feller,' Clare said.

'Whatever he is,' Nolan said sleepily, 'sure an' he's done us proud.'

'You had the meat, though,' Clare said.

'He shared it with me,' Evie said.

'What does it cost for one o' them pies?' said Nolan.

'Tuppence, if the woman brings it from the bakery.'

'Tuppence, eh?' said Nolan. 'Cheap at half the price, I reckon.'

'What else did your new friend tell you?' Clare asked.

'He told me about Belfer, an' our auntie.' Evie's fingers were wrapped about a mug of tea and she was warm in all her parts for the first time in days. 'We've the luck on our side for once, it seems. This place is a paradise compared with the tenements across the big road, so I'm told. The Blackstocks own most o' them too.'

'The Blackstocks?' said Nolan.

'Big cheeses in these parts,' Evie said. 'They've got houses all over the neighbourhood, an' Russell Blackstock's company has the contract for buildin' the new harbour. If a man's in search o' work in this part o' the world, the Blackstocks provide it.'

'Did your friend tell you all that?' said Clare.

'Aye, an' more besides.'

'What did he say about Belfer?' Clare asked.

'Belfer collects the rents for Mr Blackstock. He says who stays an' who goes. It'll pay us to keep on his sweet side.'

'How did you squeeze so much out o' a stranger?' said Clare.

'I asked honest questions an' Mr Macpherson give me honest answers.'

'What sort o' answers did you give him?' Clare said.

'I told him we're related to Eamon Cassidy.'

'Did he believe you?'

'No reason not to,' said Evie. 'I got you food, did I not now?'

'You did, you did,' Nolan said. 'Grateful we are to your Mr Macpherson. What else o' interest did he tell you, Evie?'

'The woman on Mr Macpherson's landin' is a sailor's wife. She lives there wi' her sister an' two or three babies.'

'Does your new friend work for the Blackstocks?' said Clare.

'Aye, in the coal yard,' Evie said. 'The feller across the lane at the back stables the horses for haulin' the coal from the docks to the yard.'

'I'm no good with horses,' Nolan said.

'You're no good with anythin' much,' Clare said.

''Cept me pick an' shovel,' said Nolan. 'Sure an' I'm good with those.'

Evie sat back, stretched her arms above her head, and yawned.

She was pleased at having gained so much information from Mr Macpherson and however much Clare grumbled and Nolan shilly-shallied, she was already inclined to settle here, if, that is, that paunchy old devil Belfer would let them.

Mr Belfer tossed and turned under the blanket. As a rule he was unaffected by rough weather but the wild March wind made him restless. He stared up into the darkness and felt the weight of the building pressing down upon him, the weight of the tenants too, that awkward, mutinous crew who, given half a chance, would cheat him, or Mr Blackstock, out of what was due.

At length, around four o'clock, he fumbled for a match, lit the lamp again and tried to take his mind off things by reading a book on Christian Socialism. Even that contentious subject failed to grip his attention, however, and he soon slipped into dreaming about the Irish persons upstairs and the mystery that surrounded them; the mystery, in particular, of the dark-haired girl whose modesty seemed so at odds with her pouting red lips and pale complexion.

Five came and went, then six.

He heard Mr McLean cranking the pump to water the horses and Mrs Fowler's new baby wailing for the breast and, giving up the notion of sleep, climbed out of bed to face the day.

Shivering in his nightshirt, he nipped out to the privy, then shaved and got himself dressed. He donned his waistcoat, slipped the biggest watch in his collection into a pocket, clipped a silver-plated chain into a buttonhole and, with two or three deep breaths to clear his head, climbed the stairs, rapped on the door of the late Mr Coker's room and, without awaiting an invitation, went in.

The brother was not in the room.

The one called Evie was on the floor, wrapped in a blanket, shoes for a pillow, shawl for a quilt.

The girl, Clare, was over by the window, washing herself.

Her petticoat and chemise were furled about her hips. Her dark brown hair, undone, draped her shoulders and when she swung to face him he caught a glimpse of her breasts before, with a little squeal, she covered them.

'Turn your back, sir,' the girl on the floor cried. 'Turn your back. That's not a sight for you to see. What do you want with us?'

'I've come for the rent,' Mr Belfer said.

'The woman – Aunt Cissie . . .' Evie began.

'She only paid for one night,' Benjamin Belfer said.

There was still a prickle of fire in the grate and the blackened kettle showed a wisp of steam at the spout. Unless he missed his guess the Irish had been on the scrounge, or were not so poor as they pretended to be.

'What do you think?' Evie said. 'Do you think we'll be duckin' out with your pots stuffed up our skirts? Is that why you've come bargin' in here without so much as a by-your-leave?'

'It's a shillin' a night,' Mr Belfer said, 'in advance.'

'What is it by the week?'

'Five shillin,' said Mr Belfer, 'also in advance.'

Evie's hair was the colour of ripe barley, cropped short about the neck and ears. She was almost as pretty as her sister, but far too skinny for his taste.

'Nolan will be back with money at the end o' the day,' Evie said.

'Where will Nolan get money?'

'He'll work for it.'

'Where?'

'At the wall,' said Evie. 'He's gone for to find work at the wall.'

'He'll be lucky to earn five shillin's a day there,' said Mr Belfer.

Clare tied the strings of the chemise and buttoned her bodice. She seated herself on the side of the bed and began to draw on her stockings.

'Benjamin?' Evie said. 'What sort o' a name is that? Is that a Jew name, by any chance?'

'A Jew name? What makes you think it's a Jew name?'

'It's one o' the tribes o' Israel,' Evie said, 'in the Scripture.'

'What do you know of Scripture?' Mr Belfer growled. 'You're just girls.'

'The word o' God is for everyone,' Clare said.

'Well, it isn't,' said Mr Belfer, 'not all of it, leastways.'

'Not the parts to do with Jews, you mean?' Evie persisted. 'Genesis to Zeck-hariahs.'

'Malachi,' Clare corrected.

'Aye, Malachi,' said Evie.

'The Day o' Judgement's set out in Malachi,' said Clare. 'God has the last word on Judgement in that Book.'

'Now, now.' Mr Belfer raised a warning hand, as if mere mention of God on Clare's lips constituted a blasphemy. 'That's quite enough of that.'

Clare lolled on the bare boards of the broken bed, her skirts hitched up, one stocking not properly gartered. In a droning voice that stirred apprehension as well as desire in Benjamin Belfer, she recited the verses:

' "I will come near to you to judgement; an' I will be a swift witness against the sorcerers, an' against the adulterers, an' against the false swearers, an' against those that oppress the hireling in his wages, the widow, an' the fatherless, an' that turn aside the stranger from his right, an' fear me not, saith the Lord of hosts." '

'I like the bit about the hireling's wages,' said Evie.

'An' the bit about the stranger's rights,' said Clare.

'You don't even know what those verses mean,' said Benjamin Belfer.

'I know what adultery means,' Evie said, 'an' perjury, an' exploitation, an' oppression, an' deprivin' the poor for profit.'

'Enough!' Mr Belfer snapped. 'I'm a reasonable man. I carry no prejudice against your kind.'

'Our kind?' said Clare.

'Catholics,' said Mr Belfer.

'Oh,' said Evie. 'I thought you meant socialists.'

'Them, too,' Mr Belfer said. 'Now, about the rent . . .'

'Shillin' a night for this midden,' Evie said. 'I wouldn't give you tuppence.'

'What *would* you give me then?'

The girls glanced at each other, brows raised.

'I mean – I–I'm not open to negotiation,' Benjamin Belfer blustered.

'Nee-go-tit-ay-shun,' said Evie. 'Oooooo!'

Clare laughed huskily.

Mr Belfer extracted his hand from his pocket and stroked his greasy hair. 'I suppose,' he said, 'aye, I suppose I *could* come an' go a bit, but only if you've somethin' to show me.'

Once more the brows were raised.

'What would you like to see?' said Evie.

'Money, I mean money. I mean some evidence o' good intentions, some sign you're not just fly-by-nights.'

'We're not fly-by-nights.' Clare commenced work on her stockings again, her shift bunched between her thighs. 'Our auntie will vouch for that.'

Benjamin Belfer could see the flesh of her leg as she adjusted her garter. He knew she was taunting him and that it would be sensible to order them out before Cissie Cassidy returned.

'Ask her,' Evie said. 'Ask her right now.'

'Can't,' Benjamin Belfer said. 'She starts work at six.'

'There you are then,' Evie said.

'There I am – what?'

'She thinks we'll be here when she gets back,' said Evie. 'She won't be pleased if she finds you've tossed us out.'

Mr Belfer stroked his hair again. He couldn't deny that Cissie Cassidy was an ideal tenant and would be very upset if he shovelled the Irish out into the street without telling her. Besides, Mr Coker's apartment had been vacant for the best part of a fortnight and would do better with Irish tenants than no tenants at all.

He moved to the window and looked down into the lane.

Tam McLean was leading out the horses, four huge Clydesdales linked by rope halters. He watched their feathery manes stream out in the wind and glanced up, sighing, at the surge of black clouds that showed above the rooftops.

'Tell you what,' he said, 'if your brother comes up with half the rent, I'll delay a week for the balance.'

'How's that for charity!' Clare murmured.

'It ain't charity, dear,' Evie said. 'It's business.'

'Business it is,' Benjamin Belfer said. 'Half a crown in my hand by ten o'clock tonight or out you all go, bag an' baggage.'

'Thirty pence,' said Evie.

'Thirty pieces o' silver,' said Clare.

Benjamin Belfer suddenly found the room oppressive. He

needed air. He needed breakfast. He needed to restore the balance of the day before everything tumbled out of control. He reached for the door knob – then paused. 'How is it you know so much about Scripture?' he asked. '*You* ain't Jews, by any chance?'

'Good Catholic girls,' Clare McKenna assured him.

'Steeped in sin,' said Evie, and laughed as Mr Blackstock's factor blundered out into the lobby and slammed the door behind him.

3

There *was* a wall around the builder's yard in Salamanca Street, but it wasn't the wall that everyone was talking about. It was plain, old-fashioned brick with a mortared top.

Hard by a gate stood a man in an old frock coat and battered top hat with a bunch of cardboard tickets clutched in his fist like a flower-girl's posy. Anything less like a flower-girl would be difficult to imagine, though, for the man was bearded like an oyster and his cheeks, what could be seen of them, were pitted like the board of a shooting gallery. A reeking clay pipe, glued to his nether lip, jigged and bobbed throughout his conversation.

Nolan could hardly make out a word of the guttural Glasgow accent, which was probably just as well, considering that he was signing on to work a twelve-hour shift up to his waist in thick brown river mud.

He was only too glad to be handed one of the cardboard tickets, stiff and stained as a navvy's boot, and to shuffle through the gate into the yard to join a dozen or so other unfortunates. He signed a chit for a shovel and a pickaxe and was herded through a spike-topped gate and down a long lane behind the builder's warehouse, at the end of which, to his astonishment, was a length of railway track and a portly little locomotive, belching steam.

Three flat-wagons were linked to the locomotive.

Fifteen or twenty labourers, smoking, spitting and leaning on shovels, were already assembled on the wagons. As soon as they caught sight of the new recruits they set up a great hullabaloo, chanting, cursing and crossing their pickaxes as if to ward off evil.

A fist thumped into Nolan's shoulder. 'Hoist thyself oop, lad,' said a voice behind him. 'Doan thee be fright o' them scallywags. They be all piss an' wind.'

The speaker was a gnarled, brown-skinned little man with not a tooth in his head. He thumped Nolan's shoulder once more. Nolan put a foot on the iron, levered himself on to the wagon bed, and stood up.

'By Christmas, we've got ourselves a giant,' someone shouted. 'I'll tak' him for a prop any day o' the week.'

'He'll be keepin' your head above the water, Mickey, will he not now?'

'Sure an' he will. Oy, big feller, what do they call you?'

'Nolan McKenna.'

'Dug up fresh from the Owd Sod, are ye?'

'Pardon?'

'Got manners, the lad.'

'Got no brains, though.'

'If he had brains he wouldnae be here, would he?'

'Don't need no brains to drown.'

'Drown?' Nolan said.

'He don't know nothin', do 'ee?'

'He'll larn quick enough, he'll larn.'

The last of the day's signings clambered on board. The locomotive let out a piercing whistle. Two great wings of white steam sprouted from the pistons. The wagons clanked. The men swayed.

Nolan spread his legs and braced himself as if he were still on board ship. He felt the vibrations from the engine rise through him, like sap through a tree. He dug the tip of the pick into the boards and leaned into it as the wagon lurched and the long wall of the builder's yard rolled away.

He saw the glint of iron rails curving ahead, leading, it seemed, not through but over the fretful houses of the Riverside ward, in and out of chimneypots, along earthen banks and over iron trestles. He squinted at bustling streets below, at pillared doorways and dismal windows and off to his right the masts and cranes that spiked the river and the nondescript walls of warehouses flanking the quays; then the engine plunged down into a mud-walled cutting and the view was gone and all Nolan could see was a seamless ribbon of railway track and a sunless ribbon of sky.

'Where are we going?' he shouted. 'Where are they takin' us?'

Crouched by Nolan's knee, the toothless man glanced up and grinned. 'Into the pit, son,' he yelled.

'The pit?' Nolan said.

'Where the devil takes his due,' the little man said and laughed uproariously as if wading in mud for eightpence an hour was the biggest old joke in the world.

The water from the tap in the sink had shrunk to no more than a trickle. Clare had sore need to make her linens clean again and had no choice but to carry the clothes down to the tank in the yard.

She had no soap, no bristle or switch, none of the paraphernalia that usually accompanied her to the stones of the stream that ran down to the river that ran down to the lake in the blue morning light back home.

No nodding rushes brushed her thighs as they did when she waded into the trout-brown pool to draw water. There were none of the soft smells of morning and the water cold in the big chipped jug that held the water that she poured over the linens spread across the stones in the slither of the stream, hiding her shame and looking round for a sign of a man, before she tinted the water rose.

She climbed the shallow wooden step to the lip of the tank under the old pump and peered into its rusty depths. With the flat of her hand she skimmed off the granular black dust that covered the surface of the water and dipped in the jug she had brought from Mr Coker's room. Then she climbed back down the step and looked around for a stone to serve as a scrubbing board, and just then a young man breezed out of the back close and trotted over to her.

'Well now,' he said, 'if this is not opportune. You must be the lassie who charmed my friend Macpherson an' sent him off hungry to his bed.'

'Sure an' I don't know what you mean,' said Clare.

'What are you hidin' there?'

'Nothin'.'

'There's a public wash-house at the far end o' Carpenter Street,' the young man said, 'or if you don't fancy that, Mrs McLean has a boiling tub in the back of the stables across the lane she'll let you use for a penny a load.'

'I've no need of a boiling tub,' Clare said.

'Suit yourself,' the man said.

He stepped up on to the platform, dipped his bucket into the water and, heaving it up with both hands, stepped down again.

'By God, but this is a chore I could be doin' without,' he said. 'I'll be a happy man when the water board give us enough pressure to reach the second floor. Is it not an irony that we have to live at the pump like our forefathers when the whole city is webbed with brand-new pipes drawin' beautiful clean water from Loch Katrine. *Are* you the girl? Macpherson's girl?'

'I'm the sister.'

'Two of you! Goodness me!'

Clare folded her hands and bowed her head, willing him to go away.

'I'm Harry Fairfield, by the by.'

She peeped at him from a corner of her eye. He was as slight as a boy and pale as milk. He had high cheekbones, an Adam's apple that stuck out like a door knob and queer piercing eyes, the colour of the Virgin's robe. He wore a leather vest over his shirt and a pair of patched trousers, none too clean. He set down the bucket, folded his arms and leaned against the water tank, all bright and ready for chat.

Clare said, 'What are you?'

'I'm a coalman,' Harry said. 'I work beside Jock in the yard round the corner. I gather your sister talked old Jock out o' half his supper. I think he's rather taken with your sister.'

'That's not wise of him,' said Clare.

'What does wisdom have to do with it?' Harry patted his chest. 'The heart is the most unreasoning organ in the human body. If it's wisdom you're after, don't look to the heart to provide it.'

'Do you always talk this much?'

'Usually,' Harry confessed. 'I'm a prattler by nature.'

If she listened to him long enough, Clare realised, she might fall under his spell, for in Ireland words were still a form of enchantment. Blarney, strangers called it, but it wasn't blarney to her, not since she had crouched in the chapel by the lake shore and listened to Father Garbett unleash his frightening homilies and had heard the litanies her brother Kiernan sang to amuse himself after illness chained him to his bed.

She could imagine Mr Belfer reading aloud from the Holy Book, but not Harry Fairfield whose voice, like water frothing over stones, seemed too quick and light for Scripture.

'Why are you lookin' at me like that?' he asked.

'Like what?'

'Like I was an asp.'

'An asp?'

'A snake, a viper.'

'Sure an' I wasn't thinkin' that at all,' Clare said.

'What were you thinkin' then?'

'How forward you are.'

'Aye, you're right there,' he said. 'Forward, always forward would be the motto on the Fairfields' crest – if the Fairfields ever had a crest.' He studied her in silence for a moment, then said, 'Is it forwardness or is it friendliness, that's the question for you to ask yourself, Miss . . .'

'My name's Clare.'

'So we're off on the proper foot at last,' Harry Fairfield said. 'I'm glad of that. We're just one big happy family here at number five Salamanca Street. You've met Belfer, I take it?'

'I have,' Clare answered.

'What do you make of him?'

'I make nothin' of him.'

'He's Blackstock's man, Blackstock's toadie. I'd be careful if I were you.'

'I think we're already on his wrong side,' Clare said. 'I don't think he's fond of Catholics. Is he a supporter of the Orange Order?'

'I've never thought to ask him,' Harry said. 'Mrs Cassidy's a Catholic, though, an' he's friendly enough with her. If you're kin to Cissie Cassidy he won't toss you out.'

'Mrs Cassidy's my mother's brother's wife.'

'Uh-huh,' said Harry. 'An' he's not here to deny it.'

Clare twined a tendril of hair around her fingertip. She said, 'Why would he want to deny it?'

'Why, indeed!' said Harry. 'I never met the chap m'self. He was long gone to the ground before I washed up in Glasgow.'

'How long have you been here?'

'Couple o' years, give or take.'

'Before that?'

'Here, there an' everywhere.'

'Have you no family?'

'None to speak of,' Harry said. 'Charity raised me, you might say. I wasn't reckoned to be my father's son, an' he wasn't the man for shoulderin' another man's bairn. Consequently, I was put out to school.'

'Sure an' I don't understand,' Clare said, frowning.

'Charity school, the school o' hard knocks,' Harry said. 'I can write. I can do my sums. I can whistle in tune an' recite all sorts o' rhymes without droppin' a syllable. I can dance, too.'

He executed a few nimble steps and, for an instant, Clare could almost hear the music in Mr Fairfield's head as if it came from a fiddle or a harp, then, abruptly, he leaned back against the water tank.

'What it is?' Clare said, alarmed. 'Why have you stopped?'

'I should know better than prance about like an idiot to impress a girl I've only just met. I'll finish the set another time. Will you stay in Glasgow?'

'I hope so,' Clare answered.

'I hope so, too,' Harry Fairbairn said and, lifting the water bucket, walked off, leaving, Clare noted, a shaky little trail of splashes on the cobblestones behind him.

In a pocket in the lining of her drawers were eight brown pennies, all that remained of the McKenna family fortune.

Since Nolan had not returned Evie reckoned he had found employment. Nolan, after all, was their engine, the machine that would earn their daily bread and it was up to Clare and she to keep him in good working order.

She left the tenement about half past ten and wandered along Salamanca Street which, apart from a few women and young children, was remarkably quiet at that hour of the morning. Cork was a handsome town but it seemed tiny compared to Glasgow, the quays that flanked the banks of the Lee small beer lined up against the wharves that bordered the Clyde.

She skirted an abandoned cotton mill pegged by two tall chimneys, and a new railway halt webbed with scaffolding. Spires and steeples towered above the stacks, inquisitive cranes peered over warehouse walls and on a long hill peppered with ugly villas building work was in full swing. Dust filled the air and an angry buzzing, like bees on the rampage, rose from the direction of the river where buildings were being torn down and others erected to replace them.

Nothing on this flank of the river seemed very stable or permanent and Evie, unsettled, headed back towards the tenements.

It was pure chance that brought her to the pub.

She stared up at the sign that hung out over the pavement: *The Harp of Erin. Wines, Spirits & Best Scotch Ales. Patrick Maizie, Prop.*, then, clapping a hand to her thigh and squeezing the pennies in the pocket of her drawers, she surrendered to temptation, pushed open the heavy oak door and stepped inside.

Gasaliers hung from the ceiling, unlit in the morning hour, but light from the little windows showed Evie an array of casks, kegs and barrels and a counter shrouded by a carved lintel, like a rood screen, on which stood pint pots, glasses and bottles by the score. She reeled back a little, marvelling that so much stuff could be accommodated in a building that seemed, from the outside, not much larger than a goat-wife's hovel.

'Oy, you! You there, lassie, what're you wantin'?'

The boy's face was illuminated by daylight from one of the windows, a squinched-up goblin face topped by a mass of wiry red hair.

'You after gin,' he said, 'or beer? We don't serve nae fancy drinks 'fore noon since the ice isnae hot enough. You're no' in fur a jug o' the heavy since you've nae jug, none visible, though why you keep pattin' your poncy is an interestin' question. Store the rabbit up there, eh?'

'The rabbit?'

'Never mind, love, never mind. I'll serve you since Bob's downstairs in the cellar tapping casks.' He wore a short apron and stained trousers. His shirt sleeves were tied with twine above his skinny elbows. His eyes, like his hair, were red, as if he'd been weeping. 'Well,' he said, 'you're no' here for the ginger pop.'

'Are you Mr Maizie?'

'Hah!' he snorted.

'Who are you then – the potboy?'

'Boy?' the young chap cried indignantly. 'I'm no' a boy. I'm the pot *man*. I don't go wipin' tables an' washin' glasses an' I havenae dipped ma hand in the sawdust box for a good five year. Potboy, huh? What're you after?'

'Stout,' said Evie.

'Beer, pint thereof?'

'Stout, I said.'

'All right, keep your hair on, chucks. Stout it'll be. Irish stout, I suppose?'

He trotted behind the bar, whisked a glass from a shelf, selected a handle on a gigantic engine and gave it a hearty tug.

'Stout's fourpence. You got fourpence?'

'I've got fourpence,' Evie said.

She leaned on the counter and watched the thick, black liquid coil from the pipe and foam mount on the inside of the glass. Fourpence was twice as much as she had expected to pay but her mam had once told her there was more nourishment in a well-brewed pint than in three potatoes and a bowl of stew.

'Show's your scratch.' The potboy held the half-filled glass away from her as if he feared that she might leap the counter and wrest it from him. 'No scratch, no drinkie. First rule o' the house.'

Evie furled her skirts, stuck her hand up the inside of her leg and groped for the mouth of the pocket while the boy craned over the counter to savour whatever forbidden fruits might be revealed. She fished out four brown coins and laid them on the bar. The potboy scooped them into his palm, sniffed them, then slipped them under the counter. He smiled a thin, foxy little smile, finished drawing the pint and placed it before her.

Evie smoothed her skirts, lifted the glass and supped.

She licked foam from her upper lip, and sighed.

The potboy, chin on hand, watched with interest. 'Is that it?' he said.

Evie swallowed. 'Aye.'

'I had you wrong.'

'Had me down for a tippler, did you?' Evie said.

'Nah,' he said. 'I thought you'd come about the job.'

'Job?' said Evie, swallowing again. 'What job?'

At one time St Kentigern's had been a centre of worship for immigrant Irish but the opening of an Orange Lodge in Carpenter Street and a new chapel in Partick had drawn off many of the faithful and these days Father Fingle was fortunate if anyone at all turned up for early mass.

He continued to bustle about the parish, though, in his long brown greatcoat, broad-brimmed hat and thick-soled shoes and could often be seen very late at night on his way to comfort the sick or administer last rites to the dying.

He was well known to drunkards and the wives of drunkards, to prostitutes and the men who exploited them, to wretched orphans, widows with large families, and those worn down by overwork as well as those to whom idleness had become a way of life. And he was still spry enough to sprint across Carpenter Street where the Protestants ruled the roost and apprentices shouted obscenities and threw stones at his head.

Mr Belfer was not a Roman Catholic and regarded clergymen of whatever persuasion with a mixture of admiration and disdain. But Father Fingle's name had cropped up that afternoon in conversation with Mr Orpington, an English gentleman with whom Benjamin did business and, with time on his hands, he had strolled down to the chapel and just happened to be leaning on the gate when the priest popped out.

'Sir!' Mr Belfer said, feigning respect. 'A word, if I may.'

'What do you want, Mr Belfer? Is someone in your building sick?'

'Everyone in my building is sick,' Benjamin Belfer said, 'but it's not a sickness can be cured by your mumbo-jumbo. I need a private word with you, Father Fingle, that's all.'

The priest raised an eyebrow. 'Confession, Mr Belfer, surely not?'

'Hah!' said Mr Belfer. 'No, it's about those girls you sent me.'

'Girls, what girls?'

'Two girls and an Irish boy; they *were* here, weren't they?'

'If you mean Mrs Cassidy's relatives newly arrived from the Old Country, yes, they were here.'

Mr Belfer tucked his hands under his coat-tails. 'Well, sir,' he said. 'Can you tell me if it was Mrs Cassidy they asked for specific, or was it Eamon Cassidy's widow?'

'Is there a difference?' Father Fingle said.

'The difference is that Eamon Cassidy is buried in your churchyard an' his dear lady wife is not,' Mr Belfer said. 'The point being that any Irish tramp who's been taught his letters can read what's wrote on a gravestone.'

'I take it Mrs Cassidy and her relatives have been reunited?'

'They have,' said Mr Belfer, 'but that doesn't answer my question. Did you tell them where Eamon Cassidy's widow might be found?'

Father Fingle's wits were by no means as threadbare as his coat. In fact, he suspected that he had been rather too trusting of the three young Irish who had come knocking at his door.

'Yes, I directed them to number five,' he said. 'Does Mrs Cassidy not wish to acknowledge them?'

''Course she does,' said Mr Belfer. 'That's the problem.'

'Where are they now?'

'In my house,' said Mr Belfer.

'Then all's well that ends well?'

'No, it is not, for I reckon that they cribbed Eamon Cassidy's name off his gravestone, an' you gave them the rest,' said Benjamin Belfer. 'They're no more kin to Cissie Cassidy than I am.'

'If Mrs Cassidy's willin' to accept them, does it matter who they are?'

'It may not matter to the widow lady but it matters to me.'

'They're just three poor Irish travellers,' said Father Fingle, 'in search of employment and a place to stay.'

'Does that give them the right to deceive me?'

'No, it doesn't,' the priest admitted.

'If they make trouble, it's me who'll have to answer for it.'

'If you're unhappy with their presence in your house,' Father Fingle said, 'surely you have the authority to ask them to leave.'

'They're not really Cissie Cassidy's kinfolk, are they?'

Father Fingle paused. 'Probably not, no.'

'That's all I need to know,' said Mr Belfer and, turning on his heel, walked off without so much as a nod of farewell.

'How do I look, dearest?' Evie pirouetted before her sister. 'Think I'll cut the mustard?'

'Mustard?' said Clare. 'Mustard with what?'

'This Maizie feller.'

'Are you sure you know what you're doing, Evie?'

'It's work, ain't it?' Evie replied.

'In a public house? Mam wouldn't like you workin' in a pub.'

'Well, Mam's dead an' we have to get on with things best we can.'

'I suppose so,' Clare agreed reluctantly.

She was seated on a chair by the fireplace, arms locked around her knees. It was almost dark outside and light rain, hardly more than a mist, dampened the windowpane. The room was lit by two candle stumps and the flicker of flame in the coals that Mr Fairfield had brought her late that afternoon. He had pushed the bucket of coal towards her and she had taken it, then they had loitered on the landing, chatting, for a good ten minutes before a door downstairs had creaked open, and Mr Fairfield had made himself scarce.

Evie executed another pirouette, throwing out her skirts.

''Sides,' she said, 'I ain't exactly been signed on yet. For all I know the position's been took. Do I look good, though, good enough to eat?'

'Scrumptious,' said Clare flatly.

'My friend Chiffin says I've got what it takes. He's sure Mr Maizie will hire me. He's going to put in a word in advance, Chiffin is.'

'He's only a potboy, isn't he?' Clare said. 'Potboys don't have much pull.'

'Pot man,' said Evie. 'He delivers the orders, among other things.'

'Other things? Is that what you'll be doin'?'

'I don't know what I'll be doin'.'

'Servin' men with drink.'

'Ladies go there too.'

'What sort o' ladies, I'd like to know,' Clare said.

'The Harp o' Erin; it's a real good omen, that name is.'

'I don't set much store by omens. How long will you be gone?'

'Can't say.'

'What if he comes when you're not here?' Clare said.

'If who comes?'

'Belfer – for his money.'

'Ask him to wait till Nolan gets back.'

'What if he won't wait?'

'He'll wait,' said Evie. 'If he does get frisky, you go straight downstairs to Mrs Cassidy an' tell her all about it.'

'Tell her what? That we're cheats?'

'Tell her Nolan's found work an' we'll have plenty o' money soon. Butter her up an' she'll talk Belfer into bidin' his time. If I do hook this job then we'll be rollin' in clover.'

'Clover!' Clare said. 'I don't call this clover.'

'Sure it's better than what we had back home.'

'Is it?' said Clare.

'It will be,' said Evie. 'Mark my words, it will be,' and trotted off to keep her appointment with Mr Patrick Maizie, Prop.

However impressed Evie had been by the Harp of Erin in the empty hour of the morning she was even more impressed when she entered the bar that evening. It was packed with labourers, shipwrights and dockers, the noise deafening.

Chiffin leaned on the bar rail. He wore a long canvas apron and the sort of cap a sea captain might wear, a very miniature sea captain, though, for the little cap clung to his thick red hair like a castaway to a rock. He shouted something that Evie couldn't make out and beckoned urgently. Evie battled her way through the boozers to the end of the bar.

'Where the hell've you been?' Chiffin shouted.

'Eight, you told me eight.'

'Nah, I told you early. I got folks breathin' their last for want o' a pint.' He grabbed her arm and dragged her after him. 'I hope you 'preciate just what I'm doin' for you, love, 'cos I don't do this for all the girls.' He tugged open a little door and pushed her outside into a gravel yard lit by a single gas lamp.

'Where are you takin' me?' Evie said. 'Where's Mr Maizie?'

'That's his office over there,' Chiffin said. 'He's waitin' for you.'

'You aren't leavin' me, are you?' Evie said.

'Aye, but I am,' Chiffin replied and stepped back into the Harp and left her alone in the yard.

'They've left you all alone, I see,' Benjamin Belfer said. 'Now if circumstances were different I wouldn't be averse to invitin' you to step downstairs to share my dinner, but I don't expect you'd accept.'

'I don't expect I would,' said Clare.

'Besides, the circumstances aren't different,' Mr Belfer said. 'First an' foremost I have my duty to do, so where's my money?'

'My brother hasn't come home yet.'

'Perhaps he's done a bunk.'

'He's working.'

'You sure about that?' Mr Belfer said. 'You sure he hasn't been waylaid by one of the pretty ladies who hang about Maizie's yard after dark?'

'I don't know what you mean,' said Clare.

''Course you do,' Mr Belfer said. 'Your brother wouldn't be the first chap to be tempted from the straight an' narrow by the offer of a little succour.'

'Nolan can find all the succour he needs at home.'

'Can he now?' said Benjamin Belfer. 'You give him succour, do you?'

'Aye, when he needs it.'

Mr Belfer hooked his thumbs into the broad leather belt that he had chosen to wear that evening. He had purchased the belt from a pawnshop down by the docks where bargains were to be had. He liked nice things, things with a bit of character, a bit of substance and history.

'Well, it won't be succour he's after tonight, I'm thinkin',"

Mr Belfer said. 'If he's been at the diggin' all day it'll be grub he'll want.' He looked round. 'I don't see no sign of a groanin' board.'

Clare said nothing. She was annoyed with Evie for going off and leaving her alone. She rubbed the bone comb over her thumb while the factor strutted round her like a rooster.

'Where's the other one?' he said. 'Your sister?'

'Gone out.'

'To buy food?'

'She's gone to look for work.'

Mr Belfer chuckled. 'I'll bet she has.' He glanced at her linens draped on the chair. 'Been doin' your wash, I see.'

If Evie had been here, Evie would have given him a sharp answer, but Evie wasn't here and she had never been as quick-witted as her sister.

Mr Belfer unhooked a thumb from his belt and picked up a piece of her linen. She wanted to scream and snatch the cloth away, but she was frozen with embarrassment just as she had been that day by the lake when the priest had taken her hand and pushed it under his cassock.

'For poor Irish,' Mr Belfer said, 'you've got some nice stuff.' His finger and thumb moved in a circular motion over the cloth. 'You aren't poor Irish, are you, Clare? An' you aren't related to the late Eamon Cassidy. I had a quiet word with the priest at St Kentigern's this afternoon. I know what sort o' trick you pulled to get a foot in my door.' There was no sound in the room save the faint hiss of damp sticks under the coals in the gate. 'One thing about priests,' Mr Belfer went on, 'they don't tell lies. You told me lies, didn't you, Clare?'

'No.'

'See, you're at it again. You'll have to confess, you know. Why not confess to me? Why not tell me the truth?'

'You'll tell Mrs Cassidy.'

'Is that what troubles you? Well, well!' He reached out and

caught her by the nape of the neck, his hand like a vice, his forefinger brushing the soft hairs. 'Concerned for the widow woman's feelin's, are you? Got a conscience after all, have you?'

He brought her head forward until her brow touched his. She could smell his breath, not meaty, not foul, but scented, like incense left in the air of a chapel after everyone had gone.

'Tell me,' he said, 'what you thought a poor widow woman could give you that you haven't got already?'

'Shelter,' Clare said. 'We needed shelter.'

'Shelter, aye, an' what else, Clare?' He held her easily with one hand. 'You cribbed the name from the headstone, an' invented the rest.'

'Don't tell her, Mr Belfer, please.'

'Are you a good girl, Clare?'

'I am, yes, I am.'

'An honest girl?'

'Yes, yes. We'll pay you your money.'

'When?'

'Soon as my brother gets home.'

'And if you don't . . .'

'We will, we will, I promise.'

'If you don't, know what I'll have to do?'

'Tell Mrs Cassidy.'

'Exactly,' said Mr Belfer, and, for the time being, let her go.

The man was alone in the outbuilding that Chiffin had told her was an office. It was the strangest office Evie had ever seen and Mr Maizie the strangest publican. He stood by a polished desk, his long legs crossed at the ankles. He wore riding boots, a canary-yellow waistcoat, chequered trousers, a frilled shirt and a turquoise cravat, held in place by a silver pin with a horse's head clasp upon it. He was smoking a thin cigar and a brandy glass stood on the desk.

'Are you the girl Chiffin told me about?' he said.

'I think I am,' Evie answered. 'Are you . . .'

'Patrick Maizie, aye.'

He was tall, lean and clean-shaven and, Evie thought, the most handsome man she had ever seen. There had been many handsome men at the Cork markets, dealers and cattle breeders, even bailiffs, like Mr Rogers. She had seen Lord Wring once and had thought him handsome too. None of them could hold a candle to Patrick Maizie, though, who was neither rustic nor aristocratic but somewhere in between.

Well aware of the effect he had upon impressionable young women, Mr Maizie examined the coal on the tip of his cigar and allowed Evie time to recover.

At length, he said, 'You are Chiffin's gal, I take it?'

'I'm not Mr Chiffin's anythin',' said Evie. 'I only met Mr Chiffin this mornin'.'

'*Mister* Chiffin? Good God! To the best of my knowledge no one has ever called him *Mister* Chiffin before.'

'I've come about the job.'

'Post,' said Patrick Maizie.

'Beg pardon?'

'Post, as in position,' Patrick Maizie told her. 'What you are up for, my dear young lady, is a position. Have you ever served the public before?'

Evie looked straight into Mr Maizie's wicked grey eyes. 'No, sir,' she said. 'I have not.'

'How long have you been in Glasgow?'

'A week – almost.'

'Fresh off the Irish boat?'

'Yes, sir. From Cork.'

'Do you have a husband?'

'No, sir, no husband.'

'Children?'

'No children neither, sir.'

'With whom do you lodge?'

'Me sister, sir, an' me brother.'

'Where?'

'Down the street at number five.'

'Old Belfer must be mighty pleased to have a dainty young thing like you on the premises. He's worth the watching is our Benjamin.'

'My aunt lodges there. She found us the room.'

'I see.' Patrick Maizie uncrossed his legs and lifted the brandy glass. 'Care for a snifter, Miss McKenna?'

The fact that he knew her name pleased Evie enormously. 'I think not, sir, thank you all the same.'

'Port then?' he said. 'I have an excellent year in my cabinet.'

'What year would that be, sir?'

'Eighteen twenty-two. You don't know much about wines, do you?'

Evie traced the line of her upper lip with the tip of her tongue. Any attempt on her part to deceive Patrick Maizie concerning her worldly experience would be daft. 'Not a blessed thing,' she said. 'I'm just off the farm.'

'Chiffin seems to think you're ideally suited for the post.'

'Sure an' I don't even know what the job – the post is, sir.'

'Take off that ridiculous hat.'

'Beg pardon?'

'The hat, the hat, take it off. Let's have a proper look at you.'

'Why do you want to look at me, Mr Maizie?'

'Because, sweetheart, I'm not hiring you for your knowledge of the licensing laws or for your strength of arm. I don't require you to haul casks from the cellars. I'm hiring you – if I decide to hire you at all, that is – for your looks. So take off the hat an' that shawl thing.'

She felt less confident now that he had put his cards on the table.

She dropped the flowery hat to the floor and let the shawl fall from her shoulders. She knew that she had a pretty face but, by some lights, not much of a figure. She kept her eyes down while he scrutinised her.

'What's your forename?' he said.

'Evelyn – Evie.'

'Can you count?'

''Course I can count.'

'If I present you with a guinea an' order three glasses at threepence each,' he said, 'an' four pots at fourpence, how much change do you give me?'

'Two shillings an' one pence deducted from twenty-one shillings,' said Evie promptly, 'leaves eighteen shillings an' elevenpence.'

'Very good,' he said. 'Where did you learn your arithmetic?'

'School first,' Evie said, 'but mostly at market. Try me with corn measures; sure an' I'm grand at those.'

Patrick Maizie put the cigar to his lips, took a long pull and blew smoke towards the ceiling.

The ceiling was low and crossed by heavy wooden beams. Behind the desk was an armchair, a sofa draped with plaid, a little tub chair and a velvet-covered footstool. Glass cases on the wall displayed a variety of stuffed fish and small mammals, all beady-eyed and attentive, but Evie had also noticed a line of wooden cabinets of the sort they had in banks and a big metal object that could only be a safe.

'Is this where you live, Mr Maizie?'

'No,' he said. 'This is where I work,' and at that moment seemed to lose interest in her. 'Look, you're not quite what I had in mind, sweetheart, but you do have a lively way about you, and you're pretty enough, I suppose.' He walked around the desk, tossed the cigar into the fireplace, and propped an elbow on the mantel. Two ornate gas globes hissed softly on either side of him and in the trembling yellow light he seemed older, though no less handsome. 'I'll take you on trial, how's that? Give you a week, see if you suit.'

'Do I get paid while I'm on trial?'

'You need cash, do you? Yes, I expect you do,' Patrick Maizie said. 'The hours are ten o'clock in the morning to God knows when – midnight or after – six days in the week, including public holidays. Thanks to the influence of the holy-rollers in the temperance lobby we are obliged to close on Sundays.'

'Is this a place where gentlemen drink?'

He laughed. 'Aye, where gentlemen drink. If you prove right with the gentlemen and can be trusted with cash then I'll sign you on permanent at the end of the month. How's that?'

She waited for him to tell her what she would earn and when she would be paid. Then she looked at Patrick Maizie again, at the handsome face and grey, calculating eyes, and, if it had been practical, would have offered her services for nothing just to save him the embarrassment of having to talk about money.

'Mr Maizie,' Evie said, 'how much do you pay?'

He slipped his elbow from the mantelshelf and shrugged. 'Fifteen shillings,' he said. 'Best I can do.'

'Fifteen shillings a month?'

'Fifteen shillings a week.'

And Evie shouted, 'I'll take it,' before the lovely Mr Maizie could change his lovely mind.

Kiernan had been all skin and bone even before his illness but Nolan had always been big, with hard flat muscles and a breadth to him that had all the girls back home gasping. Unlike Evie, Clare had never seen Nolan naked. Evie had been so curious about men, that, just last summer, she had spied on Nolan and his chums at the lakeside one hot evening when the boys had been lolling about just as God made them. Evie would have taken Clare with her but Clare had been too frightened of what she would see and how different it would be from the thing that lay in the pocket of little baby boys – especially after Evie had told her what grown men did with it.

It was after nine o'clock before Nolan shambled through the door. He looked like a creature dragged from a bog, so coated with filth that Clare had to stick a fist in her mouth to stop herself crying out at the sight of him.

'Nolan,' she said. 'What have they done to you?'

'Done? They've done nothin'.' He lowered himself on to a chair, smearing mud on to the floorboards, dug into the pocket of his breeches, fished out a handful of coins and slapped them down on the table. 'They've done nothin' but pay me. See,' he said, 'eight shillin's I earned today an' it'll be eight shillin's a day for as long as the job lasts.'

'Look at you,' Clare said. 'You're filthy.'

'It's muck, just muck.' In spite of his triumphant grin he seemed disinclined to move. He slumped forward, his big hands dangling between his knees. 'By Gar, though, it was hard graft down in the river. If it hadn't been for the gravel bed we'd have sunk without trace, us big fellers. They pull us out when the tide rises, haulin' us up by ladders an' ropes. Still, it's the first quay wall in Glasgow to be built on cylinders an' it'll be a long job wi' plenty o' work for diggers even when the trench is dug an' the dredgers get at it.' He hoisted himself stiffly to his feet. 'Is there hot water in that kettle an' a tub for me to be standin' up in?'

'Hot water,' Clare told him. 'No tub.'

She felt guilty because she hadn't anticipated his needs.

There was no food in the house. Mr Belfer would snatch a piece of Nolan's eight shillings but that would leave plenty to buy them supper.

She bit her thumb and stared at him as if she expected him to smack her for her carelessness. He looked so big, so ugly, not glistening with harvest sweat now or powdered with the white dust that rose from the road that went nowhere but caked with filth from the River Clyde and stinking to high heaven.

'Help me get out of these clothes before I catch me death,' he said.

She peeled off his coat and shirt, detached the undershirt from his body and tugged it off, too. He held his arms above his head.

'Where's our Evie got to then?' he asked.

'Gone to look for work.'

'She's not on the street, is she?'

'No, not the street,' Clare assured him

She told him all that Evie had told her. She was tempted to tell him about Benjamin Belfer's visit but didn't wish to burden him with her woes.

Besides, the rent had been earned and tomorrow Nolan would bring home another eight shillings and they would have a second week's rent laid by and enough left over for food and coal.

She looked around, found the ash bucket, knocked it against the side of the fireplace and shook out as much grit as she could. She lifted the big kettle and poured a stream of hot water into the bucket. She would have to boil more, lots more, to wash his clothes. She had a tiny piece of sweet soap in her pack. She knelt by the side of the bed and brought out the soap and a ragged towel. She ripped the towel in half and dropped half into the bucket.

She got up from her knees and faced him.

He was naked now, all naked, every inch of him, his back towards her.

She could see the bulging muscles of his hips swell into his broad backside. In candlelight he looked like a giant, his thighs parted and spine arched as he stretched his stiffening sinews.

Clare closed her mouth against the smell of him. She

plunged her hands into the hot water and rubbed soap into the cloth. She slapped the cloth into the middle of his back below his shoulder blades and let the water trickle down his spine into the cleft of his buttocks.

Nolan shivered at her pampering touch.

She rubbed him down as she might do a pony, washing his back and arms and shoulders, the cloth sliding against his flesh.

He groaned and closed his eyes.

She knelt on the wet floor and washed his legs and feet, cupping her hands about his calves, her hair tickling the back of his thighs.

Our engine, Evie called him, our machine: Clare knew now what her sister meant. She slapped the cloth against his backside and, closing her eyes, told him to turn around.

It was not entirely by chance, Evie reckoned, that Jock Macpherson and little Mrs Cassidy were loitering in the close.

'I have work,' she blurted out. 'Sure isn't that the good news.'

'Good news, indeed,' Mr Macpherson said.

She was too elated to hold anything back. 'I met Mr Maizie face to face an' he took me on. He says I'll be ideal for the job. Imagine me – ideal.'

Cissie Cassidy and Mr Macpherson exchanged a glance.

'What sort of job is it, dear?' Mrs Cassidy enquired.

'Sure an' I'm to be servin' drink to gentlemen.'

'Gentlemen?' said Jock Macpherson ruefully. 'Where?'

'At the Harp, of course.'

'A barmaid!' Mrs Cassidy said, and shook her head.

'Aye, a barmaid,' said Evie, 'at fifteen shillin' a week.'

'Fifteen shillings?' Jock Macpherson said. 'By Gum, you must've made a very favourable impression on old Paddy Maizie.'

'He's not so old,' said Evie.

'Forty, if he's a day,' sniffed little Mrs Cassidy.

'I start learnin' the ropes tomorrow.' Evie looked up the ill-lit staircase. 'Has my brother come home yet?'

'I think I heard him come in about a half-hour ago,' Jock said.

Evie took off the flowery hat, tossed it into the air and caught it as if it were a shuttlecock. 'If Nolan's found work too then we'll have the rent settled an' money in our pockets to buy all the things we need.'

'So you won't be wantin' this then?' Mrs Cassidy said.

She held out a brown paper parcel that leaked a little gravy.

'What is it?' Evie asked.

'A pie,' the woman answered.

'I can't pay you till Saturday,' Evie said.

'I'm not askin' for payment,' Cissie Cassidy said.

Evie had eaten nothing all day long and her belly was sticking to her backbone. She put an arm about the widow woman and kissed her cheek.

'Thank you, Aunt Cissie,' she said.

'It's the least a person can do for family,' Mrs Cassidy said.

'Sure an' that's what we are now, is it not?' Evie said, then, with her hat in one hand and the pie in the other, dashed off upstairs to break the good news to Nolan and to her sister, Clare.

4

Now that they had secured the room, Clare was determined to make it habitable. Soon after Evie left, she went out and found a corner shop and bought a broom and a bristle brush and spent the morning scrubbing the walls and floorboards. That done, she crossed the lane to the stables, introduced herself to Mrs McLean, the horseman's wife, and paid for the use of the boiling tub. She carried the steaming garments back across the lane, draped them on chairs in the kitchen, then went out again to buy bacon, butter, bread and lard, fresh eggs, sugar, tea, and three slices of iced gingerbread.

By that time her knees hurt and her back ached and she longed to slump by the fire and rest before Nolan came clumping in, demanding attention. She was half asleep when a tentative tapping disturbed her. For a moment she considered lying doggo, then, sighing, she rose, went out into the lobby and opened the front door.

'Mrs Cassidy, is that you?'

'Aye, dear. I just come by to see if you're settled. Is your sister in?'

'She's at her new job.'

'At Maizie's?'

'Aye.' Clare felt mean keeping the widow on the draughty landing after all the woman had done for them. 'Would you care to come in for a minute?'

The widow's face brightened. 'If I'm not imposin'?'

'You're not imposin',' Clare said. 'Come on.'

Mrs Cassidy stepped through the tiny lobby into the kitchen.

'My, my!' she said admiringly. 'What you've done here is a miracle. I'm glad you're a hard worker, dear. My Eamon was a hard worker, but, just between you an' me, he was a lazy beggar about the house.'

'Pardon?'

'Him, my spouse, your uncle; a right lazy beggar.'

'Oh!'

'Is that a teapot on the hob?'

'Aye.' Clare hesitated. 'Would you like a cup?'

'I'd love a cup,' said Mrs Cassidy eagerly. Ignoring the damp underwear, she seated herself. 'It crossed my mind that you an' your sister might be more like my Eamon. What a relief to find you're not.'

'Oh!' said Clare again.

'Mr Coker was a lazy beggar, too,' the widow continued, 'but he never had a wife to keep him up to the mark.' She took the teacup and sipped. 'Now, tell me all about yourself an' the others you left behind in Killarney.'

'Others?'

'Your cousins.'

'There are no cousins,' Clare said. 'It's just me, Evie an' Nolan.'

'What about the brother who was hanged? What was his name again?'

Clare swallowed hard. 'Mam never talked about him. I think his name was – was – Brian. Or no, maybe Brendan.'

'Aye, that was it,' said Mrs Cassidy. 'He never had much opportunity to father children before they sent him to the gallows, did he?'

It was on the tip of Clare's tongue to enquire what crime her 'uncle' had committed but to her relief Mrs Cassidy bobbed off on another tack.

'I hope she's careful, your sister,' the widow said. 'Paddy Maizie's not a man to be trusted. I hope Evie hasn't been dazzled by him.'

'I'm sure she hasn't,' said Clare. 'What's wrong with Mr Maizie?'

'He's a publican for one thing.'

'Sure an' there's nothin' wrong with publicans,' said Clare. 'Jesus had friends who were publicans.'

'Aye, but you do hear some funny stories.'

'About Jesus?'

'About Paddy Maizie,' Cissie Cassidy said. 'He arrived in Riverside with nothin' but the shirt on his back, a cart an' a donkey. He sold beer at the gates o' the cotton factory in Anderston Street until the council came down on him for tradin' without a licence. Next thing you know, he's leased the old cottages, had them done up and opened the Harp.'

'Where did he get the money to pay for all that?'

'I'm not one for gossip,' Mrs Cassidy answered, 'but they say he got his money from women.'

'Women?'

'Aye, women. There's a wife somewhere, though nobody in these parts has ever seen her. Children too, so they say.'

'Perhaps the wife has money?'

'Oh, she'll have money.' Mrs Cassidy nodded. 'You can be sure of that.'

Clare wondered what Mrs Cassidy might be able to tell her about Mr Belfer, not to mention Harry Fairfield, but before she could slip in a question, the widow was off again.

'Paddy Maizie's had girls by the dozen. I'm not sayin' he makes profit from these lassies, but there was all sorts o' talk at one time. Baillie Johnstone – him as is dead now – Baillie Johnstone made a fair song an' dance when the pub's licence came up for renewal an' they say Mr Maizie had to bribe him to stay in business.' Mrs Cassidy gathered herself and got to her feet. 'There is one thing to be said for lodgin' in Mr Belfer's house, though.'

'What's that?' said Clare.

'If it's a husband you're after, this is a rare place to find one.'

Clare grinned. 'Is there anyone in particular you'd care to recommend?'

'Mr Macpherson's not to be sneezed at.'

'He's too old for me.'

'He's not old. He's not that far past thirty. He's in reg'lar work an' has a gentle disposition. What's more, he's a Catholic.'

'Is he?' Clare said, surprised.

'Lapsed,' Mrs Cassidy said. 'But the love of a good woman would bring him back into the fold, I'm sure.'

'Is it marriage or missionary work you have in mind for me?' said Clare.

Cissie Cassidy was not so lacking in wit that she did not see the joke. 'You're a card, Clare McKenna, so you are,' she said. 'But I wouldn't be too hoity-toity if I were you, not if it's a husband you fancy.'

'I'm not sure I do fancy a husband,' Clare said. 'Right now all we've got in our heads is earnin' a few shillin' to keep a roof over our heads an' put meat on the table.'

'A man'll see to that,' said Mrs Cassidy. 'I mean a husband, of course.'

'What about Mr Fairfield? He's not married, is he?'

'Oh, so it's our Harry that's caught your eye, is it?' Mrs Cassidy shook her head. 'He's too quick with his tongue, that one, too smarmy for my likin'.'

'And fancy-free?' said Clare.

'That, too,' the widow said. 'Aye, that too.'

'Tell me this, Aunt Cissie, why you do advocate marriage for us when your own marriage was such a disaster?'

'Disaster? Oh no, no. My Eamon was the salt o' the earth,'

Cissie Cassidy said. 'As handsome a wee man as you'd come across in a day's march. He worked hard all his life an' never raised a fist to me even in his cups. I might take the stick to his memory now he's gone, but that's the only bad thing Eamon ever did to me.'

'Dyin', you mean?' said Clare.

'Aye, dyin',' said Cissie Cassidy, pecked the Irish beauty on the cheek and departed, leaving Clare with her teacup and her gingerbread to wait for her brother to come home.

Of the eight ramshackle tenements that flanked the Wedderburn Road four were owned by Russell Blackstock.

The Parliamentary Act of 1868 had forced private landlords to install sanitation and maintain certain levels of habitation but in the ten years that Mr Belfer had collected rents for Mr Blackstock there had been no appreciable improvement in the temper of the tenants, which was why Mr Belfer seldom ventured into Wedderburn Road unaccompanied and why both he and his escort, Mr Percival Orpington, carried a length of lead piping under their overcoats.

If Mr Belfer aspired to resemble a gentleman, Mr Orpington had long passed him in that respect.

He was a large man, bluff but not blustering, and spoke with an English accent that hinted at good breeding. He wore hand-sewn suits, hand-lasted boots, a top hat and a long Chesterfield overcoat with a velvet collar that had cost more than most of his clients earned in a year.

He was notoriously polite and in the course of conversation would raise his topper more often than he raised his voice, a habit that struck fear into the hearts of the citizens of Wedderburn Road who had no defence against hypocrisy.

'A fine night, Benjamin,' said Mr Orpington, as he stepped over the sludge in the close-mouth. 'Although I confess I prefer a bit of motion in the air.'

'Indeed, indeed,' Mr Belfer agreed. 'However, I do recommend a deep breath of that selfsame air before we enter the building.'

Mr Orpington inhaled bravely.

'Good God, Mr B.,' he said, 'why *do* these people do this to themselves?'

'It's a mystery to me,' said Mr Belfer. 'We repaired the water closet only last year, yet here we are again, sloshing through shite.'

Following in Mr Belfer's footsteps, like Wenceslas's page, Mr Orpington picked his way to the bottom of the stairs, took up position in a dark corner and allowed Mr Belfer to go on alone.

There was no glass in the windows, the woodwork had all but rotted away and draughts provided the only ventilation. A couple of ragged children, lurking on the second landing, slithered away from the man with the fat belly and went off to warn Daddy that nemesis was at hand.

On the top floor, Mr Belfer began his night's work. He rapped on a peeling door. The door, in fact, was not only peeling but cracked where, five weeks ago, Mr Belfer had been obliged to apply a crowbar to make his presence known. Daniel Towey was the registered tenant, the flat officially occupied by a wife, two unmarried daughters and an infant son.

There were usually several guests staying over, however, relatives, Mr Towey said, from across the water. The room was hardly bigger than Mr Belfer's broom cupboard and had no running water save that which seeped through the walls, but dampness hardly seemed to matter to Mr Towey or his visitors.

The door opened. Mr Belfer gripped the lead pipe a little more firmly.

The woman was clad in a filthy shift. Tipsy but not plastered, she gave him a leer and tilted her bony hips.

Since that night, five weeks ago, when Mr Belfer and Mr Orpington had smashed the pot-still on which Mr Towey's livelihood depended the collection agent had been treated with more respect.

'Come fur yur money then, Mr Belfer, have ye?'

'Aye, Jinty, that I have.'

The girl held out her hand and showed Mr Belfer six shillings in grubby coins, then, laughing, closed her fist again.

In no mood for games, Mr Belfer snared her wrist and twisted it until she cried out and her hand flew open. He tipped the coins from her palm and slipped them into his overcoat pocket.

'Thank you, my dear,' he said and shoved her back into the smelly lobby before she could rake him with her claws.

He stepped across the landing to O'Hara's house. No problem here: O'Hara was a sober, sullen, bearded man, who clerked for Russell Blackstock at the coal yard and never missed a payment or, for that matter, a meeting of the Glasgow Protestant Laymen's Association of which Wilson Blackstock was a patron. Mr Belfer collected his dues, exchanged a few words with Mr O'Hara about the state of the weather and the parentage of the Pope, then moved down, floor by floor, to street level.

Only one door was bolted against him.

Mr Belfer was unconcerned.

Mr Orpington would take care of it.

Dressed in britches, braces and a pair of stockings that had seen better days, Mr Thomas Knox was at that moment endeavouring to explain to Mr Orpington the reason for his sudden departure from his domicile, a reason so outlandish that only common courtesy prevented Mr Orpington from laughing out loud.

Instead, he doffed his topper, pressed the lead pipe across Mr Knox's gullet and pinned the lying little bugger to the wall.

'Dreadfully sorry, old chap,' Mr Orpington said softly, 'but I am not entirely convinced that your diseased kidney requires immediate attention. Somehow the alacrity of your flight in search of medical assistance and the nimbleness with which you bounded downstairs deny the validity of your story and rob it of the essential ring of truth.'

'S'help me Goad, Mr Orpin'tin, it's no' me,' Tommy Knox declared, his Adam's apple bobbing against the lead. 'It's the dug.'

'Oh, the dog!' Mr Orpington said. 'I see.'

'Bleedin' like a pig, he is, when he pishes.'

'Which dog would that be?' said Mr Orpington. 'The lurcher, the terrier, or the greyhound?'

'The greyhound. Flash is no' sae young as he used tae be.'

'None of us are, Thomas, none of us are,' said Mr Orpington sympathetically. 'I assume that your mission of mercy involves the expenditure of a sum very close to that which is owed in rent.'

'Animal doctors cost an awfu' lot o' money,' Tommy said.

'No doubt,' said Mr Orpington. 'However, is Flash not a little long in the tooth to be restored to full vigour even by the most skilled veterinarian? Will six shillings guarantee his return to the racing track?'

'Tae tell the truth, naw, he'll never be the dug he was.'

'Therefore the most you can hope for in exchange for an expenditure of six shillings is to bring relief to poor old Flash?' said Mr Orpington. 'Yes?'

Defeated by reason and unable to breathe, Tommy nodded.

'In a word, to put him out of his misery?' said Mr Orpington.

Tommy nodded again glumly.

Mr Orpington removed both the lead and his topper.

'It says a great deal for your humanitarian instincts, Thomas, that you would sacrifice your hard-earned cash and put yourself into debt for the sake of a dumb animal. I am, however, of the opinion that such a sacrifice is quite unnecessary.'

'Naw, Mr Orpin'tin, naw.'

'Do you actually have the six shillings, Thomas?'

'It's been a bad week, Mr Orpin'tin, honest it has.'

'Do you, or do you not, have the frigging cash?'

'It's all there is fur tae feed—'

'And yet,' Mr Orpington interrupted, 'you would permit your family to starve just to prolong the life of an aged canine.'

'Naw, naw, please, naw,' said Tommy Knox.

'I'll tell you what,' said Mr Orpington, 'I will assume the role of veterinarian and, at no extra charge, will personally put poor Flash out of his misery. Thus the burden of finding the scratch to fulfil your obligations to Mr Belfer will be removed, your conscience, on that score at least, will be clear and you will be free to concentrate on providing sustenance for your family. Where have you hidden the money, Tommy?'

'On top o' the dresser.'

'Jolly good!' said Mr Orpington. 'Now, stay here. I shan't be a tick.'

'Wait,' said Tommy Knox. 'Look, don't let the weans see . . .'

'The children? Certainly not,' Mr Orpington said, and with the length of lead piping tucked discreetly down by his trouser leg, picked his way upstairs.

'Is that blood on your sleeve, Perce?' Mr Belfer asked, as they stepped out of the close-mouth into Wedderburn Road.

'Heavens! I hope not.' Mr Orpington raised his arm to inspect his sleeve. 'I was exceedingly careful in the execution of my duty.' He brushed his hand over the invisible stain.

'I think it's just a little roughing of the cloth, thank you, Benjamin.'

'What did you do with the . . .' Mr Belfer let the sentence hang.

'Placed it on the midden. No doubt Thomas will give the beast a decent burial. They are amazingly sentimental about their pets, aren't they?' said Mr Orpington. 'How much better it would be for them, and for society, if they cared as much for their children as they do for their animals.'

'Indeed, indeed.' Mr Belfer extracted a watch and, holding it up to the haze that passed for street lighting, said, 'Well, Perce, an hour should see us through, then, with your agreement, I'll stand you a bite o' supper an' a glass of something French at Maizie's.'

'After we stash the dibbins, of course.'

'Of course,' said Benjamin Belfer and, touching Mr Orpington cautiously on the arm, led the way forward to tackle tenement number two.

At ten o'clock that Friday morning fifteen shillings for six days' work had seemed like money for old rope. By mid-afternoon Evie was less sure and by ten at night she had begun to regard the job as not much better than slave labour.

She was not so badly off as Bob Draper, the head barman, or her chum Chiffin, however. Their day began at half past seven and involved heaving barrels from drays in the back yard, collecting wine in the wood and cask whisky from spirit dealers, plus a hundred and one mysterious activities in the cellar, all in addition to serving drink to idlers who had a thirst to satisfy.

Between whiles Chiffin instructed Evie in the art and craft of pulling levers, showed her how to differentiate between various strengths of beer and how to read the measures used for dispensing spirits. But when noon came and a gaggle of building workers arrived in search of refreshment, she was put to rinsing glasses in a long zinc-lined trough and arranging them on shelves behind the bar where Bob Draper and Chiffin, working like demons, could reach them with a minimum of fuss. The Harp also served food; a corridor near the bar led to a smoke-filled kitchen where an elderly man fried meat and fish in a huge skillet over a gas stove and an even older woman delivered the dishes to customers in the snug.

At three in the afternoon, when the rush had quietened down, Mr Draper sent Evie into the snug where she was served with a bowl of green pea soup and three greasy slices of sausage meat piled on a piece of fried bread.

She ate hungrily, drank the glass of stout that Chiffin brought her and stared up at the big railway clock that was screwed to the panelling above the door. She watched the hand tick away the seconds and wearily calculated that her first day as a barmaid was only half over and worse was probably to come.

It was beginning to dawn on her that she wasn't a hand-picked attraction whom Mr Maizie favoured for her looks but only a lowly servant whose main assets were that she spoke with an Irish accent, was young enough not to buckle under the workload – and came cheap.

Afternoon wore on into evening, the pub filled up once more and Evie went back to rinsing pots and glasses. Shortly after ten, she glanced up from the suds and in the mirror behind the bar caught sight of two men entering the bar. She stiffened and, side-stepping along the duckboard, nudged Chiffin as he tapped whisky from a dumpy little cask on the shelf.

'Is that Belfer?' Evie asked in a hoarse whisper.

Chiffin looked in the mirror. 'Aye,' he said. 'An' Orpington's with him.'

'Orpington? Who's Orpington?'

'Not somebody you want to tangle with, chucks,' Chiffin told her. 'Not somebody *anybody* wants to tangle with. Get on back to your work.'

Evie returned to the trough but continued to watch the new arrivals in the mirror. They moved easily through the crowd, like ships ploughing through choppy waters. The boozers parted before them and an awkward silence trailed in their wake. They did not come to the counter but headed straight for the snuggery from which, a moment later, a burly young navvy and two little old women who had been eating supper emerged and hastily left the pub, followed, Evie noticed, by four or five drinkers from the bar.

Mr Draper tapped her shoulder. 'You,' he said in a rumbling voice. 'Hop out back an' tell Mr Maizie that Belfer's turned up at last.'

'Me?' said Evie. 'What about Chiffin?'

'He's busy,' said Mr Draper. 'You do it.'

Mr Draper was a tall, raw-boned man of about forty-five. He had been in the liquor trade all his life, so Chiffin told her, and knew everything there was to know about running a public house. He was well paid, Chiffin said, and would treat you fair if you did what you were told and didn't cross him.

'Is Mr Maizie in the – the office?' Evie asked.

'He'd better be,' said Mr Draper and gave her a little shove towards the passage that led out to the yard. 'Go on, lass, be quick. We mustn't keep them gentlemen waitin'.'

Evie discarded the drying cloth, hurried down the passageway and out into the cool night air. She had expected the yard to be deserted at that hour but several men and girls lurked in the shadows by the barrel stacks.

Nervously, she tugged off her muslin cap, combed her hair with her fingers and ran across the yard to the office.

She rapped on the door with the horseshoe that served as a knocker and, after a pause, the door was opened by a very tall woman, a woman who looked, Evie thought, almost more male than female.

The woman wore a sheath-like evening dress in dark blue silk. Her hair was the colour of boiling pitch and topped by a false plait. She displayed no jewellery of any kind save a crucifix of ebony wood attached to a black velvet ribbon that accentuated the whiteness of her throat and bosom.

'What do you want, girl?' the woman said.

'I've – I've a message for Mr Maizie.'

'Have you now?' the woman said. 'Well, Mr Maizie's busy.'

She made as if to close the door but Evie, though frightened, would have none of it. She said, 'Sure an' I'm to see Mr Maizie, if he's here at all.'

The woman glanced behind her and, receiving a signal of some sort, stood back and allowed Evie to step into the room. She was relieved to see Mr Maizie there; very smart and handsome he looked, lounging on the sofa in a frilly evening shirt and butterfly tie.

She dropped a curtsey and received a nod by way of greeting.

'Mr Draper says to tell you Mr Belfer's come at last.'

The woman raised her eyes to heaven and let out a groan.

Paddy Maizie heaved himself from the sofa. 'Is Belfer alone?'

'No, sir,' said Evie. 'There's another man with him, a Mr Orp . . .'

'Orpington,' the woman said. 'Good God, Patrick, are you still doing business with that piece of filth?'

'He does business with me, if you must know,' Paddy said, then, to Evie, 'Tell Belfer I'll be with him directly. Where is he, by the way? In the snug?'

'Aye, sir.'

'Mr Draper knows the drill. He'll show you what do.'

'Me, Mr Maizie?' Evie said.

'You, or someone else,' Paddy Maizie said. 'I shan't be long,' then with a weary little wave of the hand dismissed her.

Nolan lay on the bed, dead to the world. She had helped him wash, had given him a clean shirt to wear and had fed him his supper. Soon after that he had tumbled into bed as if he were drunk. She could hardly blame him for falling asleep, for he had spent half the day floundering in watery mud, wielding a shovel, and the other half, far into the night, filling the wagons that would carry the soil hauled out of the river to a dumping ground in fields far away.

Clare understood not a half of what he told her, only that there would be work aplenty for months to come and that he would have a share of it. Now, close to midnight, she was obliged to listen to her sister's complaints, while Nolly, innocent as child, slumbered undisturbed.

'Sure an' there I am,' Evie went on, 'with a full bottle o' French brandy, the best in the house, an' two big glasses, an' Chiffin, all white an' shaking, hiding behind Mr Draper, sayin' he's not going near that back room while Mr Orpington's there. An' Mr Draper telling me there's nothing for to fear since I'm not owing anybody money.'

Clare lifted the last rasher from the pan and dropped it on Evie's plate. Her sister ate with great rapidity, as if she had been given a limit of time to demolish her supper.

She had seen Evie in this excited state before and said, obligingly, 'So, tell me, dearest, what did you do then?'

'Did what I was told,' said Evie, stuffing bacon into her mouth. 'You don't cross Mr Draper, not him, for he's the power in the land. Next thing, there I am in the snug, just me an' old Belfer an' the one they're all afraid of, though he seems fine to me, dolled up, quiet-spoke an' polite. He looks at the brandy label, then at me an' thanks me kindly for my generosity, as if I'd paid for the bloody bottle meself.'

'Belfer, what did he say?'

'He asked after you, asked after you particular.'

'Did he now?' said Clare. 'How did you answer him?'

'I said you were keepin' yourself busy.'

'So I am, so I am,' Clare said.

'The one calls himself Orpington, he looks me straight in the eye an' asks in that well-spoke voice if my sister is as pretty as I am.'

'What did you say to that?'

'Told him, yes, you were the flower o' the family.'

'You didn't?' said Clare.

'I did,' said Evie. 'He looks me straight in the eye again, an' says, "You're a very lucky fellow, Benjamin." Old Belfer turns red as a carrot, grabs the brandy bottle before I can start to pour, an' tells me to make myself scarce.'

'I take it you did what you were told.'

'Sure an' I did,' said Evie. 'I dropped a curtsey an' scooted back out to the bar only to find the place is near empty, with Mr Draper washin' out the beer taps an' Chiffin, still white as a sheet, rattlin' glasses at the trough – which is my job.'

'I thought you were a barmaid,' Clare said.

'I am, I will be, when I learn the ropes.' Evie mopped up the last of the egg yolk from her plate with a pinch of bread and, wiping her lips on her sleeve, went on, 'Five minutes was all it took for a glimpse of Mr Belfer an' the other one to empty the place.'

'There's more to Mr Belfer than meets the eye, seems like?' Clare said.

'Aye, a lot more.' Evie reached for a square of iced gingerbread. 'It's all damned funny, sure an' it is, the more so since nobody will tell me anythin'.'

'Not even Chiffin?'

'Specially not Chiffin. All he would say was that Mr Patterson – he's the cook – wouldn't be pleased at havin' to stay late. The pair in the snug have to be fed, no matter what the hour.'

'So they come there reg'lar, do they?'

'Mostly Fridays, I think.'

'Collection night,' Clare said. 'I'll bet Belfer's got the rents with him.'

'You're right, dearest,' Evie said. 'I'm sure that's the way of it.'

'Did Mr Maizie put in an appearance?'

'He did. He sauntered in, calm as you like, still wearin' his dickey with the fancy necktie, an' tells Mr Draper to let us go home.'

'Leavin' them there, just the three o' them.'

Her cheeks full of gingerbread, Evie nodded. 'Now ain't that all very rum, dear, all very rum?'

'Very,' Clare agreed. 'What about the woman?'

'Never saw her again,' said Evie.

'Is she Mr Maizie's sweetheart?'

'That's probably a nice way o' puttin' it,' Evie said.

'Perhaps you'll find out more tomorrow?' Clare said.

'You can be bloody sure I will,' said Evie.

5

Bob Draper was far too discreet to gossip with a fly-by-night Irish lass even if she did have dimples and a winning smile. In honesty, he did not expect her to remain much longer than the last girl, or the one before that. In fact, there had been times over the past few years when Bob wondered if he wasn't managing a brothel or a marriage bureau, not a bar at all.

Chiffin had no such concerns. In his book the more girls the boss hired the better, for, one fine day, some female would step off the boat with his name on her dance-card, a girl not only pretty but also dim enough to take him on.

He might, of course, have purchased love of sorts by shelling out a shilling to one of the girls who plied her trade after dark in the Harp's back yard, but, for all his knowingness and bluster, Chiff was not only a virgin but a devout Roman Catholic who had no wish to condemn his soul to eternal torment by consorting with harlots. Besides, he rarely had a shilling to spare these days, for he had become the sole support of his dear old mother and three small sisters after Da had run off to Newcastle with the daughter of the woman in the next close.

'Orpington?' Chiffin pushed his chop around in a puddle of grease. 'Orpington's a right bad lot. He'd have the drawers off your back as soon as look at you if he thought they was worth a penny in the pawn. Oh aye, he'll lend you money an' talk sweet while doin' it, but if you don't pay up he'll skin your rabbit without battin' an eyelid.'

'Skin my rabbit?' said Evie.

'Take everythin' you've got,' Chiffin explained.

'What if you don't have anythin'?' Evie said.

'Everybody's got somethin' of value, even if they don't know what it is,' Chiffin said. 'Orpington always knows. Orpington works for the bank.'

'The bank? What bank?'

'The Barony of Glasgow Bank,' said Chiffin. 'Nothin' wrong with the bank itself. Safe as houses, it is, an' most o' its collectors are honest. Come to think of it, Orpington's honest too – after a fashion. He helps collect deposits from small investors every Saturday night at the Masonic Hall in Carpenter Street. If you're scared o' going anywhere near the Orange Lodge, you needn't be. With old Percival Orpington on guard at the door there's no place safer in the whole o' Glasgow than Carpenter Street on a Saturday night.'

One mutton chop, three boiled potatoes and a mound of mashed peas, washed down with a pint was reckoned to be sufficient nourishment to sustain the underlings through the long watch that lay ahead.

On Saturdays the Harp was busy from dawn until midnight, but on those afternoons when Riverside Thistle were playing a football match on the ash pitches on the hillside above Plantation Quay, a lull in trade occurred about half past two o'clock. As soon as the score was settled, though, a deluge of supporters, usually chilled and usually disgruntled, would pour down from the heights and every pub for miles around would be seething.

Evie watched her informant lift his chop in both hands and gnaw gristle from around the bone. He was not so bad, was Chiffin; that mop of red hair and those long ginger eyelashes made him look stupid but, Evie thought, he was not so daft as all that.

She polished off the spuds and, following Chiffin's lead, took her chop in both hands. 'How long do we have?'

Chiff glanced at the clock. 'Ten minutes.'

She nibbled delicately at the bone. 'How old are you, Chiff?'

'Old enough to do for you, love.'

'Come on, how old?'

'Twenty.'

'How much did you borrow from Mr Orpington?'

Chiff's jaw dropped. 'How the heck did you know that?'

'I'm a good guesser,' Evie said.

'My da borrowed five pounds,' Chiffin said, 'two years ago. Then, when he did a bunk, I was left holdin' the baby.'

'Haven't you paid it off yet?' said Evie, surprised.

'Nah, I'll never pay it off,' Chiffin said. 'I'll be in that bugger's debt till the day I bleedin' die – if you'll pardon the French.'

'They're all the same, ain't they?' Evie said.

'Who is?'

'Landlords an' money-lenders. *They* never go broke.'

Chiffin rubbed a hand over his mouth and squinted. 'You, too?'

'Aye, me too,' said Evie. 'It was pay the rent or get out. We didn't have the rent since me mam had just died an' the weather ruined the crop.'

'I thought that stuff was just stories you Irish told to break our hearts.'

'No, it's true,' said Evie. 'All true. Anyway, why would I want to break your heart? We're both in the same boat, near enough?'

He nodded. 'What age are you, Evie?'

'Sixteen.'

Chiffin sighed.

'Sweet sixteen an' never been kissed,' said Evie, grinning.

'Aye, nor me neither,' said Chiffin.

* * *

It did not occur to Clare to wonder why Harry Fairfield was hanging about the close-mouth in the middle of a Saturday afternoon.

He was dressed in a well-brushed pin-stripe suit and a spotless white shirt open at the collar. He had polished his boots and slicked down his tufty fair hair with pomade. He had the lounger's stance off to a tee, shoulders braced against the wall, legs stuck out at an acute angle, hands deep in his trouser pockets and a cigarette, half smoked, adhering to his nether lip. It took only a moment for Clare to deduce that Mr Fairfield's attention had been focused on the ground-floor privy while he waited for her to do her business.

She was both embarrassed and, at the same time, pleased to see him. She resisted the temptation to fiddle with her skirts and adjust her underclothes and greeted him with an uncertain smile.

'Are you waitin' for the . . .?'

'Nope,' Harry said. 'I'm waitin' for you.'

'For me?' Clare's voice rose. 'Why would that be?'

' 'Cause I haven't seen you for days – an' I was worried.'

'Why would you be worried about me?'

'I thought I'd lost you.'

'Haven't you heard?' said Clare. 'We're here to stay. Me brother's got a job at the wall, an' me sister's employed at Maizie's.'

'Jock told me somethin' of the sort,' Harry said, 'but I was disinclined to believe him.'

'Is he in the habit of lyin' then?'

'Jock? Nah, he's as honest as the day is long,' Harry said. 'But I've learned not to set too much store by rumours.'

He took the cigarette from his mouth, nipped off the coal with finger and thumb and tucked the stub into his jacket pocket. He rolled away from the wall, stood upright, hands by his sides, and looked at her in such a way that all the strength went out of her legs.

She let the torn sheets of newspaper that she had been carrying slip to the ground and, leaning back, searched for support. She found the wall and rested against it, her hands behind her back, her knees pressed together.

'Days?' she heard herself say. 'Only two days.'

'Two days too long,' said Harry, then, to her astonishment, leaned forward, slipped an arm about her waist and kissed her.

'There!' he said. 'I've been dyin' to do that since I first saw you. You don't know what torments I've gone through, darlin', thinkin' you might have passed out of my life without knowin' how much you've touched me.'

'Touched you?' Clare said. 'I never laid a finger—'

'In the heart, in the heart,' Harry said, with a hint of irritation that Clare failed to detect. 'You're the loveliest girl I've ever seen, but you're too modest, so modest you don't even know how lovely you are or what effect you have on a man – a man's heart, I mean.'

'I'm not lovely,' Clare said. 'I'm not—'

He touched her lips with a forefinger that tasted of tobacco. 'Hush,' he said, 'or I'll have to kiss you again just to prove my point.'

Her lips were moist, her throat dry. She felt as if she had stepped out of the privy into a dream.

Harry Fairfield was by no means the first man to flatter her but he was the first who had ever kissed her as if he meant it.

She felt every muscle in her body slacken. Her head dropped back against the wall with a little thump. The arm about her waist tightened. He drew her to him, his lean, angular body locked to her belly and thighs, his mouth upon her again, kissing her cheeks and brow and finally, once more, her lips.

'Say my name,' he murmured. 'Go on, Clare, say my name.'

'Hah-Harry.'

'Again, please, again.'

'Harry,' she whispered. 'Harry, Harry, Harry.'

'There,' he said, releasing her. 'Next time you'll know me for who I am.'

'An' who – who *are* you?' Clare asked breathlessly.

'A man who will love you till his dyin' day,' Harry Fairfield said, then, to Clare's dismay, turned and hurried out into Salamanca Street as if he, or his heart, could take no more of her.

For now.

On Saturday the last batch of pies was run out by noon. Mr Kennedy closed the bakery – though not the shop – paid his employees and dismissed them with a cheery warning not to do anything he wouldn't do. By half past one Cissie was at home preparing to wash not only the sink, windows and floorboards but also the close outside her door and the steps that led down to the street.

During the first five or six years of her tenure she had assiduously chalked the close and steps as well but, gradually, the tenement had become too down-at-heel for that nicety to have any point. At Eamon's insistence, she had put the block of pipe-clay on a saucer under the sink where it remained, grey and fossilised, to this day.

Mop, bucket and scrubbing brush were still her allies, though, for hard work offered relief from loneliness and took her mind from her worries and the prospect of the long walk to the Masonic Hall in Carpenter Street.

It was Mr Belfer who had first introduced her to the notion of 'putting a wee bit aside' for a rainy day. He had explained the principle of investment and how interest was earned and had eventually persuaded her that a shilling a week put into an account with the Barony of Glasgow Savings and Investment Bank would be money well spent.

It wasn't the 'loss' – for that's how Cissie regarded it – of a shilling a week from her meagre wage that troubled her quite so much as the trail across Riverside Road to the hall in Carpenter Street where Mr Morrison, the bank's cashier, collected 'Penny Savings' every Saturday night between eight and nine.

There was some satisfaction in watching her nest-egg grow and, now and then, she would take out her linen-backed bank book and admire the tidy little total at each quarter's end that showed how much she had earned by doing nothing; nothing, that is, but go out every Saturday evening, rain, hail or snow, and risk life and limb by entering a street where Catholics, even harmless little old lady Catholics, were liable to be set upon and abused. So far, thank God, she had not been abused much less set upon, but the trail there and back again stretched her nerves and cast a gloomy shadow over her Saturday afternoons.

She put off leaving the safety of Salamanca Street until the very last minute. Only when the Burgh Hall clock tolled the hour did she take her courage in both hands and strike out into the twilight. She had nothing to fear, of course; Protestants were just as fond of their tipple as Catholics and the pubs that backed on to Carpenter Street were no less crowded than the Harp of Erin.

None the less, she was always relieved to see Mr Orpington rocking on the balls of his feet outside the door of the Masonic Hall. In spite of his fearsome reputation at least he dressed like a gentleman and greeted her as a lady should be greeted by removing his topper.

'How are you this fine spring evening, Mistress Cassidy?' he would ask, and she, simpering a little, would answer, 'I'm as well as can be expected, thank you very much,' then, with a sweep of the arm, he would usher her into the hall.

Tonight, though, Mr Orpington not only removed his

topper but leaned over her, still rocking a little, and administered a series of little bows.

'Well now,' he said, 'if it ain't the charmin' lady from Salamanca Street. Have you come to pour more water into the well of commerce?'

Mr Orpington's unctuousness made her uneasy.

'Aye,' she said, 'aye, I have.'

'Jolly good! I do hope you realise that the mighty wheels of progress turn on little cogs like you, ma'am, and those of us whose concern is for the future are grateful for both your thrift and your trust.'

'Uh?' said Mrs Cassidy.

'I've heard from a little bird that you have new neighbours,' said Mr Orpington, rocking merrily away. 'And that said new neighbours are fellow members of the multitudinous clan of Cassidy.'

'If you mean my Eamon's relatives, aye, they've rented a room in Mr Belfer's house. Did Mr Belfer tell you?'

'He did, indeed,' said Mr Orpington. 'He also indicated – tactfully, of course – that the young ladies are not without a certain measure of appeal.'

Mrs Cassidy's discomfort increased. 'They're pretty enough lassies, I suppose,' she said, 'but I don't see what business it is of yours.'

Mr Orpington drew even closer. 'Mr Belfer is much taken with the little female who goes by the name of Clare,' he said. 'Naturally, I impart that piece of information in confidence. I wouldn't wish it to reach Mr Belfer's ears that I have betrayed his secret. Even so, I feel it's my duty to warn you that although Cupid's dart may lodge in unlikely places, our Benjamin is not a man to be trifled with. Have they, these girls, have they asked you to lend them money?'

'What?' Cissie was totally bewildered. 'What money?'

'From your nest-egg, say, from your account?'

'They haven't said a word about my nest-egg,' Cissie told him. 'I doubt if they even know I have a nest-egg.'

'Oh, I imagine that they might,' said Mr Orpington. 'Tell you what I'll do, Mrs Cassidy, I'll have a word with them, shall I?'

'A word about what?'

'About their intentions, their – ah – purpose in being here.'

'They have no intentions,' Cissie said shrilly. 'They've no interest in my money. They've got money o' their own. The boy's employed at the wall and one of the girls is workin' for Mr Maizie.' She glowered up at him, more angry than afraid. 'I don't know what Mr Belfer's been sayin' but they're my kinfolk and not to be tampered with.'

'Tampered with?' said Mr Orpington. 'I wouldn't dream of "tampering" with them, Mrs C., but promise me that if they say one single word about your nest-egg you'll inform Mr Belfer and he'll inform me and I *will* come around and have a word with them, whether you like it or not.'

'They might be Irish but they aren't thieves,' said Cissie angrily. 'I've had enough o' your nonsense. Let me past before Mr Morrison closes his book.'

'By all means,' said Mr Orpington, then, putting on his topper and promptly taking it off again, stepped graciously to one side and allowed her to enter the hall.

Night had fallen and streetlamps absorbed the last of the daylight from the western sky, yet the tall windows of the new sandstone terrace on the slope above the bowling green retained a faint lingering afterglow that gilded the elegant façade of Bellingham Place.

The close had a door of varnished oak inset with a panel of tinted glass. It was lined with shiny white tiles as high as Mr Belfer's hat and brand-new gas mantles that burned clean and bright. Mr Belfer paused to inhale the scent of wealth and privilege and enjoy a moment of self-satisfaction before he climbed the stairs to the first-floor apartment, and rang the doorbell.

He had arranged with his greengrocer to make up a basket of candied fruits: melon, a cherry, slices of apricot and pineapple, all dried and beautifully glazed. The basket had cost him all of three shillings which, by his reckoning, worked out at about fourpence per sugary piece.

The basket held out before him like a sacrifice, he waited for the woman to make her unhurried way from the drawing-room and answer the bell. At length the door opened and, stooping a little, he showed her his face in the light from the mantle on the landing.

'Oh, it's you, is it?' the woman said, turning away.

'Yes, Mother,' said Benjamin. 'It's me.'

One valuable lesson Harry Fairfield had learned from his encounters with the fair sex was that the way to many a woman's heart lay through her brother.

Nolan McKenna was by no means the first gormless lad with a gorgeous sister whose friendship Harry had cultivated and it was all too easy to lure the big Irish lump away from the domestic hearth by promising to buy him drink. Harry waited in the close-mouth while Nolan made his excuses, took leave of his sister and, spruced up and almost respectable, came clumping down the stairs with a bashful grin on his face.

'What did you tell her?' Harry asked casually.

'Sure an' I told her the truth,' said Nolan. 'I admitted I was goin' out with you for a taste of the black stout.'

'What did she say to that?' Harry asked.

'What could she say?' said Nolan. 'I'm the breadwinner, ain't I?'

Harry slapped him on the shoulder. 'Aye, it does no harm to

remind our lovely ladies who brings home the bacon. You're entitled to wet your whistle come Saturday night.'

'Are we a-goin' to Maizie's?' said Nolan.

'We are a-goin' to Maizie's.'

'Is there no other place?'

'None handy,' said Harry. 'None as makes a welcome for the Greens.'

'The Greens?' said Nolan.

'Papes,' said Harry.

'Ah!' Nolan exclaimed. 'You are one o' us then?'

'Suckled on holy water, cut my teeth on a rosary, blessed by the Pope himself,' Harry lied glibly. 'To my shame, though, I've drifted away from the Church these past few years, like so many of our ilk.'

'Our ilk?' said Nolan. 'What's that mean?'

'Our kind,' said Harry. 'Our clan, our tribe.'

'You ain't from the Owd Country, are you?'

' 'Fraid not,' said Harry. 'But we're all brothers under the skin, those of us who wear the Green.'

If Nolan harboured doubts about Harry Fairfield's claims to brotherhood he gave no sign of it and, shoulder to shoulder with the coalheaver, tramped up Salamanca Street without a care in the world.

'Me sister works in Maizie's,' he said. 'Won't matter none, I suppose.'

'Not to me,' said Harry. 'Now, which sister is that?'

'Evie, the little 'un.'

'An' the other young lady – what's her name again?'

'Clare.'

'Clare it is. What does she do?'

'Stays home.'

'Like a wife?' said Harry.

Nolan laughed. 'Aye, just like a wife.'

Harry nudged him. 'Does she make a good wife, then?'

'Good enough, I suppose,' said Nolan.

'Make a better wife to a man who wasn't her brother, though,' Harry said and nudged the big feller again.

'I wouldn't know nothin' about that,' said Nolan gruffly.

'You've never had a wife then?'

'Sure an' do I look like a man who's had a wife?'

'I mean, never had a woman in his bed?' The Irish lump flushed a queer shade of pink. Straight-faced, Harry added, 'Never had a woman at all?'

'I thought you was a Catholic?'

'What's that got to do with it?' Harry said. 'The propagatin' of the species don't hang on what a priest tells you. Some o' them priests—'

'We know all about them sort o' priests,' said Nolan.

It was all Harry could do not to break step. He continued to match his stride to that of the long-legged Irishman. He had learned long ago how to read reluctance in a man, and in women too. Behind every blush and every blink, every pause or hesitation, there was usually a tale to tell.

'What sort o' priests is that, Nolan? Bad priests, do you mean?'

'Aye,' Nolan said. 'It was trouble wi' a priest drove us from home.'

The light outside Maizie's winked in the gloaming. The air was cold on Harry's cheeks. He was oblivious to the men on the pavement or the children who shrieked in and out of the closes in some sprawling game. He caught Nolan by the arm and stopped him in his tracks.

'Look,' he said, 'it ain't none o' my business, since we're still short on acquaintance but I've a feelin' you and your sisters got the short end of the stick. Was a priest behind it?'

'Father Garbett by name.'

'Back in the Old Country?'

'Cork,' said Nolan, with a sigh. 'He took Clare . . .'

'Took Clare, do you tell me?'

'. . . took Clare an' did somethin' sinful with her.'

Harry licked his upper lip. 'How sinful?'

'She wouldn't tell us, not proper. It shook her, though, specially since our mam was dyin' an' the same priest was dashin' in an' out o' the house.'

'You don't have to say any more,' Harry said, 'if it pains you.'

Nolan glanced up at the strip of sky that ran like a dark river over the line of the street. 'I think he made her touch him – down there.'

'Is that all?' said Harry. 'That's not so terrible, is it?'

'Terrible enough,' said Nolan. 'Even worse, the bloody man sided wi' his lordship an' had us thrown off our farm.'

'Before Clare could tell what he'd done to her,' said Harry, nodding.

'So nobody would believe her if she did,' Nolan said.

'Bastard!' Harry said. 'The bastard.'

'Still' – Nolan uttered a wry grunt – 'our Evie used him to get us here.'

'You mean, he had Evie too?' said Harry.

'Nah, nah,' said Nolan. 'Our Evie's too smart for that. She wheedled him out o' five pounds by talkin' close an' quiet. She knew it would be better for Father Garbett if we left Cork; not just Cork but Ireland. We had nothin' to keep us there since Mam had died by then an' the holding had been repossessed. It was a hard time for us, Mr Fairfield . . .'

'Harry.'

'. . . a right hard time, Harry. What the priest done to Clare brought us money when we were skint. You could say he brought us to Glasgow.'

'A blessing in disguise, then,' said Harry. 'Does she know about this?'

'Who?'

'Cissie Cassidy?' Harry said.

'We come here for a new beginnin' an' we don't want to worry Mrs Cassidy wi' our troubles since she's been so kind. You won't . . .'

'Tell her? Not me,' said Harry. 'If there's one thing you'll learn about Harry Fairfield, it's that he can be trusted never to betray a confidence.' Then shoulder to shoulder once more the lads set out for Paddy Maizie's and a long hard night on the tiles.

'You can call it what you like, Clare,' Evie said, 'but I call it drunk.'

'He's tired.'

'Tired, is it? Tired, when he's sprawled out there like a pig in muck.' She kicked out at her brother but his only response was a grunt, a snort and a little shake of the shoulders. 'Well, he can sleep it off where he fell far as I'm concerned. I'll have the bed tonight.'

'Have it then,' said Clare sulkily.

'He's a bad influence, your friend,' Evie said.

'Oh, so it's Harry's fault, is it?' Clare said. 'What about you, why didn't you stop him?'

'I've more to do than count how many jugs our Nolly's swallowed,' Evie said. She had been far from delighted when Nolly entered the pub, and not much impressed with the feller who accompanied him. They had gone around the corner into the nook and she had lost sight of them. She might have forgotten they were there until, some while after ten, she'd heard Nolan's voice raised up in song and Mr Draper yell at the idiot to shut his mouth or he'd be singing the next verse in the gutter.

'Didn't Harry say anythin' about me?' Clare asked.

'Nah, he was too busy pourin' whisky down his throat.'

'He can hold his drink then, can he?' Clare said.

Evie sank on to a chair at the table and scowled at her sister. 'How do I know if he can hold his drink? Yes, yes, I suppose he can since he managed to lug Nolly back here wi'out losin' him.'

'He's a coal-heaver,' Clare said. 'He's used to carryin' heavy weights.'

Evie had a headache and every stitch she wore reeked of beer slops, fried fish and tobacco smoke. She had been hungry about half past ten o'clock but her appetite had gone now. She was too tired to fry herself an egg or even butter a slice of bread. She might have asked Clare to make her supper but she was not well pleased by her sister's infatuation with the young man upstairs.

'Where did Nolly meet him?' she asked.

'In the close, most like,' Clare answered.

'Has he been comin' in here to see you when I'm out?'

'Harry? No, I wouldn't let a man in here, would I now?'

'I don't know what you'd do,' said Evie. 'You've changed.'

'Perhaps it's havin' a nice place to live, regular money comin' in an' nothin' much to worry about that's changed me,' Clare said.

'Aye, maybe,' said Evie doubtfully. 'Thank God tomorrow's Sunday.'

'You'll be going to early mass, I take it?' said Clare, not seriously.

'Mass, what would I be going to mass for?' Evie said.

'To make confession.'

'Not me!' said Evie. 'Have you somethin' to get off your chest?'

'No,' Clare said, 'but I do have things I want to give thanks for.'

'What things?'

'For us being here, safe and sound, with a roof over our heads, a fire in the grate and food on the table. Would you have thought all this possible just a week ago, Evie?'

'No,' Evie admitted, 'that I would not. God works in mysterious ways.'

'Sure an' He does,' said Clare.

The woman sat motionless, like a little figure carved out of soapstone. She had discarded the embroidered silk wrap he had bought her and wore a ragged woollen shawl that she had carried down from the cottage in the miners' row. Benjamin hated that shawl, her knitted cap and the ugly boots that protruded from under her skirt. He longed to tell her to take what was her due and thank him for it but, as usual, held his tongue on that subject, and seated himself on the footstool by her chair.

'What's wrong, Mother? Don't you like candied fruits?'

'I like them well enough.'

He was the last of the five sons of Duncan and Jeannie Belfer. He had been born and raised in a cottage at the Red Pit out beyond Anniesland. His brothers had flown the coop as soon as they were old enough and were scattered about the globe, as far away from Anniesland, the Red Pit, and Mother Belfer as possible; he rarely heard from any of them.

'Aren't you going to have one then?' Benjamin said.

'Don't want any,' his mother said.

''Course you don't, Mother.' Benjamin sat back. 'How is he today?'

In a window corner, far from the hearth, his father occupied the Georgian wing chair that had been specially delivered from the Tabernacle Furniture Warerooms. It had been months since his father had last uttered a word, yet he looked as he had always done, strong-boned, healthy and much younger than his eighty years. He sat bolt upright, staring at the flock wallpaper, entirely oblivious to his son's presence.

'Grand,' his mother told him. 'He's just grand.'

'You, are you well?'

'Fat lot you care.'

Benjamin wriggled on the stool. 'How can you say that, Mother, after all I've done for you?'

'What've you done for us, eh? What have you done?'

Benjamin shot to his feet, knocking over the stool. 'Damn it, Mother, if you don't like it here, I'll find another place for you. Bellingham Place is one of the most sought-after addresses in Glasgow, in case you didn't know.'

'It's no skin off my nose where I spend my days,' his mother said. 'Here's as good as any place, I suppose. As for him, he hasn't known where he is since you brought us here.'

'What did the doctor say?'

'I sent the doctor away.'

'Why?'

'Doctors cost money.'

'I *have* money,' Benjamin cried.

'I don't like that girl either.'

'If you mean Mrs Walsh' – Benjamin tried to make light of it – 'she's hardly a girl. She's forty if she's—'

'I sent her away, too.'

Benjamin sighed. 'What did she say to upset you?'

'She ca'ed me a bitch 'cause I told her the toast was burned.'

'I see,' Benjamin said. 'Well, at least you still have the day maid – or have you dismissed her, too?'

'She knows her place.'

'I'll find a suitable replacement for Mrs Walsh as soon as—'

'Dinna bother. We're fine as we are.'

She plucked the basket of glazed fruits from her lap and put it down by the side of the chair. Benjamin turned up the gaslight. Mrs Walsh was the fifth housekeeper in almost as many months. No matter how much he offered them he could not persuade them to stay. He knew what was on the cards, though, and what his mother would say next.

'If you had a wife, Benjamin . . .'

'Don't start on that again,' Benjamin said.

'It's not right, a boy your age without a wife.'

It was the old song, the old chant. She wasn't urging him to take a wife for his comfort, or to provide her with grandchildren. She wanted him to take a wife so that she would have an unpaid servant at her beck and call, someone to browbeat in the sure knowledge that a daughter-in-law would not be able to resign and would be her slave, her chattel, forever.

'Turn that gas down,' his mother said. 'You're wastin' money.'

For once he did not leap to do her bidding. He walked around the Georgian chair and stooped to inspect the old man, who looked as he always did, not vacant or dead-eyed, merely, effortlessly, unresponsive. Sixty-four years of brutal labour in the Red Pit had left few scars, though, and Benjamin had begun to realise that it wasn't the job that had driven his father into mental exile but fifty-seven years of marriage to Jeannie Macrae.

Gently, he ruffled the old man's feathery hair, then, returning to the hearth, turned down the gas.

'Don't you want those candies, Mother?' he asked.

She did not answer.

'Well, do you?' Benjamin said.

'They hurt my teeth.'

Benjamin scooped up the basket and tucked it under his arm. 'In that case I'll take them away, for I know someone who *will* like them.'

She scowled. 'Who would that be?'

'My sweetheart,' Benjamin answered.

'You've haven't got a sweetheart.'

'Oh, but I have, Mother. Indeed, I have.'

'What's her name then? What's her name?'

'Clare McKenna,' Benjamin said, and, gathering up his

overcoat, kissed the dank maternal brow and left without another word.

The Bishopric of Glasgow had been established in 543 and elected into a Metropolitan See in 1492. But after the death of the fourth archbishop in 1603 it had lain vacant for well over two hundred years until the passing of the Roman Catholic Relief Bill had brought it back to life again. Now Marist brothers ran instruction schools for boys, Franciscan nuns did much the same for little girls and the great Cathedral of St Andrew, in Clyde Street, offered two and a half thousand sittings and, on Sundays, delivered mass every half-hour, in addition to vespers and benediction, rosary and stations, and confessions heard in French, Italian and Spanish as well as plain old Glaswegian.

If you slipped into St Kentigern's for Sunday mass, though, you might suppose that the heathens still held sway in Riverside, for poor old Father Fingle could, as a rule, count the faithful on the fingers of one hand.

He was pleasantly surprised when, on the fourth Sunday in Lent, his little flock was increased by three fresh faces.

They were not entirely unfamiliar faces: he recognised the Irish travellers at once and, peering over his spectacles, delivered both a welcome and an impromptu two-minute sermon about strangers in a strange land which delighted Cissie Cassidy even if it left her kinfolk more puzzled than amused.

As he proceeded through the mass, Father Fingle squinted now and then at the Cassidy clan, neat and clean if not exactly fashionable, and noted that the girls were much more engaged than the young man who seemed to be suffering some sort of malady. His broad cheeks were flushed, his eyes half shut and when he rose for the responses he groaned audibly and pressed a fist to his brow. Father Fingle knew a hangover when he saw one and marvelled at the power of female persuasion that had dragged the unfortunate laddie from his bed at that unearthly hour of the morning.

When the mass was over, Father Fingle wasted no time in hot-footing to the door in advance of the congregation. He wanted a word with Cissie's girls, because he was forever on the lookout for devout young ladies with enough education to teach afternoon Sunday school, or if not to teach, at least with enough presence to keep the infant rabble in order.

Unfortunately, his plan was scuppered by one of St Kentigern's principal patrons, who, accompanied by her ward, had been tucked away in the side sitting and had come forward last of all to take the bread. They paused to exchange words, and, crowded up behind them, Cissie Cassidy and her kin were blocked in the narrow doorway.

The woman was dressed in a severe, almost military tunic without a bustle or any of the dead animal trimmings that had recently crept into fashion. She was taller than Father Fingle by several inches, and when she placed her gloved hand in his, he felt a little tingle of something approaching awe.

She thanked him for the service, enquired after his health and placed into his hand a banknote folded up so small that it was hardly larger than a candy ball. He had long ago given up trying to persuade her that it would be much more seemly to put her donation in the plate or the poor-box. He knew, for she had told him so, that she was afraid that twenty pounds would prove too tempting for the rascals who frequented St Kentigern's.

Father Fingle took the folded banknote and slipped it into his pocket, then, smiling nervously, watched the woman and the Chinese girl, Seang Pin Saw, sweep gracefully down the pathway to the gate and out into the street where Paddy Maizie waited at the reins of a sleek victoria and, within seconds, had the ladies safe on board and clipping away towards Crosshill.

'My God!' he heard the Irish girl shout. 'It's her. It's Mrs bloody Galloway. What's *she* doin' here, I'd like to know?' But that was one question Father Fingle dared not answer, not without risk to his integrity and, perhaps, his immortal soul.

PART TWO

The Brothers Blackstock

6

It was not unusual for Sunday luncheons in Crosshill House to end in bickering. The Blackstock brothers had been at loggerheads practically since birth and when they came together on the social front sparks were sure to fly.

Those brave enough to accept an invitation to partake of lunch in the vast, echoing dining hall of the old mansion-house overlooking the docks were often treated to verbal sparring between Russell and Wilson or, if they were lucky, to a shouting match accompanied by a display of invective so colourful that it would have made a navvy blush. The secret to surviving a Blackstock lunch was not to take sides. Indeed, it was difficult to decide which side to take, for the brothers were divided on most issues by shades of opinion so fine that an outsider could not possibly fathom what the devil they were arguing about, let alone which one of them to stand behind.

Russell and Wilson Blackstock were twins but, in appearance as well as temperament, they were anything but identical. Russell had dropped into the world eight minutes before his brother which made him, legally, the elder. Though Russell had never attempted to exploit his advantage, Wilson, fiery by nature, bitterly resented it, though quite what he expected his brother to do about it, forty-three years on, remained a mystery.

They were similar in height and build, neither tall nor short, neither plump nor scrawny, but both very average on the scale of things. Wilson, however, had a long jaw, lean cheeks and protruding ears whereas Russell was regular of feature and looked, so Wilson claimed, more like a hero than a gowk. To friends and family there was nothing discernibly heroic about Russell and nothing obviously 'gowkish' about Wilson.

In fact, back in the sixties, Wilson had been presentable enough to snare Angela Galt for a wife, and it surely wasn't every day that a daughter of the Master of the Grand Orange Lodge of Scotland tripped up the aisle with the son of a humble builder's merchant. Russell, in contrast, could do no better than Jane Parker who was only the niece of one of twelve hundred and fifty-four partners in the Barony of Glasgow Joint-Stock Bank and had brought nothing but love and devotion to the marriage.

It was, however, Jane, not Angela, who had tended Papa Blackstock after his stroke; Jane, not Angela, who had wept when the old man finally gave up the ghost; Jane, not Angela, who had provided a home for Mama Blackstock and, in spite of her husband's misgivings, had insisted on offering shelter to widowed sister Libby and her ward when they had returned from the Far East and every door in Glasgow had been closed against them.

No fancy French buffets for Russell and Jane's guests, just a good, honest, old-fashioned sit-down around the long table, with all the linen and silverware that one could wish for and fare so rich and substantial that even Mr Strachan, manager of the Barony Bank and a notorious glutton, never left the table unsatisfied. The children were herded off to the nursery where a brace of nannies, assisted by sundry maids, saw to it that they were duly nourished. A few young people were invited to sit at the long table downstairs, among them the oldest son of an engineer, the twenty-year-old daughter of an architect, and the solemn, silent and very pretty young woman who Wilson, quite openly, still referred to as 'that Chink'.

Broth was followed by a smoked fish pudding, then, in

honour of Mr Strachan perhaps, a baron of Scotch beef the size of a small bungalow was wheeled in, the sight of which raised applause from the bachelor banker, and murmurs of approval all round. The ladies were fairly subdued, for they were well aware that the luncheon had less to do with friendship than business and that there would be ample time for gossip after the gentlemen had retired to the library for coffee and cigars.

All seemed to be sailing smoothly towards that end when, quite unprompted, Wilson said, 'So tell me, Ping, what sabres was your wee priestie man rattling this morning? Is he still advocating the overthrow of the British government and putting the Pope on the throne?'

'Wilson, please,' Angela murmured.

The Chinese girl focused her attention on her plate and did not respond.

'Ping,' said Mr Strachan. 'That's an unusual name even for a—'

'Her name,' said Libby Galloway, 'is Seang Pin Saw. Pin, sir, Pin, and not as my brother would have it. If you can't get your tongue around the name after twelve years, Willy, I suggest you take instruction in elocution, or pay another visit to your dentist.'

'Nothing wrong with my teeth, dearest,' Wilson said. 'I don't file them into sharp points like those savages you were so cosy with in Penang.'

The Chinese girl remained resolutely mute, while those guests who were familiar with Libby's history settled down to enjoy the fun with no more embarrassment than courtesy demanded.

Wilson turned his attention to Mr Strachan. 'Tell me, Hector,' he said, 'have you heard of my sister's wee priestie? Fingle by name, finagler by nature. He's been preaching sedition in sly ways for years – under instruction from his masters in Rome, no doubt.'

'Fingle?' At that moment Mr Strachan was more interested in beef than bigotry. 'Fingle? Isn't he in charge at St Kentigern's?'

'I think,' Russell intervened, 'that we would be wise to leave this matter for the time being, Willy. The lunch table is no place for—'

'Balderdash!' Wilson said. 'We're all of like mind here, apart from a certain female and her orphan Chink.'

'Willy,' Jane said. 'I'd be grateful if you'd change the subject, please.'

'No, no,' said Hector Strachan, 'do let him go on. I'm not unfamiliar with this Fingle person or the importance of his – what's it called? – his "mission", which is, I believe, firmly placed in the path of the proposed thoroughfare.'

There was nothing unusual in the way the luncheon had been derailed and the guests, including the banker, were perfectly at ease with Wilson's teasing. After all, Libby had no one to blame but herself for being a black sheep. If it hadn't been for Jane's generosity Libby would have remained an outcast from the family as well as Glasgow society.

'St Kentigern's isn't really our problem,' Wilson went on. 'Plans for the thoroughfare will only go forward if the remaining lands of the old Crosshill estate can be purchased cheaply.'

'How cheaply is that?' said Mr Strachan, fork poised.

'Not cheaply enough,' put in Mama Blackstock from her position at the head of the table. 'Oh, yes, Willy, it's a bit late to bemoan the fact that you didn't go the whole hog when the ground was first parcelled out. If it hadn't been for Russell's foresight we would have had none of it, not one acre. It's all very well blaming the Fenians for standing in your way but it was timidity done you in, not the Pope or his henchmen.'

'I am not,' said Wilson stiffly, 'done in, Mama, not by a long chalk.'

The engineer listened intently. Big building projects on

Clydeside would mean more well-paid work for him after the new dock was completed. The architect too was all ears. His firm had already landed contracts to design several new bridges and a number of substantial villas flanking the thoroughfare that would link the west side burghs to the city.

No one at the Blackstocks' table that afternoon doubted that in five or six years' time the Riverside slums would be replaced by fine new commercial properties, handsome domestic dwellings and all the money-making opportunities that went with them.

'Of course you're not, my dear,' said Angela loyally.

Mama Blackstock had been negotiating all her life. She understood only too well that monumental plans began not with monumental ideas but in piecemeal discussions, even arguments, over a tankard of ale or a dram of whisky or, as now, a plate of meat and potatoes.

She had watched her husband haul his way up from the hold of an Ayrshire coal barge to partnership in a coal merchants' yard and, by graft and gab, forge the right sort of connections and become a builder and property owner and well enough established by age thirty to marry the only daughter of a sheriff of Lanarkshire who, not by coincidence, also happened to be a Tory and a Freemason.

'One priest won't do for you, Willy,' she said, 'nor one stubborn landowner. If you enlist the aid of your friends then you'll find the necessary capital and the means of getting what you want.'

'And what is that, Willy?' Libby asked. 'More profit, more houses to finance your dream of being the richest man on Clydeside with not a shred of charity or grace left in you when you die.'

'I'm not a exploiter,' Wilson said, 'I'm an improver.'

'As are we all.' Mr Strachan pushed his plate away at last. 'God knows, madam, what we'd do without men like your brothers, men of foresight and enterprise dedicated to improving our fair city.'

'Hear, hear,' said the engineer.

'I second that,' said the architect.

'Do they know yet?' said Libby Galloway.

'Does who know what?' said Wilson.

'Do the poor folk in those rat-infested tenements who pay your usurious rents every week, do they know that you intend to knock down their homes and pitch them out into the streets?' Libby said.

'They will be informed in good time, dearest,' said Russell.

'In good time for what?' said Libby. 'In good time to scratch for shelter in the workhouse or the charity ward?'

'For God's sake, Libby,' Wilson said, 'they're Irish, most of them, and half of them – those that have the gumption to work at all – work for us. We're living in the second city in the Empire; what would you have us do? Sit on our hands for the sake of a few Catholic idlers who shouldn't be in here at all?'

'Let them go back to Ireland,' the engineer's son declared loudly.

Wilson laughed. 'See, there you have it, Libby,' he said, 'a simple solution uttered from the mouth of babes and sucklings.'

'He's hardly a suckling, Willy,' said the engineer. 'He is already apprenticed to the craft.'

'Is he, indeed?' said Mr Strachan approvingly.

'I am indeed, sir,' said the engineer's son. 'At the lodge—'

'Hush now, son,' said Wilson. 'We mustn't bore the ladies with talk that's more suited to a closed room.'

Libby snorted. 'Why, Willy? Are you afraid I'll hear some shattering secret that I'll carry back to my wee priestie man? If St Kentigern's stands in the way of what you care to call progress then it won't be Father Fingle you'll have to deal with, it'll be the archbishop or the vicar-general, and you'll not find them so easy to bribe and bully.'

'I don't doubt that,' said Wilson. 'If there's one thing your holy friends in high places do understand, Libby, it's money.'

'Which,' said Libby, 'is why you need another loan, I suppose.'

For all his lack of tact, Willy Blackstock did not consider finance a fit subject for conversation in mixed company. Though he had been buttering up Strachan for years, he was still unsure how much strain the friendship would bear or how much longer the Barony Bank would support his massive borrowings. He had intended to broach the subject obliquely, but now Libby had put her bloody foot in it.

He rounded on her furiously and might have blurted out something that he would later regret.

Fortunately, both Russell and Mama Blackstock were ahead of him and before either he, or Libby, could say another word, called out in unison, '*Pudding, anyone? Pudding?*' and the servants moved in to take away the plates.

'What is it?' Clare McKenna asked anxiously.

'What does it look like?' Harry said.

'It looks like custard.'

'It's ice-cream,' Harry said. 'Have you never had ice-cream before?'

'Aye, but never in a cardboard box. Where did you get it?'

'From the 'Tally's shop on the corner.' He handed her the soggy cardboard container and a little plywood spoon. 'Sup it quick before it melts.'

Clare sniffed the creamy yellow substance and curled her tongue along the surface.

'Hmm,' she said. 'It's lovely. Where's yours?'

'I had a pokey hat,' said Harry, 'but I ate it.'

'I didn't know you were goin' to buy me ice-cream,' Clare said.

'If you had, wouldn't you have come?'

'Aye' – she licked the spoon – 'but you mustn't go buyin' me things, Harry.'

'Why not?'

'It's not proper.'

'What's not proper about it?' Harry said.

'I'm not your – your sweetheart.'

'Maybe when you finish that lot, you'll be sweeter,' Harry said.

Clare had no inclination to bite her thumbs in Harry Fairfield's presence. She bit the tip of the little wooden spoon instead.

'Sweeter, I mean,' Harry added, 'towards me.'

They were seated on a bench on the strip of flayed grassland that folk in Riverside called the Parney Park. It was uncannily quiet, for shipyards and factories closed on the Lord's day and only those vessels that had a tide to catch came sliding past.

Harry had sent her a message by Jock Macpherson telling her where and when to meet him. She had put on clean linens and combed her hair and, without a word to Evie or Nolly, both of whom were half asleep, had slipped out of the house. The thought of being with Harry Fairfield had filled her with misgiving, but her heart – that organ on which Mr Fairfield seemed so keen – had given a little thump when she saw him waiting by the bench, shifting the cardboard thing from hand to hand.

She finished the ice-cream while he watched.

Her lips were cold and sticky. She wiped them on her handkerchief.

He leaned close to her, one leg folded over the other, his elbow pressing her thigh. When she was done, he took the soggy box, crushed it and dropped it behind the bench. He wiped his hand on his trouser-leg, rubbing and rubbing, without taking his eyes from Clare.

She said, 'Am I sweeter now, d'you think?'

'Hard to tell,' he whispered. 'I'll just have to find out.'

'How will you do that?' Clare asked.

'Like this,' he said and at last, at long last, kissed her.

'It isn't a good match, Mr Macpherson. Whatever you might think of him,' Cissie Cassidy said, 'Harry Fairfield's not reliable.'

Jock was making pancakes, the mixing bowl tucked under his arm.

He dropped a dollop of batter on to the hot iron and watched it form a perfect circle. He had purchased a small jar of strawberry jam and a pat of fresh butter, for he had guessed that the widow would turn up that afternoon to seek his opinion of the newcomers – an opinion that, in some respects, he preferred to keep to himself.

'That batter looks thin to me,' Cissie said.

'The batter's fine,' said Jock.

'Do you think Harry Fairfield's reliable?'

'I don't know what you mean by reliable, Cissie,' Jock said. 'Fact is, I don't see that much o' him. He works on the wagons an' I'm weighin' an' haulin'. Besides, he's usually on the early shift.'

'He took the boy out drinkin'.'

'Did he?' said Jock. 'Well, if the boys have a bit o' spare cash in their pockets, it's no' for us to tell them how to spend it.'

'I heard them stumblin' an' cursin' in the close in the middle o' the night, drunk as lords,' Cissie said.

Jock flipped over the pancakes on the griddle with a broad-bladed knife. It was warm in the room. The sun had a bit of strength to it now the days were lengthening and there was a feeling of spring in the air.

He said, 'Did he not turn out for mass? Is that what's riled you?'

'Oh, no, he turned out for mass,' Cissie sniffed, 'which is more than can be said for some folk. He wasn't quite sober, though, an' I thought it was remiss o' Father Fingle to let him take the sacraments in that state.'

'Did you tell the father you disapproved?'

'Not my place to criticise.'

'Nonsense! You're never done criticisin' that poor priest.' Jock put the pancakes on a plate to let them steam, poured boiling water into a teapot and gave it a shake. 'Were the girls in church too?'

'Aye, both o' them,' Cissie said. 'Now she's gone scamperin' out in her best bonnet an' shawl to meet that man.'

'How do you know she's gone to meet "that man"?' Jock said. 'She could have gone to meet some other man – or no man at all. Leave the girl alone.'

'I'm her auntie. It's up to me to keep an eye on her.'

'Don't tell me you followed her?'

'I think she went to the park – an' we all know what goes on in the park.'

'Aye, but not in the middle of a Sunday afternoon,' said Jock. 'Now, what's it to be: butter, jam, or both?'

'Both,' Cissie said. 'Please.'

Jock spread a pancake, placed it on a plate and put it before her.

He wondered if she had spoken to Belfer about Harry Fairfield's interest in the Irish beauty. He watched Cissie nibble on the pancake.

'How is it?' he asked, at length.

'I've tasted worse,' she said. 'Mr Orpington says they're after my money. Do you think they're after my money?'

'I didn't know you had any money,' Jock said.

'My savings with the Barony,' Cissie said. 'Mr Orpington

thinks they're after my savings. He says if they ask me for money I'm to tell him an' he'll come over an' have a word. But I just told him they're *my* relatives an' it's none o' his blessed business.'

'That's the spirit,' said Jock.

'But it got me to thinkin'; they've hardly been here ten minutes an' Evie's workin' for Paddy Maizie an' Clare's makin' eyes at Harry Fairfield,' Cissie said. 'I'm worried for them.'

Jock seated himself at the table and, reaching out, patted her hand.

'There, there, Cissie,' he said soothingly. 'You've done your best by bringin' them in here and makin' sure they have a roof over their heads, but they're not your responsibility.'

'She keeps a clean house, I'll say that for her.'

'An' did they not accompany you to mass?'

'Aye, aye, they did,' said Cissie. 'But I thought . . .'

'What?' said Jock. 'What did you think?'

'I thought it would be different, havin' a family o' my own.'

'Give it time, Cissie,' Jock said. 'Give it time.'

'Now, after what Mr Orpington told me, I'm just waitin' for them to take all my money an' run away with it.'

'Bloody Orpington!' Jock growled. 'Him an' Belfer are as thick as thieves an' since they trust nobody, they imagine nobody can be trusted.'

Cissie looked up at him, sniffing back her tears. 'Is that true?'

' 'Course it's true. Dear God, Cissie, the Irish don't even know you've got any savings.' He paused then asked, cautiously, 'By the by, how much of a fortune are we talkin' about?'

'Over fifty pounds,' said Cissie.

'My, my!' said Jock. 'That's a lot.'

'It's my nest-egg,' Cissie said. 'I mean, who'll take care o' me when I'm old an' can't work any more? I never realised what it meant to have a nest-egg until Mr Orpington told me. You hear so many stories about families squabblin' over money but I never thought it would happen to me.'

'Cissie, Cissie, for God's sake!' said Jock. 'You're makin' a mountain out of a molehill. The McKennas aren't interested in partin' you from your savings. They don't even know you've got savings an' I'm damned sure I'm not goin' to tell them, nor are you.' He paused. 'Are you?'

'No.'

'Cissie?'

'No, I'm not, no.'

'So nobody knows what you're worth – an' nobody will,' Jock said. 'You're worried over nothin'. The Irish are settled an' earnin'. You've done your best by them an' I don't doubt they're grateful.'

'Do you, do you really think they're grateful?'

'If they're not, they should be,' Jock said. 'Now have another pancake, Cissie, while they're still hot.'

'Do you know,' said little Cissie Cassidy, 'I do believe I will.'

7

Easter came and went and the McKennas settled into life in Salamanca Street. Nolly was assigned to the harbour squad. He no longer spent his days up to his waist in mud, and there was cash to spare. He bought a second-hand bed and a few other luxuries that made the room more comfortable, if no less cramped. Clare seemed happier now and accompanied Aunt Cissie Cassidy to mid-week as well as Sunday mass. She went regularly to confession, though what her sister found to confess was more than Evie could imagine.

Gossip and teasing kept Chiffin and Evie amused during dinner breaks and in those few slack moments during the day when Mr Draper could find nothing for them to do.

From Chiffin she learned that Mrs Galloway was Russell Blackstock's sister and a close friend of Patrick Maizie, a closer friend, perhaps, than propriety allowed given that Mr Maizie had a wife and children stowed somewhere out of town.

According to Chiff, Mrs Galloway had run off to Malaya with a Catholic many years ago and had caused a scandal in the family by converting to the Roman religion. After her husband had died, she had returned to Glasgow with a kiddie in tow. Whether the kiddie was hers or not remained a mystery, but it didn't take Evie long to deduce that the pretty Chinese girl who accompanied Mrs Galloway to services in St Kentigern's was the kiddie in question.

It was during a quiet mid-morning spell at the Harp that Evie first encountered Russell Blackstock. There are meetings that should never have happened and, by the laws of nature, relationships that should never have begun, and, looking back, Evie could not quite believe that fate did not have a hand in it.

She was cleaning tobacco stains from the mirror behind the bar when he came upon her. It was a cool, clear morning, the light through the windows softened by a smoky haze from the kitchen where the cook was braising beef. Mr Blackstock did not come in through the door from the street but from the corridor that led to the kitchen and the yard and, just at first, she thought that the cook had come to test her mettle by scrounging a nip of whisky on the house.

Kneeling on the broad ledge, her back to the room, she was on the point of telling him to sod off when she saw that it was not the cook but a stranger.

She turned so quickly that she almost slipped from her perch.

The man gave a little gasp, a start, and for a split second it seemed that he might leap clean over the counter and catch her before she fell.

In spite of her bunched skirts and canvas apron, she managed to steady herself and from that exalted position said brightly, 'Good morning, sir, an' what can I be doin' for you?'

'I'm looking for Mr Maizie.'

'He ain't here, sir. Perhaps he's in the office. The office is—'

'I know where the office is, thank you,' the man said. 'I've just come from the office and he isn't there.'

'Not me place to say so, sir, but it's a bit on the early side for Mr Maizie.' Evie made no attempt to come down from the ledge. ''Less you've an appointment, like.'

The man took a step towards the bar and looked up at her with just the trace of a smile. He wasn't handsome the way Mr Maizie was handsome, but he was pleasant enough, Evie thought, for someone who was old enough to be her father. His ears were tight to his head, like an otter's, all his features compact, and he was shaved so clean you could almost smell the soap.

'Tell me, young lady,' he said, 'are you permanently positioned on that shelf or do you come down occasionally?'

'I'm not sure I can come down, decent-like,' said Evie.

'Why not?'

'Me drawers are caught under me.'

The smile flitted across his lips again but he was too much of a gentleman to laugh out loud. 'Shall I send for Mr Draper to assist you,' he said, 'or would you prefer me to turn my back for a moment or two?'

'Turn your back,' said Evie. 'Please.'

He took off his hat and pretended to cover his eyes with it, then, very deliberately, turned around.

If she had known who he was she wouldn't have been so free but she had already learned that gentlemen were not averse to a little banter. She slid from the shelf to the floor, saying, 'Sure an' no peepin' now, since I might not be wearin' any drawers at all, for all you know.'

'What's your name?'

'Evie, sir: Evie McKenna.'

'You're new, I take it.'

'Aye, sir, fresh as this mornin's milk.'

'May I turn round now?'

'You may, sir, an' I thank you for your courtesy.'

She smoothed her skirts and, untying the strings, let the canvas apron fall to the board behind the counter for she had a strong, if inexplicable desire to make a good impression.

Hands on hips, head cocked, she said, 'Now, sir, would you be carin' for a refreshment while you're waitin' for Mr Maizie or will I shout downstairs for Mr Draper to come up?'

'As it happens,' the man said, 'I do have an appointment with Mr Maizie but as Mr Maizie is not one for promptness, perhaps I might break a golden rule and indulge in a half-pint of Aitken's.'

'Strong or mild?'

'Mild.'

Putting his hat on the counter, he watched her tug the lever, top off foam, and fill the glass to the brim, all without spilling a drop.

'How long have you been here?' he asked. 'In Maizie's, I mean?'

'Month, near enough.'

'Did you work in a public house before you came here?'

'No, sir, we come straight off a farm in County Cork.'

He nodded. 'You learn quickly.'

'Mr Draper taught me,' Evie said. 'Mr Draper says I have the knack.'

'Aren't you going to take my money?'

'Since it's Mr Maizie's fault you're havin' to wait, I think he'd want you to have one without charge.' She wiped the top of the counter with a rag. 'If it's not impolite, sir, might I be askin' your name, since I haven't seen you round here before.'

'My name's not important,' he said.

'Are you not from these parts then?' Evie persisted.

'I'm not often in Riverside,' he said, adding, 'not often enough, it seems.'

'It's a grand place, the Riverside,' said Evie.

'Do you lodge near here?' he asked.

'In a house down the street.'

'I see,' the gentleman said. 'Reasonable, is it?'

She was tempted to give him the rant about rat-holes and rack-rents but some instinct stopped her.

'Reasonable enough, I suppose,' she said.

'What do they charge you in rent?'

'Five shillin's the week, by the week.'

'You regard that as reasonable, do you?'

Evie nodded cautiously. 'Are you the health mannie, by any chance?'

'Good God, no! The health inspector is no friend of mine.'

After a moment, Evie said, 'Aren't you goin' to drink your beer?'

'Since it's free . . .' Lifting the glass, he drank the half-pint in a single swallow as if to prove that although he might look like a gent he had just as much stomach as a navvy or a shipwright. He put the glass down, and sighed. 'Very refreshing.'

'Aitken's strong is better,' Evie told him, simply for something to say. 'It's got more flavour an' comes out with a better top.' Then, to her relief, she heard footsteps in the corridor and Patrick Maizie put in an appearance.

'Well, well, you're here already,' he said. 'Did Libby not tell me half past the hour? No? Perhaps I got it wrong. I gather you've been given a tipple and have, I trust, been well entertained.'

'Yes,' the man said. 'Yes, I have, thank you.'

'Come then,' Paddy Maizie said. 'We'll repair to the office an' get down to it, shall we?'

'I see no reason why not.' The man glanced at Evie and gave her another of his contained little smiles. 'Thank you, young lady. I've enjoyed our conversation. I trust that it wasn't too tedious for you?'

'Sure an' it wasn't tedious at all, sir,' said Evie.

She watched Paddy gather the man with an arm and lead him towards the corridor; then she heard Paddy say, 'Do you like her, Russell? Charmin' little piece, ain't she – as her kind go?'

'Oh, yes,' she heard the man say. 'Charming isn't the word.'

'Come again then,' Paddy Maizie said, 'an' we'll see what we can do.'

Then the door closed and the voices were lost before she could hear how Russell Blackstock replied to Mr Patrick

Maizie's offer, an offer, Evie realised, that had been made not entirely in jest.

Clare had never seen such a spartan room. If she hadn't known better she would have sworn that nobody lived there. She had thought that her kitchen was tidy but Harry Fairfield's place made it look like a midden. It was clean to the point of impossibility, without a crumb, cobweb or a grain of coal dust to be seen; one chair, one mug, one plate on the table, no sign of boots or clothing, no rug on the floor, no curtain on the window and on the bed in the shadowy recess a folded sheet, a folded blanket and one spotless pillow.

'*Ta-rah!*' Harry said with a flourish. 'Home, sweet or otherwise. Yon John Howard Payne knew a thing or two when he wrote that song. You heard that song, darlin'? I'll sing it for you, if you like.'

'No thanks,' Clare said.

'I'll go down on my knees an' serenade you.'

'I didn't come up to your room to be serenaded,' Clare said.

'What did you come for then?'

'I don't know: just to see how – where you lived.'

In spite of her protest, he crooned, '*Be it evah sooo hum-bull, there's noah place loike 'ooome.*'

'Harry, be quiet. Someone will hear us.'

'There's nobody around at this hour in the afternoon.'

'Mrs Fowler's upstairs.'

'She's gone out to the shops,' Harry said. 'Anyroads, you should hear what him an' her – aye, an' the sister too – get up to when Dan, Dan the Sailor Man comes home. God, you'd think they were breakin' rocks on that bed – an' the squeals, you should hear the squeals.'

'I'd rather not, thank you,' Clare said primly.

Harry had been babbling all sorts of nonsense since they had met that late afternoon out on the drying-green, which was no 'green' at all but a patch of black ash with six or eight rusty poles embedded in it.

She had been hanging out Nolly's shirts when he came upon her. He had caught her there several times, padding from the gloom of the back close, snaring her with an arm about her waist, drawing her into the shelter of the middens and kissing her, kissing her with an urgency which she, in spite of herself, shared.

She hadn't resisted when he'd put his hands on her breasts or cupped a hand between her legs while his lips silenced her protests and his tongue had danced in and out of her mouth. She'd felt wickedness grow in her and wetness between her legs and a sullen stiffening of her breasts that had made her groan and cry out while Harry had thrust himself against her, grunting, until they were both too weak and shaken to stand up properly.

'I'll bet you'd squeal too,' Harry said, 'if you was bein' poked by a man who'd been at sea for half a year.'

'I don't know what you mean.'

'Aye, but you do, Clare,' he said. 'Anyhow, what do you think o' Fairfield manor?'

'It's very nice.'

'Is that all you have to say about it?'

'It's – it's very tidy. Now, I think I should be goin'.'

'Goin'? You only just got here.'

'I've things to be doin' downstairs.'

'Aye,' Harry said, 'so have I.'

If he had tried to kiss her at once she might well have pushed him away. But he was expert in wooing and patient enough to take her hands in his and lead her round in a weird little dance, round and round by the table and empty grate, past the bed recess and round again and then, breathless, to kick out the chair, seat himself upon it and pull her on to his knee. Evie, Clare thought, would have giggled and pretended to fight him off, but she was too nervous to be frisky and could not deceive herself that what she was doing was playful.

She leaned her head on his chest, inviting him to stroke her hair and whisper words of love into her ear, to be not only patient but gentle, as if he had never done this before; to convince her that she was truly his first love and that what he was about to do to her in that spotless room would be not an end but a beginning.

Mr Belfer was in cheerful mood. He had made a call that afternoon on a tradesman in the vicinity of Carpenter Street and had learned from the man that, to paraphrase the Shorter Catechism, the work of necessity and the work of mercy had been satisfactorily brought together and the leaking drain at the back of Mr Blackstock's most profitable property had been repaired; if not repaired, at least well enough patched to pass muster with a Health Department inspector who had been nosing around the neighbourhood of late and who, rumour had it, was far too diligent for his own or anyone else's good.

Mr Belfer had even condescended to examine the job and, finding it 'right', had persuaded the tradesman to sign an invoice for a marginally higher sum than the sum paid out in cash. In due course Mr Belfer would present the paid invoice to Mr Blackstock's agent in an office near Partick Cross in exchange for a cheque which he would deposit in his account in the Partick branch of the Barony of Glasgow Savings and Investment Bank, thereby turning a profit of eleven shillings on the transaction which, all in all, constituted a fair morning's work. Small wonder he felt so cheerful as he strolled down Salamanca Street and entered the tenement close.

At that hour of the afternoon all was peaceful in Mr Belfer's little kingdom, for the men were at work and only the women were at home; even so, he thought it best to 'do his rounds' before he retired to his room for a nap.

He moved up the stairs on the balls of his feet to the landing outside the McKennas' room, stopped there and listened, hopeful that he might share an intimate moment with the girl, Clare; might hear her singing, or sighing, or using the chamber pot, might by chance, encounter her alone and try once more to impose his will upon her, but there was no sound at all from behind the door.

He was on the point of going downstairs again when a snatch of sound so faint that he could not put a finger on it, drifted down from the second floor.

Mr Belfer slipped upstairs as silently as a Highland mist. He positioned himself outside Harry Fairfield's door and cupped a hand to his ear.

Nature had not endowed him well in the matter of manly parts and, out of embarrassment as well as rectitude, he had never been with a woman; yet listening the crescendo of gasping cries and the rhythmic knocking of a bed-frame loose against the wall from Fairfield's room he was undoubtedly aroused.

He knew at once who was there with Harry Fairfield: Clare, Clare McKenna, her dress up over her head, her belly bare, her fingers digging into Fairfield's back, her long white legs clasped around him, kicking with every thrust of the boy's backside and – *there, there, there* – crying out in a spasm of pleasure that brought sweat to Benjamin Belfer's brow and tears of jealous rage to his eyes as he realised that the girl he had hoped to make his bride was nothing but a common whore.

'Toss him out, Benjamin,' Mr Orpington said. 'He has clearly contravened the rules of behaviour you prescribed for the house. It's one thing for a husband to poke his wife practically in public, quite another for some young whippersnapper to use the accommodation to entertain harlots. As for the female herself, if you let it go this time next thing you know you'll have every Tom, Dick and Harry tramping through your close for a turn, as it were, at the pump.'

'They're not married, you know.'

'Pardon?' said Mr Orpington. 'Who's not married?'

'The Fowlers.'

'The Fowlers? I thought we were talking about the Irish girl.'

'He must take me for a fool that Danny so-called Fowler,' Benjamin said. 'His name's not Fowler. His name's Doyle. The women are Fowlers. I let that go. That was my first mistake.'

'How many children does the Fowler woman have?'

'Three,' said Benjamin. 'Bastards, every one.'

'I suppose you might defend yourself by citing common decency in that particular case,' Percival Orpington said, 'or even common law, but this other matter has to be considered more objectively, Benjamin. Do you hear me?'

Benjamin did not appear to be listening. 'Mr Coker had a woman came to visit once. Claimed she was his sister. Paid for her to stay three nights. She was no more his sister than I am. Out of the goodness of my heart, I let that go too. I've been far too soft for far too long, Perce. It's time to put a stop to it.'

'A stop to what?'

'Immorality.'

'Ah! Yes!' said Mr Orpington.

They were seated at a brass-topped table in the basement of a coffee house not far from Charing Cross. Mr Orpington had lodgings in Berkeley Street, just around the corner, though Benjamin had never been invited there.

'Are you certain it was the girl in question?' Mr Orpington asked. 'Did you observe her emerging from the amorous encounter?'

'I'm sure it was Clare. I just know it was.'

'Have you seen her since?'

'No, and I've no wish to.'

Mr Orpington drummed his fingers on the table. 'Look on the bright side, Mr B. If this girl *is* putting herself about then there's no reason why you shouldn't avail yourself of her services.'

'What do you mean?'

'If she's a whore, she has her price.'

'I do not consort with whores, Perce, not at any price. Besides . . .'

Mr Orpington cocked his head. 'Besides?'

'I had something other than bedding her in mind.'

'Did you? What sort of something?'

Mr Belfer swirled the coffee grounds in the bottom of his cup. 'Marriage,' he said.

'Marriage!' Mr Orpington cried. 'Good God, man, what's come over you? Is she such a ravishing creature that you'd have her hanging round your neck for the rest of your life? Marriage! I cannot believe it!'

'I'm forty-two years old, Perce. It's time I took a wife.'

Mr Orpington's voice dropped to a whisper. 'Have her, Benjamin, by all means have her, but, I beg you, do not rush into matrimony simply because you sense time's winged chariot thundering up your backside.' He leaned forward. 'Is it her again? Has your old mother been nagging you to get married?'

Benjamin nodded.

'All very well for her,' said Mr Orpington, 'all very well when she, in the fullness of time and obedience to nature's laws, will be gone in a year or two. And you, you, my dear good friend, will be stuck with this Irish bint and, no doubt, a gaggle of infants screaming in your ear. Ponder long and hard on that prospect, Mr B., and tell me truthfully if pandering to your dear mama's wish is worth a lifetime's misery?'

'You're right, Perce. You're right, of course,' Benjamin said. 'She's a lovely girl, though, quite lovely.'

'Oh, for God's sake, man, pull yourself together,' Mr Orpington said testily. 'Toss her and her siblings out. Do it now before she causes you more aggravation.'

'If I toss her out, she'll be lost to me forever.'

Mr Orpington threw back his head and released a little wail. 'Damn it all, Belfer, if she's a trollop, as you say, then you can have her and be done with it; though if she is a trollop, she's no fit wife for a man of your stature. If she has merely gone overboard for this coal-heaver then give *him* his marching orders and clear the field for your own advances, matrimonial or otherwise. What you *cannot* do is mope like a moonstruck calf or you will lose not only my respect but your authority in the community and, in consequence, your ability to serve effectively as Mr Blackstock's agent.'

'Yes,' Benjamin said, 'that thought had occurred to me, too.'

'Act, man, act now to save yourself.'

'I want to, Perce, I do, but . . .'

'There are no "buts" about it. Why won't you listen to me?'

'Because,' poor Benjamin said, 'I don't think you've ever been in love.'

Even in her dizzy state Clare soon became aware that she was being spied upon. It was obvious that the man downstairs had more than an inkling that Harry and she were embarked on a passionate affair and that the factor did not approve of such goings-on. He said nothing to her, nothing to Harry, though, just glowered when she passed him on the way to the water closet or the midden. In fact, he seemed to be standing on her shadow as soon as she stepped from the door and she would swear that she could hear him wheezing in the stairwell even when Harry assured her that the factor was not at home.

Late each afternoon, she would slip out to join Harry upstairs. He was always clean, scrubbed clean, for, he said, he went directly from the coal yard to the public baths in South Street to wash away the muck and put on a clean shirt and trousers. So impressed was Clare by his thoughtfulness that she did not think to enquire where he stowed his dirty clothes. After love-making, when they lay in each other's arms, Harry would encourage her to talk of the priest's seduction. He was so insistent that Clare found herself inventing details just to please him and in the telling, in the invention, found release from the guilt that had plagued her, for, it seemed, she had become fearless in her need to love and be loved by a man and not some amorphous, judgemental god.

The glib little lies that she told Father Fingle in the box at St Kentigern's no longer troubled her. She made her Acts of Contrition, said her Our Fathers and Hail Marys. She used her rosary to pray. She knelt by Mrs Cassidy's side on the hard boards of the chapel on Wednesdays and Sundays and intoned the responses that the habit of faith required of her. But what she prayed for now had less to do with the soul than the body, her body and Harry Fairfield's body, and a marriage made in heaven that, if God and the saints were on her side, would soon be sanctified on earth.

8

Russell Blackstock was, and always would be, a loyal Freemason. The Grand Lodge of Scotland had an honourable history and its organisation, by any standard of society, was eminently respectable. He had become bored, ineffably bored with Willy's Orange Order soirées, however, where principles were often reduced to big drinking, ignorant ranting against the Pope, and sweeping declarations of loyalty to a cause that, politically as well as theologically, had about as much influence on the average west of Scotland artisan as a poem by Wordsworth or a painting by Raphael.

It had been months since he had dropped in on Mr Sloane, manager of the coal yard; he preferred to let his agents get on with things without interference. He still had a soft spot for the rough-and-tumble district where so many of his employees lived, though, and from which, courtesy of several shady transactions, he had accumulated the capital necessary to finance bigger, more lucrative schemes.

Soon after breakfast, he left Crosshill and set out along the river in smoky morning sunlight. He wore a battered billycock hat and an Ulster coat that covered a multitude of sins, for it was not his intention to impress, much less intimidate anyone. He passed the abandoned cotton factory that Willy had recently purchased with a loan from the Barony Bank and, in due course, arrived at the builder's yard in Salamanca Street where he found old Ned Torrance, pipe in mouth, directing a laden brick-cart out of the gate.

'Good morning, Ned. Fine spot of weather we're having.'

'Aye,' Ned answered, the clay wagging, 'but it'll rain again afore nightfall, sur, if I know owt about it. Is it Mr Macready ye're after then?'

Russell smiled and shook his head. 'I'm after no one, Ned,' he said. 'I'm on my way elsewhere.'

'Good luck tae ye then, sur,' the gate-keeper said and, without intended insult, turned his head and spat.

As usual, Evie had lingered in bed after Clare had got up to make Nolan's breakfast. She loved the new, second-hand bed, loved it all the more when she had it to herself. She snuggled under the blanket, her back to the sunlit window, and thought of nothing at all while Clare moved about the kitchen, clinking pots and pans and shaking out Nolly's clothes. That precious extra hour in bed was worth a hasty wash, a hurried breakfast and a sprint along Salamanca Street.

She spotted him a long way off, neither hiding nor loitering but striding down the empty street at a steady pace, aiming, Evie assumed, for the Harp. He passed the door of the Harp without a second glance, though, and came towards her with a distant look in his eye, as if he failed to notice let alone recognise her.

She didn't know what to do, how to behave.

Twenty yards, ten, five: he was almost upon her.

If she had been on the opposite pavement she, like the Levite in the Gospels, might have passed him by on the other side. Face to face, there was no alternative but to stop or step aside.

He looked down at last, blinking.

'Oh,' he said lightly. 'It's you.'

'Aye, Mr Blackstock, sure an' it's nobody else.'

'Miss . . .'

'Evie McKenna.'

'From . . .'

He seemed unable to recall just where they had met before. Evie was not deceived. She was glad he'd ignored Paddy Maizie's offer to broker a second meeting, though, and had come in search of her himself.

'From Salamanca Street,' she said, 'down there at the end.'

'Of course. I remember. We met in Maizie's place, did we not?'

Fine well you know we did, Evie thought.

She said, 'I believe we did, sir.'

'You're the girl who likes sitting on a shelf.'

'You have me now, Mr Blackstock, sure an' you do.'

He seemed in no hurry to be about his business, whatever that business might be. He took off his hat and held it by his side. There were flecks of grey in his hair, though his hair was profuse and tumbled in two soft little curls over his tight otterish ears. His dark brown eyes were soft too, soft and wary. He reminded her just a little of her brother Kiernan before the consumption had pulled him down.

She laughed. 'Were you hoping to catch me on the shelf again, sir?'

'Why, do you give daily performances?'

'Oh, no, sir, far from it. I'm not as immodest as you might imagine – even though I'm Irish.'

He frowned. 'Why do you say that?'

'Say what?'

'"Although I'm Irish"?'

''Cause I am – Irish, I mean,' Evie answered. 'Ain't it obvious?'

'Patently obvious,' Mr Blackstock said. 'But what makes you suppose that I regard all Irish girls as immodest?'

'Everybody does,' Evie said. 'The Irish aren't supposed to have any brains, nor morals for that matter.'

'But you don't subscribe to that claptrap, do you?'

'Not for a minute,' Evie said.

'Yet you choose to use it as an excuse?'

'An excuse?' said Evie. 'An excuse for what, Mr Blackstock?'

'Being yourself.'

She had expected him to bid her good morning, exchange a few words about the weather perhaps, and go on his way. If he *had* come into the Riverside to catch another glimpse of her legs, she was ready for that, but not for this challenge to her character. It had never dawned on her before that she might be something other than the sum of her parts – young, Irish and female – or that a man might find more to admire in her.

'Sure an' I'll have to be goin' now,' she said, flustered. 'I'm late as it is.'

'I'll walk in with you.'

'*No!*' Evie said sharply. 'No, Mr Blackstock, please don't.'

'Are you ashamed to be seen with me?'

'It's not that, sir. It's . . .'

'Ah, yes, I know what they think of me in Maizie's,' he said. 'It's a double-edged sword, isn't it?'

She did not have to ask him to explain. 'Aye, sir, it is,' she said.

'Before you go, may I ask you a question, Evie?'

'What question?' Evie said cautiously.

'Do you worship at St Kentigern's?'

Surprised and relieved, she said, 'Yes, sir, I do.'

'In which case, you must be acquainted with my sister.'

'I've seen her, Mr Blackstock, but I ain't exactly acquainted with her.'

'How well do you know Father Fingle?'

'Not well,' said Evie. 'My sister knows him better.'

'Your sister?'

'Clare.'

'Is she devout?'

'We're all good Catholics, sir, if that's what you mean,' Evie said. 'You're not a Catholic, are you, Mr Blackstock?'

'No. My sister converted to the Roman faith many years ago and it's been held against her ever since.'

'By you?' said Evie before she could help herself.

'Yes, by me,' he said, adding, 'but less so as the years progress.'

'You've got friends in the true faith, though, haven't you?'

'Have I?'

'Mr Maizie, for one I know of,' Evie said.

'Mr Maizie's hardly a friend,' Mr Blackstock told her, then added, 'Mark you, it's hard not to be friendly with Paddy, don't you think?'

'He's my employer, Mr Blackstock, not my friend.'

'Of course,' Russell Blackstock said. 'Well, thank you, Evie. I've detained you far too long. I hope you won't find yourself in trouble.'

'Not me, sir,' Evie said, bold at last. 'I've got more excuses up my sleeve than you've had hot dinners.' Then, with a little curtsey, she stepped past him and hurried into the Harp.

'Bob's lookin' for you,' Chiffin said. 'Where the heck have you been?'

'Talkin' to Mr Blackstock,' Evie said.

Not surprisingly Chiffin just laughed.

If the Saturday trip to the Masonic Hall in Carpenter Street was the low point in Cissie's week then Wednesday evening service at St Kentigern's was the high. A trusting soul, she rarely questioned the wisdom of the priest's homespun homilies or any of the hundred and one other blessings that the Church bestowed upon her. She had no need of women's groups, Bible study meetings or charabanc trips to holy places to sustain her conviction that her spiritual welfare was in good hands, though for every shilling she put into her account with the Barony Bank, she put another into St Kentigern's poor box, just to be on the safe side.

On Wednesdays Cissie had Clare all to herself. They met at the close-mouth and, with time to spare, strolled arm-in-arm up Salamanca Street to the church. Ned Torrance and his fat wife, Faye, made slow progress towards the gate where Mrs Colgan and her brash, unmarried daughter gossiped with Mrs Durie, and then Mrs Galloway and her ward appeared from the alley that led to the back of the Harp and fell into step behind Cissie and Clare.

Cissie did not approve of converts. She certainly did not approve of Mrs Galloway. She couldn't fathom why a woman who was related to the Blackstock brothers had been accepted into the true Church, why a woman who wore expensive clothes and was collected on Sundays by a godless publican in a fancy carriage would elect to worship in St Kentigern's in the first place.

The woman reached out and tapped Clare's shoulder. 'I wonder if I might have a word with you,' she said.

'What sort of word?' said Cissie possessively.

'A private word,' the woman said and, detaching Clare's hand from the widow's arm, drew the young woman aside.

Left alone, Cissie and the Chinese girl stared at each other, then, to Cissie's astonishment, the girl raised an eyebrow, pursed her lips and made a little popping sound. Though she was embarrassed to be seen conversing with a foreigner, curiosity got the better of her and, leaning closer, Cissie whispered, 'What can that woman possibly want with my niece?'

And in an accent more Scots than Straits, Seang Pin answered, 'Search me.'

It was unusually quiet in the Harp. By nine o'clock only four customers were at the bar. It gave Evie quite a turn when

Nolan appeared in the doorway accompanied by Clare's friend, Harry Fairfield. Nolly had obviously come straight from work, for his shirt and trousers were filthy and his boots caked with mud. Harry Fairfield, though, had a shiny, almost polished look about him that reminded Evie of bum-bailiffs and constables in mufti.

'What are you doin' here at this hour, Nolly?' she asked. 'Don't tell me you've been paid off?'

''Course I ain't been paid off.' Digging into his pocket, Nolly put a shilling on the counter. 'Two pints o' Edinburgh ale, please, an' don't go fiddlin' the change.'

She said, 'You still haven't told me why you're here so early.'

'Accident,' Nolly said casually. 'Two killed.'

'Two *killed*?' said Evie. 'How?'

'Rubble cart tipped into the river at high tide,' Nolly said. 'Took two fellers with it. They weren't ours, though.'

'So that makes it all right, does it?' said Evie.

'Contractuator's fault for employin' kiddies,' Nolly said.

Harry Fairfield, standing a pace behind, added, 'Right you are, Nolan.'

'Sent us off home,' Nolan said. 'Didn't dock us for lost time neither.'

'No cloud without a silver lining, eh?' Harry Fairfield said. 'Do hurry along wi' that quaff, darlin'. I could drink the damned river dry tonight.'

Evie pulled beer from the pump with a little less care than usual and dumped the glasses down on the counter. Out of the corner of her eye she noticed Chiffin, ears cocked, wiping tables by the angle of the nook.

She slapped the coppers down hard.

'What's that?' said Nolly.

'Your change,' said Evie.

'Nothin' off for family, then?'

'Not my family,' Evie said. 'Pocket it quick, or I'll assume it's a tip.'

Carrying his glass, Nolan stepped away from the bar. Harry Fairfield lingered, studying her with interest.

'Anyone ever told you, you're quite a peach, Evie?' he said.

'Plenty o' times,' said Evie. 'I pay them no heed, though.'

Harry Fairfield shrugged and swaggered off to join her brother in the nook around the corner. Chiffin, rag in hand, came over to her and leaned both elbows on the counter.

'I hope he's not gonna make trouble,' he said.

'Who? Me brother?'

'The other one.'

'Has he made trouble before?'

'Can't say he has,' said Chiffin, 'but if they start into the singin' there's no tellin' what might happen.'

'Mr Draper will put the crimp on them fast enough.'

'Bob's not here. He's in the office doin' a tally with Mr Maizie.'

'So you're in charge?' said Evie.

'In a manner o' speakin'.'

'So if Nolly does turn tuneful, it'll be up to you to throw him out.'

'Hah, bloody hah,' said Chiffin.

'What's wrong with you tonight, Chiff?' Evie said.

'Nothin's wrong with me.'

'You're jumpy as a three-legged cat. Come on, lad, out with it. Tell Evie what ails you.'

Chiffin seemed about to say something, then, thinking better of it, flicked a few drops of moisture at her from the tail of the rag and, before she could retaliate, retreated into the snug.

Chiffin was still in the snug two or three minutes later when Mr Orpington came in and headed straight for Evie at the bar.

'Where is he?'

'If you mean Mr Maizie, he's—'

'I mean,' said Mr Orpington, 'the red-haired beggar who works here.'

'He's in the office, in the yard,' said Evie, 'with Mr Maizie.'

'You're a lying Irish bitch,' said Mr Orpington pleasantly. 'If I had time I'd take great pleasure in teaching you manners. Where's Chiffin?'

'I'll fetch Mr Draper if you don't believe—'

Orpington hooked a forefinger into the collar of her blouse and jerked her half over the counter. 'I'll fetch you, lady, if you don't open up.'

'Let her go, Mr Orpington.' Chiffin emerged from the snug. 'She ain't the one owes you money.'

'Where *is* my money, Chiffin?' Percival Orpington said. 'My patience is wearing thin. Have you got it, or haven't you?'

'I haven't,' Chiffin said, 'not all of it, leastways.'

'God in heaven, do I have to teach you the meaning of responsibility every friggin' month?' Mr Orpington said.

The customers who remained in the body of the bar headed for the door at the double. Mr Orpington caught Chiff by the hair and brought him down over a table in the centre of the room, brought him down so skilfully that the empty glasses on the table top did not even rattle. Evie shot around the counter and leaped on to Mr Orpington's back. He shucked her off as if she weighed no more than a shawl or a scarf and sent her sprawling to the floor.

'*Oy, oy*,' Nolan said. 'What do you think you're doin'?'

'Leave it be, Nolan,' Harry Fairfield muttered. 'Let it go.'

'Let it go?' said Nolan. 'I'll do nothin' of the bloody kind.'

He set his glass on the floor and offered Evie his hand. She hauled herself to her feet and wiped a fleck of blood from her lip.

'Watch him, Nolly,' she said. 'He might have a knife.'

'Come on, man, come on. Time we were all out o' here,'

Harry Fairfield said, tugging at Nolan's sleeve. 'We don't want to make trouble, do we?'

Mr Orpington held up both hands and, retreating, allowed Chiffin to slide from the table. 'My business is with this welcher here, not with you.'

'Too late,' Nolly said. 'Sure an' your business *is* with me.'

Then, like a gigantic cat, he pounced.

Seang Pin walked a few steps in front of her aunt. Libby Galloway was no more her aunt than she was her mother, of course; Pin had long ago given up trying to define, or defend, their relationship. Legally, she was Mrs Galloway's ward, all signed for and sealed by representatives of the Colonial Office, the European Magistrate, the Governor and some whiskery gent in Singapore who had been her father's sponsor before they had moved to Penang.

She remembered her mother and father vividly and most of the Malay servants who had attended her upbringing in the house on the corner of Beach Street not far from the warehouse where Mr Galloway and her father stored the pepper and spices in which they traded. She also remembered the priest in the Catholic Mission out on Waterfall Road and the nuns who taught there and how devoted they were to the Virgin, and how they had prayed to the Virgin to comfort her when a great fire had roared through the warehouse and carried off to heaven not only her father and mother but Mr Galloway too. She did not often dwell on that time in her life, however. She had been brought to Scotland and put to school in Scotland and though she could never hope to disguise her features she regarded herself in most respects as Scottish as a mutton pie.

Mrs Cassidy was clearly none too pleased at being seen in public with a person whose skin was not white. She would not have to put up with it for long, though, for Libby would turn off at the lane that led to Paddy Maizie's office and would persuade old Paddy to run out the carriage and drive them home.

Pin hoped that she would have a chance to ask Paddy to lay the half-crown she had wheedled from Uncle Russell on the nose of *Jim Dandy* at tempting odds of eleven to four in the Eglinton Stakes at Ayr on Saturday and her thoughts were occupied with horses and odds when the door of the public house whacked open and two grown men, locked in a ferocious embrace, tumbled on to the pavement.

Mrs Cassidy shrieked.

Libby caught Pin by the waist and pulled her back.

The Irish girl cried out, 'Nolly!'

Pin recognised Mr Orpington, even without his topper, but the young man with the floppy fair hair and massive thighs was more of a stranger, though she had noticed him in church once or twice. She pursed her lips and uttered a curious little popping sound that signified not bewilderment but admiration.

'*Good God!*' Aunt Libby shouted. '*What is this? Stop it, stop it at once or I'll send for the constables.*'

You can send for a battalion of the Seaforth Highlanders, Pin thought, but it will do no good, for that pair will not be parted until one has beaten the other into the dirt.

She craned her neck for a better view.

'Get him, Nolly. Kill him, Nolly,' Clare McKenna cried and, wrapping an arm around Pin's waist, proudly informed her, 'That's my brother, you know. He can lick any man alive.'

Pin could well believe it.

Tenement windows rattled up, skeins of small boys appeared out of closes, a crowd gathered in what had been, only a moment ago, an almost empty street. Paddy's potboy and Clare McKenna's sister slithered from the door of the pub and crabbed along the wall.

'Kill 'im, son, kill the effin' bastard,' someone shouted.

'G'arn, Irish, knock his soddin' block off.'

'Eye-rish. Eye-rish. Eye-rish!'

Though famous for her reticence, Pin heard herself chanting too, 'EYE-RISH. EYE-RISH. EYE-RISH,' and even Libby leaned forward, fists clenched, the ebony crucifix swinging out from her bosom, and delivered sharp little blows into thin air as if to add her weight to that of the Irish labourer who had suddenly become the hero of the hour.

Evie brought warm water in a bowl and Clare unbuttoned her brother's shirt. No less a person than Libby Galloway dipped a clean cloth into the water, added a drop of gentian violet from a bottle that Bob Draper had provided and gingerly bathed the gash on the young man's forehead.

'Lucky,' Paddy Maizie said. 'Very lucky, I reckon, that Orpington wasn't carrying a knife.'

'He's an animal,' Libby said. 'An absolute beast.'

Paddy rocked in a chair in a corner of the snug, puffing on a cigar and sipping brandy. 'Orpington was only doing his job, Libs.'

'Terrorising defenceless girls, is that what you pay him for?' Libby snapped. 'Give me that glass.'

She plucked the brandy glass from Paddy's fingers and offered it to Nolan who was slumped in a chair, his head resting on a cushion, eyes closed. He hadn't lost consciousness but his thinking was hazy. He seemed to recall holding the Englishman in a head-lock and pummelling away at his biscuit until the feller caught him off balance, overturned him and cracked his head on the pavement. If he hadn't been so mad he might have let the feller go at that point but he had hung on to the feller's legs for dear life, for he reckoned if he let go the feller would stamp all over him.

'Where is Orpington, by the way?' said Paddy.

'Ran off,' said Libby, 'like the craven coward he is.'

'Well, I wouldn't be sayin' he *ran*,' Evie put in.

'Crawled off, more like,' said Clare.

Nolan opened his eyes as the rim of the glass brushed his lips. He had a vague recollection of grabbing the feller's foot as it came towards him and rolling into a forest of dirty bare feet and trouser-legs, of hearing the feller scream when his ankle bone broke.

'By Gar!' said Evie. 'I thought they were goin' to lynch him.'

'Yes, our Perce ain't awfully popular in these parts,' Paddy Maizie said.

He regretted having missed the excitement but at least the bar had filled up; there was nothing like a bit of violence to encourage thirst. Besides, Paddy thought, the good citizens of Riverside will no doubt want to toast the bold young Irishman who'd had the gall to stand up to Percival Orpington.

'It's high time you got shot of him,' Libby said.

'Shot of him?' said Paddy.

'Sacked him, fired him,' Libby said. 'I've told you a thousand times, Patrick, you should not be associated with a man like that.'

'He does have his uses,' Paddy said.

'Oh, I know what he is and what he does,' said Libby. 'I wonder, however, just how useful he'll be to anyone now.'

Paddy got to his feet: no point in arguing with Libby when she was in a crusading mood. He said, 'Your brother's welfare appears to be in good hands, Evie. I think Bob might need your services in the bar.'

'Aye, Mr Maizie,' Evie said and, with a last anxious glance at Nolan, went out to help Chiffin and Mr Draper at the counter, while Paddy sauntered off into the kitchen to see to Mrs Cassidy who was having her nerves calmed by applications of hot tea, liberally laced with brandy.

* * *

Libby ran her thumb down the lip of the wound, leaving a smear of gentian across Nolan's broad brow. His eyes were wide open now and he seemed, she thought, to have recovered most of his wits. He smiled that white smile again and, stretching his magnificent neck, indicated that he might cope successfully with a little more to drink.

She gave him the glass.

'Better?' she asked.

'Aye, much better, thanks.' He looked around. 'Where's Harry?'

'Oh,' Clare said, 'he took himself off home.'

'Did he now?' Nolan put the glass on the table, pushed against the arms of the chair and got unsteadily to his feet. 'I'm thinkin' it's time we went home, too, dearest, since I could be doin' with gettin' me head down.'

She was so quiet and passive that he hadn't really noticed her before.

She held up his mud-stained jacket and, giving it a shake, helped him into it. She was taller than Evie, taller than Clare, as slender and straight as a pickaxe shaft, he thought, as she tugged at his collar to make it neat and then, still without a word, buttoned him up.

Nolan looked down at her.

She tilted her chin and looked up at him.

'What's your name again?' Nolan asked.

'Seang Pin,' she answered. 'And yours?'

'Nolan McKenna,' he said. 'You can call me Nolly, if you like.'

As soon as he heard Nolan leave for work next morning, Mr Belfer rose, dressed, and galloped upstairs to the McKennas' apartment.

Clare opened the door to his knocking. She wore a thin cotton shift, her feet and legs bare, her hair hanging down her back like a mourning veil.

'Evie said it would be you,' Clare informed him.

'Evie?'

'Me sister,' Clare said. 'You remember me sister?'

He continued to stand there, his belly stuck out before him like a sail in the wind, powerless to erase the image of Clare naked on Fairfield's bed.

'Is – is Evie inside?' he said.

' 'Course she is.'

'May I come in?'

Clare smiled, more amused, it seemed, than frightened. Where, he wondered, had her fear gone? Why, when he had such a hold over her, did this chit of a girl frighten *him*? Graciously, she allowed him to enter the kitchen.

Evie was still in bed. He could see her breasts, pink-tipped under her shift. They had no modesty at all, these McKenna girls. He was disgusted at himself for accepting them for what they were, for not kicking them out.

'I need to know what happened last night at the Harp,' he said.

'Didn't Aunt Cissie tell you?' Evie said.

He was hot-browed, sweating under his waistcoat. He pulled out a chair and seated himself upon it. 'Not enough,' he said. 'I mean, why were you conveyed home by Libby Galloway? What's your connection with her?'

'Oh!' Clare answered. 'We've a lot in common now.'

'What did happen at Maizie's last evening?'

'If it's information you want, you'll have to trade for it,' said Evie.

'Trade for it?' said Benjamin. 'What do you mean?'

Clare padded about behind him. He could smell her: a warm-bed smell, like new baked bread.

'We're not under your thumb no more, Mr Belfer,' Evie told him. 'We've got friends in high places.'

'Since when?'

'Since last night,' said Clare.

'Aunt Cissie didn't tell you everythin', did she?' said Evie.

'Well, she told me something.'

'Did she tell you about Clare?'

No, Benjamin thought, she doesn't have to tell me about Clare: I know all about Clare: I know what Clare does and who she does it with: I know how she squeals when a man is upon her.

He licked his lips. 'What about Clare?'

'See,' said Evie, 'you don't know very much at all, do you?'

'I'm not here to argue. I'm here to find out what happened to Mr Orpington.'

'Me brother saw him off,' said Clare.

'What's more,' said Evie, 'Mr Orpington's out.'

'Out?'

'Sacked.'

'Stuff and nonsense!' Benjamin said. 'Mr Blackstock would never sack—'

'Mr Blackstock?' Evie said. 'Now which Mr Blackstock would that be?'

It was on the tip of his tongue to tell her the truth but he was not quite so far gone as all that. Even when Clare leaned across him to put a cup of tea on the table and he glimpsed of the curve of her bare breast, he had just enough sense left to keep mum.

'I see,' said Evie. 'So you don't want to trade information after all?'

The situation was ridiculous; a man of his calibre could not afford to be mesmerised by a young girl, however pretty and desirable.

'I could give you information,' he said. 'Believe me, I could tell you things that would make your hair curl.'

He turned and stared at Clare, and saw her blush. He had

Clare on the ropes, no doubt of that, but the tow-headed creature in the bed was still confident, still cocky.

'You don't know what Mrs Galloway wants with us, though,' Evie said, 'nor why you won't have the assistance of your friend Orpington when you make your rounds of the Riverside in future.'

'I doubt if my friend Orpington will be gone for long,' Mr Belfer said. 'Mr Orpington has served the Blackstocks well for ten years; you've been here about ten bloody minutes. When push comes to shove who do you think the Blackstocks will support?'

'Well' – Evie swung herself from the bed – 'we'll see.'

'I've no doubt we will,' Benjamin said and, lifting the teacup, offered the McKenna girls, Clare in particular, a genial little toast by way of reconciliation if not – not yet – surrender.

Clare and Evie did not have long to wait. Mr Belfer had hardly left the apartment before the door opened and Nolan stumped into the kitchen. He threw his cap on the bed, hauled out a chair and sat down.

'Paid off,' he said glumly. 'I got sacked.'

'*What!*' Evie shouted.

'Who paid you off?' Clare cried.

'Old Ned Torrance took back me ticket. Said he was sorry but word had come down from the office.'

'There must be some mistake,' said Clare.

'No mistake,' said Nolan. 'Paid me what was due an' told me there was no more work for me on the wall.'

'Liars, liars an' cheats!' Evie shouted. Beside herself with rage, she pranced round and round, like a demon.

'Sure an' it seems old Belfer was right,' Clare said.

Nolan looked up. 'Belfer?'

'He said *you'd* get the hook, not Orpington,' Clare said.

'Well, that settles that; if the Galloway woman wants somebody to help out with her precious orphans she can look elsewhere.'

'It's spite, sure an' that's what it is,' Evie raged. 'Somebody gave somebody else a wink an' a secret handshake. Sure what's Nolly to them but a thick Irishman.'

'That's goin' a bit far, Evie,' Nolan said.

'Is it?' Evie snapped. 'Do you think you'd have been paid off if you'd been an Orangeman? Aye, bloody old Belfer's right. Irish navvies are ten for the penny but a brute like Orpington's worth his weight in gold to somebody – an' I intend to find out who that somebody is.'

'Wait, Evie,' said Clare in alarm. 'Don't do anythin' rash.'

'Rash? You're a fine one to talk about rash, givin' you're bein' poked by a fly-by-night coal-heaver every bloody afternoon.'

Clare clutched the rim of the sink.

Nolan looked up and round, bewildered.

'Did you think you could keep a secret in this buildin', Clare?' Evie went on. 'Besides, just the way you look at him . . .'

'Who, at who?' said Nolan. 'Not Belfer?'

'She's not *that* stupid, no,' Evie said. 'Ask *her*, Nolly. I've better things to do right now than listen to her make excuses.'

'Harry!' Nolan shook his head. 'It must be Harry.'

'What if it is?' Clare said. 'It's none o' your business, neither of you.'

'It'll be our business if he knocks you up, though.' Evie gathered her clothes and, not caring that Nolan was in the room, began to dress. 'Right now our business is to get Nolan back on the Blackstocks' books.'

'He intends to marry me,' Clare said.

'Does he?' said Nolan.

'He loves me. Harry loves me.'

'Well, perhaps he does,' said Evie. 'Perhaps we will be hearin' weddin' bells before the summer's out. But before you start sewin' your trousseau, maybe you'd care to poach me an egg, for I'm damned if I'm goin' into battle on an empty stomach.'

9

There was nothing architecturally imposing about the building at the corner of Chartwell Street. The entrance was pinched between two pitted sandstone pillars and a glass-panelled door allowed you to peep into the hallway and decide whether or not you had the nerve to enter.

Nerve was not something that Evie McKenna lacked, not when her dander was up. She stormed into a hallway that, to her surprise, was completely empty: no doors, no desks, no doorman, just an oblong cage draped with hawsers and, tucked behind it, a flight of steep stone stairs, going up. She hesitated, lost already, then heard whistling and footsteps and a young man in a spotlessly clean brown overall came skipping down the stairs.

'If you're waiting for Davy to bring down that contraption,' he said, 'you'll be here all day.'

'What is that contraption?' Evie asked.

'It's a hydraulic lift. Installed last year. More trouble than it's worth.'

'I'm lookin' for Mr Blackstock.'

'Wilson or Russell?'

'Russell – Mr Russell.'

The young man gave her the eye. 'Is he expectin' you?'

'Yes,' Evie lied glibly. 'Yes, he is.'

'You'll find him on the third floor, most like.'

Evie thanked him and watched him hurry out into the road.

Snake-like things were sliding about in the cage, gruff voices echoing in the oily shaft. Hitching up her skirts, she headed quickly for the stairs.

The fireplace was surmounted by a portrait of a stern-faced gentleman in a swallow-tail coat. The walls were lined with cabinets and document cases. Two huge windows looked out over the roof of the rubber works towards the river.

Russell Blackstock and four young men were gathered round a massive mahogany table littered with maps and plans. Evie's arrival had, it seemed, interrupted a lively discussion.

'I'm sorry,' she said. 'I was told Mr Blackstock was ready to see me.'

'And so he is,' Russell Blackstock said. 'George, take the boys out for a cup of coffee in the counting house. I shan't be long.'

'How long, sir?'

'Five minutes,' Russell said.

Evie stepped to one side as the young men quit the room. They eyed her in passing and when the last one, George, closed the door she heard a great burst of laughter from the corridor.

'Don't mind them,' Russell Blackstock told her. 'They're not used to seeing ladies in the office.'

Evie's indignation had evaporated and, with it, her confidence. She pressed her elbows to her sides to stop herself shaking. She had taken Mr Blackstock to be a person of small means and influence and had assumed that his association with Paddy Maizie and Mr Orpington meant that he was only a half step up from the street dwellers. How wrong she had been. He was much more important than that. This huge humming-top of a building belonged to him and everything that came out of it had his stamp upon it.

'You're trembling,' Russell Blackstock said. 'Surely you're not afraid of me? I thought you Irish were afraid of nothing.'

He guided her to a high-backed chair and pressed her down into it.

'Are you here because of what happened at Maizie's last night?'

Evie nodded. 'More particular, Mr Blackstock, what happened to my brother at the builder's yard this mornin'. Do you know about that?'

'There isn't much goes on in this part of Glasgow that I don't know about. As for last night's little fracas, my sister told me the whole story.'

'It wasn't Nolan's fault.'

'I don't think it matters whose fault it was.'

'Aye, but it does,' said Evie. 'It matters to us.'

'Libby tells me she's asked your sister to help at the orphans' picnic.'

'Somethin' Clare is very willin' – *was* very willin' to do,' Evie said, 'but that's on the slates now, Mr Blackstock, since me brother was given his marching orders.'

'Your brother will find other work, I'm sure.'

'Why did you sack him, Mr Blackstock? Isn't Nolan a good worker?'

'From what I gather, he's an excellent worker.'

'Then why pay him off?' said Evie.

'It isn't your place to question how we conduct our business.'

'It was Nolan or Mr Orpington, wasn't it? One o' them had to go.'

'Who told you that?' Russell said.

'Mr Belfer.'

He lifted a large sheet of paper from the pile on the table. 'Do you know what this is?' he asked.

'No, sir, I don't.'

'This,' he said, 'is a rough plan of the west bank of the river as it will be in ten years' time.'

'Sure an' what does that have to do with my brother?'

'Nothing,' Russell Blackstock said. 'That's the point.'

'You mean he doesn't count?'

'Oh, no,' Russell said. 'Everyone counts, every man and woman will have a hand in it whether it be with a shovel, a pen or a stitching needle. But the men who assemble the labour force, who organise it and put it to best use, who ensure there's money enough to pay for it – they count for a little more.'

'You haven't answered my question. What about my brother?'

'I have no satisfactory answer,' Russell said. 'Look at you, Evie. You're an immigrant girl of – what – sixteen or seventeen who washes glasses in a public house. What right have you to challenge us about who we employ?'

'Mr Orpington's your man, ain't he?'

'Orpington's not my man. I don't employ him.'

'Whose man is he then?' said Evie.

'Orpington is anyone's man,' Russell Blackstock said. 'On every squad, every crew, every street corner, you'll find an Orpington. He won't be sporting a top hat and collecting cash at a usurious rate but he will be keeping the peace – peace of a sort, that is.'

'Keepin' the likes of us in our place, you mean?' said Evie.

'That,' said Russell Blackstock, 'is more or less what I mean.'

'Oh, that's cruel, that's callous.'

'Perhaps so, but bear in mind that discipline, purpose and structure are essential to a progressive society, which is why,' Russell said, 'when it comes to it, we must protect the Orpingtons of this world. How old is your brother?'

'Twenty.'

'I can probably find a job for him at the coal yard.'

'Would it pay as well as the diggin'?'

'No.'

'Then no thanks, Mr Blackstock. Don't worry. We won't starve.'

'Hasn't it occurred to you, Evie, that we can sack you too?'

'Why would you do that, sir?' Evie scrambled to her feet. 'Is it spite moves you? I never took you for a spiteful man.'

'Be easy,' Russell said. 'Your job at Maizie's is quite safe. However unwittingly, your brother defied us. For that reason we can't keep him on our books.'

'It's because Nolly's a Catholic, isn't it? If he was a Protestant you wouldn't sack him. Isn't that the truth of it?'

'Yes,' Russell Blackstock said, 'that's the truth of it.'

'Damn it, an' damn you then.' Evie pushed past him and headed for the door. 'You can keep your rotten job, for all I care.'

'Evie,' he called out, but she ignored him and, before he could even think to pursue her, had gone clattering down the steep stone stairs to the street.

When Willy wasn't out in the wilds inspecting brickworks or stone quarries, he could most often be found at a table in the Toll House, a private club for gentlemen noted for their financial acumen if not their religious forbearance.

Russell tracked him to a corner table in the dining-room where he was cutting up beefsteak and chatting across to a party of executives from the Barony Bank who, fortunately, were eating at a separate table. Russell apologised for the intrusion, ordered a chop and seated himself directly between Wilson and the bankers.

'I didn't expect to see *you* here,' Willy said. 'What's up? Are Sheckles and Freckles, or whatever they call themselves, causing trouble about the sewage pipes?'

'It's the Trust who aren't happy. The engineers are on our side.'

'A pox on the Trust,' Willy said. 'They're still smarting

because the contracts came our way. If we hadn't nailed down the leases, of course—'

'Did you put out an order to sack Nolan McKenna?'

'What?' Wilson said. 'Who?'

'Come on, Willy, don't play the innocent with me.'

Wilson popped a cube of beefsteak into his mouth. Russell cracked open his napkin and spread it on his lap and waited for Willy to finish chewing.

'If,' Wilson said, at length, 'you mean that Irish hooligan who attacked Orpington outside Maizie's place, yes, I sent him packing.'

'May I ask why?'

'Can't have our boys brawling in the street, can we?'

'Nonsense,' Russell said. 'Our boys are never done brawling in the street. You've never turned a hair before now. I'm astonished you've even heard of Nolan McKenna, given that he's on the harbour squad, my squad, not yours. Who got to you? Was it Orpington?'

'Good Lord, no!' said Wilson.

'It certainly wasn't Libby.'

'Libby's far too fond of consorting with riff-raff these days,' Wilson said, 'between that damned chapel and that damned orphanage, let alone the fact that she's poking an Irish publican.'

'Is she? I'm not so sure that she is.'

'Don't,' said Wilson, 'be naïve.'

He glanced over Russell's shoulder, smiled and nodded at the bankers, and popped another piece of meat into his mouth.

Russell leaned forward. 'Don't tell me you sacked a daft young Irishman you've never even heard of just to get back at Libby? Even by your standards, Willy, that would be unbelievably petty.'

'Libby has nothing to do with it,' Wilson admitted grudgingly. 'I just can't fathom why you're so upset about one Irish navvy. Is it the girl?'

'Girl? What girl?' said Russell, startled.

'The wee Irish tart from Maizie's who you have your eye on. I heard that she even came to the office to see you this morning.'

'Have you lost your senses completely?'

'No, but I'm beginning to think you have.'

'Belfer!' Russell said. 'Belfer's been spreading evil rumours again, hasn't he? When did he get to you?'

'Last night,' said Wilson. 'Nabbed me coming out of the Masonic Hall.'

'How did he know you'd be there? Belfer isn't a brother.'

'Given that there was a public notice in the newspapers, the meeting was hardly secret. What Belfer pointed out in no uncertain terms was just how much Orpington knows about our – what shall I say – our somewhat shadowy dealings in the old ward. In addition, our Libby has been nagging Paddy Maizie to break off with Orpington, and we can't have that, can we? I sent a note to the yard first thing this morning to wipe McKenna off the books.'

'Simply to keep Orpington happy?'

'Aye, and, with luck, to chase those blasted people out of the Riverside.'

'I see,' Russell said. 'Yes, Willy, I see.'

'I should have consulted you first, perhaps,' Wilson said, 'but you haven't been yourself of late and I thought I'd relieve you of the burden.'

'Most kind of you,' Russell said.

'You haven't been yourself, have you?'

'No, I suppose not,' Russell admitted.

'It's a symptom of age.'

'Your age, too, Wilson,' Russell reminded him.

'It's true; neither of us are getting any younger,' Wilson said.

'I'm sorry if I queered your pitch, Russell, but this rather too public squabble was better settled once and for all. What did the girl have to say?'

'Nothing of any consequence. She flounced off in a temper.'

'Well, there are plenty more fish in the sea, old man, if that's the sort of thing you're after.'

'I'm not after anything of the sort.'

'Just a passing fancy, was she?'

'Not even that,' said Russell.

Bob Draper had already squandered a good half-hour placating young Chiffin who was convinced that Percival Orpington was about to crash through the door in search of revenge. When Evie McKenna, with a face like fizz, appeared in the bar a full hour late, Bob knew that he was in for a day of it.

Prudently he uttered no word of reprimand as she stalked around the counter, poured a nip of whisky and knocked it back. He watched her pour another, more modest measure and down that, too, then, still sullen and scowling, reach for her apron and cap. He did not pooh-pooh his employees' fears. He was well aware that Orpington was dangerous and that dark things went on in the office across the yard, and had done so for many years.

Skulking in the shadows of the gallery, Chiffin leaned over and called out, 'Have you seen him, Evie? Have you seen Orpington out there?'

'Nah,' Evie said, without looking up. 'I haven't seen Orpington. I have seen Russell Blackstock, though, since that's where I've been. An' for two pins I'd throw up this bloody job here an' now, sure an' I would.'

Chiffin hopped down the stairs and caught Evie by the arm.

'Mr Blackstock? You spoke to Mr Blackstock?'

'Fat lot of good it did me. Nolan got paid off. Russell Blackstock gave him his books.'

'Gave him his books? For why?' said Chiffin.

It was on the tip of Bob's tongue to explain a few facts of life to the pair but if they were aware of his presence at all they were too upset to care.

''Cause he's a Pape an' therefore a trouble-maker,' Evie said.

'I'm sorry, Evie,' Chiffin wailed. 'It's my fault, all my fault.'

'Why's it your fault?'

'If I'd paid Orpington none of this would've happened.'

'Why didn't you pay Orpington?' Evie said, then, shaking her hands in the air, answered her own question. 'I know, I know: you didn't have the cash.'

'It's the sister, the youngest, she's been sick again.'

'Sure an' if you told me that, Chiff, I'd have lent you some o' the money.'

'I can't go takin' money from you,' Chiffin said.

'Why not?'

'I prefer to stand on my own two feet.'

'While pigs like Russell Blackstock get fat on the proceeds,' Evie said. 'That's not right.'

'Right or not,' said Chiffin, 'it's the way things are.'

'It's not the way things should be,' Evie said, 'or the way things *could* be. We should be standin' up to them.'

'An' get sacked,' said Chiffin. 'I've got mouths to feed, Evie.'

'We've all got mouths to feed,' Evie McKenna said, 'an' damn' well the employers know it. I learned a thing or two this mornin', Chiff, believe me I did. I learned a thing or two just seein' him there in his office.'

'You went to the office?' Chiffin said, aghast.

'Aye, I did. Why should I not?'

'God help you, Evie, you'll be next for the axe.'

'He said my job here's secure.'

'He lied to you once, what's to stop him lyin' to you again?'

Chiffin said, then, turning, brought Bob into the conversation. 'Is that not right, Mr Draper?'

Bob had been moved, a little, by the sight of the youngsters consoling each other as they struggled to make sense of a system that was older than the city itself. He had come to terms with the inequities of capitalism long ago and did not believe in rebellion or revolt. If you were willing to bow to its demands, the system gave you enough to keep your head above water. There were those who comforted themselves with drink, others who sought the support that religion offered but, boiled down, earning a living wage absorbed most of your attention and distracted you from dwelling on how the big money was made, who made it and the lengths to which they would go to hang on to it.

He, Bob Draper, knew better than to interfere.

He said, 'She'll just have to wait an' see, won't she?'

'That's no answer, Mr Draper,' Chiffin told him.

'It's the only answer you're going to get,' Bob said and, with a growl that was not unfriendly, chased the hapless couple back to work.

If being without much of a conscience meant being without much of a brain, there were times when Harry Fairfield could be incredibly stupid. It did not occur to him, for instance, that his failure to back a pal when the cards were down might affect his relationship with the Irish beauty, or that she might consider blood to be thicker than water and loyalty more important than love.

Scrubbed clean and slick as a piston, Harry trotted along Salamanca Street with nothing on his mind but the turbid ache in his groin and the fun he was going to have relieving it. He skipped blithely upstairs and rapped on the door of the McKennas' flat to let Clare know that her presence was required, with some urgency, on the bed upstairs.

Hardly had his knuckles left the woodwork when the door whipped open, a massive hand caught him by the collar and yanked him into the lobby.

'What the bloody hell . . .' Harry got out.

'Come for your ration, Harry, have you?' Nolan said.

'Wha' – what're you talkin' about, man?'

From the corner of his eye Harry saw Clare peering from behind the kitchen door, and realised that the jig was well and truly up. Dazed and scared, however, he couldn't be sure which jig was which, or for which particular misjudgement he was being brought to book.

'I'm talkin' about you takin' off like a rabbit,' said Nolan.

'Aw, that!'

'Aye, that,' said Nolan, 'an' a lot worse besides.'

'I – ah – I saw you had things in hand, man,' Harry gasped. 'If I'd thought you needed my help I'd've pitched in of course.'

'You ran, Harry, you friggin' ran.' Nolan screwed his fist into Harry's shirt and lifted him three inches from the floor. 'That's not the worst thing you've done, though, is it?'

Harry rolled his eyes towards the kitchen door: Clare had gone. He thought – though he couldn't be sure – that he heard her sobbing in the kitchen.

'Don't – don't know what y' mean,' he said.

'You've been pokin' me sister,' Nolan said.

Harry felt like a doll hanging there, a showman's puppet. He stretched his spine and reached for the floor with his toes.

'Did – did she tell you that?'

'Didn't have to,' Nolan said. 'Sure an' it's true, is it not now?'

'Well, she thinks she's in love with me.'

'I'm not. I'm not. I'm just not,' came Clare's voice from the kitchen. 'You said you loved me an' were goin' to marry me.'

'Is that right, Harry?' Nolan asked.

'Naw. I mean, I never promised her . . .'

'Are you callin' me sister a liar?'

'She wanted me, wanted – it.'

'Now you're callin' her a tart, are you?' said Nolan grimly.

'I never called her anythin', man,' Harry said. 'For Christ's sake, put me down, will you?'

Nolan lowered him to the floor but did not release him.

'Well,' Nolan said, 'you've had the bridal night, so when's the weddin'?'

'Weddin'?' Harry squeaked.

'Sure an' you are goin' to make an honest woman of her, are you not?'

'It's not a great time for me to take on a wife.'

'When *would* be a great time?' said Nolan. 'Would next week be a great time? Next Monday, say?'

'Listen, she's not expectin', is she?'

'I'm not. I'm not,' Clare called out. 'Nolan, I'm not.'

'Clare might not be expectin',' Nolan said, 'but *I'm* expectin'. Expectin' you to do the decent thing.'

'She just said she doesn't want—'

'She doesn't mean it,' Nolan said. 'If you're not willin' to take my word for it, go in there an' ask her yourself.'

Harry rolled his eyes towards the half-open door once more. Clare had stopped weeping and there was no sound from the kitchen.

'Get in there,' Nolan said, 'an' ask her nice,' then, giving Harry an encouraging shove, pushed him forward into the room.

Russell's mansion at Crosshill was certainly large but it was not by any stretch of the imagination splendid. The double villa that Wilson had built for his family on the boulevard at Kelvinside was both spacious *and* splendid and, Willy believed, represented one in the eye for Russell who remained stuck on Clydeside, too close for comfort to the crowded coal yards, docks and tenements that he, Wilson, had managed to leave behind. He was forever mindful, however, that Russell and he were linked not just by blood but by the financial empire that Papa had handed down to them and he still regarded his father's rise from the depths of poverty to a peak of bourgeois respectability as something so far above the ordinary as to be almost miraculous.

It was a placid early summer evening, the trees in leaf at last as Willy rode up the newly cobbled street in a hackney cab. In stables behind the house, he kept a pair of horses and a cabriolet but he used the carriage only to take the family to church and preferred to dot about the city in hired hacks charged to company expenses.

The villa stood out proudly against the sky, the shape and scale of it more suggestive of a fortress than a haven. Downstairs in the kitchen the cook would be preparing dinner. Upstairs in the nursery the maids would be making four of his five children ready for bed. Giles, his valet, would remove his dusty clothes and dress him in the half-formal, half-casual attire that he wore in the evening. Then he would join Angela and together they would go upstairs to pet the children and listen, for a minute or two, to an account of how their offspring had spent the day; then, since no guests were due, Angela and he, and Ronald, his eldest, would proceed to the dining-room to eat.

Wilson paid the cabby, entered the pillared portico and reached for the gigantic iron bell-pull that would announce to the household that the master had returned. As a rule only Leonard, the butler, answered the bell, but this evening, to Willy's surprise, Leonard was accompanied by Mrs Crockatt, the housekeeper, and by Giles and Angela, too.

Giles took away Wilson's hat, gloves and overcoat.

Leonard closed the door.

Mrs Crockatt pressed her hands to her bosom.

Angela said, 'There's a man here to see you, Willy.'

'A man?' Wilson said. 'What sort of a man?'

'His name, sir,' Leonard said, 'is Orpington. I tried to send him away, but he's a crippled gentleman and would not take No for an answer.'

'He's in the library, Willy,' Angela said. 'He's been cooling his heels there for an hour. He's very insistent.'

'Uh-huh,' Wilson said. 'I'll wager he is.'

'What shall I do, sir?' Leonard asked. 'Shall I throw him out?'

'That,' said Willy, 'would not be advisable. No, I'll speak with him. Angela, will you see to it that dinner is held.'

'I will, dear,' said Angela obediently, and went off downstairs with Mrs Crockatt while Willy, a deal less in charge than he appeared to be, headed post-haste for the library.

'Have you read all these books then, Mr Blackstock?' Percival Orpington asked, waving his malacca cane at the glass-fronted cases that lined the room.

'No,' Willy answered curtly.

'It's a very fine collection, sir, if I might be permitted to say so,' Percival Orpington went on. 'I am particularly admirin' of the set of Edward Gibbon's works you've had bound in half morocco. I have a weakness for Gibbon, too, though my edition ain't so handsome.'

'What do you want, Orpington?'

'You'll excuse me not risin', Mr Blackstock,' Percival Orpington said, 'but as you will have no doubt observed I am encumbered with a leg – an ankle to be anatomically precise – encased in stookie which renders risin' never mind standin' somewhat of a challenge.'

'How did you get here?'

'Cab, sir, cab from my door to your door.'

Mr Orpington was perched on a Georgian armchair. He

was dressed in a suit of fine-woven tweed, a striped vest and one high-buttoned boot. The other boot had been replaced by a heavy plaster stocking the colour of oatmeal.

'Let me ask you again,' Willy said, 'what are you doing in my house, disturbing my wife and staff, and delaying my dinner?'

'Delayin' your dinner, sir? Oh, excuse me.' Mr Orpington twirled the cane and tapped the plastered leg. 'Not for worlds, sir, would I wish to delay your dinner. I'd have taken my business to Mr Russell if the lady – your sister – had not been residin' in his house. I don't think your sister likes me.'

Wilson had taken up position by the fireplace. He was almost as much in awe of Percival Orpington as the tenement dwellers but he was also decidedly piqued that the fellow had invaded his home.

'For God's sake, Orpington, come to the point.'

'The point, Mr Blackstock, is compensation.'

'Compensation? For what do you wish to be compensated?'

'Injury sustained in pursuit of duty.'

'In a brawl, a public-house brawl?'

'It was your interests I was pursuing in that pub, Mr Blackstock. I was attempting to collect money on your behalf when I became the victim of an unprovoked assault.'

'On my behalf?' said Willy. 'I don't employ you. You don't work for me.'

'For the other Mr Blackstock, then,' said Percival Orpington. 'It's all the same, ain't it?'

'No, it isn't all the same,' said Willy. 'It isn't the same at all.'

'Far as I'm concerned, it's the same,' Mr Orpington insisted. 'Has been since you and the other Mr Blackstock got a little too finicky to do your own dirty work. It was dirty work then, sir, and dirty work it is still, though I think you've forgotten how dirty since you quit the Riverside.'

'Doesn't Belfer pay you?'

'Mr Belfer does pay me. Mr Maizie pays me too. And, I confess, I'm paid a little bit extra for services rendered to the Barony Bank. Look at my leg, though. The ankle's broke in two places and I'm out of commission for God knows how long. That ain't Mr Belfer's business, nor Mr Maizie's – nor the Barony Bank's for that matter. When you get to the root of it, Mr Blackstock, you and your brother reap the rewards, so you and your brother should pay for my misfortune.'

'Is that what it says in the contract?'

Percival Orpington's lips compressed into a tight line and colour drained from his ruddy cheeks. 'There is no contract, never was a contract, as well you know. A handshake was good enough for you in those days and should be good enough for you now.'

'What's that handshake going to cost me?'

'Fifteen pounds a week until I'm fit to resume my duties.'

'How long is that liable to be?'

'Ten weeks, maybe more.'

'How would you have this money paid?'

'Lump sum,' Mr Orpington said. 'In cash.'

'Setting aside the question if you're entitled to compensation at all,' Willy said, 'one hundred and fifty pounds seems somewhat excessive. How do you arrive at this figure?'

'Estimated loss of earnings.'

'Good God, my site managers don't earn that much.'

'Your site managers don't do what I do,' Mr Orpington said, 'and your site managers don't know what I know.'

Wilson paused. 'And what do you know, Mr Orpington?'

'How you got your hands on those tenement properties in the first place and, now you've skinned them, how you intend to sell them to the bank.'

'Why,' Wilson said, 'would we want to sell them to the bank when they are still bringing in revenue?'

'You'll sell them to the bank for an inflated sum and the

bank will lease them back to provide you with enough capital to demolish and rebuild.'

'What an ingenious scheme, Mr Orpington. I just wish I'd thought of it.'

'In the thought the deed is born,' Percival Orpington said.

'However, as there's no such thought and certainly no such deed in our minds,' Wilson said, 'I'm afraid your claim for compensation will have to be adjusted to a more realistic level.'

'What sort of level?'

'Forty pounds,' said Willy. 'Lump sum.'

Mr Orpington lifted the cane and placed it across his knees. 'One hundred and twenty,' he said. 'I can't go no lower.'

'And I won't go that high,' said Willy.

'In that case, I'll have to take my claim elsewhere.'

'What do you mean by elsewhere?' Willy said.

'To folk who'll listen to what I have to tell them.'

'Who, for instance?'

'Interested parties – that's all I'm sayin', sir.' Mr Orpington twirled the cane again, planted the tip on the carpet and hoisted himself to his feet. 'Since I don't have the strength to do my work, I'll just have to sit about and put together all the things I know about you and your brother. Information like that has to be paid for, since, you might say, I ain't got no other leg to stand on.'

'Where did you come by your information?'

'I come by it over the years, piecemeal.'

'From Belfer?'

'From Mr Belfer, among others,' Mr Orpington said. 'It ain't how much a man knows that's important but how a man makes that knowledge work for him.' Leaning heavily into the cane, he crabbed towards the door.

'Wait,' Wilson said.

Mr Orpington turned.

'The least I can do,' Wilson said, 'is discuss your proposition with my brother.'

'It isn't a proposition, sir. It's a fair claim for compensation.'

'Of course it is,' said Willy. 'I may have been a wee bit hasty in not considering it more carefully.'

'I won't be palmed off,' Mr Orpington said, 'nor paid off neither.'

'Paid off? Certainly not,' said Willy. 'For your information, Mr Orpington, the fellow who attacked you is no longer on our books. At Mr Belfer's suggestion, we got rid of him first thing this morning.'

'I'm pleased to hear it,' Mr Orpington said. 'But that's a matter of pride, Mr Blackstock, not money.'

'We all have our pride to contend with, though, don't we?'

'We do, sir, that we do,' Mr Orpington agreed and, balanced on one leg, offered Willy a handshake to clinch some kind of a deal.

In her brother's absence, Evie was offered not only congratulations but even free glasses of beer by the customers who had suffered most at Percival Orpington's hands, customers who, unlike Chiffin, lacked the foresight to realise that Orpington had not gone forever but would return one day to demand, with interest, his pound of flesh. Meanwhile, there was rejoicing in the tenements of the Riverside and in Paddy Maizie's pub a fair quantity of liquor was poured down a fair number of throats.

Evie was too busy and too upset by what had happened to feel like celebrating, and, wisely, said nothing about Nolly's sacking for fear that news of the injustice would dampen trade. It was moving towards eleven o'clock before Mr Draper released her. She hung up her apron, said goodnight to Chiffin and headed for the door.

It was a warm night without a breath of air. The river, at low water, smelled ripe, and sounds carried far. Evie walked down Salamanca Street, sniffing and close to tears at her failure to change Mr Blackstock's mind. She was so absorbed in misery that she failed to notice the figure in the stable lane and so on edge that she let out a muffled shriek when he addressed her.

'Miss McKenna?' he said softly. 'Evie?'

'Who is it? What do you want with me?'

Mr Blackstock stepped out of the shadows.

Guilt and relief welled up in her. She let out a little cry that, in the still night air, set off a dog to barking. She put her hands to her cheeks and murmured, 'I'm sorry. I'm sorry.'

'What do you have to be sorry for?' Russell Blackstock said. 'If apologies are in order I should be offering them to you.'

'Have you taken my job from me, sir?'

'Oh, is that what you think? No, I haven't taken your job. In fact, I've been giving serious consideration to what you said this morning.'

'I'm sorry. I'm truly sorry.'

'Evie – no,' Russell said, then, thrusting out his hand, 'See, I've brought you proof of my change of heart.'

'Proof, Mr Blackstock?'

'A letter to Ned Torrance instructing him to restore your brother's ticket, to take your brother back on to the books. Have your brother give the letter to Torrance at the gate first thing in the morning.'

'Why, Mr Blackstock? What made you change your mind?'

'Let's just say that I didn't have all the facts at my disposal. Now I've heard your side of the story, it sheds a different light on the matter. Here, young lady, take the letter before I change my mind again.'

Evie plucked the envelope from his fingers and gave him a crooked smile.

'Sure an' I don't know how to thank you, sir,' she said, then, on impulse, placed a hand on his chest and, reaching up, kissed him on the cheek before she turned and ran for home.

If Evie had expected her brother to be overjoyed at her news she was doomed to disappointment. Mr Blackstock's letter lay neglected on the table; Clare, it seemed, had stolen her thunder once more.

'Engaged?' Evie said. 'Who's the lucky feller? Him upstairs. I suppose?'

'Aye,' said Clare. 'Who else could it be?'

'That treacherous, two-faced swine,' Nolly said, 'pretended to be me pal when all he wanted was to bed me sister. Well, he'll have to do the decent thing now, whether he likes it or not.'

Evie knelt by the bed where Clare lay, fully dressed.

'Are you carryin' his child, Clare?' she asked.

'Sure an' I am not,' Clare answered indignantly.

'Why do you want to marry him then?' said Evie.

'The bastard's had his fun,' Nolan said, 'now he's got to pay for it.'

'Clare had her fun too, did she not?' Evie said. 'What was done was done with her consent. He didn't force you, did he, Clare?'

'He didn't have to force her,' Nolan said.

'It's you, Nolan,' Clare said, 'you just want rid o' me.'

'Why would I want rid o' you?' Nolan said. 'Who's goin' to wash me clothes an' have me supper ready when you've gone?'

'Gone?' said Clare. 'Movin' upstairs isn't what I'd call gone.'

There was no sign of supper and the fire in the grate had almost gone out. Evie was aggrieved at Nolan's lack of gratitude, his lack of interest in the letter that had cost her so much. She buttered a slice of bread, watered the last of the milk and, seated at the table with her back to the big bed, ate her meagre supper while Clare and Nolan bickered.

'I'm not sure I *can* marry him,' Clare said. 'What if he isn't a Catholic? I promised Mam I'd never marry a man who wasn't a Catholic.'

'Didn't you have time to ask him about that before you lay down an' opened your legs?' Nolan said.

'That's enough, Nolly,' Evie said, without looking round.

'Or did it not matter to you what he was so long as he had a—'

'Stop it, stop it, for God's sake,' Clare cried.

'We'll need to talk with Father Fingle,' Nolan said. 'He'll keep us on the straight and narrow. Harry told *me* he was a Catholic.'

'An' you believed him,' said Evie.

'I never thought it mattered,' Nolan said, 'since I didn't know what he was doin' to Clare.'

Evie finished the milk and got up from the table. She pulled the curtain around the bed, took off her clothes, and, nudging Clare to one side, slid wearily between the sheets.

'Go to your bed, Nolan,' she said. 'You've work first thing in the mornin' – an' don't forget to take that letter to Mr Torrance.'

'Oh aye,' Nolan said. 'The letter. Thanks.'

'Soon as I get home tomorrow night,' said Evie, 'we'll sit down an' sort it out with Harry Fairfield.'

'Fix a date for the weddin', you mean?' Nolan said.

'Yes,' Clare said reluctantly, 'an' fix a date for my wedding.'

10

Of all the beneficial habits that Libby had acquired during her marriage to Peter Galloway the three that stood her in good stead upon her return to Glasgow were early rising, morning prayers and eating a hearty breakfast.

Throughout Pin's schooldays Libby took breakfast with her ward at their own special table in the morning-room, just the two of them. As befitted a young lady of the middle class, Seang Pin had been educated at Our Lady High School. Libby had become involved in the work of the orphanage attached to the school and had taken it upon herself to organise outings and other special treats for the children. Whatever slanders Willy might put about, the Our Lady Orphanage was not a reformatory where beatings and starvation were the order of the day and all sorts of unspeakable perversities were enacted after dark. The children were well cared for, given a basic education and, as a rule, found remunerative employment when they became old enough to work.

After Pin left school Libby and she continued to take breakfast at the little table in the morning-room with an intimacy that Jane Blackstock envied, though it would no doubt have surprised Jane to discover that after prayers each morning Libby and Pin would fall to discussing horse flesh and that, before the morning was out Pin would lay a series of small bets with Patrick Maizie, Libby's publican friend.

On that warm May morning, however, Libby and Seang Pin were not assessing the merits of *Jim Dandy* or *Bold Derry* but the worth of a certain Nolan McKenna who, if he had been running at Ayr, might well have been carrying Seang Pin's colours.

'Oh!' Libby said. 'So the Irishman's caught your eye, has he? He's certainly a fine figure of a man and would, without doubt, help keep our little monsters in hand.'

'You are always saying that we need more male helpers.'

'It's true. After the last fiasco,' Libby said, 'when there was hardly a teacher under the age of fifty . . . Yes, I confess, we do need someone with a better turn of speed. If it hadn't been for you, we'd have lost a good half-dozen of the wee devils over the sea wall.'

'Mr McKenna is young and fit.'

'Mr McKenna is a working man, not free on Saturdays.'

'Uncle Russell might be able to sort that out for us.'

'Us?' said Libby.

'For the orphanage.'

'Of course, for the orphanage,' said Libby. 'May I point out, however, that your uncles are not in favour of little Catholics being carted off into the countryside to enjoy themselves.'

'Perhaps if we promised to drown a few . . .' Pin said.

'Indeed,' said Libby, grinning, 'an annual sacrifice to the river gods might appease even your Uncle Willy.'

Pin poured and drank a thimbleful of coffee.

'Will you ask Mr McKenna – and Uncle Russell?' she said, at length.

'Pin, Pin.' Libby shook her head. 'Have you learned nothing about the eccentricities of our society? The Irishman is not like us.'

'Was Mr Galloway like you?'

'I was young and silly in those days.'

'Would you not make the same mistake again?' said Pin.

Libby laughed. 'Yes, chicken, of course I would.'

'Admittedly Mr McKenna is not a businessman, like your

Mr Galloway,' Pin said. 'No more, however, is he a Protestant. Besides, he might wish to come to the picnic to chaperone his sister.'

'Who, by the by, has not yet given me an answer.'

'Perhaps she will speak with you at church on Sunday.'

'Perhaps she will,' Libby said, fondly brushing Pin's hair with her fingertips. 'We'll see.'

'And Mr McKenna?' Pin asked.

'We'll see about that too,' said Libby.

Father Fingle lived alone. Though three or four elderly parishioners took it in turn to clean for him, he cooked for himself and was just polishing off a breakfast egg when the door knocker rat-a-tatted.

Still in carpet slippers and a scruffy old bathrobe, he shuffled to the door and found the beautiful dark-haired Irish girl hopping agitatedly on his doorstep. He invited her into the parlour, excused himself long enough to wash the egg stains off his face, give his hair a brush and get rid of the bathrobe, then, more intrigued than he had a right to be, came back to find her staring at his beautiful little statue of the Virgin.

'Well, Clare, what troubles you?' He seated himself in the least comfortable of the parlour's three worn armchairs. 'Is it the picnic?'

'The picnic?' Clare said.

'I was under the impression that Mrs Galloway had asked you to assist at the orphans' picnic next month.'

'Oh that!' Clare said. 'No, Father, it isn't that at all.'

'What is it then?'

He listened to her tale of woe, nodding as if his head would fall off. He had heard it all before, of course, a dozen variations on the same old story: the temptation of Adam, or, in this case, Eve. He put a tactful question or two and was relieved to discover that the illicit union had not been illicitly blessed and that there was still time, as it were, to redeem the situation.

When questioned about her young man, though, the McKenna girl was oddly evasive. Father Fingle knew by experience that disparity of cult was not an insurmountable obstacle to a long and happy marriage, but for all that something in Clare's account of the relationship troubled him.

'Your young man, you must bring him to talk to me,' Father Fingle said.

'If he'll come,' Clare said.

'If he won't come then there can't be a marriage before God.'

He sounded more disapproving than he had intended. After all he didn't want to chase the young woman into her lover's arms without commitment or consent. He had met too many disbelieving husbands, too many lying spouses, to respect a promise made on the spur of the moment. Better a difficult marriage between different faiths, however, than no marriage at all.

'My brother will make sure he comes to see you, Father,' Clare said.

'That's not good enough,' Father Fingle told her. 'The essence of any marriage forged in the grace of the Church must be love between the parties.'

'Harry does love me, you know.'

'In that case he'll come without coercion,' Father Fingle said. 'I take it he *has* asked you to become his wife, that consent to the betrothal is mutual.'

She hesitated for a fraction of a second before she answered, quite long enough to sound another warning bell in the priest's head.

He got up from the armchair and made a little tour of the parlour while the girl watched him, frowning. What did she really want, he wondered: a nod, a few hasty arrangements, a dispensation or two, meaningless penances, then a ceremony that would bind the young man to her in the hope that he would honour a promise by which he set no store at all? She would not be the first young woman to confuse carnal gratification with true love.

He heard himself say, 'You must talk to your young man – Harry, is it? – talk to Harry very seriously. Make sure he fully understands what's at stake. If he really cares about you, he'll come to see me willingly.'

'But will you marry us in church?'

'I make no promise on that score,' Father Fingle said. 'It's up to Harry to take the first step before we proceed down the road to a proper Christian union.'

'I want to be his wife,' said Clare. 'I do.'

'Send him to me, then,' said Father Fingle.

'When?'

'Tonight at nine o'clock.'

'He'll be here,' Clare McKenna promised, nodding.

But wise old Father Fingle was not so sure, not so sure at all.

She had expected more from the priest at St Kentigern's. In a woolly sort of way she had assumed that she was due some favour, some dispensation to make up for the suffering that Father Garbett had inflicted upon her when she was young and innocent of men, as if one sin of the flesh might cancel out the other. In hindsight she felt sorry for the gnarled wee man in the cassock who had pulled her hand against his upright flesh and had been moved to defile her by the same instinct that had driven her into Harry Fairfield's arms.

Long ago she had heard her father and Kiernan argue that if God had not wanted man to procreate God would not have given Eve unto Adam, that it was lusting not love that shoved the world along its evolutionary track. She had understood none of the argument then or why Kiernan had laughed and her father had raged, or why – now – she felt purged not only of guilt but of righteousness, cleansed by the very act that she had been taught to abhor.

She worked hard all that morning at the tub in the stable, scrubbing thick knots of cotton and flannel. She washed not only her linens but all the sheets and blankets too, rinsing away her sins in an aura of horse dung and horse pee while Mrs McLean's cats crouched in the empty stalls and eyed her warily with their yellow-green eyes.

She pegged the washing out on the ropes that laced the yard behind the tenement, for it was a fine, warm day with the sun coming round to bring light to the yard. She was wet with the work, hot beneath her skirts, the cotton clinging to her thighs. She was thirsty, hot and hungry, yet filled with restless energy that her long morning's labour at the tubs had failed to diminish.

She went upstairs.

The tenement room was bathed in sunlight.

She took off her clothes and washed her body in the trickle of water from the tap at the sink, paddling in the puddle on the floor like a child in the rain. She plunged her face into the sink and soaked her hair. She dried herself carefully, patting and primping, wrapped one towel around her body and another around her head and, pulling the stew pot from the stove, seated herself at the table and ate straight from the pot, dipping and digging with spoon and fork, mopping up the rich brown gravy with hunks of bread.

She drank tea, cup after cup.

Then she dressed herself in the loose box-pleated blouse and tie-back skirt that she kept for special occasions and twisted up her damp black hair and pinned it with a little peeling diadem of tortoiseshell.

Then she lay down on the mattress to wait for Harry.

* * *

It was generally agreed that trade overcame all obstacles and that the Clyde Trust had squandered vast sums of public money deepening the river. What, Willy Blackstock chanted, did the peasants care about the engineering principles that had brought the river into a state of equilibrium by creating a current proportionate to the form of the channel, or, for that matter, about the financial jookery-pookery required to raise the wind to build the huge retaining walls and jetties? The average citizen saw only the mineral barges, lighters and dredgers that nipped about like water skippers and the two hundred men and half that number of horses who removed the gravel and shale and planted concrete shoes for the elegant iron cranes: never a thought, Willy went on, for the real miracle – the money, and where the money came from.

Willy did not go so far as to shake his fist at the idlers who gathered on the little iron bridge above the Crosshill horse ferry or swear at the ladies who meandered along the half-finished promenade, though, in his opinion, their interest was so shallow that they might as well have been watching the elephants at Hengler's Circus.

Given the sprawling nature of the site, let alone the clouds of dust that shrouded it that Friday afternoon, it was sheer bad luck that brought the young women into Willy's view. He had been passing through Crosshill and had stopped off only briefly to consult one of Russell's smart young engineers on a matter of brick facings when, looking up from the porch of the draughtsman's hut, he saw above him on the iron bridge three blobs of pastel colour floating against the sky.

He blinked and wiped his bushy eyebrows as one blob of colour rose above the others and he recognised, incredibly, a parasol.

A bloody parasol!

'Do you see that?' he asked the engineer.

'Oh, aye,' the young man answered with enthusiasm. 'I do.'

'Girls?'

'Too true, Mr Blackstock.'

'What are they doing?'

'Wavin' to you, sir, I think.'

'Me?' said Willy, scowling. 'No, they can't be waving at me.'

'Aye, but they are,' said the sharp young man. 'Hark to the angel voices, sir, an' you'll see that it's you all right.'

'*Uncle Wilson? Uncle Wilson?*'

'In the name of God! What now?' Willy growled and, slapping on his hat, set off for the ferry steps that lay behind the hut.

'And this is my friend Norma, from school,' Seang Pin said, 'and this is her maid, Farquhar.' The maid dropped a deferential curtsey while Norma offered a lace-gloved hand with all the imperiousness of a princess.

Willy took the hand, grunted by way of greeting, and shook the girl's slender fingers. She was tall, blonde, blue-eyed, fine-boned, and, if she'd been able to control her giggles, might have struck him as autocratic. She lofted up the parasol again and gave it a wriggling little twirl as if the touch of his hand had thrilled her to the core.

'Pleased to meet you, Mr Blackstock,' Norma said. 'My papa has often talked of you.'

'Has he, indeed,' said Willy, unimpressed.

'Francis M'Gunnigal,' said Norma, undeterred. 'He makes glass.'

'Yes, I know him,' Willy said. 'So, pray tell me, what's Frank M'Gunnigal's daughter doing down here on the docks?'

'We're looking for Uncle Russell,' Pin put in.

'Russell?' Willy said. 'What do you want with Russell?'

'Nothing, really,' Pin said.

The M'Gunnigal girl giggled again and the maid stifled a guffaw.

Willy's cheeks reddened. He had a feeling he was being made fun of by three females hardly old enough to wipe their own noses. Only the fact that M'Gunnigal was the biggest glass supplier in Scotland prevented him chasing them away.

'We just came to say hello, didn't we, Pin?' Norma M'Gunnigal said, twirling the parasol. 'Can we go down there, Mr Blackstock?'

'No.'

'Why not?'

'It's no place for girls.'

'Why not?' Norma persisted.

'Because it's dangerous.'

'It doesn't look dangerous, Mr Blackstock.'

'Look, I don't know what you're up to, Pin,' Willy said, 'but a building site is no place for young ladies. May I suggest you . . .'

The blonde girl lifted herself on tiptoe and peeped down at a team of workmen who were excavating a deep pit just ahead of the concreters.

'Oh, Pin, I say, is that him?' Norma said. 'The tall one?'

'Hmm,' Pin answered.

'Oh, he *is* a big fellow – and *very* handsome.'

Wilson swung round just as the girls, including the maid, rushed to the guard rail and leaned upon it. Even before he looked down on the site, Willy had a sinking feeling that he knew just which particular digger had claimed their attention.

'Mr McKenna, Mr McKenna, up here,' Norma's angel voice piped up. 'Pin's here. Pin wants you.'

'Stop it, Norma,' Pin said. 'You're embarrassing me.'

Then the girls were waving, all three, even the maid.

Sleeves rolled up, shirt open, the big young Irishman grinned from ear to ear and waved back.

'McKenna!' Willy said through his teeth. 'Bloody McKenna,' and, abandoning the girls to their flirting, set off in search of his brother.

The coal trade in summer was never quite so stiff as it was in winter. Fires still burned in the tenements, of course, for dinners had to be cooked and water boiled but, courtesy of Mr Sloane, the yard manager, Jock and the other heavers were allowed to slip off a wee bit early.

It was just after six when Jock arrived in Salamanca Street. Fine weather had brought everyone out of doors and the normally quiet street rang with the cries of children and the bellowing of gossiping women leaning from wide-open windows. Being a solitary soul, Jock did not much care for this time of year when every last shred of privacy was stripped away and it seemed as if the contents of the kitchens had been shaken on to the pavement.

They were waiting for him at the close-mouth, Cissie and Clare.

Dressed in a spotless blouse and skirt, the girl looked more beautiful than ever, though she had been crying and her pale cheeks were reddened by weeping. She might, Jock thought, have thrown herself into his arms if Cissie hadn't already been holding her.

He said, 'What's up?'

'Harry – have you seen Harry?' Cissie said.

'Um,' Jock said. 'Aye, I did see Harry as a matter o' fact.'

'Where is he?' said Cissie. 'He hasn't come home yet an' this poor girl's worried sick about him.'

Jock glanced into the cool grey recesses of the close and had half a mind to make a run for it.

'Is he dead?' said Clare. 'Sure an' don't be tellin' me he's dead.'

'Now, now,' said little Mrs Cassidy, 'you've no reason for thinkin' he's dead, have you, dear?'

'Where is he then?' Clare cried. 'Why hasn't he come home?'

Jock had picked up strong hints that Harry was paying court to the McKenna girl but, not keen to become involved, had steered clear of chinning the young man about his intentions.

'Harry isn't dead,' he said. 'I saw him earlier.'

Cissie sensed his reluctance. She took a step towards him, gripped his ragged sleeve and gave it a tug as if to coax the truth from him.

Jock drew in a deep breath. 'He's gone, lass.'

'Gone? What d'you mean – gone?'

'He drew his wages an' left at the end o' the early shift.'

Clare swung round and stared up at the tenement. 'Then he's here,' she said, puzzled. 'He must be here, waiting for me.'

'Have you tried his door?' Jock asked.

'That's where I found her,' Cissie said, 'sittin' outside his door.'

'He's in there. He must be in there,' Clare said. 'Perhaps he's sick. Aye, he must be sick. He has to see the priest tonight. He has to see the priest to arrange our weddin'. I'll go up again an' see if he's awake yet.'

'I think . . .' Jock began, but Cissie checked him.

'We'll go with you, dearest,' Cissie said. 'Won't we, Mr Macpherson?'

Jock nodded glumly, for he was already quite sure that Mr Harry Fairfield had scarpered.

By the time Benjamin Belfer came panting upstairs quite a crowd had gathered on the landing outside Harry Fairfield's apartment. The Fowler sisters, the Jardines – tenants from the top floor – and sundry small children as well as Cissie Cassidy, Jock Macpherson and Clare McKenna were milling about, and Jock, at the Irish girl's urging, was just about to attack the door lock with a coal-hammer.

'Wait, wait, wait,' Benjamin called out. 'Doors cost money, you know. What is all this? What's a-goin' on here?'

He was answered by a babble of voices, each anxious to express an opinion.

'Mr Fairfield – sick.'

'Mr Fairfield – deathbed.'

'Not seen since yesterday.'

'Not come home since . . .'

'Whoa!' Benjamin shouted. 'One at a time. You, Clare, you tell me what all the fuss is about.'

'Harry – Harry won't answer.'

'Perhaps because he isn't in there,' Benjamin said. 'He'll be down at Maizie's, like as not, dippin' his face in a pint pot.'

'*No*,' the girl screamed. '*He promised he'd come home*.'

She was close to hysteria, Benjamin realised. He had been dozing in the armchair by the open window when the racket had wakened him; another two minutes and the coal-heaver would have smashed down the door and somebody would have had to pay for the repair. He stepped hastily to the door of Fairfield's flat and spread out his arms. Macpherson lowered the coal-hammer and the girl, weakened by high emotion, fell against Cissie Cassidy who, somehow, managed to support her.

She looked, Benjamin thought, as if the sky had fallen on her. She was all tousled and torn and tear-stained, her eyes huge and her mouth slack, but still as beautiful as ever even if she had been abandoned by her deceitful lover who, by the smell of it, had vanished without paying the rent.

'I,' Benjamin said smugly, 'have a key.'

He fumbled in his pocket, brought out the key that fitted all the doors and held it up between finger and thumb, almost as if he expected applause.

'It's not my habit,' Benjamin announced, 'to go pokin' about in people's rooms when the said people ain't at home.

In this case, however, seein' as how you're all here to witness what I am about to do, I—'

'Just get on with it,' Macpherson told him gruffly.

Benjamin stooped, inserted the key in the lock, turned it and pushed open the door. He held out an arm to stop the Irish girl rushing past him. He was convinced that the room would be empty, the young fly-by-night gone, but the experience of finding Mr Coker's body, sprawled on the floor with mice and cockroaches crawling all over it was still too fresh in his memory to ignore and, in a rare moment of consideration, he entered the room first.

No body: no nothing. The room was clean and bare.

At least Fairfield hadn't stolen the furniture.

'He's not here,' Mr Belfer said and, squeezing to one side, allowed both Clare and Cissie Cassidy to step inside and see for themselves.

But there was nothing to see, no trace of Harry Fairfield, not a bootlace or a button, not a breadcrumb or a flake of soap. Everything had been taken, everything that did not belong to the landlord, everything except the house key and two half-crowns pinned under a teacup in the centre of the table. With a little '*ooo*' of surprise Benjamin plucked up and pocketed the coins while the girl darted frantically about the barren room, crying for Harry to come out and show himself.

Then with a shriek, she threw herself on the bed.

And Jock Macpherson said, 'I think I'd better fetch the sister.'

And Benjamin, not unmoved, said, 'Aye, I think you'd better.'

The home-coming game that Russell played with his children had gone through several variations over the years. At present it involved Nanny Milliken, Jane and sometimes his mother forming a line behind the girls and, as he stepped through the front door, chuffing out of the morning-room, elbows pumping in unison, to steam to a halt in the hall before him.

Feigning surprise, he would say, 'My goodness, it's the Crosshill Express, come to take me to dinner,' and would lift each of the not-so-little morsels in turn and give her a kiss, and would kiss Jane and his mother, too, though not, emphatically not, whiskery Nanny Milliken.

Tonight, though, the Crosshill Express had been derailed by the appearance of Uncle Wilson who had no time for games and stood smack-dab in the middle of the hallway, his arms folded across his chest.

His first words were, 'So it's come to this, has it?'

'Come to what, Willy?' Russell said, as patiently as possible.

'That you'd side with a damned Irish navvy instead of your own brother,' Wilson snarled. 'Has this wee trollop got you so bewitched you'd humiliate me just to please her?'

Russell glanced towards the morning-room where his daughters were piled up behind Nanny Milliken, and Jane, eyebrows raised, was all agog. He took Wilson by the arm, hurried him across the hall into the dining-room and closed the door.

'Now,' he said, 'what's all this about, Willy?'

'You know damned well what it's about.'

'McKenna?'

'Aye, McKenna.'

Russell shook his head and said calmly, 'Don't tell me you're going to let a digger come between us?'

'You overturned my order . . .'

'I gave him back his job, yes.'

'. . . overturned my express order without even consulting me.'

'Well, you sacked him without consulting me,' said Russell. 'Do you want a drink – tea, whisky?'

Willy ignored the offer. 'We've two hundred men, give or

take, on our books,' he said. 'What, tell me, makes this man so special if it isn't your interest in his sister?'

'How many times do I have to tell you that I have no interest in Evie McKenna – or any girl, for that matter.' Russell's voice strengthened and took on edge. 'And I'd thank you not to hurl these slanderous accusations about in front of my wife and family.'

'Because you do have something to hide, eh?'

'I've nothing to hide,' Russell said. 'Nothing.'

'You know her, though, don't you? I mean, you spoke to her?'

'Of course I know her,' Russell said. 'Half the men in Riverside know her. She's a barmaid, for heaven's sake. And, yes, I admit I did speak with her – but only to get at the truth.'

'The truth! Hah! You'll never get the truth out of a Pape.'

'That's your opinion, Willy, not one I happen to share.'

'You want to keep her here, don't you?' Willy said. 'You think you're safe because she's in your debt and will do whatever you ask her to. And you have the audacity to talk about me.'

'I don't talk about you.'

'At least,' Willy said, 'I'm no damned hypocrite. Everyone knows where they stand with me.'

'That's true,' said Russell.

The dining-table had been set. The smell of cooking drifted in from the double door that led out to the kitchen stairs. The brothers stood six or eight feet apart, their raised voices echoing in the vaulted room. Then Willy, appearing to capitulate, seated himself on the edge of one of the dining chairs and put his hands on his knees. He looked, Russell thought, rather weary, worn down by the heat of the day, or perhaps by his own splenetic outburst.

'Did Libby approach you?' Wilson said.

'About what?'

'McKenna.'

'Of course not. Why do you ask?'

'The Chink came down to the wall today, accompanied by a female friend,' Willy said. 'They said they were looking for you but the fact of it is they'd come to ogle the McKenna boy.'

'They're only young lassies, Wilson. You can't blame them for that.'

'He's a digger, a bloody digger,' Willy said. 'It's all her fault, really.'

'Libby, you mean?'

'Aye, Libby and her socialist inclinations. Nobody knows their place any more. Since she ran off and married that Papish no-good all those years ago everything's gone from bad to worse.'

'I'd hardly call a new double villa in Kelvinside worse,' Russell said. 'I admit I was as shocked as anyone when Libby ran off with Peter Galloway, but please remember that we were young and struggling ourselves at that time.'

'Aren't we struggling now?'

'No,' said Russell. 'We're not.'

'We're stretched beyond our limit.'

'Is that what all this is about?' Russell said.

'The bank won't support us forever.'

'I don't see why not,' said Russell. 'Strachan's approved your proposal, hasn't he?'

'In principle,' Wilson said, 'only in principle. We still need the income from the Riverside properties to provide us with operating capital.'

'I know we do.'

'So who'll collect the rents and ensure good order if Orpington—'

'Oh, Orpington? You're still concerned about him, are

you?' Russell said. 'Pay him off, Willy. Pay him whatever he asks, and let's be rid of him.'

'He's too useful,' Willy said, 'and he knows too much. He won't be happy when he finds out you've brought McKenna back.'

'The devil with Percival Orpington,' said Russell. 'We've Paddy Maizie on our side – Libby will keep him in order – and we have Belfer.'

'Belfer!' said Willy with a snort. He slapped his hands to his knees and got to his feet. 'God, Russell, how I wish we could be shot of these people.'

'These people,' Russell said, 'are our bread and butter.'

'If it wasn't for us, they'd starve,' Willy said.

'And if it wasn't for them *we'd* starve,' said Russell.

'Huh,' Willy said, 'you've fair changed your tune.'

'Not before time, perhaps,' said Russell.

'All right,' Willy said, 'if you feel so strongly about it, let the Irishman stay on the books. It's your squad, after all, not mine.'

'And Orpington?'

'I'll see to Orpington,' Willy said, then, forefinger wagging censoriously, added, 'But just you be careful, old man, just you have a care. We've come this far by pulling together, more or less, and now is no time to go weak-kneed and surrender to whim and fancy.'

'If you mean the girl . . .'

'I don't mean the girl.'

'What do you mean then?'

'I mean those people,' Willy said. 'At the first sign of weakness they'll drag us down, and we don't want that to happen, do we?'

'No,' Russell said, 'we don't want that to happen.'

'Then make damned sure it doesn't,' Willy said and, with a curt nod to Jane in passing, strode across the hall and let himself out of the house.

PART THREE

The Orphans' Picnic

II

The horses, though huge, were not in any way unruly. The same, alas, could not be said for the orphans of Our Lady or the dozen or so neglected wee souls that Father Fingle fished out of the tenements and led in a crocodile to the meeting place in Hillpark Street.

Here the carters, generously sacrificing a day's wages, had assembled their charges, massive Clydesdales and Shires and one magnificent Percheron, horses that on every other week-day throughout the year could be found hauling heavy loads up hill and down dale throughout the city. There were nine high-sided drays and a hay-wagon, no flat-beds. The carters, Catholics to a man, took great pride in providing transport for the orphans and in outdoing each other in the number of ribbons, banners and bells with which they decorated not only their carts but their horses as well.

It was a very fine display and drew a crowd of onlookers, not all of whom wished the expedition well. The usual gang of louts had slouched down from Wedderburn Road to jeer at the show of Green and call down curses on the heads of the nuns, priests and helpers. There was no stone-throwing, however, for a certain Mr Maizie, prompted by Libby Galloway, had rounded up *his* bully-boys to see the procession safely out of Riverside.

The archbishop was well aware of what was going on in his smallest parish but he was far too grand – far too busy, actually – to attend in person. Instead, he sent six crates of ginger beer and three trays of pies as his contribution to the feast, and made sure that the Diocesan Inspector for Schools and, oddly, the Registrar for Deceased Clergymen turned up to wave the party off which, at precisely ten thirty, they did.

For once there was no rain, not a cloud in the June sky, as the carts rolled away from the walls of the orphanage and set out for the sunlit uplands of the Hannan estates, west of Anniesland.

Old hands among the orphans were perhaps a mite disappointed that the picnic grounds were not, this year, on the shores of the Clyde, but a committee, headed by Libby Galloway, had found a somewhat less watery site and Sir George Hannan, or at least his agent, had agreed to allow a stretch of parkland close to the Daffodil Wood to be used instead.

Libby, Pin and two teaching sisters had driven out to inspect the place and had found it in all respects ideal. There were trees to climb, flowers to pick, even a shallow stream to paddle in and, of course, a great flat area of grassland sprinkled with nothing more disgusting than sheep droppings upon which to hold races and play games.

Cheers went up as the first of the drays trundled away.

There was singing and yelling, scared wails from one recruit new to the annual outing who had never ridden in a cart before. There were bugle calls – every parade had a bugler – the clatter of hooves, the rumble of wheels, some sisters crying, one or two praying, and a host of women, old and young, hanging from tenement windows as the procession, flanked by Mr Maizie's burly friends, wended past and, with the carters picking up the pace, left all the troubles of the Riverside behind.

With a small boy clinging to his back and an even smaller girl tucked under one arm, Nolan McKenna lumbered towards the trestle tables on which were stacked one hundred and ten brown paper bags, plus a few extra to allow for 'accidents'. Each bag contained a meat pie, a wedge of cheese, a slice of gingerbread, a chocolate bar and an orange. Ginger beer in brown bottles was distributed from crates piled high on the grass close by. The nuns in charge were hard pressed to cope, for however well trained and orderly the orphans were 'at home', in the wide open spaces of the Hannan estate the shackles of restraint had fallen swiftly away, and, come feeding time, it was every man for himself.

'Gangway, gangway,' Nolan shouted. 'Hungry hunters here on board.'

The boy on his back was not quite right in the head and the girl, one of Father Fingle's deserving cases, had a withered leg.

How Nolan McKenna had latched on to them was a mystery. Pin had hardly taken her eyes off him from the second the carts had entered the field and the children had scattered hither and yon in spite of all that the nuns and co-opted helpers could do to contain them.

She had watched him lift children down from the drays two at a time, had watched him unload the barrel of ale that Mr Maizie had sent out to refresh the carters and heavy bags of grain for the horses; had watched him set up the trestles in the wink of an eye; had watched him spare a moment to speak with his sister, Clare, and, putting an arm around her, give her a comforting hug, though Pin could not imagine why an adult would need to be comforted in the midst of such a mêlée. She watched him now from her stance by the ginger beer stall, the poor daft boy on his back and the crippled girl on his hip, and saw him reach out and snatch three brown paper bags and, with a wolf-howl of triumph, step carefully back through the legion of children, small and not so small, that jostled around the tables.

Something very strange was happening, Pin realised, for she

could not wrest her gaze from the enormous Irishman. In fact, she had hardly stopped thinking about him since she had first properly clapped eyes on him, brawling on the pavement outside the Harp. He looked so much at ease today, so gay and light-hearted, so much in control that she found herself smiling at the sight of him and, as her friends and family would testify, she was a girl not much given to smiling, whatever the circumstances.

Nolan lowered the little girl to the grass and handed her one of the brown paper bags. She was a sad wee pinched-faced creature in a ragged dress. When she gazed up at Nolan there was awe in her eyes, as if she could not quite believe that a man as big and young and golden – or any man at all, for that matter – would notice her, let alone show her kindness.

Nolan swung the boy from his shoulders and set him down too; an ugly lad with scaly skin and popping eyes who drooled when he spoke. If it hadn't been for Nolan, Pin knew that she would not have been able to bring herself to look at the boy, never mind approach him. She cradled three warm bottles of ginger beer in the crook of her arm and, smiling, walked as if on air across to the patch of grass that Nolan had staked out for himself and his party.

Seated cross-legged on the grass, he was helping the little girl open her lunch bag when Pin's shadow fell across him.

'Refreshment, Mr McKenna,' Pin said.

'Beer?' he said, grinning. 'By Gar, this wifie's brought us beer.'

The boy laughed and laughed and rolled over on his back like a dog.

Nolan said, 'Sober up, man. Sure an' you ain't had none o' it yet.'

He took a bottle from Pin's arm, dug his teeth into the cork, tugged it out, spat it on to the grass and handed the bottle to the little girl.

'Drink up, me hearties,' he said, then, pausing, watched her tentatively lick the sweet, lukewarm foam that poured over the neck of the bottle. 'Don't you know what it is, Rosie? Have you never had ginger before?'

The little girl shook her head.

'Ah, God!' Nolan whispered, wiping a big hand across his face.

And at that moment Pin did not feel Scots or Chinese or very much of anything, except lucky to be alive in that green field with Nolan.

It did not take long for Clare to pull herself together. When it became clear that Harry had indeed abandoned her, she had pitched into a frenzy of scrubbing and scouring. She had squared up to Father Fingle, had taken her medicine and, in due course, received the host. Of course, she did not admit to anyone, least of all herself, that what she missed most was not Harry's company but the wicked, blissful pleasures of love-making.

She found Nolan and Evie's solicitousness tiresome and was impatient with Mrs Cassidy who, for some unfathomable reason, seemed to believe that what had happened was her fault. Even bullying, blustering Belfer treated her now with something approaching respect.

It was only to appease Mrs Galloway that Clare agreed to help at the orphans' picnic and reluctantly allowed herself to be cajoled into visiting the orphanage to meet the nuns and some of the children. The visit to the high-walled building in Hillpark Street did nothing to cool the little pool of molten rage that bubbled deep inside her, however, rage not at Harry Fairfield for making her look a fool, but rage at herself for the lewd and fretful longings that were, it seemed, to be her lover's only legacy.

She did not enjoy the ride along the Great Western Road, rocking in the high-sided cart with a crowd of excited kiddies clinging to her skirts. She said little or nothing to the teaching sister, a woman twice her age, who perched on an orange box in a corner. But as the houses dropped away and the sky widened Clare's self-absorption dwindled and by the time the procession reached the field gate she was at least willing to be civil.

'There you are, Clare,' said Father Fingle. 'I see you've gathered quite a crowd of young admirers.'

'Only 'cause I've a corkscrew, Father,' Clare said, amiably enough. 'Those bottles weren't meant to be opened by small fingers, I'm thinkin'.'

The priest looked down at the pile of empty crates then at the horseshoe of orphans, mainly boys, who had gathered round the ginger beer stall. He took the implement from Clare's hand and, with considerable dexterity, began opening the last of the bottles and setting them out, one by one, in a line along the trestle to his left.

The mob grew tense.

Father Fingle pursed his lips to hide a smile and glowered down at one moon-faced reprobate. 'What are you hanging about here for, Duncan Calder?'

'Ah huvnae hud ony yet, Faither.'

'Oh, Duncan, Duncan!' the father said. 'What a white one.'

'He's hud three,' said Duncan's boon companion George, who, when it came to a choice between loyalty and ginger beer knew where his preference lay. 'Ah've hud nane.'

'Huv tae,' said Patie Paterson from the rear. 'Hud fower.'

'Ah'm still thursty, but,' said Duncan, who did not give up easily.

Father Fingle set down the last bottle from the last crate and handed the corkscrew back to Clare who tucked it, like a dagger, into the waistband of her skirt. All eyes now were on the line of opened bottles, on the soft dribbles of froth that slid down the sides. The older boys knew that the father would not let them go away empty-handed – they would remain patient – but the youngsters, Duncan, George and Patie, would they, Clare wondered, break under the strain?

'Thirsty enough to remember your manners?' Father Fingle said.

Duncan pondered for a second. 'Aye, Faither.'

'Then come up here, young man, and hand one bottle to each of your companions, starting with the girls at the back. And if – I say if – there happens to be one bottle left at the end, it's yours.'

Duncan swung round, counting heads as fast as basic arithmetic would allow then with an air of resignation that was almost noble, stepped quickly to the table and began, two-fisted, to dish out the bottles.

Father Fingle drew Clare back a step or two from the table.

'How is it with you now, Clare?' he asked. 'Are you back on your feet?'

'I was never off my . . . I mean, aye, Father, I'm fine.'

'Take my word on it,' the priest said, 'it was a good thing for you that Fairfield left you in the lurch. If you had gone on with it, I would probably have married you in bad faith.' Father Fingle glanced over his shoulder as if he feared that he might be overheard, then he went on, 'I'm sorry to have to tell you this, Clare, but your Mr Fairfield already has a wife.'

Clare's mouth popped open. 'Wha . . . what?'

'A wife and a child – in Kingsway.'

'But he lives – he lived in Salamanca Street,' Clare said.

'Apparently he told his wife that he had work on the road.'

'How could he possibly afford to pay two rents?'

Father Fingle shrugged. 'That I can't say. You have my absolute assurance, however, that there is already a Mrs Fairfield. I traced Fairfield through the coal yard to his former parish, Kingsway; the name's recorded on his employment sheet.'

'He's a traveller, a wanderer. He told me so himself.'

'A wanderer?' said Father Fingle. 'Well, it seems he wandered only as far as the high road between Kingsway and the Riverside.'

'This woman – this wife,' Clare got out, 'did he desert her too?'

'Not entirely,' Father Fingle said. 'I gather from the minister of Kingsway parish church that your Mr Fairfield returned every so often, usually at night, to leave a little money and, I imagine, to exercise his – ah – his conjugal rights.'

'Harry wasn't religious.'

'No, but the woman in question was born and raised in Kingsway and is well known to the Reverend Mr Oakes. Fairfield was married, *legally* married to this poor girl. You had a very narrow escape, Clare.'

'Where's Harry now? Has he gone back to this woman?'

'It seems not,' Father Fingle said. 'I gather from correspondence with Mr Oakes that Fairfield hasn't returned to the Kingsway. Perhaps he has gone wandering this time. By the by, Clare, there's no purpose to be served in calling on Fairfield's wife. Promise me that you won't go out to Kingsway. Promise me too that if Fairfield returns to Salamanca Street you'll have no more to do with him, no matter what promises he makes.'

'He promised me marriage,' Clare said, though that wasn't quite true. 'If he hadn't promised to marry me I wouldn't have done what I did.'

'Quite!' said Father Fingle. 'None the less, you committed a sin.'

'For which I've been forgiven.'

'You must not commit that sin again. Do you hear me?' Father Fingle said sternly. 'In time some young man will come along and fall in love with you, and you with him, and you will marry in the grace of God.'

'And what will I tell this imaginary person?' Clare said.

'Tell him?' said Father Fingle.

'When he finds out I'm not pure?'

For all his worldly experience there were limits to the father's knowledge. He had heard talk of how a woman could trick a man by pretending to be pure when she was not, but he had not pursued that area of information. He believed in honesty between husband and wife, trust as the bedrock of a sound Christian marriage. He knew before she asked it what Clare's next question would be.

'Will you still marry me in church even though you know I'll be startin' my married life with a lie?' she said.

Father Fingle looked to the distant horizon, to the smoke that smudged the pale blue sky but, finding no inspiration there, sighed. 'No, Clare, that would not be right,' he said. 'Best tell your husband the truth. It may be that the man also has things he'd like to get off his chest so that the slate will be clean between you before you embark on a life together under God.'

'Aye,' Clare said. 'I thought you'd say that.'

'*Is* there another man, another suitor?'

'God in heaven, Father! What do you take me for?' Clare said. 'No, there's no other man, nor will there be another man. I've had enough of men to last me a good long while.'

'You must not allow bitterness to affect you.'

'I'm not bitter, Father,' Clare told him. 'I asked for what I got. But, by Gar, next time a man talks sweet to me you can be sure I'll not be taken in. If I do take on another man some day it'll be with my eyes wide open an' me head rulin' me heart.' Then, abruptly, she turned from the trestles and went striding off towards Daffodil Wood on the hill above the picnic ground.

'Clare, Clare . . .' Father Fingle cried after her.

'Sure an' I have to pee, Father,' she called out, loudly

enough to make the small boys snigger, and went on, running now, towards the shelter of the trees.

It was three hours or more until sunset but already the air was cooling and shadows creeping over the deserted field. The day was over, everyone knew it. No one sang on the long road home. Even the most rambunctious boys sprawled in melancholy heaps and gazed quietly back at the meadow and the trees as if to imprint them on their memory. Nolan hunkered in a corner of the cart with the little girl on his knee. He had run with her in one of the races and had carried her, against all protests, to victory. He had put her on his shoulder, had taken the daft boy by the hand and had gone with the others to explore the wood and the stream. He had picked weeds and called them flowers, had paddled in the shallow brown water and scared the little fishes. He had dried Rosie's feet with the tail of his shirt and discreetly examined her pinched toes and skinny little leg, and had given Pin a look, such a look, and had rubbed his face with his hand again.

Now Rosie was almost asleep, the daft boy, slumped against the Irishman, nodding too, his mouth wide open. Pin held on to the side of the dray with one hand and on to Nolan McKenna with the other and wondered what it would be like not only to fall asleep but to waken, safe in his big strong arms. She was surprised when he glanced up at her, and said, 'May I ask you an intemperate question, please?'

She nodded. 'Yes.'

He said, 'What are you?'

'I'm not sure I know what you mean.'

'Well, you're not just a Chink – I mean Chinese, are you?'

'I'm what they call Straits Chinese. I'm from Malaya, from Penang, though I was born in Singapore.'

'You don't talk Chinese.'

Seang Pin lowered herself to the floor of the cart and put an arm about Nolan's waist for support.

'Are you curious about me, Nolan?'

'I am,' he said. 'I admit, I am.'

'I do speak Chinese. Mandarin to be exact.'

'Like the orange?' Nolan said.

'Yes, like the orange,' Pin said.

'You're not a heathen, though.'

'I never was a heathen,' Pin said. 'I believe in the same God as you do, in Christ our Lord and Mary His Mother. I was brought up Catholic. My mother was Malay, but my father was raised by missionaries and put out to work with a spice trader in Singapore when he was old enough.'

'Why was he raised by missionaries?'

'There are too many children in China, too many mouths to feed. Soon after he was born my father was abandoned on the edge of the town, left to die. Fortunately for me, he was found and taken to the Mission.'

'Where is he now, your father?' Nolan asked.

'In heaven,' Pin said, with a little shrug. 'He, and my mother, were caught in a terrible fire that swept through the warehouse my father owned in partnership with Mr Galloway.'

'Is that why Mrs Galloway brought you back here?'

'Yes.'

Pin had told her story to her school friends often enough; she was not ashamed of her origins. There was something a little different about this telling, however, with this man as her audience. He had not asked her why she didn't wear a pigtail or if her feet had been bound, or any of the silly questions that were usually put to her. He had asked her about the god she worshipped, as if that was more important than the shape of her eyes or the colour of her skin.

'So you belong here,' Nolan said.

'Sitting in a cart with orphans? Yes, Mr McKenna, I suppose I do.'

'Sure an' that's not what I meant.'

'I know,' Pin said. 'I know what you meant, Nolly.'

She waited for him to tell her something about himself, to reveal to her at least as much, if not more, than she had revealed to him. He said nothing, though, simply crouched there in silence with the girl child on his lap and the drooling boy, dead to the world and snoring, resting against him. His size, his energy, even his brash Irish brogue made him seem naïve but Pin, unlike her friend Norma, no longer saw him in that light, for there was a force about him, a gentle rhythm to which she could not help but respond.

She tightened her arm about his waist and rested her head against his shoulder while the cart rolled back into the city and the tenements closed about them once more.

Sunlight still glinted on windows high up and gilded the chimney-heads like funerary ornaments but the upper reaches of Wedderburn Road were already wrapped in summer night's shadow. On Father Fingle's instruction the carters dropped off his deserving cases one by one, to see them safe – if that was the word – home again. Mothers and sisters, a brother or two, came out to greet them and lead them indoors to listen to the tales they had to tell.

At Rosie's close, however, there was no such welcome, only a woman, drunk and abusive, craning from a top-floor window, screeching like a crow.

Nolan lifted the little girl from the cart and put her on the pavement. He would have carried her into the close and up the flight of stairs if Father Fingle had not put a hand on his sleeve.

'No, son,' the priest told him. 'You can do no more for her now,' and Rosie went on, alone, into the dark mouth of the close, clutching her empty ginger beer bottle in her arms, like a doll.

12

If he had learned anything from his mother – and he certainly hadn't learned much – Benjamin Belfer had acquired a degree of cunning that he fondly interpreted as tact. He did not jump upon Clare McKenna in her hour of need, did not grab her by the neck and shower her with kisses but, throughout the month of June, generally managed to make it known that he was willing to be her friend. For his courteous attentions he received a just reward: Clare no longer snapped at him or flayed him with sarcasm and even went so far as to invite him in for a cup of tea and a chat when he came to collect the rent.

Did Mr Belfer have any news of Harry Fairfield?

No, alas, he did not.

Did he have any news of Mr Orpington?

On that score too he was devoid of information.

In fact, he had encountered Perce outside the coffee house near Charing Cross but Perce had been short with him, not rude exactly but curt, and had limped off without offering to buy him a drink.

Did Clare see much of Mrs Galloway?

Every Sunday at church.

Did Evie see anything of Mr Blackstock?

Now why would Evie see anything of Mr Blackstock?

Benjamin had no answer to that question and tactfully took the conversation off in another direction while the lovely Clare McKenna poured him a second cup of tea.

Close to the end of the month seaman Daniel Doyle

returned from his voyage to the Antipodes. Burned to the colour of a walnut shell and lean as a ferret, he bounded into the close one afternoon with his dunnage on his shoulder and a gleam in his eye so fiery that you could have cooked your dinner on it. He knocked on Mr Belfer's door to let him know that he was here again, then leaped off upstairs, calling out to the Fowler sisters to get their drawers off *tout de suite* for Daddy was home and dying for a cuddle.

Ten minutes later Betty Fowler took the children to play in the park.

Ten minutes after that Benjamin knocked on Clare's door to warn her not to be alarmed by any unusual noises in the close.

'What unusual noises?' Clare said.

'The noises may not, of course, seem unusual to you,' said Benjamin, adding hastily, 'by which I mean mortar and sandstone may muffle them so that you're unable to distinguish what they signify.'

'Sure an' I don't know what you're talkin' about,' said Clare.

'Danny Doyle's come home from the sea.'

'Oh?' Clare said, then, as a great yell followed by several piercing shrieks came ringing down the stairs, said '*Oh!*' again – and blushed.

'The longer the voyage, the louder the noise,' Benjamin said. 'I'm afraid it might go on for several days.'

'Several days?' said Clare. 'My, my! Why don't you put a stop to it?'

'I'm a man o' the world,' Benjamin said. 'What you might call a realist. Mr Doyle pays rent in advance so a bit of rowdiness every half year or so is excusable, don't you think?'

'I don't know what to think,' said Clare.

Another peal from upstairs, laughter loud and long: Clare cocked her head and listened. Benjamin slyly observed her reaction. The blush, he noted, had faded from her damask cheek, her lips were pursed in a manner more amused than disapproving. She showed no inclination to retreat indoors.

'There'll be another baby on the way before the summer's out,' Benjamin said. 'No cause without effect, eh?'

'Does he – I mean – both of them?' said Clare.

'So it appears,' said Benjamin.

'Greedy beggar,' Clare said, and laughed.

If June was a dry and peaceful month, July, as a rule, was the opposite. That it would be wet went without saying for the gods had never been known to let Fair Week go by without at least one terrible tract of rain or, worse, persistent drizzle. Orange and Green conflicts were common. The lodges had opposition now in contingents of Home Rulers, and Orange walks during the trades' holiday, when shipyards and manufactories were closed, usually spelled trouble.

To Evie's disappointment, there was no sign of Russell Blackstock in the Riverside. She had no reason to be disappointed, of course. They had bumped together in unusual circumstances, she had overstepped the mark and had been lucky to get away with it. Even so, she'd hoped that he might come in search of her, might venture into her territory since she could not, in conscience, venture again into his. Four days into July, without any warning, he turned up again.

It was well after eleven, late even for a summer's night. The horses were stalled, the McLeans in bed. Only the cats were out and about, hunting in the cool night air. Mr Blackstock was hiding in the lane. He called out Evie's name and when she came to him, took her arm and led her away from the mouth of the lane. He wore no hat, no gloves, no necktie or cravat. His shirt had a wing collar and the collar was open, springing away from his throat.

'Evie,' he said, 'do you trust me?'

'I do,' Evie whispered thickly.

'Tomorrow, first thing, I require you to seek out Paddy Maizie and inform him that the Harp will be attacked.'

Evie blinked. 'Attacked?'

'Some Orangemen are hell-bent on making trouble,' Russell Blackstock said. 'I have it on good authority that they intend to set upon the Harp during the course of the walk to Glasgow Green and inflict as much damage as possible.'

'Why don't you tell Mr Maizie yourself, or have your sister do it?'

'I don't want it known that I'm the source of the information.'

'Why damage Mr Maizie's place?' said Evie. 'Why not the chapel?'

'Too many ministers are opposed to Orangeism; an attack on any sort of church building, even a Catholic chapel, would not sit well with them.'

'Most o' your workmen are Catholics,' Evie said. 'If the Harp goes up in smoke, they'll find a way to blame you for it an' work on the harbour will be held up because of it. It's all to do with business, isn't it?'

'Of course it is.' She heard him laugh. 'You've hit the nail on the head.'

'What I still don't understand, Mr Blackstock, is why you need me to deliver your message. Surely Mrs Galloway . . .'

'Libby would fly into a temper and rush to accuse my brother Wilson, and that would undoubtedly lead to all sorts of complications.'

'Is that the only reason you're askin' me to do it?'

'Yes.'

'I thought perhaps you – you liked me,' Evie said.

'If I didn't like you, Evie, I wouldn't expect you to trust me.'

'I thought it was me who had to be trustworthy.'

'To keep a secret, yes.'

'Is that all?' Evie said.

She couldn't see his face clearly enough to mark the change. He slid his hands to her shoulders and held her close for a moment.

'Yes,' he said. 'Yes, Evie, that's all.'

'I'll do anythin' you ask of me,' she said.

'Then deliver my message to Paddy Maizie,' Russell said.

He drew back a little so that he could see her face in the faint light from the lamp in Salamanca Street. She was hardly much older than his oldest daughter and no prettier than Jane had been when Jane was her age. He felt old suddenly, old and awkward, and disappointed by his lack of fire.

'Tell me,' Evie said, 'will you march with your brother?'

'No,' he said. 'I've given all that up.'

'In that case will you not stand with us?'

'Why would I do that?'

'You have to stand some place, do you not now?'

'Perhaps – but not with you, Evie. No, not with you.'

She expected him to vanish into the darkness but he was too polite for that. He took her by the arm, led her back to the mouth of the lane once more and watched her cross the street to the close.

But when she turned to wave goodbye, he had gone.

Jane was in bed but not asleep. She was propped on pillows, reading, spectacles with oval lenses perched on her nose. Russell saw himself reflected in the lenses as he leaned to kiss her. She put the book to one side, removed the spectacles, lifted her chin and closed her eyes. She always closed her eyes when he kissed her. He liked the nervous flutter of her lashes against his cheek. She had discarded her longcloth nightdress in favour of a filmy thing embroidered with forget-me-nots.

He stepped away from the bed and began to undress. He had washed his hands and face in the bathroom downstairs but wondered if he still had the smell of the girl upon him.

'I'm sorry I missed the children,' he said.

'And dinner,' said Jane.

'Yes, and dinner.'

'Where did you eat?'

'At the Toll House.'

'With Willy?'

For all he knew Wilson had called here this evening. Cautiously, he said, 'No, with Struthers.'

'Struthers?'

'A brother from lodge Western.'

'Oh!' said Jane.

He took off his trousers, folded them neatly and, stepping into the dressing closet, placed them on the trouser rack. He peeled off his shirt, vest and drawers and stuffed them into the laundry basket.

He selected a clean nightshirt from the shelf.

'What are you doing in there?' Jane called.

'Making ready for bed,' he told her.

He held the nightshirt over his arm and looked down at himself. He was fairly trim for a man of his age, a little thick around the middle but not stout. He did not know whether it was the memory of holding the girl in his arms or the prospect of being welcomed to bed by his wife that had roused him.

'Did you play cards?' Jane asked.

'Billiards,' he said.

He took a deep breath and stepped, naked, out of the closet.

'Well, well!' Jane said. 'It must have been an exciting contest.'

'Rather dull,' he said, as casually as possible. 'Dull, but protracted.'

'Did you beat him?'

'Yes.'

'Were you playing for high stakes?'

'More for fun than anything,' Russell said.

He felt self-conscious standing before her without a stitch.

She stared at him, unabashed. 'It's very late,' she said.

'I know,' he said. 'After midnight.'

'Still warm, though, so very warm.'

'Almost tropical,' he said.

'Aren't you going to put on your nightshirt?'

'In view of the heat I thought I might not.' He moved to the side of the bed. 'I'm sure I'd be more comfortable without – if you can put up with it.'

'I think I might be able to put up with it,' Jane said. She had fine hair, not sparse but fine. It wisped across her brow when she shifted her weight. 'Will I have to put up with that too?'

'Possibly.'

'Possibly?'

'Probably,' he said.

She fell back upon the pillows, tossed aside the covers and lifted her nightdress. She was as slender as the day he had married her in spite of having borne four children. He knelt upon the bed and slid a hand behind her head. He lifted her up, kissed her mouth and felt the flutter of her lashes on his cheek.

He slipped a hand down between her legs.

'Are you ready, dearest?' he asked courteously.

'Yes,' she answered him. 'Yes, Russell, yes.'

And, no longer thinking of the Irish girl, he entered her.

'Oh,' Evie said. 'I'm sorry. I thought Mr Maizie would be here by now.'

'He is,' Pin told her. 'He has just popped out to relieve himself.'

'I'll come back later,' Evie said.

'Wait,' Pin said. 'He'll be no more than a minute or two.'

The girl was seated on the ottoman. She looked, Evie thought, very fresh in a summer frock, but prim, almost too prim. On her lap was a folded newspaper, as if she had been swatting flies. There were no flies in Mr Maizie's office, though, and, Evie suspected, no flies on Mrs Galloway's protégée either.

'Bantry Bay in the second race at Ayr on Wednesday.' Pin tapped the newspaper. 'Poor Patrick owes us three pounds and twelve shillings.'

'Us?' said Evie.

'My Aunt Libby and I enjoy a flutter now and then,' Pin said. 'How is your brother, by the way?'

'My brother?' said Evie.

'Nolly.'

'Nolly – sure an' he's grand.'

'He will be at church tomorrow.'

'Will he?' said Evie.

'He will,' Pin said. 'He promised.'

'Did he?' said Evie.

'Your brother is a man of his word.'

'Is he?' said Evie.

'Honesty is the bedrock of his character.'

'How well – I mean, what do you know about Nolly's character?'

'I am a good judge,' said Pin. 'He has hidden depths.'

Nolly had talked a great deal about the Chinese girl after the picnic and had certainly been unusually eager to prise himself out of bed for Sunday morning mass but, in Evie's book, that hardly added up to hidden depths.

'Have you been meetin' him on the sly?' Evie asked.

'Only at mass.'

'Is Nolly – I mean, have you taken a notion for our Nolan?'

'I have,' Pin said, looking up. 'Do you object?'

'Object? Well – I mean – he's only a bloody labourer.'

'My father was only a bloody coolie,' Pin said.

'Nolan isn't good enough for you.'

'That is for me to decide,' said Pin.

Evie reddened. 'Does Nolan know how you feel about him?'

'If he does not,' Pin said, 'he will soon enough.'

'He can't support you,' Evie blurted out. 'He doesn't earn enough.'

'He supports you, does he not?' Pin said.

'I work.'

'Your sister does not work.'

'How do you know so much about us?' Evie asked.

'Nolly told me.'

'When?'

'At the picnic,' Pin said calmly.

'So that's it, is it?' Evie said. 'It started at that damned picnic.'

'It would have happened in any case,' said Pin. 'Nolly is the man for me. I have made up my mind.'

'What about us?' Evie said.

'What about you?' said Pin.

'We need a man to look after us.'

'Then find one of your own,' said Pin and, rising, stepped forward to greet Paddy Maizie as he came in through the door.

Though she had tended the animals on the holding back home and understood the mechanics of conception, Clare experienced no more than vague unease when, for a second month, her bleeding did not occur. She put it down to hot weather and, for that reason, also dismissed the queasiness that affected her first thing in the morning. If her mama had been alive, her mama would have spotted the signs at once, but with no one sensible to turn to for advice, Clare refused to acknowledge that she might, in fact, be pregnant.

It would not have pleased her to learn that her condition was being discussed, hypothetically, by childless Aunt Cissie and big, bluff, hairy bachelor Jock Macpherson. It would have pleased her even less had she known that Danny Doyle's common-law wives had already concluded that the stuck-up miss downstairs had been thoroughly knocked up and that there would be at least one more mouth to feed in Belfer's close come Christmas.

The irony of her situation might have been less apparent if Mr Belfer's wooing had been a shade less determined and the inevitable strain, on Clare's part, of pretending that everything was normal had not been accompanied by Danny Doyle's loud mating calls and the racket of not-quite-perpetual intercourse that drifted down from upstairs.

It was, Evie said, disgusting.

Clare did not think it disgusting. She, like Nolan, found it more amusing than anything else and it said much for her powers of self-delusion that she could still joke about the sailor's sexual appetites even as she entered her third month and her breasts began to swell and her nipples darken.

Benjamin, of course, was enchanted.

What had begun as lust had transformed itself into love and as high summer approached had become a passion so exalted that he did not know how to define it or what the devil to do about it. Courtship was one thing, consummation another, and the Belfer of old, the Belfer of the lead pipe and the crowbar, the Belfer who could discuss with Percival Orpington a female's less visible parts without turning a hair had become, of all things, virtuous.

Clare was aware that Mr Belfer was attracted to her and was, at first, less flattered than amused by his attentions. Instead of lasting fifteen minutes their weekly tea-takings ran on into the afternoon as Mr Belfer – Benjamin – inexpertly plied the craft of suitor and fished to discover just what Clare thought of him and, in passing, what she thought of Mrs Galloway.

'But, Benjamin,' Clare said, 'I hardly know the woman.'

'Don't you converse with her every Wednesday an' Sunday?'

'We exchange a few words, that's all.'

'A few words about what?' said Benjamin. 'About me, perhaps?'

'To the best of my recollection,' Clare said, 'your name has never crossed Mrs Galloway's lips.'

'You must talk about somethin',' Benjamin persisted.

'The weather,' said Clare innocently. 'The church.'

'The church? What does she say about the church?'

'She's tryin' to persuade me to help out at Sunday school when the new season starts in September,' Clare said.

'I thought it was the priest's job to teach Sunday school.'

'Father Fingle has enough to do,' said Clare. 'Over a hundred children attend the school, not counting infants; helpers are needed just to keep order.'

'Have you accepted Mrs Galloway's invitation?'

'Not yet,' Clare said. 'I'm thinkin' about it, though.'

'Do you like children?'

'Not specially,' Clare said. 'But I feel I should do my bit.'

'To please Libby Galloway, you mean.'

'For the church, for the faith,' said Clare.

'Ah, yes, the faith,' said Benjamin sagely.

'Father Fingle says our faith is a cord that binds us to our past and commits us to our future,' Clare said.

'What of your future, Clare? How do you see your future?'

'I haven't thought about it.'

'It's time you did,' said Benjamin. 'None of us are gettin' any younger.'

'I'll give it careful consideration,' said Clare.

Benjamin paused. 'Give what careful consideration, my dear?'

'Mrs Galloway's invite.'

'Oh! Yes,' said Benjamin, hiding his disappointment.

'What did you think I meant?'

'I thought you meant lookin' for a husband.'

'I'm not lookin' for a husband.'

'You can do better than some penniless coalman,' Benjamin said.

'An' find some wealthy old feller instead?'

'Is that the sort of chap you fancy?' said Benjamin.

Clare laughed and instead of giving him the answer he wanted, went off to unearth the rent money.

Mr Maizie strode into the bar and with a gesture less languid than usual summoned Bob Draper into the snug.

Chiffin sidled up to Evie who was polishing the counter.

'Old Paddy's in a hurry,' he said.

'Perhaps there's been a problem with deliveries,' Evie suggested.

'No problem with my deliveries,' said Chiffin. 'It's you, ain't it? It's somethin' you said to Paddy not half an hour ago.'

Evie had no excuse to hand. 'Nah,' she said lamely.

'You were with him long enough,' said Chiffin. 'What's the news? Is it Orpington? Has Orpington come back?'

'If he has,' said Evie, 'I haven't heard of it.'

'I have his money, some o' it anyway,' Chiffin said. 'I'd hate for him to come to the house again an' scare my sisters, but I'm buggered if I'm goin' lookin' for him. You would tell me if Orpington was back, wouldn't you, Evie?'

'Sure an' I would.'

She was tempted to inform him that Mr Maizie was briefing Bob Draper on the Orangemen's march but if she did, then Chiff would be bound to ask how Mr Maizie had learned about the Orangemen's plans and she would be obliged to invent more lies to keep Mr Blackstock's name out of it.

Paddy and Bob emerged from the snug.

'The march, Chiffin,' Bob said gravely.

'Aye, Mr Draper, what about it?'

'It's comin' our way, apparently.'

'Are we puttin' up the shutters for the day?' Chiffin asked.

'We're not putting up the shutters at all, son,' Paddy said.

'Are we gettin' in the polis, then?' said Chiffin.

'Huh!' Bob Draper said. 'Fat lot of use the constables are to us, since most o'them favour the other side.'

'We're on our own then?' Chiffin said.

'Oh, we'll find some help somewhere, son,' said Mr Maizie and with a nod in Evie's direction went out into the yard and closed the door.

Benjamin was embarrassed at being seen abroad with his parents. He squirmed at the disdainful looks that his shawl-clad mother and his doddering old dad attracted on the pavements of Bellingham Place. Even dainty little maidservants and lanky, limp-haired footmen stepped hastily away from the Belfers as they took a rare afternoon promenade to escape the stifling heat of the apartment.

Arranging the outing had been as complicated as planning an invasion of France. His father had resisted, his mother had complained and Mrs Loomis, who had replaced Mrs Walsh, proved to be no help at all. It had taken the best part of an hour to dress his father and another twenty minutes to persuade his mother that it was safe to leave Mrs Loomis in charge of the house before the arduous descent to street level could even begin.

The old man had been mute and fairly compliant until his feet touched the pavement and sunlight smote his eyes, then, under the impression that he was being taken to jail for some unimaginable crime, he kicked up a terrible fuss, struggling, weeping and begging forgiveness. It took Benjamin some while to calm him down and steer him along the pavement towards the iron railings that bordered the gardens. Leaning heavily into her stick, muttering complaints, his mother followed a step or two behind.

It was pleasant enough in the shade of the elm that backed the bench upon which Benjamin placed them. There was a view of dockside cranes, a granite fountain, nursery-maids and nannies with their charges and, not far off, two or three gentlefolk strolling on the gravel paths. From behind a nearby privet hedge came the *tick-tock* of bowls from games upon the green.

From his vest pocket Benjamin removed a leather cigar-case and extracted a waxy cheroot. He cut it in half with a penknife and putting both halves in his mouth lit them with a match. He carefully placed one half into his father's mouth and, to his relief, saw that at least the old man had not forgotten how to smoke. He gave the other half cheroot to his mother who sniffed it suspiciously before she put it to her lips.

She inhaled, coughed, sighed, and inhaled again.

Benjamin sat back and watched his parents puff away contentedly.

Odd, he thought, how a twopenny cigar brought them more obvious pleasure than all the expensive luxuries he had lavished upon them.

His mother took the cheroot from her mouth, leaned forward, and spat.

Still bent almost double, she peered up at him. 'Where is she?'

'Who?' said Benjamin.

'This sweetheart o' yours.'

'Sweetheart?' said Benjamin.

'This Clare McKenna,' his mother said.

'Oh!' he said. 'Clare! Clare's very well. We had tea yesterday. She asks after you.'

'Where is she, but?'

'She lives in Salamanca Street.'

'Naw, where *is* she? I want tae meet her.'

His father turned his head and stared at his wife as if the conversation had caught his attention. For a flicker of a second Benjamin wondered if the old man's grasp on reality had suddenly returned; then, loudly, the old man broke wind and, satisfied with his contribution, suckled on his cheroot and stared absently at the cranes that reared above the trees once more.

'Meet her you shall, Mother,' Benjamin said, 'when the time is ripe.'

'Is she no' ripe already?'

'I don't know what you mean,' said Benjamin.

'Has she no' been poked?'

'Mother! Clare is a lady.'

'A lady, is she? Livin' in Salamanca Street wi' you?'

'She doesn't live with me,' said Benjamin.

'Well, that's wise o' her,' the old woman said. 'Who'd want tae live wi' you, Benjamin? The only way you'll ever get a lassie tae the altar is tae have her podded first an', if you ask me, you're no' up tae it.'

Benjamin bit his lip and tried to check his temper.

His mother went on remorselessly, 'When you was new born we thought you was a lassie, so shy was your parts.' She laughed at the memory. 'Had tae fetch a doctor in tae inspect you afore we had you named in kirk. Heh, but that was a sight tae see, how he fished about an' brought you down afore he could say for sure whether you was a Benjamin or a Betty.'

'For God's sake, Mother, it's forty years ago,' Benjamin hissed.

'Ach, you're still too puny down there, I expect; like a wee whelk that's lost its shell, your dada used tae say.' For a horrible moment Benjamin thought that his mother was about to ask him to expose himself just to prove her point.

He scrambled to his feet. 'Come along. I think it's time we went back.'

'Is it dickie!' his mother said. 'We've only just got here.'

'Too much sun ain't good for him.'

'Well, it's good for me – so we'll stay a while longer.' She tucked the shawl tightly about her, tipped her chin up and closed her eyes. 'What's wrong wi' this girl o' yours, any-roads?'

'Nothing's wrong with her,' said Benjamin.

'Is she a hunchback?'

'Of course she's not a hunchback.'

'Club-footed, then?'

'Mother, she's a beautiful young—'

'Why are you reluctant tae bring her tae meet me?' his mother said, then, opening one eye, added, 'Is it me you're ashamed of?'

'Of course I'm not ashamed of you,' Benjamin lied.

'Then fetch her tae me.'

'What? Now?'

'Next week,' his mother said. 'Without fail.'

'Very well,' Benjamin said. 'If it can be arranged – next week.'

'An' then we'll see for ourselves.'

'See what?' said Benjamin.

'Whether or not she's got one in the pod.'

13

The seventh Sunday after Pentecost was the hottest day of the year. Before the week was out great storms of wind and rain would gather in the west and sweep across Clydeside but stifling heat that Sunday meant a sleepless night for the McKennas. Come morning, Clare, whey-faced and nauseous, did not have the strength to get up and it was left to Evie and Nolan to accompany Aunt Cissie to church.

Sweat laved the brow of poor Father Fingle as he dispensed the elements of the mass and even Seang Pin was less than daisy fresh by the time the service was over and the congregation, what there was of it, trooped out into the street.

'Good morning, Nolly.'

'Good mornin', Pin.'

Nolan took off his cap and held it across his chest like, Evie thought, a lovesick swain. She stood by his side, glowering at the Chinese girl. Mrs Galloway chatted to the priest at the gate and Cissie hovered by the pavement's edge in the hope that Mr Maizie might offer her a ride home.

'Good morning, Evie,' Pin said.

''Mornin',' Evie growled.

The sky was an odd colour, streaked like an unripe plum. Every window in every tenement was open to trap a non-existent breeze and the stench of the river mingled with the odours of cooking, and drains.

'Hot, ain't it?' Nolan said.

'Awfully,' Pin agreed. 'It's almost like Singapore.'

She stood toe to toe with Nolan and looked up at him as if he were a crane or a steeple. What disturbed Evie was the dreamy smile on Nolan's face as he looked down at Pin.

'Time we were leavin',' Evie said.

Neither Nolan nor Pin paid her any attention. They seemed unaware that conversation had stalled or, perhaps, that conversation was required at all. Just then Mrs Galloway came up and led Evie off to speak with Father Fingle.

'Is it true,' said Father Fingle, 'that you think the Orange brigade intend to burn down the Harp?'

'It's not what I think, Father,' Evie said. 'It's what've I heard.'

'Where did you hear it?' Father Fingle said.

'In the pub.' Evie felt bad lying to a priest. 'I told Mr Maizie about it.'

'Will they also attack the church?' the father said.

'They didn't say anythin' about the church.'

'They? They? Who are these people?' said Libby Galloway. 'Are they known to you, Evie? Do they have names?'

'No, they were strangers.'

'Very strange strangers,' said Libby, 'if they discussed plans to burn down the Harp while standing at the bar of the Harp.' She turned to the priest. 'I think, Father, we may take it that we've been given all the warning we're going to get.'

'It might only be talk,' said Evie.

'I'm sure it's not,' said Libby. 'Who told you, Evie?'

'Men – men at the bar.'

'I don't know if you're aware of it, Evie,' Libby said, 'but so-called celebrations of the victory of Protestants over Catholics under William of Orange on the banks of the Boyne two hundred years ago are not confined to your country. There are riots here in Glasgow, riots that last for days. Haven't you heard the bands practising? In Partick last July hundreds were injured when Green and Orange clashed. The women are as bad, if not worse. They pick out the victims. They point and cry "Catholic, Catholic" then leave it to the men to club the poor fellow to the ground.'

'Does this happen here in Riverside?' asked Evie, alarmed.

'North of Riverside Road is where most of the trouble starts,' said Father Fingle. 'So far we've been protected.'

'Protected?' said Evie. 'How are you protected?'

'By force of numbers,' Libby Galloway explained. 'Some years ago my brother Russell decided to employ Irish Catholics on his labouring gangs. My other brother, Russell's twin, was furious, for he, Willy, is uncompromisingly opposed to popery. Russell brought in contracts, however, large and valuable contracts that he was able to cost only because he had Catholic labour at his disposal. Being a true blue hypocrite, Willy eventually surrendered and began employing Irish Catholics, too.'

'I reckoned it was business,' Evie murmured. 'Look, Mrs Galloway, I'll have to be off home now. Me sister's not feelin' up to the mark.'

'On Saturday,' said Libby, 'you'll have more to worry you than a sick sister. If the procession turns right at the top of Wedderburn Road then more than the Harp will go up in flames. The sheriff will read the Riot Act and the soldiers will arrive to support the police, and it's you who'll suffer.'

'Me?' said Evie, more alarmed than ever.

'Everyone who wears the Green, and even some of those who don't,' Libby said. 'If someone did warn you what to expect, then that person knows precisely what's being planned.'

'Did someone tell you, Evie?' Father Fingle said. 'Someone who might know?'

Evie glanced over her shoulder at Mr Maizie who sat at the reins of the carriage at the kerb. He was watching her, head raised. She had given her promise to a man she admired, a man who had held her in his arms, but, it seemed, that promise had already been broken. She glanced too at Nolly, he of the hidden depths, and had a fleeting vision of him lying dead in the street.

'Someone did tell me,' she said. 'Someone in the know.'

'Who was it, Evie?' the priest said gently.

'He made me promise not to tell you his name.'

'It was my damned fool of a brother wasn't it?' Libby said.

And Evie, knowing the game was up, said, 'Aye.'

The mechanical fan was a well-made object with fly-wheels and ratchets and a stout mahogany handle that Benjamin had polished to a high shine. The copper blade did no more than stir the sluggish air, however, and a few seconds of furious cranking produced only more heat. Benjamin had bought the device from a pop-shop by the docks and it had lain untouched on a shelf for several years. Now, clutching the object like a posy, he went upstairs to present it to Clare, and to discover why she had stayed home when the rest of the family had gone off to church.

The old tenement was as hot as a baker's oven. Most of the doors in the building were propped open. The door of the McKennas' flat was ajar.

He knocked tentatively.

'Who's is it? Who's there?'

'It's Benjamin, Clare. What's wrong?'

'I'm poorly.'

He put the fan down on the stoup and stepped through the lobby into the smothering heat of the kitchen. Small wonder that the girl was sick. Eyes half closed, mouth open, she lay on the larger of the beds, covered only by a sheet. Her hair, unbound, formed damp little curlicues across her neck and shoulders.

'Are you fevered, my dear?' Benjamin asked.

'Hot, I'm hot.'

He came to the side of the bed and placed his hand on her brow. Her skin was moist but she did not seem to be burning.

He said, 'Have you vomited?'

'I tried, but nothin' came up.'

'Do you still feel queasy?'

'No, not now.'

He closed his fingers lightly upon her wrist as he had seen the doctor do to his old man when his old man had come down with miner's spit.

'Ah!' he said sagely. 'Ah-hah!'

'What, what is it?'

'You don't seem to have a fever.'

Crouching by the bed, he continued to hold her hand. Clare closed her eyes as if his touch soothed her. He felt the soft, plump pad at the base of her thumb and calluses, not too horny, along the finger joints. He squeezed her hand gently as if to reassure her that he meant no harm.

She opened her eyes and gave him a wan smile. 'Water,' she said weakly. 'From the jug. The tap's dried up again.'

He released her hand, went to the sink, found the jug, poured water into a cup and brought the cup to her. Kneeling, he lifted her head. The water wetted her lips, and her tongue, like that of a cat, curled as she sipped. His hand slipped between the pillow and damp sheet and he realised that she was naked. He fanned his fingers across her shoulder blades and drew her up, the sheet clinging to her breasts like cheesecloth. He thought of the coal-heaver and what the coal-heaver had done to her and how he might do the same to her now, when she was too weak to fend him off. He got up once more, went to the sink and fetched a bowl of water and a towel. He dipped the end of the towel into the water and bathed her face with it. She sighed again and, before he could stop her, peeled down the top sheet and, catching his hand, brought it to her breast.

'Do you like me, Benjamin?'

'Yes,' he said thickly. 'Yes, Clare, I like you very much.'

'Well, you can't have me,' she said. 'I'm not for you.'

'I could take you,' Benjamin said. 'Take you, an' nothin' to stop me.'

'But you won't, will you?'

'No,' he said. 'I won't.'

'Sure an' I think you love me,' Clare McKenna said.

Benjamin, warily drawing back, said, 'Yes, I think I probably do.'

Paddy Maizie had long ago grown used to Libby's outbursts. He liked it when she stalked about the office on those long legs of hers with her hair flying in all directions, her arms waving and that damned ebony crucifix bobbing against her chest hard enough to leave bruises. He had never seen Libby Galloway's chest, of course, and never would. Whatever tales were told about him, Paddy was a man of principle. He might dress like a dandy and be as handsome as a fallen angel but he did not care to share his nigh perfect self with women other than his plump wife, Nuala, who had married him in all good faith and to whom, through good times and bad, he had remained resolutely faithful.

Now and then he had cast a speculative eye over the young tarts who plied their trade in his yard and he had been fond of some of the girls who had drifted through the Harp, but he had never given in to his urges and had preserved not only his integrity but his pride. He remained, as it were, a great deceiver who did not have to expend one ounce of energy maintaining his reputation as a rake. Women adored him; men admired him; his wife, children and horses loved him – and the rest, as far as Patrick Maizie was concerned, was jam.

'What's botherin' you now, my love?' he asked.

'My brother, my damned brother,' Libby snapped.

'Which particular brother would that be?'

'Both of them. They're as bad as each other,' Libby said. 'On the one hand Willy is conniving to turn Saturday's walk into a pitched battle and, on the other, Russell has betrayed his sworn oath by telling us of Willy's plans.'

'Russell didn't tell us; he told the Irish girl.'

'The Irish girl, the Irish girl!' Libby ranted. 'Good God, Patrick, I've had just about enough of these people. Immigrants are one thing but infiltrators are quite another.'

'Infiltrators?' said Paddy, arching an eyebrow.

He was sprawled on the ottoman, sipping coffee and smoking a cigarette. It was raining outside, pouring in fact. A high wind lashed the empty yard and made the tiles chatter, but the office was remarkably cosy.

'You know what I mean,' Libby said. 'They come here, find work and *infiltrate* themselves into the community, *our* community.'

'I thought you liked the Irish,' said Paddy.

'I didn't expect my brother to take up with one of them.'

'It's hardly a capital crime havin' a fancy for a sweet young thing,' said Paddy. 'It ain't your brother you're worried about, is it? It's Pin throwin' herself at the big man.'

'How can you sit there, grinning like a Buddha,' Libby said, rapidly changing the subject, 'when the Harp might go up in flames.'

'The Harp won't go up in flames,' said Paddy. 'Heck, if this rain keeps up the beggers won't be able to light a match, let alone start a conflagration.'

'Patrick,' Libby said, 'have you got something up your sleeve?'

She came to the ottoman, placed one foot on the leather seat and leaned into him. Many a man would have quailed before her, but not Paddy.

'Who?' he said. 'Me?'

'Stop playing the fool, Patrick. You know as well as I do that turning out your bully-boys won't solve the problem. If blood is shed in the vicinity of the Harp the councillors will seize the opportunity to take away your liquor licence, then where will we be?'

'Act of Amendment, the year of 'sixty-two,' said Paddy. 'Good order and rule must be maintained within the house and premises; yes, I think I've heard about that one.'

'You won't be able to bribe your way out of it this time,' Libby said.

'For God's sake, Libby, don't nag me,' Paddy said. 'Plant your tail on the leather and give it a rest.' He shifted to make room for her and only when she was seated, went on, 'If anybody accuses Russell of blabbin' lodge secrets he can deny it without a blush. Nobody will believe the word of a young Irish barmaid who's infatuated with a man so far above her.'

'Is she infatuated with him?' Libby said, surprised.

'Sure and how would I be knowin' that?' said Paddy. 'After all, they say you're infatuated with me – and that's not the truth, is it, sweetheart?'

'Huh!' Libby snorted. 'No, that's not the truth.'

'It's all a grand guessing game, a riddle-me-ree,' said Paddy. 'You can prattle all you like about love and family loyalty but it comes down to money in the end. Here we are, running an orderly establishment that provides us both with a nice bit of change and your brother Russell a hole to bury his rent money in – and now the bank wants it.'

'Wilson wants it, you mean?'

'Willy needs the Harp, St Kentigern's chapel and most of the tenements in Salamanca Street to secure a massive loan from the Barony Bank, and he doesn't care who he tramples on to get it.'

'Russell won't stand for it,' said Libby.

'Russell might have no choice, my love,' Paddy informed

her. 'It's a tight corner for him as well, given that he has the harbour scheme to finance. I suspect he has every penny of his capital invested in that contract and must keep his labourers happy if he hopes to finish the work on time.'

Libby stretched out her long legs and appeared to be admiring her high-button boots. 'I suppose it was inevitable that it would come to this in the long run,' she said. 'My brothers have pulled together for the benefit of the family for as long as I can remember, but they've always been rivals.'

'Much as I'm loath to say it, sweetheart,' Paddy went on, 'my concern is with hanging on to the Harp. How you sort things out with your brothers ain't really my business.'

'I know,' Libby said.

'Which, however, doesn't mean I won't support you,' Paddy said. 'I wouldn't be where I am today if you hadn't helped me get started.'

'It was to our mutual benefit,' said Libby.

'Is that all I am to you?' said Paddy. 'A reliable source of income?'

'Not that reliable,' Libby said, giving him a dig with her elbow. 'Now, Mr Maizie, out with it. What devious plan do you have in mind to thwart the Orange brigade, not to mention my brother Wilson?'

Paddy smiled his handsome smile and, tapping the side of his nose with his forefinger, said, 'You'll see, my love, you'll see.'

In spite of Danny Doyle's sexual shenanigans, Betty Fowler continued to 'do' for Mr Belfer; that is, she stumbled downstairs every morning to rake out and set the fire, make his breakfast, sweep, dust and polish and, once every week, get down on her swollen knees to swab the linoleum.

If Benjamin was tempted to probe for details of what was taking place upstairs, he gave no sign, for he had never been in the least attracted to either of the Fowler sisters, who were both large women who reeked of babies. He was not particularly fond of Danny, either; the lean, sallow-skinned wee fellow was just too vigorous for Mr Belfer's liking. Thus, he was glad when Betty appeared with tears in her eyes and announced that Danny had signed on for another voyage and would be leaving – her phrase – on the noon tide. With much wailing and lamentation, the sisters and their children turned out in the teeming rain to wave the spry little seaman farewell.

Benjamin delivered a handshake, muttered a hollow promise to look out for the sisters and the offspring then retreated hastily into his room to count the money that Danny had given him to cover a half year's rent in advance.

If there was one thing Benjamin enjoyed it was counting money. For a chap more used to dealing in tarnished coins, banknotes were a special treat. He counted them once, arranged them according to denomination, counted them again, then, just for amusement, laid them out on the table like a fortune-teller's cards and placed on top of each a single silver shilling taken from the metal cashbox he kept hidden beneath the sink.

What better way to pass a dismal summer's afternoon than playing with cash, Benjamin thought, and, digging into the box, brought out a handful of coppers to decorate the table top further. It was all very artistic, very creative, and he crooned happily to himself while the clocks ticked and the fire hissed and the rain beat down upon the windowpane.

He was so absorbed that he did not hear movement in the close until someone knocked at the door. He reared up and looped an arm over the edge of the table as if he feared that some unseen force might suck away his profits.

'*Who is it? Who's there?*' he called out.

'It's Clare, Mr Belfer. Sure an' if it's not convenient . . .'

'*Yes,*' he said; then, '*No. Wait,*' and swept the coins and banknotes into the metal cashbox and stuffed it hastily under the sink.

'I'll call back another time, shall I?' said Clare.

'I'm comin', just comin',' Benjamin cried. 'Hold on.'

He slicked a hand over his hair, tucked in his shirt, hitched up his trousers, and threw open the door.

'Well,' he said, 'if this ain't a pleasant surprise.'

'I brought you some pancakes,' the girl said, 'hot from the pan.'

'How thoughtful,' Benjamin said.

'You were kind to me when I was sick,' Clare said. 'It's just a bit of a thank-you, that's all.'

She held a plate in both hands, a plate mounded with soft, pale brown pancakes that gave off wisps of steam. Benjamin glanced down at it, then up at Clare. She was no longer weak and pallid. She had done herself up in a clean skirt and a blouse with lace at the collar. She had fixed her hair with ribbon and three or four gold-headed pins. She had dabbed some powder on her cheeks, too, and was that a touch of rouge upon her lips? he wondered.

'Are you not goin' to be askin' me in?' she said.

Benjamin swallowed the lump in his throat.

'Of course,' he said and, stepping back a pace, allowed her to enter his dwelling place.

It had been almost five months since Clare had peered into Mr Belfer's kitchen. It was not quite as she remembered it, not spacious or shiny, and the shelves were littered not with valuable antiques but with what amounted to junk. It did have a large sink, though, brass gas-fittings and a big polished stove, linoleum on the floor, a comfortable-looking tub-chair and, at the rear, a bed recess so deep that it was almost like another room. It was also clean, not antiseptically clean like Harry's room, but much cleaner and tidier than a bachelor's room had a right to be, even with Betty Fowler coming in.

Benjamin put an arm about her waist and guided her to the chair.

He seemed nervous, she thought, or perhaps just eager to get his hands on her. He helped her into the chair and stood by her, his belly poking over the chair's curved arm.

'I don't need your help,' she said. 'I'm quite well now.'

'Good,' he said. 'I'm relieved to hear it.'

'Everybody's feelin' better now the hot spell's over.'

'Yes,' he said. 'We are all the better for a drop o' rain.'

If she had suggested that the moon was made of green cheese he would probably have agreed with her.

'I hope I'm not keepin' you from anythin' important,' she said.

'Important.' He shot a glance in the direction of the sink. 'No, nothing important, my dear. Indeed, it's fortuitous you've called on me this afternoon since you've been much on my mind.'

'Have I?' Clare said. 'In what way have I been on your mind?'

'What I said about harbourin' affection – considerable affection . . .'

'Did you say affection, Mr Belfer?'

'Benjamin.'

'Benjamin: I don't recall that word enterin' our conversation.'

'Well, it was said – an' I apologise for it.'

'Did you not mean it, then?'

'It was meant most sincerely but under the circumstances it should not have been said out loud.'

'Under what circumstances?'

'When you were sick.'

'I'm not sick now, Benjamin.'

'No,' he said, 'no more you are.'

'What exactly is it that needs an apology?'

He continued to stand close by, staring at her bosom. She could hardly blame him. She had grown so opulent in that direction that even Nolan had remarked upon it. For the best part of a month she had blinded herself to the signs and symptoms. In the past couple of days, however, it had become apparent that Harry Fairfield had left her with something more tangible than a broken heart to contend with, though she was unwilling, just yet, to pay a midwife or a doctor to confirm her condition.

'What *did* you say, Benjamin? Didn't you say you loved me?'

'In a manner of speakin', I did.'

'Didn't you say you wanted me?'

'I might have said somethin' of the sort.'

'I was a poor weak girl; you could have taken me where I lay, sure an' what would I have been able to do about it?'

'Oh!' Benjamin said. 'How can you think that of me, Clare? I'm a gentleman for one thing an' would never take advantage . . .'

'You may be a gentleman, Benjamin – I don't doubt that you are – but you're also the landlord's agent an' have a right to take what you want with nobody to deny you.'

'The law's there to deny me,' Benjamin reminded her.

'The law!' Clare said. 'Aren't you the law in Salamanca Street? Aren't you the man with the money?'

'Money?' Benjamin said.

'Enough money to look after a young woman properly.'

He knew she had been with Harry. He had no doubt heard enough of what had gone on upstairs to realise that she was no longer the frightened virgin who had arrived off the boat from Cork.

A month ago, before the orphans' picnic, he might have forced himself upon her and been reasonably certain she would keep her mouth shut for fear of what he might do if she squealed. But she had friends now, friends who had more influence than Benjamin Belfer might imagine. There was more to it, though, more – and less – to Benjamin Belfer than met the eye. She had guessed that the bully was a coward, the braggart no better than a timid boy.

She had promised her mother that she'd marry a Catholic. She had promised her mother that she would remain pure. The slavering old priest on the shore of the lake had put paid to that, and Nolan, her brother, showing off his parts, and Harry upstairs: Harry who had taught her that there was more to love than love itself, and who had shown her where her clout lay. If she *was* carrying a child there were worse things to do about it than set her cap at a man who would treat her well and keep her in comfort and ease.

'Do you mean me?' said Benjamin.

'I don't know,' said Clare. 'Do I?'

He crouched down, his knees cracking a little, and spoke softly. 'If this is a negotiation, my dearest, then there's a reason for it. The reason, far as I can see, is that you're in desperate need of a husband. An' if you are in need of a husband there can only be one reason for that.' He laid a hand across her belly. 'How far are you gone, Clare?'

'I'm not sure,' Clare said.

'Not far, though, not far?'

'No, not far.'

He sprang to his feet, and clapped his plump hands. 'Hah!' he said. 'Hah, yes! Ideal!'

'Ideal?' said Clare. 'It's not ideal for me.'

'I know I'm not what you'd choose for a husband if you had time on your side an' nothing swellin' your belly,' Benjamin said, 'but you're in sore need of a man to take care of you right now, an' I'm willing to be that man.'

'Benjamin, I'm carryin' Harry Fairfield's child,' Clare reminded him.

'That's all to the good, far as I'm concerned,' Benjamin said. 'But there are things we have to do before we get down to makin' arrangements.'

'Things?' said Clare, frowning. 'What sort o' things?'

'Things,' said Benjamin, 'like meetin' my mother.'

14

Bands from three lodges competed for attention as the marchers converged on Riverside Road. The official parade, four hundred strong, turned into Wedderburn Road, heading for the rally on Glasgow Green. Fifty hand-picked men broke off, however, and swung into the top of Salamanca Street. Moist air muffled the flutes and the only sounds that Evie could make out at first were the thud-thud-thud of a bass drum and the stutter of kettles.

Onlookers lined the main thoroughfares for, in a dreary month, the Orange walk offered a welcome diversion. South of Riverside Road, however, the streets were all but deserted as the jumbled cacophony of bugles and flutes, pipes and drums drifted closer through the misty grey veils of rain.

Bob stood outside the door of the Harp, arms folded, head turned towards the sound of the drums. Chiffin was stationed at the rear of the building to keep watch on the office. No shutters had been put up, no bars upon the doors, for Mr Maizie had decided that he would not be browbeaten into closing his premises. So far, though, there had been no sign of Mr Maizie and it crossed Evie's mind that perhaps the proprietor had taken cold feet and had abandoned his staff to their fate, whatever that fate might be.

She stood outside the pub with Mr Draper and the cook. The cook had fought many a pitched battle with the Proddies in his younger days and had brought along a sack to cover his head and a pitchfork to lean on. Evie wondered where Mr

Maizie's bully-boys had got to. They were certainly cutting it fine.

At St Kentigern's Father Fingle, quite alone and unprotected, leaned on the gate. He had refused offers of support from those aged parishioners who were willing, if not eager, to protect the church from harm. Cissie had gone to the bakery, Nolan to work on the wall. The coal yard had been closed and Jock Macpherson had taken refuge with Clare, Mrs Jardine, the Fowler sisters and their children in Harry Fairfield's old room which lay to the rear of the building where, Mr Belfer said, windows were unlikely to be shattered.

It was about half past eleven when the parade finally hove into view, a noisy, colourful display, with men and boys strutting to the beat of the drums, the skirl of bagpipes and the wet, warbling notes of the flutes.

There was still no sign of Patrick Maizie, or his hired hands.

Evie said, 'Where are they?'

Bob said, 'You'll see.'

The timing was exact to the minute. As soon as the platoon of trouble-makers swung into Salamanca Street, a crocodile of small children, led by a nun, appeared from the lane by the graveyard. The children were excited by the clamour and not in the least afraid. They skipped after the sister and, just as orderly as the marchers, filed through the gate past Father Fingle and on up the path to the church.

Confronted by the orphans, the bearers of the banners faltered, the marchers piled up behind them, the drum beats became irregular, bagpipes deflated, and the solitary bugler lost his lip.

Evie ran out into the road for a better view.

At first it was unclear what was happening. Hasty discussions took place among the leaders of the break-away and the solitary horseman that the superintendent of police had appointed to keep order. A commanding figure in his tall helmet and blue cape, the officer rode forward to the gate of the church and, leaning from the saddle, exchanged words with Father Fingle while the orphan flock chirruped and cheered, for to them the appearance of a mounted policeman was all part of the entertainment.

Evie watched the copper ride back into the cluster of marchers. She expected the baton to come out and violence to erupt but with the arrival of four gentlemen in toppers the matter was swiftly resolved, the platoon reassembled, banners went up and the procession advanced once more. Hugging the side of the street, it gave St Kentigern's a wide berth, as if, Evie thought, small children offered more defence than a battalion of militia. The main parade continued to stream past on Riverside Road but a crowd of curious onlookers crossed into Salamanca Street to see what was going on there.

Behind the railings of St Kentigern's, the orphans cheered and jumped up and down while Father Fingle fingered the beads of his rosary, well aware that one stone, one handful of muck, one fool in Green leaping from the crowd would be sufficient excuse for retaliation and bloodshed.

The break-away was a hundred yards short of the Harp when the door of the pub opened and Mr Paddy Maizie stepped forth. He was followed by a second line of orphans, a dozen or so in all, who had been shepherded through from the yard by Libby and Seang Pin and who, cheering and waving enthusiastically, occupied the pavement in front of the pub.

Flanked by Mrs Galloway, Paddy Maizie and a Chinese girl, the odd-looking crew was too passive to pose a threat to hard-headed Orangemen who, thoroughly confused and frustrated now, had no choice but to tramp past the Harp without raising so much as a finger let alone a fist.

'Will they come back here after the rally?' Libby asked.

'It's possible,' Paddy said, 'but I doubt it. It was supposed to be a show, you see, a public demonstration. If I'd brought out my boys and a riot had ensued we'd have been blamed for it, which would have played straight into your brother's hands.'

'Did you apply to the archbishop's office?' Libby said. 'I can't imagine the archbishop agreeing to allow his orphans to be put in danger just to keep your pub from being burned to the ground.'

'I can be very persuasive when needs arise,' Paddy said.

'You're not going to tell me how you did it, are you?'

'Nope,' Paddy Maizie said smugly.

The parade had gone off along the road to Glasgow Green where members of lodges from all across the city were gathering to hear fiery speeches from spurious doctors and ministers imported from Ulster and, bad weather notwithstanding, generally have a high old time.

The orphans of Our Lady were already having a high old time. Paddy had laid on ginger beer and chocolate-coated biscuits and the cook, a man of many talents, had brought out a melodeon and was singing some old sea shanties that were just risqué enough to amuse the kiddies without sending the sister into a swoon. Chiffin's little hat had been 'stolen'. Evie and Seang Pin, aided by several giggling wee girls, were intent on making sure that he wouldn't get it back without a fight, while Father Fingle and Bob Draper doggedly guarded the beer engines from sneak attack by young Duncan Calder and his cohorts.

'Did it cost you money?' Libby asked.

'Stop fishing, sweetheart,' Paddy said. 'If you must know, it cost me a lot more than money. The trick worked this time but it won't work again.'

'They're after you, Patrick, aren't they?' Libby said.

'Sure an' they're after all of us,' said Paddy.

'But they won't get us, will they?' Libby said.

'Not if I can help it,' Paddy said and, snapping his fingers, told Chiffin to stop playing the fool and fetch out another tray of biscuits.

Benjamin told her that he owned a spacious flat in Bellingham Place and that soon after their wedding they would leave Salamanca Street and go to live there.

'How will you make your collections?' Clare asked.

'I'll come back to Riverside two or three times a week.'

'Won't Mr Blackstock object?'

'Provided the rent money comes in on time he won't say a dickey-bird. In fact, we might not bother to tell him.'

'Evie's bound to let it slip,' Clare said.

'Evie? What does she have to do with Mr Blackstock?'

'She's his friend.'

'Is she, do you say?' said Benjamin. 'Well, well, well!'

'Anyroads,' said Clare, 'I haven't agreed to marry you yet.'

'You're just bein' coy, aren't you?' Benjamin said.

'Sure an' I am not bein' coy,' Clare told him. 'Since your proposal came out o' the blue, I need time to think about it.'

'My proposal might've come out of the blue,' said Benjamin, 'but the baby in your belly didn't.' He paused. 'You're not still hopin' Fairfield will come back, are you?'

'No,' said Clare. 'Harry won't come back.'

'If he did, though, what would you do?' Benjamin said.

'I'd send him away with a flea in his ear,' said Clare.

She hadn't told Benjamin that Harry already had a wife; the less Benjamin knew, the better. She was by no means convinced that she wanted him for a husband. She had not forgotten how wicked he could be and she was puzzled by his willingness to raise another man's child. She was, however, impressed by the elegant sandstone terrace of Bellingham Place, by its polished oak doors and shiny white-tiled closes.

'Do you really own a house here, Benjamin?' she asked.

'An apartment,' Benjamin said.

'Where did you get the money to buy such a place?'

'I put down half the purchase price an' arranged a mortgage for the balance. Mr Blackstock put in a good word on my behalf.' He took off his hat and ran a hand over his hair. 'Well, here we are, my dear. Now, remember what we talked about, what you're to tell my mother. Please, do not let me down.'

Then, before Clare could protest, he rang the doorbell.

If Clare was impressed by the flat she was a deal less impressed by Benjamin's mother whose notion of a warm welcome consisted of a snort of derision and whose sole concession to hospitality was to let Clare enter the drawing-room. The lamps had not been lighted dismal. The old man in the wing chair, Benjamin's father, did not so much as turn his head when Clare was introduced and continued to stare blankly from the window.

If Benjamin was anxious to please Clare, it soon became clear that he was even more anxious to please his mother. She almost felt sorry for Benjamin who, try as he might, seemed incapable of wringing a kind word, or any word at all, from the old woman. He stumbled through introductions, feigned heartiness, perpetrated a lame joke or two, stood by his mother's chair, knelt by her side, enquired after her health and asked if there was anything he could do to make her more comfortable; to all of which the old woman merely grunted and cast black looks in Clare's direction as if the small sorrows that accompanied old age had been magnified by her presence.

At first Clare remained meek as a mouse and pretended to respect the woman's great age and salt-of-the-earth rudeness but then, without asking permission, she got to her feet and toured the room, looking up at the gasoliers, down at the Turkish rugs, at flock wallpaper, couches, footstools and armchairs. When she reached the window bay she peered down at the crown of the old man's head as if he too were part of the furnishings.

'How old is he?' she enquired.

'Eighty,' Benjamin answered.

'An' her?' said Clare. 'Your mam?'

'Eighty-one.'

'By the look o' them they're not long for this world,' said Clare. 'It'll make no matter if you move them out.'

'Move them out?' Benjamin said, bewildered.

'Is that not what you said, my love?' Clare went on. 'Ain't it your intention to transfer them to your house in Salamanca Street after we marry?' She floated back from the window. 'We'll need a lot of space when the kiddies begin to arrive.' She held out her hand. 'Come, dearest, show me the rest of the flat so we can pick the best room for a nursery.'

She yanked Benjamin towards the door before he could protest and from the corner of her eye watched the old woman sit upright.

'Kiddies?' Mother Belfer said. 'Nursery?'

'Oh, there you are,' Clare said. 'I thought you were asleep.' She glanced up at Benjamin. 'Have I spoken out o' turn? Have you not told your mother about the baby yet?'

'Benjamin,' the old woman said, 'what's goin' on?'

'Nothing, Mother, nothing,' Benjamin said. 'Nothing's settled yet. It's all still up in the air.'

'Up in the air?' said Clare. 'That's no way to talk about our baby.'

'Your baby?' Mother Belfer rasped. 'He hasn't given you a baby?'

'How did it get there, then?' said Clare. 'It's not a 'maculate conception, you know. My Benjamin did his bit, more than his bit, I'd say. Now he's got to pay the price an' marry me. Ain't that right, my love?'

'It – I mean – aye, damn it, that's right,' said Benjamin.

The old woman groped for her stick and hoisted herself to her feet. She hobbled across the room to the window bay and, poking her husband with the stick, shouted, 'Do you hear, Daddy? Do you hear what he's done to us?'

Daddy did not answer. Even when his wife struck him across the shoulder, he seemed unaware that he was being asked a question.

'Benjamin's knocked up this Irish bitch,' Mother Belfer went on, 'now he's goin' tae throw us out into the street. Daddy, are you listenin' tae me?'

'Leave him alone,' Benjamin said.

'What – are – you – goin' – tae – do – about it?' the old woman shouted, each word accompanied by another blow from the stick.

'Mother, for God's sake!' Benjamin exploded and, tearing himself away from Clare, strode across the room and caught the stick as it rose again.

For half a minute mother and son wrestled for possession of the stick until, with a cry, the old woman released her hold, tumbled over the arm of the chair and landed upon her husband, who let out a piercing scream and with a sudden shocking burst of energy surged to his feet, hurled her to the floor and began to stamp on and kick at her, not in fury but in panic.

At first Clare was paralysed by the black depths that her malicious teasing had uncovered, then, while Benjamin continued to struggle with his father, she ran across the room, wrapped her arms about the old man and pulled him down into the chair again.

'There, there,' she crooned soothingly, 'hush now, it's all right, we're here, Benjamin's here, hush, hush,' and, to her relief felt his bony limbs slacken and become limp, saw his head tilt back until he was staring up at her, not vacantly but with something that approached recognition.

'Jeannie?' he muttered. 'Jeannie Macrae, is that you? Gi'e's a kiss, ma honey, gi'e's a kiss, ma Jean,' then reason faded, like a ship receding into fog, and he was vacant again, lost again, and Clare, very gently, let him go.

Night now, dead of night: Willy, in full trig, summoned him to rise and when he had done so led him, still clad in his nightshirt, along a narrow corridor under an arch and into a vast, shadow-filled room.

Willy held him by the hand, not the arm, and when he looked down he saw that Willy wore the red glove and that the glove was leaking blood and that his hand, too, was bloody. When he opened his mouth to speak, Willy said, sternly, 'Silence before the court,' and he saw before him the court whereof his brother spoke: John Andrew, Robert and Hughie, and, flanking them at a long, long table, the Lord Advocate and the Lord Justice Clerk and Dr Quintin Rathbone who had been on the platform at the Green that very afternoon, ranting in the rain. Rathbone looked dry enough now, though, with his mouth full of salt bacon and a glass of claret in his fist.

Rathbone wiped his mouth with a napkin and bellowed, 'Have you, Russell Blackstock, builder and constructor in the city of Glasgow, not undertaken a binding oath and engagement to conceal our secret ceremonies and transactions, to conceal and not discover the rites associated, murder and treason not excepted, or an oath or engagement of similar import? Answer to the court or forever hold your tongue.'

He opened his mouth but no words came.

'He did, damn me, he did,' he heard Willy say. 'I was there when he took the vows. I'm always there when he takes his vows. I have seen this boy do things you would not believe, sir, but we are no longer bound by boyhood oaths. It is his word against mine and it is my word that will prevail.'

'The jury is empanelled and the case has come to trial,'

said a voice that sounded as if it might belong to Percival Orpington.

The men at the table nodded and, one after another, said, 'Aye, aye, aye,' all solemn and hallowed.

'What is the verdict?' said the voice.

'Where is the evidence? Where is she?' said Willy. 'I was there when he was admitted to the Lodge Crosshill, Number six-three-eight, and a pistol was fired and some person unknown called out, "Put him to death," and we are called upon to do that now, sirs, for heinous crimes against his family.'

He saw John Andrew stoop and bring from beneath the table a stone jug with a candle burning in it and it was the representation of God in the midst of the burning bush and he knew that while he could bear false witness to his brother he could not bear false witness to the burning bush. He cried out but no sound came forth, for his lips were sealed with stolen kisses.

'We will read from the fourth chapter of Exodus,' Quintin Rathbone declared and thirteen lighted candles appeared upon the table and Willy blew out one of the candles and called him 'Judas' and then the Lord Advocate yelled, 'Not proven, not proven,' and there was wailing round the table and a man he had never seen before put a pistol to his head, an ancient flintlock like one Dad had kept in a drawer in the dresser in the house in Riverside, and Willy, from a great distance, cried, 'No, no,' and the faceless man squeezed the trigger.

The pistol went off with a blinding flash.

Russell sat up, sweat-drenched and terrified.

Stirring, Jane murmured, 'Russell, are you all right?'

'Yes, yes, go back to sleep,' he told her and, shaking like a leaf, disentangled himself from the sheets and staggered across the darkened room to the water closet where, kneeling, he disgorged into the bowl the remains of the ceremonial dinner that Wilson had forced him to eat and the acidic residue of the claret that had accompanied the speeches afterwards.

He knelt on the stone floor, shivering, brow resting on the rim of the bowl until everything came out, then, groaning, he got to his feet, found the basin, drank water straight from the tap and splashed his face. He fumbled a towel from the peg on the wall, dabbed his face dry, drank more water, then, still shivering, went out into the passageway.

The bedroom door was ajar.

He heard Jane snoring, lightly, but the nightmare was still with him. He could not separate it from the events of the day. Wilson had dragged him to the Green and stuck him on the platform, albeit at the back, and he had been obliged to look out over the seething mass of men and women gathered there. Afterwards, he had been Wilson's guest at a grand dinner in the Orange Hall in Glassford Street, safe from the gangs that rampaged up the High Street and, he learned later, fought hand-to-hand with gangs of other persuasions in Partick.

All he could think about as he sat there listening to Rathbone rationalise the irrational was how he had protected his folk, his labourers, by breaking the seal of silence. Nightmares were a small price to pay for behaving honourably and decently; honourably and decently, that is, for a hypocrite whose loyalties were not only divided but had been chopped into little pieces by circumstances over which he had no formal control.

He loitered in the passageway, then, looking up, saw that dawn had broken. Summer, of course, July: dawn arrived early even when the sky was heavy with cloud. He shambled down the passageway to the window, a tall, well-constructed window. Hood, jamb and flush sill had been replaced last autumn and the spider-leg cracks that had marred the old mortar facings had all been repaired: Willy's boys had done a good job.

It was pretty across the river, the sky soft and milky before the sun spread light over the city: Sunday, a day of rest, everything quiet and tranquil.

He was cold, though, the damp nightshirt cooling on his skin.

He must return to bed soon, snuggle against Jane, let her warmth warm him enough to sleep again; sleep and, with luck, not dream of Willy, ancient rites, broken vows, or of Evie, the pert little Irish girl, who was lying asleep in a tousled bed in his tenement in Riverside.

'Oh, damn!' he said. 'Damn, damn, damn!' and holding a finger tight to his lips, hurried back to the water closet to be sick again.

'Marriage?' Father Fingle said. 'But the young man is married already.'

'Not marriage to Harry,' Clare said. 'Marriage to Mr Belfer.'

'Belfer? Benjamin Belfer?' said Father Fingle.

'The same,' said Clare.

'But he's . . . I mean, are you sure this is a wise choice, Clare?'

'It's not a matter o' choice,' said Clare. 'It's a matter o' necessity.'

'You're carrying a child,' Father Fingle stated.

'I am.'

'Not Belfer's child?'

'No.'

'Does Belfer know you're expecting?'

'He does.'

Father Fingle stroked his chin or, rather, rubbed his hand against stubble for his shave that morning had been hurried. 'I take it his offer to marry you isn't an act of altruism.'

'Sure an' I don't know what that means.'

'It means he's not doing it out of the kindness of his heart.'

'He says he loves me,' said Clare. 'Fact, I think he does love me.'

'Have you engaged in acts of congress with Mr Belfer?'

'Pardon?'

'Sexual intercourse.'

'No,' said Clare. 'Benjamin isn't that way inclined.'

Doubts on that score Father Fingle kept to himself. He was disturbed by the young woman's announcement and her request for advice if, that is, she was actually asking for advice and not just twisting him round her finger. He had taken Clare McKenna for an innocent who had fallen into carnal sin through no fault of her own: now he was not so sure.

'I cannot marry you in church, Clare,' he said.

'Why not?'

'Belfer – Mr Belfer will not agree to it.'

'He'll marry me anywhere I choose,' said Clare.

'Perhaps so, but will he agree to uphold the conditions that our faith requires?' Father Fingle said. 'Will he, for instance, allow the children of the union to be raised Catholic?'

'Benjamin isn't Orange, you know.'

'I don't know what he is,' the father said. 'Do you? Does he?'

'Is it because I'm a sinner?' Clare said. 'Is that why you won't do it? Mary the Magdalene was a sinner, an' Jesus said—'

'Enough,' Father Fingle snapped, with a rare flash of annoyance. 'I won't be lectured by a girl who . . .' Tutting, he walked several paces away from her to give himself time to cool down.

When, after morning service, Clare McKenna had requested a few minutes of his time in private, he had taken her out to the graveyard behind the church. The graveyard was all that he had by way of a garden in which to stroll and rest his mind from turmoil. Few folk came to visit the dead in St Kentigern's. Most of the relatives had drifted away or were, he supposed, dead themselves and buried elsewhere; how lonely the untended graves seemed, how lonely the bones that lay beneath. Here he had pondered the mystery of Mary the Mother, and the inexplicable fact that if Joseph and Mary were husband and wife only in appearance, then, by the law and dogma of the Roman Church, which determined that marriage was a sacrament, the holy couple were themselves recreant, and sinners of a sort.

When he turned back, the girl was waiting for him, hands on hips, her eyes dark with anger. 'Tell me, Father,' she said, 'do you think it's better for my baby to be born out o' wedlock an' never have a legal father than for me to be married in the church?'

On the spur of the moment he could think of no reasonable answer. He shook his head and stammered, 'In the sight of God . . .'

'I don't think God gives a tinker's curse about me. His eye may be on the sparrow, like the Book tells us,' Clare said, 'but when it comes down to it, sure an' I have my doubts that He ever looks my way at all.'

'Clare! Oh, Clare!' Father Fingle exclaimed. 'Marriage is a sign of fidelity between—'

'Aye, you've given me a faithful answer, Father. For that I'll thank you, if for nothin' else,' Clare said. 'You'll not be bothered by me again; not by me, nor my baby, nor my husband, when he becomes my husband. If it takes the rearin' o' a bastard to make you happy, you can keep your Church, an' your God. I'll get on with it on my own.'

'Clare, wait, please . . .' the priest cried.

But she was too quick for him and, lifting her skirts, ran out through the iron gate into the street before anyone, or anything, could stop her.

* * *

They did not hold hands but now and then, when her steps failed to match his longer stride, their elbows touched and they flinched a little and, pretending that nothing had happened, continued with the airy conversation that Pin had started and that he, Nolan McKenna, day-labourer, was doing his best to finish.

'Can you read?' she asked him.

'Now what sort o' question is that? I can read with me eyes closed.'

'Can you write, too?'

'I can write in pen or pencil – or blue chalk, if you like.'

'Count in numbers?' Pin said.

'One to a hundred, in inches, feet an' yards.'

'Do you know your Catechism?'

'Inside to out. In Latin.'

'Ho, ho,' Pin said. 'Now, my man, that is not the truth.'

'Nah,' he admitted ruefully. 'Not the whole truth, any-roads.'

'You have no Latin, do you?'

'Only enough for the mass.'

'Latin is not important,' Pin said.

'Not for a digger it's not,' said Nolan. 'Do you have the Latin?'

'Some,' said Pin modestly.

'And the Greek?'

'A little Greek, too,' she admitted.

'I thought they didn't teach them things to girls.'

'They teach all sorts of things to girls these days,' Pin said.

'I never had but a year or two at school,' said Nolan. 'Me old man taught us what we needed to know, mostly religion an' politics.'

'Radical politics?' said Pin.

'Pointless bloody politics,' said Nolan, then, touching her arm, added, 'If you'll pardon me language.'

'I notice you do not say pointless bloody religion?'

'Well, religion can be pretty bloody, too,' said Nolan.

It was at Pin's insistence that they were walking together down Salamanca Street. Paddy Maizie's rig was behind them, the horse ambling in the shafts, the wheels of the carriage turning slowly. Libby was perched on the front seat by Paddy's side and, being a little short-sighted, peered ferociously at the couple on the pavement in front of her, a scrutiny of which Nolan was blissfully unaware and that Seang Pin did her best to ignore.

'Do you like children?' Pin went on.

'I suppose you could say I do.'

'They seem to like you.'

'Do they now?' said Nolan. 'Maybe 'cause I'm so big.'

'That's true,' said Pin. 'Children do like big things.'

'How about you?' said Nolan. 'Do you like big things?'

Caught off guard, Pin said, 'My opinion is of no consequence since I am no longer a child.'

'You're not much older than a child,' said Nolan.

'I am, indeed I am. I am a . . .' She checked herself. 'Be that as it may, Nolly, I have been delegated to ask if you would consider becoming a teacher in our Sunday school.'

'Your Sunday school?' said Nolan.

'St Kentigern's Sunday school.'

'What would I be expected to do?'

'Keep order,' Pin said.

'Aye, I could do that,' said Nolan, 'but I'm none too sure I could do much along the teachin' line.'

'You would set an example.'

'Hoh!' said Nolan, hiding his pleasure. 'Fine example I'd make with me rough tongue an' rough hands.'

'The children of this parish are well used to rough tongues,' said Pin. 'It's not the tongue or the hands that matter; it's what's in the heart.'

'Well, I've a rough heart too, if the truth be known,' Nolan said. 'Who told you to ask me to do this thing? Was it the father?'

'He agreed to it. It was my Aunt Libby's suggestion originally.'

'Are Sunday school teachers that hard to find?' said Nolan.

'In the Riverside, they are,' said Pin.

'How many children in the class?'

'Eighty to ninety.'

'How often?'

'Every Sunday; three o'clock to five.'

'Will I have to pray?' said Nolan.

'You will.'

'Will I have to read to them?'

'On occasions.'

'Will you be there?'

'I will.'

'Every Sunday?' Nolan asked.

'Every Sunday,' Pin answered.

'Then sign me on,' said Nolan.

'Look at them,' said Libby. 'They can hardly keep their hands off each other.'

'They're young, sweetheart,' Paddy said.

'I should never have agreed to Pin's suggestion that we invite that common fellow to become a Sunday school teacher.'

'You don't really think he's a common feller, do you?'

Libby snorted ruefully. 'You know me too well, Patrick Maizie.'

'When you were Pin's age, were you never in love?'

'Pin's age?' said Libby. 'No, I was older – and far too reserved to go strolling down the street with him in broad daylight.'

'Better broad daylight than in the dark,' Paddy remarked.

Libby dug an elbow into his ribs. 'Why do you always have to be right?'

'I'm an Irishman; we're always right,' said Paddy, 'even when we're wrong. Have you seen your brother yet – Willy, I mean?'

'He's expected for lunch today. He'll not be in the best of tempers,' Libby said. 'In fact, if the state of my brother Russell is anything to go by, he'll be like a bear with a sore head.'

'You'll have heard there was rioting in Partick?'

'Father Fingle mentioned it. Much damage?'

'Broken heads, mainly,' said Paddy. 'Broken windows, too.'

'We were fortunate to escape unscathed,' said Libby. 'Perhaps fortunate isn't the best word. You did well to extricate us from involvement, Patrick. One mounted policeman sent to control that rabble – what an insult that is. I'll be having words with Willy about it, I tell you.'

'I reckon Willy will be havin' words with you,' Paddy said. 'He's not bringing the famous Dr Rathbone to lunch, by any chance?'

'Dear God!' said Libby. 'I hope not.'

'Put the wind up you proper, didn't I?' Paddy laughed. 'Have no fear, sweetheart; Rathbone went back to Belfast on the night boat, drunk as a lord and singin' like a linnet, by all accounts.'

'How *do* you know these things?' said Libby.

'Wee birdies tell me,' Paddy said.

Drawing on the check rein, he brought the carriage to a halt twenty yards shy of the couple at the close-mouth.

'Now,' he said, 'is young Nolan going to throw her over his shoulder an' carry her upstairs, do you think, or are they just going to stand there gazing into each other's eyes till the cows come home?'

'Neither,' Libby said and, rising from the bench, called out to her ward to make her farewells, for there would be the devil to pay if, today of all days, they happened to be late for lunch.

15

Cissie waited outside the church for ten minutes then set off home on her own. Nolan was preoccupied with the Chinese girl and Clare had gone to talk to Father Fingle and she had no idea where Evie was. She had almost reached the close when Clare came rushing up behind her in floods of tears, threw herself into Cissie's arms and blurted out a garbled story about babies, marriage and the church.

Cissie led the sobbing girl into her ground-floor room, seated her in the one and only armchair and listened sympathetically to Clare's tale of woe.

'As if that wasn't bad enough, Aunt Cissie,' Clare concluded, 'we lied to you. We're not related. It was just a trick to get a place to stay an' a hot meal. We'd never even heard o' Eamon Cassidy till we came here. We stole the name off his gravestone an' made the rest up.'

Cissie patted Clare's hand. 'I've known that for ages, dearest. It didn't take me long to realise you'd never met any of Eamon's relatives. I never said anythin' because it would have had Mr Belfer crowin' like a cockerel. I thought if you stayed here long enough you'd become my family.'

'Oh, Aunt Cissie, what a mess I've made of things.'

'It's a mess that can surely be fixed, though,' Cissie said. 'Has Mr Belfer really asked you to marry him?'

'Aye,' said Clare. 'I think he needs a wife to teach his mother a lesson. The miserable old bitch leads him a merry dance.'

'I didn't know that Mr Belfer had a mother,' Cissie said. 'Where does he keep her?'

'In a lovely flat in Bellingham Place.'

'Bellingham Place!' Cissie exclaimed. 'My, my! How posh!'

'Too posh for her,' said Clare. 'His father's there too but he's not right in the head, poor chap. Benjamin says we'll move there after we're married. I'm not so sure I want to. I reckon he only wants me to take care o' the old couple.'

'In exchange, though, he'll give your baby a name.' Cissie knelt on the patch of carpet that adorned the floor in front of the hearth and looked up at Clare. 'Well, well!' she said. 'I never thought Mr Belfer had it in him.'

'Father Fingle has refused to marry us in church.'

'Is that why you're upset?'

'I promised my mam I'd only marry a Catholic.'

'If your mam were alive, she'd understand.' Cissie got to her feet. 'In any case there has to be a registry wedding for to make it legal; that's the law for us Catholics. What's really brought on the tears, Clare?'

'I thought I was a strong person,' Clare said, 'but I'm not. I've been silly an' selfish, an' now I'm bein' punished for it.'

'Babies aren't a punishment,' said Cissie. 'Babies are a blessin'.'

'Aye, if they have a father.'

'Mr Belfer will make a better father than that other one. At least Mr Belfer's got steady work an' a comfortable house, an' seems fond o' you.'

'He only wants to poke me.'

'You can't blame him for that,' said Cissie. 'It would be a dour man, indeed, who didn't want to poke a lovely lassie like yourself. What does your sister have to say to all this?'

'I haven't told Evie yet. I've told no one but Father Fingle.'

'Well, I might not be your auntie, dear,' Cissie said, 'but I'm old enough to give you advice.'

'What sort o' advice?' said Clare, with a hint of caution.

'The first thing you must do is visit Mrs Haggarty,' Cissie said. 'She's the most reliable midwife you'll find on this side o' the Clyde. She did real well by me when I was carryin'.'

'I didn't know you had children.'

'I don't,' Cissie said. 'A fault in the womb meant I couldn't bring any of my poor bairns to full term. If it hadn't been for Mrs Haggarty I'd have died that last time. Better than any doctor she is when it comes to babies.'

'She's not one o' those sort of women, is she?' said Clare.

'One o' those . . .? Oh, Lord, no!' said Cissie. 'She never misses a mass at the Immaculate Conception if she can help it, an' she does for the wives o' half the policemen in Partick. Nothin' fly-by-night about Mrs Haggarty.'

'Where will I find her?'

'Ask in the dairy at the top end o' Carpenter Street,' said Cissie. 'She lives above the shop an' her oldest boy drives the milk cart. Once she confirms what you think you know, then you can stride ahead with your plans.' The kettle on the stove hissed steam and Cissie, still talking, masked a teapot and measured out tea. 'Have you given Mr Belfer a definite answer yet? Have you promised him your hand?'

'My hand?' said Clare. 'It's not my hand he's after. I've told him I'll consider his proposal an' give him an answer real soon.'

Mrs Cassidy filled the teapot. 'If it turns out you're not expectin',' she said carefully, 'will you still marry him?'

'Do you know, Aunt Cissie,' Clare answered, 'I do believe I will.'

'But why?' Evie shouted. 'I mean, how can you even consider marryin' that fat pig after the way he treated us?'

''Cause she's in love?' Nolly suggested mildly.

''Cause she's knocked up more like,' said Evie. 'You are, aren't you, Clare? You've gone an' got yourself knocked up.'

'What if I have?' said Clare. 'It's none o' your business.'

'Is it not?' said Evie. 'Can you imagine what carin' for an infant in this place will be like? There's hardly room for the three of us as it is.'

'There's folk up in the Wedderburn sleepin' ten to a room,' said Nolan, 'so I reckon four of us could struggle through.' He came around the back of the chair and placed his hands on Clare's shoulders. 'A baby, eh? You're the sly one, Clare, not sayin' a word. When will the wee soul make an appearance?'

'January, I think.'

'That bloody Fairfield. I'd tear his eyes out if he was still here,' said Evie.

'He didn't know I was pregnant.'

'If he had,' said Evie, 'he'd have run all the faster.'

Clare said, 'Harry couldn't have married me. He already has a wife.'

'What?' Evie cried. 'Did you know that when you let him poke you?'

'No,' said Clare. 'If I had it wouldn't have made much difference.'

''Cause you was in love with him?' said Nolan.

'Love!' Evie sneered. 'Just because that Chinkie girl's makin' eyes at you, Nolan, suddenly you think you're an expert on love. Anyroads, this has nothin' to do with love.'

'That's true,' Clare said. 'An' that's why I'm goin' to marry Benjamin.'

'An' leave us in the lurch?' said Nolan dolefully.

'What about the old woman, his mother?' said Evie.

'She won't live forever,' Clare said. 'Besides, I can offer Benjamin a lot more than she can.'

'What if Belfer wants more than you're prepared to give him?' Evie said.

'There's nothin' I'm not prepared to give him, in bed or out of it. He can't do worse to me than what I've suffered already.

I know he won't harm my baby, 'cause in the eyes o' the world it's his baby too.' Clare pushed Nolan away. 'My mind's made up. Benjamin Belfer may not be a great catch but, by Gar, he's the best I'm likely to find on short notice.'

'Better marry him quick then,' said Evie.

'I intend to,' said Clare, 'just as soon as I've seen Mrs Haggarty.'

'Who the devil's she?' said Nolan.

'A midwife Aunt Cissie recommends,' Clare said. 'Oh, an' by the way, you can stop tellin' fibs now, for Aunt Cissie knows who we are. She guessed almost right off that we were tellin' her a pack o' lies.'

'Huh!' said Nolly. 'We couldn't even do that right.'

'Well, I'm doin' what's right,' said Clare. 'What's right for me an' what's right for my baby. I'm goin' to marry Mr Belfer.'

'Hell mend you then!' Evie cried and, in a jealous rage, flung herself down on Nolan's bed and turned her face to the wall.

Libby Galloway was not superstitious. It had galled her considerably when her house servants in Penang had slipped out of a night to appease some imaginary sprite by nailing a gee-gaw or tinsel ornament to a tree in the garden; even more when they returned, all agog, from the fortune-teller's house with one of the ubiquitous slips of red paper on which some hint of a rosy future had been scribbled. Libby needed no red paper prophecy to inform her that the family lunch in Crosshill House that Sunday would be the last time the Blackstocks would break bread together for many months to come, though even she could not have predicted just how bitter the rivalry between her brothers would become or how swiftly it would bring them down.

Fortunately, there were no guests present, for it was obvious that the morning services had not filled Russell, or Wilson, with spiritual light, or eased their headaches and grumbling stomachs.

'All your own fault, boys,' Mama Blackstock informed them. 'If you will go carousing till all hours of the night, you have to take the rough with the smooth next morning. Will I fetch out the castor oil, Russell?'

'No, Mama, thank you all the same.'

'Willy – a vinegar poultice, perhaps?'

'God, no!'

'Then get some food inside you and please stop moaning.'

The soup was a rich beef broth that proved too much for Russell. Wilson, on the other hand, ate manfully and by the time the entrée arrived he appeared ready to tackle the pork chops and sour apple sauce with a degree of relish.

Pin was daintily toying with a chop and smiling a faint, self-satisfied smile that Willy chose as his point of entry.

'What are you grinning at, Ping?' he said.

Seang Pin looked up.

'You,' Willy said, 'I'm talking to you, girl.'

'Willy,' Libby and Mama Blackstock said in unison. 'That's enough.'

'Enough?' Wilson said. 'I haven't even started yet.'

'It's not Pin's fault you're not up to the mark,' Mama Blackstock said.

'It's not me that's not up to the mark.' Willy wiped pork fat from his chin with his napkin. 'What is she grinning about? Has that big Irish nobody been ticklin' her fancy already?'

'Willy, for God's sake, stop it,' Libby said.

'No, I will not stop it. It's time it was out in the open.'

'Time what's out in the open, Willy?' Russell said.

'I'll get to you in a minute,' Wilson said. 'First, I want that girl to tell me what she and her Irishman are up to.'

'Nolan is not my Irishman, Uncle Wilson,' Pin said. 'If

I have my way, however, he will become my Irishman or, rather, I will become his Chink.'

'My goodness!' Angela Blackstock exclaimed. 'She's fallen in love with a labourer. How dreadful!'

'What more do you expect from a coolie?' Willy said.

'Your father was next best thing to a coolie, Wilson,' Mama Blackstock reminded him. 'He may not have been born with a brown or yellow skin but he wasn't much more than a coolie, however you choose to look at it. Pay your uncle no heed, Pin. I don't think he's quite sober yet.'

'I'm as sober as a judge, Mama,' said Wilson. 'However, I don't imagine we can expect much more from the girl given the examples that have been set for her in this household.'

'And what,' said Libby, 'is that supposed to mean?'

'Chinks or Paddies,' Wilson said, 'what's the difference? They're all heathens, aren't they? Cut your throat as soon as look at you, cut your throat – or stab you in the back. Am I not right, Russell?'

'Why ask me?' Russell said.

'True,' Willy said. 'Why bother asking you, when you're the biggest back-stabber of them all?'

'If you have something to get off your chest, Willy,' Russell said evenly, 'might I suggest that we discuss it in private – after lunch.'

Willy squared his knife and fork upon his dinner plate. He was, Libby thought, dangerously controlled. His attack on Pin had been nothing but an opener and, with a sinking feeling in the pit of her stomach, she watched him tilt his head and stare across the table at his twin.

'Oh, yes, Russell, that would suit you to a tee, wouldn't it?' he said. 'Keep it all secret, keep it all in the dark.'

'I don't know what you're talking about, Willy,' Russell said.

'Don't tell Mama, don't tell your dear wife, don't let it slip to anyone how you stabbed me and your brethren in the back,' Willy went on. 'Do you take me for a complete idiot, Russell?'

'Now and then,' said Russell, 'now and then, I admit, I do.'

'Have you any idea what you did yesterday? Any idea of the damage you caused by warning Maizie about the route of the walk? Oh, don't pretend it wasn't you. It couldn't have been anyone else. I'd be willing to give you the benefit of the doubt, if you hadn't been spotted cuddling up to that wee Irish tart in the lane off Salamanca Street.'

For a split second Russell shifted his attention to his wife, then, leaning both elbows on the table, cupped his hands to his chin and focused on his brother once more. There was no sound in the dining-room, only the far-off laughter of the children from the nursery upstairs.

'My God, Wilson, did you have me followed?' Russell said.

'Of course I had you followed,' Wilson said. 'Fat lot of good it did me, or the cause, as it happened. How was I supposed to know you're so infatuated with that Irish whore that you'd deny your Masonic oaths. I knew you wouldn't tell Libby in case she came to me, screaming her head off to protect her wee priestie man and her dear Paddy.'

'I'm just as eager as you are to have the lands of the Riverside lease-free and in our possession, Willy, but not at any cost,' Russell said. 'Paddy Maizie has been our friend for years and the Irish families in Salamanca Street are our employees, our responsibility. To keep my mouth shut would have been more of a betrayal than dropping Paddy a hint that you'd instructed your wrecking crews not just to break a few heads and smash a few windows but to put Maizie out of business and begin the sordid process of clearing the tenements.'

'Clever, Willy,' Libby said, 'but not clever enough, apparently.'

'Keep out of it, Libby,' Wilson told her.

'No, I will not,' Libby said. 'If you're so petty as to let

bigotry drive you to these extreme measures then you've no right to accuse Russell of anything, particularly playing fast and loose with a barmaid.'

'He was seen with her late at night,' said Wilson. 'Look at him! He doesn't even have the brass neck to deny it.'

'Russell, is this true?' Jane Blackstock asked.

'Of course it isn't true,' said Libby loudly.

'Russell,' said Mama Blackstock, 'have you nothing to say?'

'I met with the girl, Evie, after she left the pub,' Russell said. 'I told her what I'd overheard and asked her to pass on a message to Paddy, that's all.'

'Why,' Jane said, 'why did you go to her? What is she to you?'

'Nothing,' Russell said. 'She's nothing to me.'

'She is Nolan's sister,' Pin put in. 'She is not a whore, Uncle Wilson, whatever you may think of her.'

At that moment the door from the kitchen opened and a maid appeared to clear the dishes. Mama Blackstock waved her away. Angela rose from her place at the table and wrapped a consoling arm around Jane's shoulders. Jane shook her off, got to her feet, rested her fingertips on the tablecloth so lightly that she might have been testing the quality of the linen.

'I do not know what your intention is, Wilson,' she said, 'or what purpose you hope to serve by driving a wedge between my husband and me but I am no longer willing to listen to your slanders. I'd be obliged if you, your wife and son would leave our table and our house immediately. Pin, go upstairs, fetch Angela's children and the nursemaid and see to it that they are made ready for the road.'

'Oh, now, Jane, surely you don't mean . . .' Angela began.

'I do mean,' Jane said. 'You are no longer welcome here.'

'Are you going let to this woman insult us, Mama?' Wilson said. 'Are you going to allow her to toss us out as if we were riff-raff?'

'It isn't up to me, Willy,' Mama Blackstock said. 'Ask Russell.'

Wilson threw down his napkin and pushed back his chair so violently that the whole table shook. Ronald, his son, followed suit. Pin was already on her way out of the dining-room, heading for the staircase in the hall.

'I see,' Wilson said. 'It's a conspiracy, is it, a bloody conspiracy to leave me high and dry? And you're all in it together. Even you, Mama. But Russell was always your favourite, wasn't he, always your blue-eyed boy? Well, by God, we'll see who has the last laugh when it comes to a final reckoning.'

With that he stalked around the table, took his wife by the hand and his son by the arm and steered them out of the dining-room, across the drawing-room and into the hall where his children and nanny, all subdued, were tiptoeing down the staircase.

Pin opened the outside door and Wilson and his family, duly hatted and coated, trooped out of Crosshill House to wait for the cabriolet to come round from the stables to take them home.

'Goodbye, Uncle Willy,' Pin called out, with more than a hint of irony.

And slammed the big front door.

Benjamin was half asleep in his armchair when Clare knocked on the door. He roused himself at once and when he learned who it was invited her to enter. A stew pan simmered on the stove and the room was filled with the smell of cooking meat. Clare was dressed in a close-fitting jacket and a neat little bonnet, the jacket patched on the purse flap and frayed at the cuffs.

Benjamin was too excited to notice.

'Don't stand on ceremony, my dear,' he said. 'Do come in.'

'Are you havin' your dinner?'

'No, not yet awhile. Will you join me? There's more than enough for two.'

She had that solemn look again, not sulky but subdued. She stepped over the threshold but did not advance into the room.

'Will you walk out with me, Benjamin?' she asked.

' 'Course I will,' he said. 'Is it still rainin'?'

'No, it's dry for the moment.'

He kicked his boots back under the chair, pulled out his shoes and put them on, reached for his coat and hat and, pausing only to pull the stew pan to the side of the stove, offered Clare his arm. They went out into the street linked like an old married couple, and turned towards the river and the park.

The footpaths had dried out but the verges were still muddy and the trees dripped huge droplets upon the sodden grass. Rain had drifted away to the east but another band of brooding cloud was building and with the arrival of the evening breeze wet weather would sweep in again. Clare held his arm loosely, her hand, ungloved, extended across the back of his hand.

'It's very quiet today,' Clare said, at length.

'Some folk will be sleepin' it off,' Benjamin said. 'Others, I don't doubt, will be nervous about showin' their faces after yesterday's fracas.'

'Will there be more trouble to come?' said Clare.

'I'll be surprised if there ain't,' said Benjamin.

'You will be careful, won't you?' Clare said.

'Careful?'

'When you're makin' your rounds.'

'Oh!' he said, pleased. 'Oh, yes, dear, I'm always careful when business takes me north of Wedderburn.'

'I told my sister an' Nolan about us,' Clare said.

'How did they receive the information?'

'Badly,' Clare said. 'But I don't care about them.'

'Don't you?' Benjamin paused. 'Do you care about me?'

'Your mother doesn't like me.'

Benjamin guffawed. 'Clare, my dear,' he said, 'as you'll soon learn, my ma hates everyone, without exception. You'll never win her round, so don't even bother trying.'

'Have you heard of Mrs Haggarty?' Clare asked.

'Everyone's heard of Mrs Haggarty. She is, by all accounts, an excellent midwife,' Benjamin said. 'But what does Mrs Haggarty have to do with us?'

'I'm goin' to visit her this week,' Clare said.

'To see if everythin's in order, I suppose.'

'Yes.'

'Does your answer to my question hang on what the midwife tells you?'

'No.'

'No?'

Benjamin stopped walking and drew her round to face him. He altered his grip on her arm, moving his fingers higher so that she could not cut and run. For one split second, he experienced a desire to pinch her by the neck and wring an answer out of her. Instead he placed a forefinger on the point of her chin and forced himself to smile, indulgently.

'Ask me again, Benjamin,' Clare said. 'Ask me properly.'

'And if I do?'

'I'll give you me answer here an' now.'

'Straight?'

'Straight,' Clare said.

He glanced this way and that, scanning the pathways of the Parney as if he expected a tribe of tenants to rush out of the bushes, then, hand on thigh, he lowered himself to one knee, took Clare's hand, to steady himself as much as anything, and sucked in a breath of damp, grassy air.

'Clare McKenna,' he said gravely, 'will you marry me?'

'I will.'

'Pardon?'

'I said I will; I'll marry you, Benjamin Belfer.'

'No matter what the midwife tells you?'

'No matter what,' said Clare.

PART FOUR

Clare's Wedding

16

'Wedding bells,' said Jock Macpherson. 'Who'd have thought it. She seemed far too sensible a lass to become embroiled with a man like Belfer.'

'She became embroiled with Harry Fairfield, didn't she?' said Cissie.

Jock cleared his throat. 'I take it she is expectin'?'

'Confirmed by Mrs Haggarty.'

Jock wrinkled his nose. 'When's the happy event?'

'January.'

'A cold month for a wee scrap to enter the world,' Jock said.

'The wee scrap will be well taken care of, never fear,' said Cissie.

'Will there be a celebration?'

'I have my doubts,' said Cissie. 'Clare's fallen out with Father Fingle. He's tried to talk her round, but she won't listen. She an' Mr Belfer'll be joined by declaration before the registry officer in Partick.'

'Are you tellin' me Clare's given up receivin' mass?'

'Turned her back on her faith, aye,' said Cissie.

'Belfer's influence, I expect,' said Jock.

'I'm sure she'll come back after the kiddie's born,' said Cissie. 'Not to St Kentigern's, though, for she'll not be residin' in this parish.'

'What? Are Belfer an' she leavin'?'

'They're movin' to Bellingham Place,' said Cissie.

'By God, that's a step up.'

'It is, Mr Macpherson, it is,' Cissie said. 'Mr Belfer's feathered more than one nest, it seems. He has a property in Bellingham Place where he keeps his aged parents.'

'What about your nephew an' niece? What'll they do when Clare goes?'

It was on the tip of Cissie's tongue to tell Mr Macpherson that Evie McKenna was not her niece, or Nolan her nephew, but she was still embarrassed by her gullibility and did not wish to admit that she had been taken in by the plausible Irish waifs.

'Perhaps Nolan will not be far behind his sister at the altar.'

'Is he courtin' too?' said Jock.

'Bein' courted, more like,' said Cissie and, lowering her voice, added, 'by a girl with a coloured skin.'

'Like a birthmark, you mean?' said Jock.

'No, a Chink,' said Cissie. 'She's a devout Christian, I'll give her that, but she's close connected to the Blackstocks, so it'll not be easy for her to marry a common labourer.'

'If she's foreign maybe a labourer's the best she can hope for,' Jock said. 'What'll become of Evie if the others wed an' move away?'

'One o' them will take her in, I'm sure – or she can lodge with me.'

'She might be tempted to find a man of her own,' Jock suggested, as casually as possible.

'If she hasn't been tempted already,' Cissie said.

'Please, Russell,' Jane Blackstock said, 'do not palm me off with a lie. Is there another woman in your life?'

'If you mean have I taken a mistress, the answer's no,' Russell said.

'Wilson talked of a girl, a barmaid . . .'

'Evie McKenna,' Russell said. 'She works in Paddy Maizie's pub. I've spoken with her on – oh, three occasions.'

'In a back street after dark?' Jane said.

It was only mid-afternoon and without doubt he would have to suffer interrogations from Libby and his mother, too, before bedtime. While the wreckage of Sunday lunch was being cleared away, he had slipped into the morning-room to treat his fluttering stomach with a small glass of brandy, knowing full well that one of the women – Jane, Libby or his mother – would follow him.

'Do you want her?' Jane said.

He tried to sound convincing: 'No, of course not.'

'I'm not a fool, Russell. I realise that you often find me tedious.'

'Of course I don't find you tedious,' he said.

'Is she young? I mean, very young?'

'I really have no idea,' he said, then, 'Yes, she's young.'

'And pretty?'

'Yes, she's pretty.'

'Dark-haired, or fair?' Jane said.

'I don't really see the point . . .' he said, then, 'Look, Jane, I won't put myself in a cleft stick. I've nothing to apologise for and you have nothing to forgive. The girl is – well, just a girl. She has spark, I will admit. When Willy sacked her brother, Pin's friend, from the harbour squad – without, I might add, consulting me – she came hot-foot to the office to berate me.'

'Is that all she did?' said Jane. 'Berate you?'

'She argued her brother's case convincingly,' said Russell. 'I made sure he got his job back, which, naturally, raised Willy's hackles even more.'

'And she, this girl, was duly grateful, I suppose,' said Jane.

Russell put the brandy glass to one side. He got to his feet and walked to the window. The sky was lidded with blue-grey cloud and the breeze had risen enough to lick up angry little waves on the surface of the Clyde. He stood with his back to the room, looking out.

'Yes, she was grateful,' he said. 'But not so grateful that she would give herself to me for the asking.' He swung round to face his wife. 'I used Evie McKenna to convey a message, and that, I confess, was a misjudgement on my part. I stepped into a trap that Willy had set for me. Don't you see what this is about, Jane? Not you and me and some inconsequential girl in a tenement in Salamanca Street; not smashing windows or setting fire to a public house or fomenting enough trouble to attract the attention of the magistrates.'

Jane unlaced her fingers and put a hand to her mouth. If fifteen years of marriage had taught him nothing else at least he had learned to read her gestures, and knew that she was listening intently.

'We are in debt, dearest,' he went on. 'The Blackstocks are in debt up to the ears. The company's mortgaged to the hilt and Willy wants shot of it. He has his own connections in the Barony Bank and Strachan and others of similar ilk – lodge brethren – will finance his building schemes. But not mine. Why not mine? Because I'm building a harbour for the Clyde Trust and there's no quick profit in that venture. Private land development is a different matter. Profits in that field are substantial and, relatively speaking, the return on capital is rapid.'

'What does that have to do with this girl, this Evie?'

'Nothing,' said Russell. 'And everything.'

'Oh, come now, Russell,' Jane said scathingly, 'do not be enigmatic.'

'My father, rest his soul, was more ambitious than honest,' Russell said. 'He made a fortune by exploiting immigrants. He had no conscience about it. He firmly believed that only those of strong will prospered and the rest – idlers and weaklings, he called them – deserved to be sheared like sheep.'

'He was a rack-renter,' Jane said. 'I know.'

'He started by leasing a single rat-infested tenement that he rented out room by room to immigrant Irish Catholics. He bought another tenement, and then another, and was lauded by his peers for his acuity. Not only did he skin those desperate men by inflating the rents, he employed them in his builder's yard, too, and within ten years the Riverside ward had become his kingdom.'

'A kingdom that you inherited,' said Jane.

'That Willy and I inherited,' Russell corrected. 'Sad to say, Willy and I continued to operate on the same unscrupulous principles that we'd learned from Papa. We were properly educated, educated like gentlemen, in fact. We were fully aware that what we were doing was wrong. Nevertheless, we moved on, Willy and I, moved upward and learned to dine with lords and ladies. For all that, we still trail behind us, like a rusty chain, the debris of our origins.'

He kept his voice low, not hectoring or lecturing, but confiding, for it had become necessary to make her understand that being a man of wealth and influence did not mean that he was without conscience.

'In plain terms,' he continued, 'Willy wishes to sell our tenement properties to the Barony of Glasgow Bank. The properties, if not quite worthless, are worth a great deal less than the land on which they stand.'

'Because of the proposed new road,' said Jane.

'Exactly,' said Russell. 'The new highway that will link the city to the outlying boroughs. It's a wonderful idea, a visionary idea; a brand-new route flanked not by warehouses, quays and rotting tenements but by fine new villas and mansion houses. But what will become of the folk who pour their hard-earned cash back into the system and, more importantly, do the work at wages low enough to make the scheme possible; not just the labourers but all those people who make up the community? You don't know them, Jane. I do. I grew up among them and I have sympathy for them.'

'Wilson doesn't care, does he?' said Jane.

'Willy cares not two hoots.'

'And he is furious because you do?'

'Yes, he blames me for putting obstacles in his way,' Russell said, 'but those obstacles are not of my making, not my doing. The projected line of the thoroughfare is tight, particularly along the quarter-mile at the bottom end of Riverside. Willy knows that I, not the company, own four tenements there. I bought them from Papa before he drafted his final will. My tenements aren't the only stumbling blocks, however. The real stumbling blocks are Paddy Maizie's public house and St Kentigern's church and grounds.'

'Has Willy opened negotiations with the archbishop?'

'Not yet.'

'Will the Church's administrators agree to sell St Kentigern's?'

'They might.'

'And Maizie?' said Jane.

'It isn't Maizie we have to worry about,' Russell said. 'He's not the owner of the Harp of Erin, as it happens. He has a partner, a sleeping partner.'

'Who?'

'My sister, Libby,' Russell said, 'who won't go down without a fight.'

The prospect of marriage excited Clare more than she cared to admit. Evie was still sulking and Nolan less than enthusiastic about having Benjamin Belfer as a brother-in-law. Father Fingle too was annoyed with her and had called at the flat three times to try to persuade her to return to St Kentigern's. Clare was adamant, however, and declared, quite heatedly, that she'd rather be a lapsed Catholic than an unmarried mother and that as far as she was concerned she was finished with the Church forever. Aunt Cissie too put in her pennyworth and even the midwife, Mrs Haggarty, gave her a lecture on the subject of true faith, a lecture that Clare, lying on a blanket on a strange kitchen table with her skirts up and drawers down, was unable to avoid.

Benjamin steered clear of religious issues. He was happy enough to have her down for tea or, more often, to trot upstairs and join her for a spot of luncheon which she, in quaint old style, still referred to as her dinner. He was even happier when the mood came over her and she volunteered to sit upon his knee and let him kiss her and touch her breasts. Clare, for her part, shifted her bottom on his lap and opened her knees to test the strength of the man she had chosen to be her husband. She might even have led him to bed in the quiet of an afternoon if he had pressed her but Benjamin seemed grateful enough for the small liberties that she allowed him, and did not ask for more.

What Benjamin did ask for, however, was a date for the wedding.

'How about Monday,' he suggested. 'Next Monday.'

'Monday week might be more convenient.'

'Why?'

'I have things to do, dear.'

'What things?' said Benjamin.

'Clothes to wash, a dress to repair . . .'

'Are you havin' second thoughts, Clare?'

'Sure an' I am not.'

'Monday week, then,' Benjamin said. 'At half past two o'clock.'

'I'll need a bridesmaid, an' you'll need a best man.'

'Why?' Benjamin frowned.

'As witnesses,' Clare said. 'An' because it's the right thing to do. I'd like my sister to be there, an' Nolly if he can get the time off.'

Benjamin sighed. 'I'm not averse to makin' a show,' he said, 'but, under the circumstances, a bit of discretion might be no bad idea.'

'Aunt Cissie will come,' said Clare. 'Your mother, too, maybe?'

'My mother!' Benjamin said. 'God, no, not her.'

'She'll be insulted if she isn't invited.'

'She'll only make trouble,' Benjamin said. 'Besides, my father can't be left on his own, not even for half an afternoon.'

'I thought you had a housekeeper to look after him?'

'Well, yes, I do – Mrs Loomis – but it might not suit her.'

'Might not suit you, you mean,' Clare said. 'There's discretion, Benjamin, an' there's secrecy. Are you ashamed to be seen marryin' me?'

'How can you think that, my dearest?' Benjamin said. 'I'd have the world there to witness our nuptials if things were different.'

'A best man, you need a best man to make a speech afterwards.'

'Afterwards?'

'At the weddin' breakfast.'

'A breakfast?' said Benjamin. 'In the afternoon?'

'It needn't be elaborate,' said Clare, 'or expensive.'

'Well, that's somethin', I suppose,' Benjamin said. 'Where do you propose we should hold this – ah – weddin' breakfast?'

'Mr Maizie has a room.'

'Maizie's,' said Benjamin gloomily, 'is an Irish pub.'

'Ain't I Irish?' said Clare.

'Aye, I suppose you are.'

'So you're happy enough to marry an Irish girl but not to break bread in an Irish pub?' said Clare. 'I thought you ate there regular, anyroads.'

Benjamin blew out his cheeks and scratched his ear. 'I do,' he said. 'But that's Fridays, an' that's business.'

'Well, this is Monday,' Clare told him. 'An' it's not business.'

'You're set on this, aren't you, Clare?'

'Dead set,' she told him.

'And afterwards?'

'We'll come back here,' she said. 'Come back here as man an' wife. That's why I need a proper weddin', even if it can't be before God.'

'A proper weddin',' Benjamin said, capitulating. 'Yes, damn it, why not! We'll make it a day to remember.'

'An',' Clare said, insinuating herself on to his knee, 'a night, too?'

'What?' said Benjamin, trying to hide his alarm. 'Yes, and a night too.'

Nolan told Ned Torrance that he would need a half-day off. Ned told McCandlish, the ganger, and the ganger told Mr Hall, who was managing the site, and Mr Hall told Russell Blackstock at a meeting the following morning. Mr Blackstock told Hall to tell McCandlish to tell Torrance that Nolan McKenna would be permitted to leave work at midday but to make sure he was docked three-quarters of the day's wage for the privilege.

In due course, Ned told Nolan, who, with a whoop, told Pin, who told Libby, who told Jane, who told Russell who, of course, already knew. But none of them, not one, could believe that the pompous old bachelor who had terrorised the good folk of Riverside for so many years was finally tying the knot and that he had copped not just any old woman but a young, raven-haired Irish lass who was not only a perfect beauty but a Roman Catholic to boot.

'A Pape!' Wilson raged when the news reached his ears. 'Great God in heaven, what's possessed the fellow? I don't care if she's the bloody Queen of the Nile or that – that other one who started the Trojan War, Belfer has no right, no bloody right to marry out of the faith.'

'What faith is that, dear?' Angela asked.

To which question, of course, Willy had no answer.

'Has nobody thought to ask him?' Bob Draper said, when Evie brought him news of the impending nuptials, together with a request for private use of the snug. 'Hasn't your sister asked him?'

'I'm not on speakin' terms with my sister right now,' Evie said.

'If she was my sister,' Chiffin said, 'I wouldn't speak to her neither if she got spliced to a man like Belfer.'

'He's not a Catholic, or an Orangeman,' Bob Draper said. 'I suspect he might be one o' the new Christian Socialists we've been hearin' so much about. Not a church wedding, Evie?'

'Nah! Certificate.'

'Hmm.' Bob nodded. 'Sausage rolls?'

'Pardon?'

'I can order sausage rolls from Kennedy's, if you like.'

'It's not a grand affair,' said Evie, then, with a tut, 'Order what you like.'

'Why don't you ask the blushin' groom on Friday when he brings in the dibbins,' Chiffin suggested. 'He mightn't be keen to tell you where he says his prayers but he's not likely to thump you for quizzin' him about sausage rolls.'

'Good idea,' Bob said. 'You ask him?'

'Not me,' said Chiffin, backing away. 'Let Evie do it.'

'All right,' Evie said. 'I'll have a word – one word – with Clare.'

'How many guests?' said Bob Draper.

'I don't know,' said Evie. 'Six or eight.'

'Who's to be the bridesmaid?' said Chiffin. 'You?'

'Aye,' Evie admitted grudgingly.

'All in lavender an' wearin' lace drawers?' said Chiffin.

Evie punched him on the arm to wipe the grin off his silly face.

'More to the point,' Chiffin said, 'who'll stand by Belfer? He don't have a friend in the world.'

'He does, you know,' Bob said.

'Who's that then?' Chiffin asked, and blanched when Mr Draper answered, 'Orpington.'

It hadn't occurred to Benjamin to invite his old chum to the wedding. He had thought of Perce not at all in the past few weeks. He did not, of course, neglect his collections or fail to supervise ongoing repairs to Mr Blackstock's properties, and take his under-the-counter cuts. Percentages and back-handers were necessary to meet the mortgage payments on the flat in Bellingham Place and pay the wages of the housekeeper, Mrs Loomis, who, fortunately, seemed to be made of sterner stuff than her predecessors. Marriage would bring many changes, though, not least of which would be the cost of supporting a wife and, come January, a child.

He booked the services of the registrar and presented documents necessary to prove residence. He consulted Draper at the Harp and organised the so-called wedding breakfast that Clare seemed so keen on. He even persuaded Nolan to stand as groomsman to add a degree of credibility to the affair. Then, on Wednesday afternoon, he took himself down to the row of pop-shops behind the docks and, after much searching, found a plain gold ring, not much worn, at a reasonable price, and, more by chance than intention, a pair of grey suede gloves and a nice top hat that some swell, down on his luck, had pawned and never redeemed. He had them wrapped in brown paper to keep off the rain and, pleased with his purchases, picked up a hackney to carry him home.

It was quiet in the streets, for shipyards and factories had not yet disgorged the day shift and the labourers and other shiftless souls who occupied the tenements in Salamanca Street were still out earning a crust. With the parcel tucked under one arm, Benjamin entered the close. He fumbled in his pocket for his key, then, with a start, noticed that the door to his apartment was open.

He pushed it with his shoulder and peered into the gloom.

'Well, well, well,' Mr Orpington said, 'if it ain't my old chum returned from his wanderings. About time, too. I've been here for hours, you know. It's just as well I'm a gentleman of leisure with naught but time on my hands.'

The muscles in Benjamin's stomach contracted and a sharp pain nipped his breastbone. 'How did you get in?'

'Ways and means, old son, ways and means,' Percival Orpington said. 'Been shopping, have we?'

'Uh – yes,' Benjamin said guiltily, and put the parcel down on the table.

'Something nice, it is? Something nice to keep the wife happy?'

'It's a hat.'

'Been down at old hookey's, have you, tartin' up your wardrobe for the grand occasion? What did you buy? A topper, I'll be bound.'

'Yes, a topper,' Benjamin confessed. 'It's – it's good to see you, Perce. You're lookin' very fit, very – uh – trim. Has the ankle healed?'

Mr Orpington was seated in the armchair, a cushion behind his head. He had stirred the fire and added coals, Benjamin noted, but hadn't lighted any of the lamps. His top hat and gloves lay on the linoleum by the side of the chair and, resting against the arm, was a silver-topped malacca cane.

In answer to Benjamin's question Mr Orpington stretched out his leg and, plucking up the cane, tapped it lightly against his shin.

'Healed, but not properly,' he said. 'I can squeeze my foot

into a boot now but pain still takes me when I walk, an unfortunate weakness that hinders my pursuit of employment.' He glanced up. 'Kind of you to enquire, though, when you have so many other things on your mind.'

Though his apprehension had not decreased, Benjamin was well practised in the art of bluff and still capable of putting on a bold face.

'I gather you've heard I'm to be married?' he said.

'I have, indeed,' Orpington said. 'I've come to offer my heartiest, and to enquire where my invite might be. Got lost, has it, lost in the post?'

'Family only, I'm afraid,' Benjamin said. 'Keepin' it small, you see.'

'Small – yes,' Orpington said. 'Bet the bride ain't so small, though.'

'Have a care, Perce, just have a care.'

Orpington hardly seemed to move; a twist of the wrist and a dip of the shoulder and the tip of the cane prodded Benjamin's belly. 'Is that a threat, Benjamin? Are you threatenin' me?'

'Take it how you like, Perce.'

Mr Orpington laughed and lowered the cane.

'Defendin' a lady's honour, are you?' he said. 'My, my, that's a turn-up for the book. Still, I'll remember to respect your sensibilities in future. It is the Irish bint you're taking on board, ain't it?'

'Clare McKenna, yes.'

Benjamin rested his buttocks against the table. Out of habit, he was inclined to placate Mr Orpington, to offer him brandy or wine, but he had no wish to restore his friendship with the man and, folding his arms, said, 'What do you really want, Perce, since I know you don't care two figs about who I marry?'

'No pullin' the wool over your eyes, old son,' Orpington said. 'Sharp as a carpet tack you are. No, I don't expect an invitation to your wedding celebrations. It's business brings me here.'

'The collection business, do you mean?'

'I mean the accommodation business,' Mr Orpington said.

From his coat pocket he produced one of several handwritten cards that Benjamin had displayed in local shop windows. The card was grubby and yellowed around the edges and had been folded more than once. Mr Orpington smoothed it between his palms and held it up.

'You have, I believe, a vacant room just begging for a tenant,' he said.

'It's gone, Perce. Sorry.'

'Ah, Benjamin, Benjamin!' Mr Orpington said. 'It ain't gone, or if it is you must be harbourin' a phantom 'cause it's still a-lyin' empty.'

'It's promised.'

'To whom?' said Mr Orpington pleasantly.

Benjamin was all too familiar with that reasonable tone. As nonchalantly as possible he slid from the table and stationed himself by the drawer in which he stored his knives.

'Irish couple,' he lied. 'He's lookin' for work in Riverside.'

'How long has it been promised?'

'Week.'

'They ain't here yet, are they?'

'That's true, but a promise . . .'

'Promises to Irish persons aren't binding, Benjamin; you know that,' Mr Orpington said. 'I'm here, now, with cash in hand.'

'Now?' said Benjamin. 'You want to move in now? I thought you lodged in Berkeley Street?'

'I do. Leastways, I did. But' – he patted his leg – 'this sorry feller put me out of commission, and a man with no commission has to economise.'

'If it's a loan you need . . .'

'I ain't no borrower, Belfer. It ain't a loan I need: it's a room, and that there room you have upstairs will suit to a tee,' Mr Orpington said. 'I'll settle four weeks in advance and move in tonight.'

'Tonight?'

'Soon as I can find a carrier to heft my stuff.'

'Why the rush?' Benjamin said. 'You in trouble with the law?'

'Nope – and I ain't doing a moonlight either,' Percival Orpington said. 'Fact is, I haven't worked in weeks and, while I ain't strapped, I've had to dip into my reserve too deep for comfort.'

'What about the bank? The Barony?'

'What about it?'

'Have they dropped you, too?'

'Everyone's dropped me,' Orpington said. 'I've got clients out there just desperate to pay me money, but I haven't been up to collectin' it. I'll be back with the bank in a month or, with luck, sooner. Meanwhile . . .' He got up suddenly and, parrying the cane, clipped the edge of the table several times. 'Meanwhile, I need a cheap, clean room to lie up in to let my ligaments knit. I have no one, Benjamin, no nagging wife, no kiddies, no furry animals to shit on your doorsteps. It's just me, poor crippled feller that I am, and I cannot understand why you, my oldest, dearest friend, and companion of many a raucous escapade, why you won't—'

'All right, all right,' Benjamin said. 'You can have the damned room, Perce, but I want to make it clear that I'll brook no trouble in my building.'

'Trouble?' Orpington said. 'Me?'

'The Irishman who done for your pin, he lives here too, one floor up,' Benjamin said. 'I hope you ain't comin' here in search of revenge.'

Mr Orpington laughed. 'What? And risk losin' another

scrap? No, Benjamin, old son, I may be proud but I'm not stupid. Besides, I gather this young feller is soon to be your brother-in-law, and I got far too much respect for you to foul your nest – or mine, for that matter.'

'It's five shillings by the week.'

'And by the month?'

'Eighteen.'

'Very fair. Very manageable,' Orpington said. 'Half, and a piece, less than what I'm paying in Berkeley Street. You've saved a life, Mr Belfer.'

'I'm please to hear it, Mr Orpington.'

'I'll fetch my stuff, then.'

'I'll have the room swept and aired for you,' Benjamin said.

'And warn the neighbours while you're at it?'

'Warn the neighbours, Mr Orpington?'

'Not to knock me down on the stairs,' Orpington said and, with a crooked little grin, limped out on to Salamanca Street, leaning heavily into his cane.

17

Evie was too upset to eat. She pushed the minced-beef pattie around on her plate with her fork while Nolan, who had finished supper long ago, sat on a chair with his feet on the hob, sipping tea from a mug as if he hadn't a care in the world.

'You could've knocked me down with a feather,' Nolan said, 'when I strolled into our close an' the first person I see is that Orpington feller. I thought he was a-goin' to strike me down with that stick o' his, then he waves a white hankie in my face an' offers me his hand. "Let bygones be bygones," says he, "since we're goin' to be neighbours," an' I say, "Neighbours?" an' then he tells me he's rented the room upstairs.'

'You shook his hand, I suppose?' said Evie.

'Sure an' I did,' said Nolan. 'You know how I am, Evie: never one to harbour a grudge.'

'He flung me down,' Evie said. 'Leopards don't change their spots, Nolly. I want to know what he's up to, squattin' on our doorstep.'

'He needs a cheap place to live,' said Clare.

She sat on the side of the big bed with threads and ribbons spread on the blanket about her and a summer dress laid across her lap. It was late now, light had long gone from the sky and the wick in the lamp on the corner of the mantelshelf needed trimming. She bent her head and peered at the needle as she worked it through the material.

'Glasgow's full o' cheap lodgings,' Evie said. 'Why has he come here?'

‘ ’Cause he knows Benjamin,’ said Clare. ‘Benjamin’s his friend.’

‘Some friend!’ said Evie, with a sigh.

‘Benjamin’s promised he won’t be at the weddin’,’ said Clare.

‘The weddin’, the weddin’, that’s all you think about, Clare,’ Evie said. ‘Next thing, it’ll be the baby, the baby. Don’t you ever spare a thought for the rest of us?’

‘Why should I?’ Clare said. ‘You never spared much thought for me.’

‘Sure an’ I always looked out for you, Clare,’ said Nolan.

‘Did you?’ Clare said. ‘I never noticed.’

‘An’ I suppose that before too long you’ll marry your Chinkie, Nolan,’ Evie went on, ‘an’ I’ll be left high an’ dry at the mercy o’ that beast upstairs.’

‘Marry Pin?’ said Nolan. ‘No chance of that.’

‘She’d have you tomorrow if she had her way,’ said Evie. ‘It’s only Libby Galloway that prevents her runnin’ off with you.’

‘Is it?’ Nolan looked over his shoulder. ‘Libby Galloway, do you say?’

‘Aye, an’ the Blackstocks,’ said Clare. ‘They’ll never let her marry you, Nolan, even if she is a Chink.’

‘Why not?’ Nolan said. ‘ ’Cause I’ve no money?’

‘ ’Cause you’re common as muck,’ said Evie.

‘Thanks very much,’ said Nolan.

‘We’re all as common as muck,’ said Evie. ‘For two pins I’d pack my bag an’ go home again.’

‘What?’ said Nolan. ‘To Cork? What’s left for you in Cork?’

‘Nothin’,’ said Evie. ‘Nothin’ left for me anywhere, it seems.’

Cissie Cassidy said, ‘If you don’t stand still, Mr Macpherson, you’re goin’ to get pricked again. It’s not easy pokin’ a needle through such heavy material, you know, an’ it’s not made any easier with you wrigglin' like an eel every time I come near you.'

'It's not you, Cissie,' Jock said. 'It's this blasted kilt. It itches.'

'I'm not surprised it itches,' Cissie said. 'By the look of it, it's been in that trunk o' yours since Methuselah was a boy.'

'It was my father's,' Jock said. 'He gave it me when he died.'

'By the smell of it they should have buried the kilt with him,' Cissie said.

'Heather,' Jock said. 'My daddy stored it in a creel o' heather.'

'Mildew, more like,' Cissie grunted. 'Is this a real Macpherson tartan?'

'I doubt it,' Jock said. 'I think it's Black Watch. My grandfather was a piper with the Royal Highlanders when he was young.'

Cissie discreetly averted her eyes from Mr Macpherson's bare knees and hairy thighs which were visible under the trailing edge of the garment. She'd heard that Highlanders wore nothing but nature beneath their kilts but she had no wish to find out if the story was true.

'Do you play the bagpipes?' she asked.

'Not me,' Jock said. 'I didn't have the wind for it.'

'Pity,' Cissie said. 'You could have given us a tune on Monday afternoon.'

'There'll be wailin' enough at Clare's weddin', I reckon,' Jock said, 'without me addin' to it.'

'There!' Cissie said, snipping off a loose thread with her scissors. 'That's as good a job as I can make of it. Put on the jacket an' let me look at you.'

Jock took his tweed jacket, which was almost as hairy as he was, from the back of a chair and slipped it on. He planted his hands on his hips and spread his legs in the pose of a Highland warrior.

'Well, Cissie, what do you think?'

'Very handsome,' Cissie said. 'You'll need to trim that beard, though.'

'I will, I will.'

'An' those eyebrows.'

'Those, too,' Jock promised.

Cissie took three or four steps back across the kitchen and studied him again. 'By gum,' she said. 'You are a sight to see, Jock Macpherson.'

'Will I pass muster on Monday, d'you think?'

'You'll be the belle o' the ball, Jock,' she assured him. 'If she won't dance with you then, blow it, I will.'

'If who won't dance with me?' Jock said.

'Evie McKenna,' Cissie said. 'Isn't that who you're out to impress?'

'Havers, woman!' Jock said, blushing. 'I'm old enough to be her father.'

'You wouldn't be the first old man to set his cap at a maid.'

'That's enough o' that now, Cissie, if you please,' Jock said. 'I'm not settin' my cap at anyone, least of all Evie McKenna.'

'She's a sweet girl, you know,' said Cissie.

'I'd hardly call her sweet,' said Jock.

'If her sister can marry a man like Mr Belfer . . .'

'Stop makin' a match for me, Cissie,' Jock said gruffly. 'I'm happy enough as I am.'

'Are you?' Cissie said. 'Would you not be a deal happier if you had a wife to look after you?' She paused, then added, 'Or a wife to look after?'

'It'd be a brave chap who'd take on a nippy sweetie like Evie McKenna,' Jock said. 'She doesn't need looked after, that one.'

'I think she does,' said Cissie. 'Besides, you look brave enough in that kilt to take on a dozen Irish barmaids.'

'One would be enough,' Jock said, then, instantly realising his mistake, blustered, 'Are you finished, Mrs Cassidy?'

'I am,' said Cissie. 'Unless you'd like me to pluck your beard?'

'No, thank you,' Jock said stiffly. 'I think you've done enough damage for one day, don't you? Tea?'

'Yes, please,' said Cissie and, smiling to herself, began to pack her threads and needles into her sewing basket while the big, hairy Highlander, still in kilt and sporran, noisily filled a kettle at the sink.

It had taken Libby the best part of the day to shake off her ward. Over the past week, Seang Pin had clung to her like a limpet, asking questions to which Libby had no sensible answers.

'Tell me, Aunt Libby, is it better in your opinion for a woman to marry an older man who has secured his place in life or a young man who still has to make his way in the world?'

'Why do you ask?'

'I am curious, that's all.'

'I have no opinion, one way or the other,' Libby said.

'Nolan's sister is marrying an older man.'

'In her case extenuating circumstances prevail.'

'She is pregnant, do you mean?' said Pin.

'There can be no other reason why she'd marry a man like Belfer,' Libby said. 'I trust you'll learn a lesson from her mistake.'

'Do you mean that one should not lie with a man, or that one should be careful if one does?' said Pin.

'What sort of a question is that?' Libby said. 'And what significance does the pronoun have, this abstract "one"? Have you lain with a man, is that it, or are you contemplating lying with a man? Has the Irishman been pressing you to—'

'Lord, no!' Pin interrupted. 'Nolly would never do that.'

'And you, would you do that?'

'Certainly not,' said Pin. 'It would be a mortal sin.'

Libby sighed, hoping that the conversation had burned itself out.

After a pause, Pin said, 'Did you sin with Mr Galloway, Aunt Libby?'

'Good God!' Libby exclaimed.

'Did you?'

'No.'

'You ran off and married him,' Pin said.

'If you're thinking of running off . . .'

'Why did you not bear children, Aunt Libby?'

'God did not see fit to bless me with children.'

'It wasn't because . . . I mean, you did – try?'

'I'm beginning to find this conversation distasteful,' Libby said.

'But you did – try?'

'Yes, we tried, of course we did. Now, enough.'

Only in the mid part of the day could Libby be sure that she would have a little time to herself, for every afternoon, rain or shine, Seang Pin would put on her bonnet and cape and head out of the house for the ferry bridge from which she would scan the building site until she spotted Nolan; then she would wave and, so Libby had been informed, would catch a blown kiss or two, for the fair-haired Irishman had no shame and simply laughed off his workmates' scornful comments or, if their remarks became too rude, would show them his fist to shut them up.

Seang Pin's romance might have provided Libby with light relief if she hadn't had more important matters on hand. The feud between Wilson and Russell had come to a head; lawyers and accountants were already waiting in the wings. Mama Blackstock had called on Wilson in an attempt to patch things up, but her mission, it seemed, had failed.

Friday mid-afternoon found Libby in the cottage behind the Harp, sipping a glass of wine, while Paddy Maïzie, languid as ever, sprawled on the ottoman, puffing on a cigar. 'I wish you'd stop pacin' up and down, sweetheart,' he said. 'You'll wear a hole in my carpet 'fore long. Sit down and drink your wine, like a good girl.'

'It's all very well for you, Patrick; you don't have to make decisions.'

''Course I do,' Paddy said. 'I have to decide what necktie to wear and what horse to have saddled when I go out for a ride of a morning.'

'Stop playing the fool,' Libby said. 'Surely even your fuddled brain can grasp the import of what's happening, and how it will affect us.'

'It'll take the accountants months, if not years, to tally assets and divvy up your brothers' holdings prior to dissolving the partnership,' Paddy said. 'Time enough to worry when the deed's near done.'

'I cannot understand what's come over Russell,' Libby said. 'Willy thinks he's infatuated with your little barmaid.'

'If Russell fancies a fling he can probably have one just for the askin'.'

'Has he had her, Patrick?'

'Nah!' Paddy shrugged. 'I can see what he sees in her, though. She's pretty and has a tongue on her that could slice lemons. I think she reminds him of his not-so-flamin' youth. She's the opportunity he never had back when he was a lad in these parts; his second chance, in a manner o'speaking.'

'He's happily married. He doesn't need a second chance.'

'You know that, Libby, and I know that,' said Paddy. 'What's more, I think old Russell knows it too, which is why he's teasin' himself with the thought o' what he might do if he wasn't the sort o' feller he's turned out to be.'

'Enough cod philosophy, Patrick,' said Libby. 'Kindly address yourself to the question of what I should do now Wilson's turned his attentions to Riverside. Should I sell to Russell?'

'Nope,' said Paddy. 'Not Russell.'

'Who then? Surely not Willy?'

'Certainly not Willy,' Paddy said. 'If you sell the Harp to Willy he'll have the place razed to the ground an' the heart ripped out o' the Riverside before you can wink.'

'Four old tenements, one Catholic chapel, and an Irish public house hardly constitute the heart of a community,' Libby said.

'Depends where you stand,' said Paddy, 'and who stands with you.'

'You don't think I should sell at all, do you?' Libby said.

'Nope, not yet.'

'Wilson won't rest until he pushes us out, you know.'

'He'll have to push damned hard, I reckon,' Paddy said. 'Fact is, Libby, the Riverside is bound to be swallowed up in course o' time. It's progress, honey; not even you can stand in the way o' progress. But it won't be Willy Blackstock that'll call the tune – no, nor Russell either.'

'Who will it be then, Patrick?'

'The banks,' Paddy said. 'However much we fret and fume, it's the banks who pay the piper in the long run.'

'What do you think I should do?' said Libby.

'Sit tight, sweetheart,' Paddy said, 'sit tight.'

'And let my brother Willy hang himself?'

Paddy Maizie nodded, and said, 'Just so.'

Evie knew that by Riverside standards the McKennas were not poor. She recalled only too well what it was like to live in fear of the bailiff's knock or the arrival of the landlord's lackey demanding rent; how her father and brother – Mam too at the end – had been ground down by the threat of eviction after the failure of a crop or a slump in market prices, and how often Clare and she had gone to bed cold and hungry. Whatever quirk of fate had brought her to Glasgow and the tenement in Salamanca Street, whatever ills had befallen her since, at least there was food on the table and coal for the fire and even a little extra cash to put in the tea-caddy on the mantelshelf for a rainy day.

'What's this?' said Chiffin.

'It's money,' Evie told him. 'Twenty shillin's to be precise.'

'For what?'

'For you, Chiff.'

'What are you after, Evie?'

'God in heaven, Chiff, don't be so suspicious. It's a loan from me to you.'

'But why?'

Evie paused. 'Orpington's back.'

'Jesus, Mary an' Joseph!'

Chiffin bunched his fists against his chest like a squirrel. His mouth opened and closed but no words came out, only a high-pitched whimper.

'For God's sake, pull yourself together,' said Evie.

'Whu – whu – where is he?'

'Our place. He's taken a room in our tenement.'

'Oh, Jesus! Jesus, save me.'

'The beggar's short o' hard cash, so I've heard. No doubt he'll be callin' on you soon. How much do you owe him, all told?'

'A lot, an awful lot. It's been near eight weeks since he collected anythin' an' the interest mounts up faster than I can count.'

'Do you have anythin' saved, anythin' at all?' Evie said.

'Theresa's been sick.'

'Yes, I know that.'

'I had to pay for a doctor.'

Evie pushed the little heap of silver coins across the counter towards him. 'This'll cover the interest, with some left over. Orpington won't know you've cash up your sleeve, so he won't squeeze you too hard. Can't you pay off the original sum?'

'I'll never be able to do that.'

'Stop it,' Evie said. 'Stop bubblin'. I'll help you all I can.'

'I can't take your money, love,' Chiff said. 'I mean, it's not that I'm not grateful, but . . .'

'Wouldn't you rather be in debt to me than in debt to Orpington?'

He managed a crooked grin. 'What's your rate, Evie?'

'Half a percent a year, over twenty years.'

'What if I can't pay?'

'I'll send my brother over to sort you out.'

'Well, that's a scare, that is,' Chiffin said. 'Where did you get the money, Evie? You didn't borrow it, did you?'

'I'm not that daft.'

He cupped his hands on either side of the coins as if he feared that they might roll away and be lost in the sawdust.

'I've six shillin's saved,' he said. 'See, I knew he'd come back one day.'

'There you are then,' Evie said. 'Take it to him.'

'Take it to him? Not wait till he comes for it?'

'Let's keep the bastard on the hop,' said Evie. 'If he doesn't show up here tonight, come back with me an' I'll have Nolan step upstairs with you while you drop the money into Orpington's hand. Catch him unawares an' let him see you're not frightened of him.'

'But I am frightened of him,' Chiffin said.

'You needn't be, not with my sister married to Benjamin Belfer an' my brother teachin' at St Kentigern's side by side with Mrs Galloway's girl. What's more,' Evie said, 'you've got some money now.'

'Aye, but it's your money, Evie. I don't have any money o' my own.'

'Maybe not,' Evie said, 'but you've got me for a friend.'

'Have I?' said Chiffin.

'Like it or not,' said Evie, 'you have.'

⋆ ⋆ ⋆

At the age of ten Mr Orpington had been sent from a foundlings' home on the outskirts of London to a job in the mercury furnace in Shoreditch; just another disposable child who raked ashes from under the ranges and slept in the barn next to the furnace-master's house. He was still amazed that he had survived the choking fumes from the cucubits in which the ore was boiled or, after he'd stepped up, hadn't been burned to death by the concentrated sulphuric acid in the stoneware retorts in the Apothecaries Hall where chlorides of mercury were produced for the use of medical practitioners and embalmers.

He had worked in the Hall for four years, had lodged in a rookery off St Giles and had slept with a girl not much older than he was, a ragged, skin-and-bone urchin who had believed that he would look after her which, indeed, he did until she died of something or other and he had moved on again, up west a way, where, being a sturdy, handsome young devil, even if he did smell a bit like a pickled corpse, he had soon found himself another woman.

Older and wiser, Clara had given him a taste of the high life by introducing him to her father, Mr Bainsbridge, who operated a knocking-shop at the bottom end of the Haymarket.

It was Mr Bainsbridge who had taught him the value of quiet words coupled to a strong arm and, over the next few years, had made him into the man he was today. He might have settled in the Haymarket if he hadn't lost his temper one night and had done something unforgivable to Clara Bainsbridge and, as a result, had been forced to go on the run.

Fifteen years ago, give or take, he had wound up in Glasgow and found employment with the Blackstock brothers or, rather, with old man Blackstock who, beneath his silk hat and frock coat, had been just as ruthless as he was and had recognised a valuable asset when he saw one.

At first he had been commissioned to do the heavy work that

old Mr Blackstock could no longer do for himself: a threat here, a beating there, a word of warning to a tardy contractor or a supplier whose goods turned out to be faulty. Then he had drifted into employment with the boys, the twins, who, at that time, had hardly known how to wash their own faces let alone manage properties, and, with a little spare time on his hands, he had developed some profitable little sidelines of his own.

Naturally, there had been women, lots of women, and none of them bought off the shelf either, for he was far too shrewd to shell out for something he could have for nothing. He had happily jigged a councillor's wife for half a year, and had enjoyed both daughters of a legal gentleman for whom he had done a bit of business. He had lived with, and sponged off, a genteel lady of a certain age for the best part of three years until her sons had ganged up on him and had whisked her away to an asylum in Edinburgh. After that, he had found himself respectable lodgings in Berkeley Street and a meek little servant, Ida, who was so terrified of him that she would do anything, absolutely anything, he asked of her, in addition to cleaning, cooking and laundering his clothes.

Early that summer, however, soon after he'd come down with the leg and was laid up in bed stuffed full of chloral hydrate, Ida had quietly gone through his drawers and had pawned his shirts and neckties, his pins, cufflinks and some of his books. She had even unearthed his strongbox and slunk off with all the cash he had on hand which, as it happened, was approximately half the sum he had received in compensation from Willy Blackstock.

For this disaster he blamed not so much Ida, and certainly not himself, but almost everyone else, including the brothers Blackstock, Benjamin Belfer and, most of all, the burly, blond Irish boy who, in Mr Orpington's opinion, was the author of all his woes.

'*You!*' he snarled, as soon as he opened the door, then,

lowering the cane and tugging down his nightshirt, got control of himself. 'Well, well, Mr McKenna, what a pleasant surprise, even if the hour is what one might call late. Who's that you have there? Why, if it isn't your lovely sister and – I'll be blowed – isn't that my little ginger friend, Chiffin, hidin' behind you?'

'Sure an' it is, Mr Orpington,' Nolan McKenna answered. 'He has come to pay you what he owes, since he knows you're close to down an' out.'

'Close to . . . Haw, haw! I see. That's a joke.'

' 'Course it is,' said Nolan McKenna. 'Chiff, pay the man his money.'

The girl pushed the lad forward. Even in the miserable light from the oil lamp in the kitchen, Percival Orpington detected loathing in the girl's eyes. He propped his cane against the doorpost and held out both hands.

'How – muh – much, Mr Orpin'ton, sur?' the boy asked.

Perce had lost count of the tally in a mist of chloral hydrate and raw red rage. He had also lost his account book which, he assumed, Ida had taken off to the pawn too. He had not, as yet, opened another one and, if things went according to plan, might not have to.

'Ten shillings?' Percival Orpington said. 'Ten bob will do nicely.'

'How many weeks does that cover, Mr Orpington?' the girl said.

'What? Oh, I dunno.' He had been in bed, half asleep, and his mind was not in arithmetical mode. 'Say, ten – ten weeks.'

'So wuh – we're clear for another fortnight?' said Chiffin.

'Are we?' said Mr Orpington. 'Yes, I suppose we are.'

'Good,' Nolan McKenna said. 'If interest's fixed at a shillin' a week, I'm sure Mr Chiffin can manage that amount. It is fixed at a shillin' a week, ain't it?'

'That seems satisfactory,' said Mr Orpington, still with his hands hovering in mid-air like a beggar on a street corner. 'Do you have ten shillings, Chiffin? I mean to say, if it's inconvenient . . .'

Chiffin dropped four half-crowns into his hands.

'Is that us square, Mr Orpin'ton, sur?'

'Yes, that's us square.'

'No receipt?' the girl said.

Anger rose up in him again, a great rush of anger that almost overwhelmed him. He reached for the cane and for two pins would have smashed it across the smug little Irish bitch's face if the brother hadn't been there. As it was it was all he could do to control himself, to say, 'My word is usually good enough by way of a receipt.'

'Nolly?' the girl said.

'Sure an' I think we can accept Mr Orpington's word instead of a wrote-down receipt,' Nolan said, 'specially since we're neighbours now an' know where to find him if we need him.'

'Neighbours, haw, if you need me, haw,' said Percival Orpington and, with a smile as stiff as the blade of a knife, thanked Chiffin for his prompt payment, and bade his visitors goodnight.

He closed the door quietly and heard them laughing as they went downstairs. He leaned his brow upon the woodwork and breathed through his nose.

Then, wheeling, he stumped into the bare kitchen, hurled the four half-crowns against the wall and smashed the cane down upon the bed, beat and thrashed the blankets and bolster in blind fury, vowing that when the time was ripe he would take revenge not only upon Nolan McKenna, Belfer and the Blackstocks, but upon that smug little Irish bitch as well.

18

To Clare a civil marriage seemed like a sham, too impersonal and perfunctory to have any meaning in the sight of God. Until the last minute she had hoped that Father Fingle would relent, but he did not, nor did he turn up at the registrar's office or at the Harp to wish her well and, by his presence, confer an informal blessing on the union. She remained calm throughout the exchange of vows and the signing of documents. In a frock coat, frilled shirt, suede gloves and top hat Benjamin looked even more pompous than usual, less like a country squire than a government inspector. She noticed, though, that his hands trembled as he put the ring on her finger and scrawled his signature on the crowded page in the huge leather-bound book that would record their marriage for posterity and render them indivisible under law.

The trickle of excitement that had sustained her over the past week had dried up completely by the time he led her out of the registrar's office and down the steps to the pavement where a dozen friends and neighbours, including Mrs Jardine and Betty Fowler, had gathered to shower her with rice and paper rose petals and cluck at how pretty she looked in a low-necked summer dress and a big hat with a skimpy little veil that left her face wide open to inspection. To demonstrate impartiality, they hurled rice at Benjamin too and cheered as he steered his blushing bride across the busy thoroughfare and, with the rest of the wedding party trailing behind, hurried her at something approaching a trot down Wedderburn Road en route to the Harp and a mid-afternoon breakfast.

The weather was dry, though no sun shone and the wind was strong enough to swirl a fine, sandy dust into the faces of the guests as they trooped through the streets. Evie was to the fore, scurrying along, scowling, while little Cissie Cassidy, flanked by Nolan and Jock, brought up the rear.

Bob Draper, Chiffin and Paddy Maizie waited outside the Harp to shake Mr Belfer's hand before the happy couple were shown to the water closet, where, after urgent calls of nature had been attended to, it was assumed that the groom would kiss the bride at last.

Still scowling, Evie flew past the reception committee without a word, knocked through the door and headed for the bar where, to her consternation, a row of wine glasses waited to be transferred to the snug and two of the establishment's regular boozers were propped up, drinking stout as if nothing unusual was taking place. She had just poured herself a brandy to settle her nerves when Chiffin sidled up behind her and, infected by wedding fever, perhaps, endeavoured to put an arm about her waist and kiss her as if she, not Clare, were the bride.

'Get off me, Chiffin,' Evie snapped, pushing him away.

'Aw, come on, love, gi'es a hug.'

'I'll give you a black eye if you don't leave me alone.'

Nonplussed, he stepped back. 'What's wrong with you, Evie? Ain't you happy for your sister?'

'Knocked up an' married to that fat pig – why should I be happy?'

'Well,' said Chiffin, 'for one thing, you look good enough to eat.'

'Aye, like a sausage roll.' Evie downed the brandy, wiped her lips on her wrist and turned on him. 'Who ordered wine?'

'Mr Belfer.'

'What for?'

Chiffin shrugged. 'Toasts, I suppose.'

'Who else is here?'

'Mrs Galloway an' the Chink.'

'Not Orpington?' said Evie.

'Do you think I'd be standin' here if Orpin'ton was on the premises?'

'Nah, maybe not.' Evie conceded. 'Anyone else?'

'Like who?'

'Mr Blackstock, for instance.'

'Now what would Mr Blackstock be doin' at your sister's weddin'?'

'He's employed Belfer for years,' said Evie. 'I thought, perhaps . . .'

'You're dreamin', girl,' said Chiffin, 'just dreamin'.'

Evie sighed. 'Aye, I suppose I am.' Then, as Nolan ushered Aunt Cissie into the bar, cocked her head and offered Chiffin her cheek. 'Make it quick, Chiff,' she said. 'I have to go an' pee.'

Chiffin laughed, shook his head, dabbed her powdered cheek with his lips and watched her hurry off to the water closet where her sister and Benjamin Belfer were still locked in a somewhat less than passionate embrace.

'Handsome is as handsome does, I always say,' Aunt Cissie Cassidy remarked after her third glass of port. 'My Eamon was considered handsome afore the drink pulled him down, even if he was on the short side to start with. If God'll forgive me – which I'm sure He won't – my Eamon was none near as handsome as our Mr Macpherson here when he's done up in his kilt.'

'Now, now, Cissie, that's enough o' that,' Jock told her.

Undeterred, the widow dug an elbow into Evie's ribs. 'If you had one bit o' sense in that head o' yours, Evie McKenna, you'd see what a catch you're missin' now he's washed his face an' trimmed that filthy beard.'

'Do have another ham sandwich, Mrs Cassidy,' Libby Galloway suggested, hastily whipping the plate from the serving table.

'Nah, nah, I'm stuffed. But I'll have another one o' them port-and-lemons, please, since you're offerin'.' Cissie held out her sticky glass. 'It's not every day I gets served by a lady.'

'You're not gettin' served any more, not by a lady or anyone,' Evie told her. 'If you carry on at this rate we'll have to carry you home on a plank.'

'Wouldn't be the first time,' said Cissie grandly. 'I went home on a plank often enough when Eamon was alive. You could lift me in your strong arms, Jock, an' pop me into your sporran an' carry me off an' have your way with—'

'Another toast,' Nolan cried loudly. 'Charge your glasses an' we'll drink to my other lovely sister, eh? To Evie.'

'Evie,' Jock mumbled.

'Aye, to Evie,' Chiffin said. 'I'll drink to Evie any time.'

Evie removed the glass from Cissie Cassidy's fingers and passed it to Libby who prudently lost it among the crockery on the long table. Cissie was too far gone to notice. She dropped her chin on to her breast, closed her eyes and crooned a wistful little melody to herself.

In the sudden lull, the first quiet moment since bride and groom had taken their leave, the ticking of the clock above the door seemed deafening.

'Time we were makin' tracks, I think,' Jock said.

'No,' said Seang Pin from her seat in the corner. 'Not now.'

'Yes, now,' said Libby. 'Patrick, would you be good enough to fetch our overcoats and hats and, if you will, find us a cab?'

'Why?' Pin said. 'Why do we have to leave so soon?'

'Because,' said Libby, 'it's almost dinner time.'

'I could not eat another thing,' said Pin.

'Tell you what,' said Nolan. 'Stay a while, Pin, an' I'll walk you home.'

'Oh, no,' said Libby. 'We're not having that, young man.'

'Havin' what, Mrs Galloway?' said Nolan. 'Don't you trust me?'

'In a word,' Libby said, 'no.'

'I'm a Sunday school teacher, for God's sake; if you can't trust a Sunday school teacher, sure an' who can you trust?'

'You're not a Sunday school teacher just yet,' Libby said, a little more reasonably. 'When you have proved yourself . . .'

'When will that be?' said Pin. 'Some time or never?'

'It was a grand weddin',' Jock said. 'Let's not spoil it by arguin'.'

'No,' Pin said. 'Tell me, Aunt Libby, when will that be?'

It was after seven and in a couple of hours or so the sun would set, night would steal over Clydeside and the leeries would come round and light the streetlamps.

However honest and upright Nolly might be, Evie couldn't blame Libby Galloway for taking a stand against the budding romance. It would come to nothing, anyway, Evie thought bitterly: Nolan was muck, just as she was muck. It was hard on both of them to have fallen into the trap of supposing that they were better than they were simply because chance had landed them in this odd, disjointed neighbourhood.

'Tell you what,' said Paddy Maizie, placing a fatherly arm around Pin's shoulder, 'why don't I run out the coach an' horses and drive you home?'

'I do not want to go home,' said Pin.

'We'll take Nolan with us,' Paddy promised. 'You can sit in the rear with Nolan, an' I'll bring him back with me. How does that sound?'

Head bobbing, eyes closed, Cissie continued to sing her little song, the words too slurred to be recognisable.

'Oh, very well,' Pin said, 'if the arrangement is suitable to Nolly.'

'Suits me fine,' said Nolly. 'Breath of air'll do me good.'

Chiffin was sent out to the yard to tell the ostler to fetch the horse and carriage; and, quite suddenly, the party was over.

Evie looked up.

Jock was standing over her.

'Are you workin' tonight, or are you goin' home?' he asked.

'Goin' home,' said Evie.

'Good,' he said. 'I'll need a hand to put Cissie to bed.'

They looked down at the widow, nodding and crooning to herself, half asleep already on the chair by the wall.

'What's she's singin' about, I wonder?' Evie said.

'Love,' Jock said. 'It's a love song from the old days.'

'How do you know that?' said Evie.

'I used to sing it myself, once upon a time,' Jock said.

'But no longer?'

'No longer,' Jock said and, stooping, lifted the little widow woman and settled her, like a baby, against his shoulder. 'Are you ready to go now, Evie?'

And Evie answered, 'I am.'

Benjamin had taken off his topper and gloves but seemed reluctant to remove his frock coat. He sat stiffly in the armchair with his hands on his knees while Clare, awkward and embarrassed too, scrubbed potatoes and shelled peas for a supper that neither of them wanted.

She had not changed out of her wedding dress and still wore the little half-veil, though she had folded it up so that she could see what she was doing at the sink. She was unused to Benjamin's kitchen and too stubborn to ask where he kept his knives or if he preferred his potatoes mashed or boiled. She kept her back to him, moving from the sink to the dresser and back again with a sliding side-step so that she would not have to meet his eye.

She had hoped that he might treat her to supper in a restaurant in town with candles on the tables and music playing; it would be like the affairs in *Under Two Flags* or *Held in Bondage* or other 'Ouida' stories that she'd bought for a penny in tattered editions at the markets in Cork before Father Garbett had destroyed her illusions and she'd lost all inclination to read about love.

Benjamin did not invite her to supper up town, however. It probably hadn't crossed his mind that a woman in her condition might take pleasure in the niceties of love, or that love was involved at all in what they had done that day and what, when the clock struck eleven, and retiring became inevitable, they would do that night in bed.

'They did us very well, did they not, dearest?' Benjamin said.

'Aye, they did,' Clare agreed. 'Very well.'

'A beautiful bit of ham, wasn't it?'

'Bought fresh from McNair's this mornin',' Clare said.

'Was it? I didn't know that. Who told you that?'

'Mr Draper.'

Clare cleaned a fleck of earth from the eye of a potato with her fingernail. The wedding ring, polished and shiny, slipped about a bit now that her hands were wet. She looked at the unfamiliar shelves above the sink, at the tins, jars and packets that Benjamin had accumulated.

'You like black pepper, I see,' she said.

'I do – an' mustard, too.' He paused. 'Tasty.'

'White vinegar, not brown?'

'Yes, white.'

She filled a pot, the first that came to hand, from the tap that jutted from the panel above the sink. The flow was strong, a great thick jet that splashed out of the pot and wetted the front of her dress. She turned off the tap, dropped six potatoes into the water and carried the pot to the stove. Then, squatting on her heels, she peeped through the bars at the fire.

'We'll need coal soon, Benjamin.'

'It's in the bucket behind the kindlin' basket.'

She remained crouched, drying the front of her dress in the heat of the fire and staring at the tiny spurts of flame that the coals gave off, little blue spurts, soft as sighs, that you only got from best domestic.

Benjamin cleared his throat, and said, 'Well, Clare, it seems that we're married now at last.'

'Aye, we are.'

'Did you ever imagine that one day you would be Mrs Belfer?'

'Sure an' I can't say I did.'

She looked at him directly, half expecting him to be leaning forward, ready to spring upon her. She had not forgotten how cruel he had been to her not so very long ago, how Evie and she had teased him and how much they'd despised him. Now that she was his wife he could do whatever he wished with her and might even make her pay for her impudence. He hadn't changed position, though, and sat with his hands on his knees, stiff as a statue.

'Are you hungry, Clare?' he asked.

'No.'

'Nor me,' he said. 'Put the supper things aside. I've something to show you.'

'What?' she said; then again, 'What?'

She danced on the balls of her feet to hold balance as he reached up and brought from the mantelshelf an oblong enamelled box which he opened with his thumbnail. He hunkered beside her and showed her the collection of keys that the box contained, small keys and long keys, all quite fine and clean.

'My clocks,' he said. 'Since we seem to have some time on our hands, I'll show you how to wind my clocks, shall I?'

And Clare, a little too brightly, said, 'Dearest, what a good idea.'

* * *

The room on the ground floor, across the close from Mr Belfer's, though small, had none of the austerity of Harry Fairfield's room or the grubby clutter of the McKennas' kitchen. Cissie's taste ran to plaster ornaments and cane-framed prints in lurid colours, acquired, mainly, from church bazaars. Every item had its place among the antimacassars, embroidered mottoes, and the chipped teapots that were regularly dusted but never used.

The table was covered with a mock-velvet cloth, the bed with a mock-silk spread and the cushion on Cissie's armchair with a painted case that depicted two parrots nibbling on a coconut. Grate and cooking range were glossy with black lead, the brassware, what there was of it, gleamed and it wouldn't have surprised Evie to discover that the coal in the bucket by the hearth had been scrubbed and polished, too.

Cissie had been transported down Salamanca Street in Paddy Maizie's rig, sprawled in the rear seat, Evie and Jock holding her arms to prevent her sliding into the gutter. Jock had lifted her from the carriage and had carried her into the close while Paddy had turned the rig around and gone back to fetch his second lot of passengers, Libby, Nolan and Pin, whom he would convey to Crosshill House.

It was, as Evie had anticipated, a fine, calm evening, the sky clear enough to show a rising moon and a sprinkling of stars. She had lingered a moment outside the close, listening to the clatter of the horse's hoofs diminishing, listening too, not for telltale sounds from Benjamin Belfer's room, but for a voice from the lane, an urgent calling of her name that would mean that Russell Blackstock had not forgotten her. No call had come, of course, and, disappointed, she had gone into Cissie's apartment to undress the aunt-that-wasn't and tuck her into bed.

When that was done and the widow lay on her back in the alcove bed, eyes closed and mouth open, snoring gently, Jock said, 'Should I sit with her for a wee while?'

'She looks peaceful enough to me,' said Evie. 'She won't waken now.'

'I'll pop in before I go to work in the mornin',' Jock said. 'She'll need wakened early if she's to get to Kennedy's on time. Cissie never had much of a head for drink.'

'Did you know her husband?' Evie said. 'Eamon, I mean?'

'He was dead before I came here, though not long. He had a fearsome reputation as a boozer an' he didn't treat Cissie that well, so I've heard. She's not really your aunt, is she, Evie?'

'Nah,' said Evie. 'It was all pretend.'

'You don't have to pretend now, though.'

'With my sister married to Belfer, you mean?'

'An' your brother so pally with the Blackstocks.'

'It's the girl, the Chink; she's taken a mad fancy for Nolan, though I can't think why. No, we're not pretendin' now, Jock. We took some real knocks back home in Ireland, an' had to look out for ourselves.' She laughed. 'I even managed to scrounge a half a meat pie from a hard-hearted old Highland man, an', by Gar, that took some doin'.'

'He's not so old as all that, Evie, your Highland man.'

'Nor so hard-hearted neither,' Evie said.

'He's just a coal-heaver, though, an' never like to be much else.'

'But he doesn't have a wife hid away in Kingsway, does he?'

'Not him,' Jock said. 'She wasn't wise, your sister.'

'She got carried away,' said Evie.

'Aye, that sort o' thing can happen,' Jock said. 'When it does, common sense flies straight out the window.'

'Has it ever happened to you?' Evie asked.

'Once, just once,' Jock answered. 'But she preferred another.'

'I suppose you're too set in your ways to go lookin' for a wife now?'

'Just because I can look after myself doesn't mean

I wouldn't favour a wife,' Jock said. He paused, and added, 'If the right girl came along.'

'There's always Mrs Cassidy.'

'Cissie's a good friend – but she wouldn't be a good wife for me.'

'Why not?' said Evie. 'She thinks you're very handsome, specially in your kilt an' sporran.'

'I want a family,' Jock said, 'an' Cissie's too old to provide one.'

'Oh!' said Evie, taken aback. 'A family? You mean – babies?'

'Aye,' Jock said quietly. 'Babies.'

'Men aren't supposed to want babies, only the pleasure o' makin' them.'

'Not all men are like Harry Fairfield.'

'That's true,' Evie said. 'My dad was a family man. It damned near killed him earnin' enough to keep us all fed.'

'Do you think marriage is a trap an' babies a burden?'

'I'm not sure I do,' said Evie. 'I never thought about it much.'

'Nor did your sister,' Jock said, 'which might be why she put the cart before the horse.'

'Our Clare could have done better for herself, if she'd only been patient,' Evie said. 'Why did she have to marry bloody Belfer?'

'The question you have to ask yourself is why Belfer married her.'

'That's easy. It's 'cause he wanted her,' Evie said. 'He wanted her from the minute he clapped eyes on her. Even young girls have a sense o' these things, you know. He'll have what he wants from her now, I fancy.'

'An' a family ready made?' Jock said. 'Are you frightened she won't be happy with him, Evie?'

'No,' said Evie. 'I'm frightened that she will.'

* * *

They ate lamb chops, mashed potatoes and peas smothered in a delicious gravy that Benjamin poured from a tall glass jar and had Clare warm up in his 'special' saucepan. There was fresh bread, too, and, afterwards, a rich fruit cake coated with icing that Benjamin said was their wedding cake and cut into slices with a silver-plated knife that he'd purchased for sixpence in a pawnshop near the docks. He talked at great length about pawnshops and the items he'd found there and proudly pointed out the various bargains on his shelves.

Clare dutifully admired his acquisitions and ate two slices of rich fruit cake washed down with a glass of fizzy wine that Benjamin assured her was cheaper than champagne, but just as intoxicating. They would save some of the wine for supper tomorrow, he said, and put the bottle away beneath the sink.

Tomorrow he would buy fresh herrings from the fish-man at the corner of Wedderburn Road and show her how to steep them in white vinegar, and they would finish the fizz and have a feast fit for a king: 'A king *and* a queen,' he added, with a smile.

It was after ten before voices in the close indicated that Mr Macpherson and Evie were leaving Aunt Cissie's at last, and, a few minutes later, Nolan came whistling in from the street. Ten or fifteen minutes after that Clare heard another sound on the stairs. Benjamin said it would be Mr Orpington returning from one of his meetings and she would hear the click of his cane if she listened carefully. Obediently, Clare listened and made out the click of the cane and, very faint and muffled, the sound of a door being opened and a door being closed. Then, because this was a week night, the tenement fell silent and there were no sounds save the ticking of Benjamin's clocks and the sifting of ash in the grate and the drip of the tap that Benjamin said needed a new washer.

He seated himself in his armchair, unbuttoned his frock

coat, and watched Clare wash the plates and pots in the basin at the sink.

'There,' he said, 'the saucepan goes there, the plates on the top shelf, an', if you don't mind a bit of advice, dearest, I prefer to put the scraps in a pail with a lid to avoid attractin' unwelcome visitors, by which I mean mice.'

Clare was tired now and the fizzy drink had left a metallic taste in her mouth, as if she'd been sucking a halfpenny. It would have been fine, she thought, to kiss Benjamin good-night, toddle off upstairs and slip into bed beside her sister, pull the sheet over her head and, all safe and snug, fall fast asleep.

'Now,' Benjamin said musingly, 'now, would it be better for you to visit the privy first, or shall I? There's a chamber pot beneath the bed, but, on consideration, it might be more suitable if you went outside before me, my dear, to allow you a modicum of privacy to do whatever it is you have to do to make yourself ready for – for bed.'

'I'll use the pot if you like,' Clare said.

'What? Oh no. No, no.'

'I'll empty it in the mornin'.'

'Betty does that.'

'Betty? Will she still be comin' in?'

'I see no reason why not,' Benjamin said, 'for all she costs. Besides, she knows my ways.'

She was tired of listening to his voice and, after drying her hands on a towel, edged around the table to the armchair. She saw his hands grip the arms of the chair and his thigh muscles tighten as if he were about to leap up and vault over the table.

'Benjamin,' she said, 'I'm your wife now.'

She smoothed her dress and, kicking off her shoes, seated herself on his knee and kissed him on the mouth; kissed him and pulled back and, when he did not respond, kissed him again and ran her tongue across his upper lip as Harry had taught her to do. Then she spread her knees, hitched up her skirts and petticoat a little, and felt him squirm.

'I'm your wife now, Benjamin,' she said, 'an' this is our weddin' night.'

'But you – your condition . . .'

'No harm will come of it, Benjamin.'

'The woman, Haggarty, did she say . . .'

Clare pushed her hand between her knees and kneaded his thigh. She plucked his hand from the arm of the chair and planted it on her breast. She felt his fingers close about her, and his squirming ceased.

'Clare,' he said. 'Oh, Clare, I love you so much.'

'An' I love you,' she heard herself say, harshly, and, pushing his hand to one side, unbuttoned her dress and fiddled with the band that supported her breasts. 'Here,' she said. 'Don't you want to feel me?'

'You're lovely, Clare, so lovely. I – yes.'

He shoved one hand beneath her clothing, ran his forefinger down the line of her breast, then grabbed her and squeezed so hard that she almost cried out.

'Oh, God!' he said. 'Oh, God!'

She arched her back just enough to show him what she wanted him to do and felt his mouth upon her flesh, the day's stubble on his cheek rough against her skin. He licked and nipped her, too greedy to be gentle. Bare almost to the waist, she lolled against the arm of the chair and let him do as he wished with her, until, abruptly, he pushed her from his lap and struggled to his feet.

'That's enough,' he said.

'What's wrong?' said Clare. 'Benjamin, what's wrong with you?'

'If you don't need to use the privy, I do,' he said and, without another word of explanation, hurried from the kitchen and closed the door behind him.

* * *

Russell had taken Jane and the children to an early evening concert in the Madison Halls, nothing too solemn or weighty. They had returned only a half-hour or so before Libby and Seang Pin, and dinner was served late. It was later still, almost eleven, before Libby persuaded Pin that the day was over and, with the girl gone upstairs at last, tracked her brother to his study.

He was drinking whisky and studying a sheaf of invoices when Libby entered. He was not at ease in his armchair but stood by the desk staring glumly down at the papers as if he hoped that they might spontaneously combust.

'Russell,' she said, 'I need a word with you.'

'It's not about the girl, is it?'

'No, it's not about the girl,' Libby said.

'It wouldn't have been right for me to show my face at Maizie's, you know.'

'I know,' Libby said. 'I didn't expect you to be there.'

'Did she?'

'Who – the bride?'

'The girl, Evie,' Russell said.

'I thought that was all over?' Libby said.

'In spite of what Willy says,' Russell said, 'she was never for me.'

'Ships that pass in the night, hmm?' said Libby. 'Don't you find it ironic that Willy will accuse you of lusting after a little barmaid when he spends half his time drinking with tradesmen in Orange Lodges? He's just as vulgar as you are, Russell – as I am, too. We're caught in the middle and can do little about it.'

'Caught in the middle? What do you mean?'

'Neither one thing nor the other,' Libby said. 'Neither tradesmen nor artisans and not well enough bred to be gentry.'

'Whose fault is that?' said Russell.

'No one's fault,' said Libby. 'Has Wilson started proceedings yet?'

'He has.'

'Paddy says it'll take years.'

'Not if I know Willy, it won't,' said Russell.

'Will you sell him the tenements?'

'I may have to, of course, to complete the harbour project.'

'I have money,' Libby said.

'I know you do.'

'What's more, Russell, I have property.'

'A half share in the Harp, yes.'

'You didn't know my husband, did you?' Libby said. 'You made no effort whatsoever to get to know him. He was damned in your eyes from the first because he was Catholic. Catholic or not, Peter Galloway was no fool, believe me. He spoke three languages and umpteen dialects and dealt equally with men and woman of all creeds and colours without a trace of superiority. And when he died, he left me a tidy fortune.'

'Are you saying that you can buy me out?'

'I'm simply offering you a choice, Russell.'

'What sort of choice?'

'I'll sell you my leases at a reasonable price, on condition that you do not sell them on to Wilson or to the bank.'

'How am I supposed to finance this purchase?'

'That's up to you,' said Libby.

'What's the alternative?'

'I'll buy the leases on your tenements.'

'And do what with them?'

'Keep them,' Libby said. 'Keep them from Willy.'

'Do you hate him that much?'

'I don't hate him at all,' said Libby. 'I only hate what he stands for, his greed, his bigotry and his stupefying sense of moral superiority. Willy's my brother, however, and there are thousands just like him, men on the rise, men who are better prepared than we are to carry Glasgow into the next century.'

'Are you preaching Christian Socialism now?'

'I'm not preaching anything, least of all socialism,' Libby said. 'I'm on your side – at least, I *think* I'm on your side.'

'Four tenements,' said Russell, 'take a great deal of managing, Libby, or is it your intention to let them fall down of their own accord?'

'Certainly not,' said Libby. 'I'll put them in a good state of repair and make them a damned sight more habitable than they are now.'

'It isn't as simple as you imagine, Libby. It isn't like charity work. You won't have nuns and priests scampering to do your bidding. You're an excellent organiser, I'll admit, but managing rent-bearing properties – that's not for you.'

'I'll have help.'

'Who? Paddy Mazzie?'

'Among others.'

'From all you've said I assume you don't intend to employ men like Orpington and Benjamin Belfer?'

Libby shook her head. 'Not if I can possibly avoid it.'

'Then you'll go broke within a year.'

'That,' Libby said, 'is a risk I'm willing to take.'

'Out of a sense of obligation to the poor and needy, like the giving of alms?' said Russell. 'Are you trying to reserve a special place in heaven, is that it? Salamanca Street's a long way from heaven, Libby.'

'Will it be better for them when Willy knocks down their homes?'

'They'll find other rooms to rent, other places to live. They always do,' Russell said. 'Look, I've no wish to go to war with Willy. I may not agree with what he's doing but I do understand why he wants to shake off the burden of slum-ownership and make better use of our leases.'

'Father's legacy, you mean,' said Libby. 'Father's tainted legacy.'

'A coal yard, an old stables, a dozen decaying tenements . . .'

'Wilson doesn't give a damn about progress, Russell. He's not building homes for the men who'll dig out your harbours and lay the facings on your quays. He's building for himself and those like him, men on the rise, who'll ride roughshod over everything and anyone.'

'I applaud your idealism, Libby,' Russell said, 'but you can't stand in the way of progress.'

'Perhaps not,' Libby said, 'but I can delay it for a little while.'

'Have you any idea what buying out the leases will cost?'

'No, not an exact figure.'

'No matter how much you inherited from your husband and how much profit you've harvested from your partnership with Maizie, take it from me, Libby, you don't have enough capital to finance this scheme.'

'Possibly not,' Libby said, 'but I know someone who does.'

'And who might that be?' said Russell.

And Libby said, 'Seang Pin.'

19

Marriage was the strangest thing, Clare thought, her marriage to Benjamin Belfer, that is, for his demands upon her were so few. He didn't object when she went upstairs to clean her sister and brother's room while Betty Fowler scrubbed and polished the ground-floor apartment. He allowed her to spend time at the wash tubs but insisted on shopping for groceries himself. He prepared the evening meal and instructed her how to cook it, thus smudging the distinction between the duties of a husband and the duties of a wife still further. And late at night, when the building fell silent and there was no help for it but to undress and go to bed, he would shilly-shally as if the last thing in the world he wanted to do was slip between the sheets.

At first Clare supposed that he might be afraid of damaging the baby. She tried to tell him that the infant was wrapped up safe and sound in the folds of her womb but Benjamin was unwilling to accept her assurances.

When they lay together in the broad double bed, with nothing but one layer of flannel and one layer of cotton separating them, he would inch away from her as if he, not she, were the blushing bride, and when she rubbed against him, he would become unnaturally rigid, as if, like that creature in Greek mythology, she had turned him into stone.

'Don't you want to, Benjamin?' She pressed her breasts against his shoulder blades and her belly against his bottom. 'I'm ready when you are.'

'Time enough for that sort o' thing later.'

'Later?' She blew lightly on to the hair at the back of his neck. 'We've been married near a week, dearest.'

'I'm not like your bloody coal-heaver, Clare. He'd have poked you a dozen times by now, I suppose.'

She lifted herself on an elbow. 'I made no secret about Harry Fairfield. You knew all about him when you married me. I thought you wanted me.'

'All I want is a dutiful wife.'

'What am I, then?' Clare said sharply. 'Green cheese?'

It was warm in the alcove bed. She could smell his sweat, not foul but sweet, almost cloying, for he was no digger or coalman. When he washed at the sink, which he did with great thoroughness, he used a large yellow sponge, and when he shaved he shaved with lavender-scented soap, and, unlike Nolan, changed his vest and drawers every day.

'Don't you even want to look at me?' she said.

There was no light in the room save a faint glow from the embers in the grate. She thought of Harry; how he had flaunted himself before her in broad daylight, showing off his lean belly. How flattered she been, lying naked on her back in a pool of sunlight with everything on display, how ready she had been to receive him when he straddled her.

'You don't have to see me, Benjamin,' she said. 'Feel me. Here, put your hand on me an' feel me. See, I'm ready for whatever you have to give.'

He struck her with the flat of his hand, cuffing her swiftly and accurately on the side of her head. 'You're not a whore I'm payin' by the minute. Do you understand?'

Her head rang and her ear stung but in the heat of his outburst she detected desire as well as anger. She lay back against the pillows and stared at the ceiling.

'Clare?' he said, softly now. 'Do you understand me?'

'Yes, Benjamin,' she answered meekly. 'Yes, Benjamin, I do.'

The trades' holidays were well and truly over and, with August drawing to a close, even upper-crust families were returning home from their summer sojourns by the sea. Neither Russell nor Willy had seen fit to take a house at the coast this year, for, appearances to the contrary, money was tight and they could not afford time off from the work they had on hand.

The same could not be said for Cameron James, legal adviser to the Administrator Apostolic of the Western District of the Metropolitan See of Glasgow. To Cameron James playing golf was infinitely preferable to working. In fact, he had just spent three weeks on the links of St Andrews beating the very devil out of a golf ball, or, to be accurate, several dozen golf balls, and he was not at all happy at being back in harness.

He was a man of middle height, with thinning fair hair, and, after three weeks battling east coast winds, had the weather-beaten complexion of a gardener or a ferry-man that did not sit well with his double-breasted morning coat, high-standing collar and extravagant Ascot necktie.

Fortunately for his clients, Cameron James was a better lawyer than he was a golfer and, for some years now, had been known in legal circles as 'The Great Conveyancer'. Anyone who had business with the archdiocese was at perfect liberty to make an appointment with the archbishop or the vicar-general and would be politely received at 33 Rose Street between the hours of noon and two o'clock, Tuesdays and Fridays. But the chap you dealt with when it came to Church-owned property was Mr Cameron James, whose expertise in transfers of title deeds and leases was equalled only by his discretion.

In his elegant office in St Vincent Street, the metaphorical drawbridge had been raised, the moat filled and three clerks posted to deter eavesdroppers, and, at last, Mr Cameron James was ready to talk turkey.

'Madam,' he said, 'am I to understand that you wish to purchase the chapel that presently stands at 77 Salamanca Street, and the burying ground that adjoins it?'

'That is correct,' said Libby.

'May I ask why you wish to make such a purchase?'

'To protect the chapel from being sold to parties who might wish to demolish it.'

'Even if St Kentigern's and its burying ground are to be made available for sale,' said Mr James, 'do you imagine that I would recommend my clients to sell to a sister of Wilson Blackstock, a notorious Orangeman?'

'It's true that my brother Wilson has designs upon the property, but I'm not acting on his behalf, or even with his knowledge.'

'You're a convert, are you not?'

'I am a practising Catholic, yes.'

'And the young lady?'

'She is also a Catholic,' Libby said. 'Mission educated.'

'May I enquire which Mission that might be?' said Cameron James.

'Waterfall Road, sir.' Pin answered for herself. 'In Penang.'

'Also, if I'm not mistaken, a former pupil at Our Lady?' said James.

'Yes, sir,' said Pin politely.

'Although we haven't met before, Mr James,' said Libby, 'I believe you know perfectly well who I am.'

'Of course I know who you are. You're a friend of Patrick Maizie and a generous patron of Our Lady orphanage. I am merely breaking the ice.'

'Well, now the ice has been broken,' Libby said, 'would not my time, and yours, be better spent in getting down to brass tacks?'

'Brass tacks it is then, Mrs Galloway,' said Cameron James. 'What do you know of the law in respect of Church-administered properties?'

'Precious little,' Libby admitted.

'And of burying grounds?'

'Even less.'

'Burying grounds are, as a rule, provided by the heritors of the original estate. In the case of St Kentigern's, however, the burying ground was bundled with the land on which the church stands, for the simple reason that Catholic ownership was illegal at the time the deeds were drawn up.'

'Are you saying, in effect, that the archdiocese owns the lot?'

'Ownership is a relative term, Mrs Galloway,' Cameron James went on. 'Churches are *extra commercium* and strict laws apply to the sale of existing buildings and the erection of new ones.'

'Do these laws apply equally to Catholic churches?' Libby said.

The lawyer smiled. 'Aye, that's the rub. They apply only in part to establishments owned or leased by the archdiocese, largely because the Scots legal system took little or no account of the possibility of a Catholic Emancipation Act ever coming into force and has not caught up yet.'

'In short,' said Libby, 'if I wish to buy a Catholic church I am not constrained by law from doing so?'

'You are only constrained in what you may do with it,' said Cameron James. 'May I ask, what do you intend to do with it?'

'Give it back to the diocese,' said Libby.

'And charge the diocese rent, I assume?'

'A nominal rent,' said Libby, 'at a fixed rate.'

'I take it you're aware that St Kentigern's is in a poor state of repair?'

'Only too well aware,' said Libby.

'Also, that the parish is shrinking?' said Cameron James.

'It will shrink all the faster if the proposed new road cuts through it,' said Libby. 'If St Kentigern's remains, repaired and refurbished, at least there will be a church for the Catholic community of Riverside to hang on to.'

'What will your brothers have to say to that?'

'They will be furious.'

'I trust,' the lawyer said, 'that you are not involving the archdiocese in a spiteful family squabble. That would not be right or fitting.'

'Less right and fitting than putting St Kentigern's into the hands of the Barony Bank,' said Libby. 'That, in effect, is what you'll be doing if you transfer ownership of the leases to either of my brothers. Before we proceed, Mr James, answer me this: has the archbishop received permission to sell the grounds of St Kentigern's mission, and is it in his mind to do so?'

'I cannot betray Church confidences, I'm afraid,' said Cameron James. 'Sales are private matters between the papal authorities and Archbishop Eyre.'

'Is the archbishop awaiting an offer?'

'That I cannot tell you.'

'Will you put my proposal to him in principle?' said Libby.

'By all means,' said Cameron James. 'If I might be so bold as to ask, Mrs Galloway, why are you pursuing this scheme? Your brothers will think you're mad, you know.'

'My brothers have always thought me mad,' said Libby.

'Now you intend to prove it, do you?' said Cameron James.

'Precisely,' said Mrs Libby Galloway. 'Now I intend to prove it.'

Pin said nothing until they were seated at a table for two in the tea-lounge of the George Hotel and she had scoffed two rounds of hot buttered toast and an iced fairy cake; then she enquired, 'Aren't you going to tell me, Aunt Libby?'

'Tell you what, child?'

'Why you took me with you today?'

'I thought you might find it of interest to see how business is done.'

'Oh, I did,' said Pin. 'I found it of great interest. However, I think you are not telling me the whole truth.'

'In a matter of weeks,' Libby said, 'you will attain the ripe old age of eighteen, and will be free of me.'

'I do not wish to be free of you,' said Pin.

'I am gratified to hear it,' Libby said.

'You are all I have in the world.'

'If anything happens to me, Russell will always look after you. He and I may be at loggerheads but he cares for you, too, you know,' Libby said. 'But the fact of the matter is that I have kept you so close to me that my friends are your friends and my enemies are your enemies. And that is not how it should be. Soon, very soon, you will be able to choose what you want to do with your life. You may, for example, wish to go back to the Far East.'

'My home is here,' said Pin, 'not in the Far East.'

'Then you might choose to marry.'

'Marry without your permission, you mean?'

Libby nodded. 'Without my permission, or my approval.'

'Marry, say, Nolan McKenna?'

Libby nodded again. 'If that's your wish.'

'It's certainly something I've thought about.'

'Before we rush off in that direction,' Libby said, 'have you any idea what you're worth, Pin?'

'Worth?'

'Financially,' Libby said.

'I know Papa left me something and that you have been in charge of it.' She fixed her aunt with a penetrating gaze. 'Are you going to tell me, Aunt Libby, that I have no money and, free or not, must continue to depend upon Uncle Russell's charity?'

'Quite the contrary,' Libby said. 'Your father's estate amounted to over seven thousand pounds, English. As your guardian, I invested that sum with the Bank of Scotland. Rather deceitfully, I made no mention of it to anyone in the family. I preferred to let Russell take care of us because we needed a home, a proper home and a family. Of course, Russell knows that I have money of my own invested in the Harp in partnership with Mr Maizie.'

'Why did you do such a thing?'

Libby laughed. 'To infuriate Willy, I suppose. No, that's too glib. I was looking about for something that would be as far from Blackstock interests as possible when Father Fingle introduced me to Paddy Maizie who had just lost his trading licence and who was so eager to open a public house, an Irish house, that he would have sold me his soul if it had been worth anything.'

'Were you taken in by his charm, Aunt Libby?'

'Not me,' said Libby. 'I saw through Patrick straight away. I saw that he was honest and generous and that he would not cheat me for his own ends.'

'Did he remind you of your husband?' said Pin.

'You know,' said Libby, 'I do believe he did. For whatever reason, I elected to finance the purchase of the Harp and entered a partnership arrangement with Patrick, who was not entirely without funds of his own.'

'And is, as we are, a Catholic?'

'The Harp has been good to me,' Libby said. 'I can't deny I've enjoyed my friendship with Patrick, not least because it's chaste. Paddy appeals to a disreputable side of my nature.' She gave herself a little shake, firm enough to cause the ebony-wood crucifix to bob against her breast. 'Be that as it may, the thing I have to tell you, Pin, is that on the day of your eighteenth birthday you will receive statements of your accounts with the Bank of Scotland and the sums they contain, sums that, in total, add up to almost thirteen thousand pounds.'

'Dear God in heaven!' said Pin. 'I'm rich.'

'Moderately so,' said Libby.

'Why have you said nothing of this before now?'

'In case Willy found out,' said Libby. 'He may regard you as some kind of heathen incongruity who has no right to be in Glasgow, let alone part of the Blackstock clan, but that wouldn't stop him trying to part you from your inheritance.' Libby paused, closed her eyes, opened them again. 'Which, in fact, is what I am about to do now, my dearest.'

'What do you mean?'

'I want you to help me buy property in Riverside.'

'St Kentigern's, do you mean?' said Pin.

'The purchase of St Kentigern's, if it can be managed, is my affair, my little act of folly, if you will. I wouldn't expect you to be involved in that.'

'In what then?' Pin said.

'In buying out Russell's tenements.'

'Becoming a slum landlord,' said Pin, 'like your father?'

'Not like my father,' Libby said. 'That's entirely the point.'

The girl sat back in her chair and stared at her buttery plate. For all her experience Libby could not read her ward's expression or guess at what thoughts were rushing through her head.

'Aunt Libby,' Pin said, at length, 'why are you doing this? Why do you wish to buy up these dirty old buildings?'

'To make amends,' Libby said.

'For what?' said Pin.

'The sins of the fathers,' Libby said.

'In that case,' Pin said soberly, 'count me in.'

For a church with so few regular worshippers St Kentigern's managed to attract a fair number of children to its Sunday school. If Nolan had expected bedlam he was pleasantly surprised to discover that the children were relatively well-behaved and that even the very youngest were interested enough in learning about Jesus and the lives of the more respectable saints to keep quiet for four or five minutes at a stretch. Nolan may have been no great shakes as a storyteller but he did not have to raise his voice to command attention.

'You,' he'd say quietly. 'Where d'you think you're goin'?'

'Miss – Miss Tracy's class.'

'Hurry along, then, hurry along.'

And the dawdler would scurry off, red-faced with embarrassment.

When Sunday school was over and the children had dispersed, Nolan and Seang Pin were left alone in the church. Mrs Galloway did not, it seemed, teach at Sunday school but, according to Pin, had relented enough in her attitude to permit Nolan to escort her home to Crosshill.

'She's changed her tune all of a sudden, hasn't she?' said Nolan.

'Perhaps she has realised that I am no longer a child,' said Pin. 'I'll be eighteen in a few weeks, you know.'

'Eighteen! Ah, eighteen!' said Nolan with a mock sigh. 'I remember when I was eighteen. Seems like only yesterday.'

'You fool, Nolly,' Pin said, laughing. 'However, you had better mind your Ps and Qs now, old chap, for soon I will be able to marry without permission.'

'Does that mean Mrs Galloway will no longer be your guardian?'

'She will no longer be my legal guardian,' Pin said, 'but nothing will change between Aunt Libby and me.'

'So there's no such thing as marriage on your mind, Pin?'

'Who'd marry me? I'm not even white.'

'Aye,' said Nolan, 'what sort of a muttonhead would want a beautiful girl like you for a wife.'

'Would the muttonhead change his mind if he knew I was well off?'

'Are you?' said Nolan. 'Nah, you're not worth tuppence.'

'What if I was – if I am well off?'

'Wouldn't make no difference,' Nolan said.

'Then it's just as well I'm not,' said Pin and, taking his arm, led him out on to the steps of the church where a nun and some young helpers were chatting.

'Fine evening, Sister, is it not?' said Pin.

'It is,' said the nun brusquely. 'Where is Mrs Galloway?'

'At home, as far as I am aware,' said Pin.

'She isn't leaving you alone with that man, surely?'

'There are worse men to be left alone with, Sister Catherine,' Pin said.

'It isn't right, you know. It isn't right,' the nun muttered.

'What isn't, Sister?' said Pin. 'A Chink being escorted by an Irishman, or an Irishman escorting a Chink? In any case, I'm sure I'll come to no harm with Mr McKenna by my side,' and, with that, stepped down into Salamanca Street, dragging Nolan, not at all reluctantly, in her wake.

'I must say, Benjamin,' Clare said, 'I'm surprised at us not visitin' sooner. Does she even know we're married?'

'Oh, she knows,' Benjamin said. 'Trust me, she knows.'

'Are you hurt because she didn't turn up at the weddin'?'

'I'd have been more hurt if she had,' Benjamin said.

'Not a word from her, though,' said Clare, 'not the scratch of a pen, as much, offerin' us her good wishes.'

'Scratch of a pen? My mother can't read or write.'

'That's a sore affliction,' said Clare. 'How did she learn her Scriptures?'

'What use would Scriptures be to my mother? In the Red Pit at Anniesland there was nothing to be gained from praying to a God who allowed the Red Pit to exist at all.'

'Have you no religion, Benjamin?'

'None worth the name.'

'The baby, though, our baby – we will have him baptised, won't we?'

'Aye,' said Benjamin, 'if that's your wish.'

'It is my wish.'

'I was under the impression you'd renounced the Church,' said Benjamin.

'I might've given up goin' to church for a while but I certainly haven't renounced my faith in God an' all His many mercies.'

'I'm tempted to ask what many mercies,' said Benjamin, 'but I'm feared you'll give me another o' those lectures about the Day o' Judgement.' He chuckled. 'My, but you had me on the griddle that day, you an' your sister.'

'Serves you right,' said Clare. 'Eyein' us up like that was naughty.'

'I was nothin' of the kind eyeing you up.'

'You were, too,' said Clare.

'Well, can you blame me?' said Benjamin. 'Beautiful girls like you.'

'Your mam doesn't think I'm a beautiful girl,' said Clare. 'She thinks I'm a fiend out o' hell for stealin' away her son.'

'She's only concerned about herself,' said Benjamin. 'She's been badgerin' me for years to find a wife so she'd have someone to order about.'

'Well, if you think I'm goin' to dance attendance . . .' Clare began.

'I don't,' said Benjamin. 'What's more neither does my mother. She expected me to pick a meek wee thing who wouldn't say boo to a goose.'

'An' instead you picked me.'

'You stood up to her,' said Benjamin. 'Stood up to her in a

way I've never dared do, an' she hates you for it, an' hates me for bringin' you into her house.'

'If it's her house,' said Clare, 'let her keep it.'

'I thought you liked Bellingham Place?'

'I do, Benjamin, I do, but not if I have to share it with your mam,' said Clare. 'She has a housekeeper, a spacious apartment, food on the table an' fuel for the fires; what more can she expect from you?'

'Devotion,' said Benjamin. 'Devotion an' admiration. So, let's see what she has to say for herself now I'm a married man. Shall we?'

'By all means,' Clare said. 'Ring the bloody doorbell, Benjamin, an' let's get this ordeal over with.'

It was the first of the harvest moons and the biggest that anyone in Belfer's tenement had ever seen. It rose so stealthily that its enormous size did not become apparent until it appeared through the gap between lane and gable and seemed to fill the whole night sky.

All up and down Salamanca Street folk came out to watch the moon rise and dream those dreams of city-dwellers, of barley fields and farms and the smell of wood-smoke, and if there had been a piper or some young lassie singing unaccompanied then sentiment would have taken over completely and tears would have flowed in copious profusion.

'It's the dust,' Jock said.

'The dust? What dust?' said Evie.

'It's the dust causes the magnification,' Jock went on. 'The moon's close to the earth this season o' the year, an' the layer of dust—'

'Havers!' said Cissie.

'No, no,' said Benjamin, 'Macpherson has a point.'

'Dust!' said Evie scornfully.

'Big fires in Canada,' said Jock.

'Canada?' said Clare. 'What does Canada have to do with it?'

'Right you are, Jock,' said Benjamin. 'Forest fires in Canada send clouds o' dust sailin' over the Atlantic into our atmosphere.'

'Is that a Canadian moon then?' Cissie asked. 'Is that why it's so big?'

Benjamin and Jock sighed in unison.

'It's the same moon we see in Cork every autumn,' said Evie, 'only our moons are bigger.'

'Never!' said Benjamin. 'I'm a lot older than you are, my dear, an' I've never seen a moon that size before.'

'Aye, but you've never been in Cork,' Evie retorted.

'Three different moons,' said Cissie. 'One for us, one for the Irish, another one for the Canadians.'

'Have you been at the port again, Aunt Cissie?' Clare enquired.

'Chance would be a fine thing, dear.' Cissie pushed a tray of hot buttered scones through the window of her ground-floor room. 'Here, have a bite to keep you goin' before that partic'lar moon falls down on us.'

'Whoever's moon it is,' said Nolan dreamily, 'it's gorgeous.'

'Dear God!' said Evie. 'Look at him. He'll be howlin' at it in a minute.'

'He's only in love,' said Clare. 'Give him a scone. That'll shut him up.'

The mid-evening soirée had sprung up after Jock had fetched Evie and Nolan to the close-mouth to admire the lunar phenomenon. Cissie, who had been baking in her kitchen, had been drawn by familiar voices on the pavement and had propped open her window just as Mr and Mrs Belfer, arm-in-arm, had appeared around the corner from the direction of the park.

In addition to a spectacular moonrise, it was such a balmy

evening, with just the faintest taste of autumn in the air, that no one wanted to go indoors. Benjamin brought out a kitchen chair for Clare to sit upon, Evie perched herself on Cissie's windowsill, and the men, as men will, formed a defensive half-circle around the women.

'In love?' said Benjamin. 'Is your brother really in love?'

'Aye, he is.'

Evie passed the tray of scones to Jock who passed it to Nolan who had to be roused from his contemplation of the moon to hand it on to Clare

'Who's he in love with?' said Benjamin.

'I told you, dearest,' said Clare. 'He's fallen for a Chinese girl.'

'She's half Malayan,' said Nolan, coming out of his reverie long enough to help himself to a scone. 'You've met her, Benjamin. She was at the weddin'.'

''Course she was,' said Benjamin. 'Lovely girl, lovely.'

'Jewel o' the Orient,' said Clare.

'Not as lovely as my Irish jewel, though.' Benjamin selected a scone, placed it tenderly on his wife's lap, and patted her shoulder. 'It's a funny old world we live in, ain't it?'

'What's funny about it?' Evie said. 'It never seemed funny to you before.'

Benjamin stared up at the moon which, having done its bit for the citizens of Riverside, had begun to retreat, shrinking imperceptibly as it went. He said, 'Well, I'm just wonderin' why we've never done this sort of thing before.'

'What sort of thing, Mr Belfer?' said Cissie.

'Met like this, talked like this,' Benjamin said.

'Perhaps because you were only interested in screwin' the rent out of us,' Evie began. 'Now you're one of us, whether we like it or not.'

'One of you?' Benjamin blinked. 'Am I? Good God! I do believe I am.'

* * *

Dinner, and bedtime, had been delayed to allow the Blackstocks of Crosshill House to run outside and marvel at the moon. With the river on their doorstep they had the advantage of an open sight-line and, laid along the horizon, all the hills in silhouette in the sun's long-lingering afterglow.

Nanny brought the children down, Libby and Pin shepherded them across the roadway to the railings and, leaning as if on a quarter-deck, they dutifully gasped at the sight of the huge moon, red as a blood orange and pitted like custard pudding, and asked a host of questions that only Libby seemed willing to answer, for Pin, like her soul-mate in the tenements, was lost in a world of her own.

On the step before the front door, Russell and his mother lingered, watching not so much the rising of the moon as the rising of the next generation.

'I hear that Libby has been to the lawyer?' Mother Blackstock said.

'Yes, she told me,' Russell said. 'Cameron James.'

'He has handled no business for us before, has he?'

'No,' Russell said. 'And he's handling no business for us now.'

'Will Libby act against your interests, too, Russell?'

'Libby.' He paused. 'Libby remains unfathomable.'

'Not to me,' said Mother Blackstock. 'I can read your sister like a book. She's been harbouring grievances of one sort or another for umpteen years. She intends to thwart Willy's plans for expansion no matter what it costs her. Has she offered to buy your tenements?'

'Yes.'

'Then sell.'

'I'm not sure I can,' said Russell. 'I'm mortgaged on those properties, too, and the Barony—'

'Libby will assume responsibility for the debt and there's precious little the Barony can do about it.'

'If only Dad were still alive, he'd know what to do for the best.'

'Your father never did anything for the best,' Mother Blackstock said. 'Are you still salting away cash with Maizie?'

Russell hesitated, then nodded. 'I'm sorry I ever got into that. Maizie is just too close to Libby for comfort.'

'He is trustworthy, though.'

'Oh, yes, my cash is safe enough with him. The problem is that Libby knows a little too much about the arrangement, not to mention the schemes Dad set up that, frankly, should have been buried with him.'

'Give Libby what she wants,' said Mother Blackstock. 'You've no reason to operate in Riverside now. Cameron James handles business for the Catholic diocese, doesn't he?'

'Yes, he does.'

'Libby's hoping to buy the church grounds, isn't she?'

The children had begun to drift away from the railing, for the air was cooling now and a chill little breeze was coming in off the river. Libby and Pin were acting as policemen though there was no traffic on the road at that hour.

'It's a very complicated issue,' said Russell.

'The Catholics won't release one hectare to you, or to Willy.'

'If the offer is high enough, they might,' said Russell.

'Will you negotiate with Willy?'

'No,' Russell said.

'Then stand aside and sell your tenements to Libby,' his mother said. 'Let your sister do what she feels is right.'

'Even if it ruins her?' said Russell.

'Even if it ruins you,' his mother said.

'Surely you don't want to see me brought down?'

'Of course not,' Mother Blackstock said. 'But if Willy insists on going ahead without you, you'll have to gamble on your own.'

'To finish the harbour project, do you mean?'

'To finish the harbour project and move on,' his mother said.

The first of his children rushed through the gate and headed past him into the hall in search, no doubt, of supper.

'Move on to what, though?' Russell said.

'Better things,' his mother said.

And then, quite gaily, she followed her grandchildren indoors.

Clare lay on top of the quilt in the half dark of the bed recess. She had put on her best nightdress, the one with the embroidered collar, and had propped a pillow behind her shoulders. She had almost yielded to the temptation to throw modesty to the winds, undress completely and lie naked, challenging him to prove himself a true husband or explain once and for all his reluctance to make love to her. In the end, she had settled for a nightdress.

Benjamin had extinguished all but one of the gas lamps. He sat in shadow in the armchair, coat off and waistcoat unbuttoned, not reading but, hunched a little forward, staring intently at the flickers in the grate as if, Clare thought, he might find the answer to all his problems spelled out there.

She did not call to him to come to her, for then, surely, he would go out to the privy in the close and might be gone for a half-hour and the day would end badly, and the rapport that she – and he – had experienced outside on the pavement would be replaced by that clenched and sullen rage again, and the dismal dance of avoidance would begin.

She cleared her throat. 'I thought your father was a wee bit better today, didn't you, Benjamin?'

'Hmm, a little perhaps.'

'Do you think he knows who I am yet?'

'I doubt it.'

'He doesn't push me away, though.'

'He was always fond o' pretty girls,' said Benjamin. 'Too fond, if you believe half the stories my mother tells.'

'He must have been a vigorous man in his day.'

'To do the job he did, month after month, year after year, you had to be vigorous, I suppose,' Benjamin said. 'She's tryin' to get rid o' Mrs Loomis, you know. Did you hear her goin' on about it?'

'Has she sacked her? Did I hear that right?'

Benjamin sat back and rubbed his brow with his wrist.

'Aye, she's sacked Mrs Loomis two or three times but the woman will not leave without a signed letter from me. My mother has no answer to that manoeuvre, for she knows I'll sign no such letter, ever. She may tell Mrs Loomis to leave till she's blue in the face but the woman's too clever for her. That's what sticks in her damned old throat, I think, that she can no longer call the tune. Provided Mrs Loomis is there to look after them, we're safe enough here.'

'Then here we'll stay,' said Clare.

'It's such a fine apartment, such a fine address: Bellingham Place,' said Benjamin wistfully. 'Would it not be grand for us to live there?'

'Sure an' we will live there,' said Clare. 'Some day.'

He appeared suddenly at the side of the bed, surprising her.

'Ain't that why you married me, Clare?' he said. 'To have a fine spacious apartment to live in an' an address to make you proud.'

Clare stirred, shifting her legs and rolling on to her hip to look up at him, the nightdress, catching between her thighs, taut across her belly. There was no hint of anger in him and when he looked down on her she could see sadness in his eyes, a strange, hang-dog sort of sadness, devoid of all desire.

'No,' she said warily. 'I married you 'cause you asked me to.'

'You know I love you, Clare?'

'I know.'

'Is it enough for you to have me love you?'

'It is enough, aye.'

'God, but you're beautiful,' he said. 'So beautiful.'

'Is that enough for *you*, then, Benjamin?'

She could not shake the memory of Harry Fairfield and the pleasures he had coaxed from her, wicked pleasures that required no art or guile. Now she was married to a man who said he loved her but she was afraid that being loved without loving would not be enough for her forever, or even for very long. She might reach for him, wrap her arms around him, easily unbalance him and pull him down to her, but she sensed that she had badly misinterpreted the nature of the bargain between them – and did nothing.

'What my mother says is true,' Benjamin said in a voice hardly above a whisper. 'She knows I can't give you a child. She knows that however much we show off to her, it's a sham.'

'Benjamin, your mother . . .'

'Wait,' he said, turning from her.

She watched him fumble with buttons and belt, saw his trousers fall about his ankles, and then, hobbled, he turned towards her. She raised herself up, more in fear than expectation, and watched him lift his shirt.

His belly was round and smooth as a boulder in a stream.

Beneath it was a single tussock of coarse black hair.

Beneath the hair was a small, twisted piece of flesh that appeared to be attached to nothing of any consequence, like a lamb doctored too soon.

'Oh, God!' Clare said. 'Oh, Benjamin, you poor, poor man.'

'Now do you see?' he said.

'I do, I do,' Clare said, and covered her face with her hands.

PART FIVE

Ships That Pass

20

By the end of September Percival Orpington's ankle had healed enough to bear his full weight and the cane had become more of an affectation than a necessity. He had returned to the Barony Bank as a guard and accompanied Mr Morrison, cashier of Penny Savings, on his rounds. He was once more on duty at the Masonic Halls, north of Riverside Road, and Cissie Cassidy saw more of her upstairs neighbour on Saturday evenings than she did at any other time. No matter how often he raised his topper, though, she regarded him with suspicion now and gave him short shrift when he tried to pump her for information about the McKennas.

On Friday afternoons – Mr Orpington was seldom at home in the evening – Benjamin went upstairs to collect the weekly rent. Mr Orpington would open the door dressed in a gaudy silk dressing-gown and slippers. Sometimes he would have a newspaper in his hand, sometimes a book, and he looked, Benjamin thought, more like the sort of chap you would find in a gentleman's club than in a single room in a down-at-heel tenement in Riverside. The old friends were friends no more and Mr Orpington had not sought to return to his post with the rent-collector. But when they met he was never less than amiable and the pair would trade jokes and local tittle-tattle, though, rather to Benjamin's relief, he was never invited to cross the threshold.

'Haw, Benjamin, so it's that time of the week again, is it?' Mr Orpington would say. 'What, tell me, will you do if I don't have the dibbins? Attack me with that weapon you have in your trousers?'

'I'll reason with you first, Perce,' Benjamin said.

'Reason with me? I'm the chap who does the reasoning, if you recall. Always better at it than you were. Do you still carry the pipe?'

'I do still carry the pipe, though not when I'm doing this place.'

'No welchers here, old chap, nobody sneakin' off down the back stairs or hidin' in the water closet? Got them all tamed, have you?' Mr Orpington said.

'All meek as lambs,' said Benjamin. 'No fly-by-nights in this building.'

'What about the sailor?'

'Pays in advance.'

'Are both women his?'

'Sisters.'

'And how's your dear old ma?'

'What? Oh, she's as well as can be expected.'

'And your lady wife? Is she bloomin''?'

'Like a rose, Perce, like a rose.'

'Good, that's good. Here's your rent, then, Mr B.'

'Thank you, Perce. Until next week?'

'You know where to find me,' Mr Orpington said.

And, although that wasn't strictly true, Benjamin nodded none the less.

If Percival Orpington kept himself to himself and held his plans in his head, the same could not be said for Wilson Blackstock. As autumn slithered towards winter, Willy became more and more visible and more and more voluble. He was here, there and everywhere, renegotiating contracts with suppliers of brick and concrete, title, glass and timber, and spreading scurrilous rumours about his twin brother's financial incapacity and lack of moral scruples as he went.

At lunch and dinner times he was often to be found in the Toll House, conferring with architects and engineers, city and ward councillors and officers of the Barony Bank. Angela saw little of him, his children practically nothing, except at Sunday's church parade, a duty that not even Willy could duck. He still found time to attend an occasional lodge meeting, however, and was just as vociferous there as elsewhere, calling down curses on his disloyal twin who, according to Willy, had gone over to the other side and sold his Protestant birthright for a mess of pottage.

Most of Willy's friends were well aware that Russell was no blackguard but they did not care enough to defend his reputation. Scenting a bit of profit for themselves, they backed rumour with rumour until half the city, it seemed, was humming with conjecture about events that had never taken place and never would take place until, that is, Wilson Blackstock was free of his brother's influence and plans for the river route that would link Glasgow to the western suburbs had finally been approved.

Willy was sleeping fitfully, when he managed to sleep at all. He was eating far more than was good for him and had a bloated, unwholesome appearance and a complexion that veered from ruddy to almost apoplectic. He shouted at everyone, even lawyers, and when he bumped into Russell on the stairs or in the street, he was so lacking in control that he would bark at him like a dog or, worse, point a finger and yell, '*Papist, Papist, Papist bastard*,' until someone dragged him away.

Even Mother Blackstock had given up trying to mend fences and all social contact between Willy and Russell's families ceased. Russell, meanwhile, rode out the storm with something approaching indifference and forged on with the harbour project with the men and materials at his disposal before Wilson and the Barony, between them, could reduce his lines of credit. Income from rents was more useful than ever and the six and a half thousand pounds he had filtered from the system without Wilson's knowledge, and which he kept hidden in Paddy Maizie's safe, provided some comfort. Buffer money, his father had called such unrecorded sums and buffer money was how Russell thought of it now: money that would allow him room to manoeuvre on the off-chance that Willy ever did find an effective way to drive him to the wall.

On the first Monday in October Libby turned up unannounced on the second floor of the Blackstocks' office building. She was fortunate to catch Willy in transit, for he had just dropped by to check specifications on a delivery of roof bevels that had arrived from the carpenter's shop at the end of the week and that did not appear to conform to builders' requirements. He had unfurled the original plan and section and was poring over it when his sister walked in.

'Oh,' said Willy, scowling. 'It's you, is it?'

'Good morning to you, too, Willy,' Libby said. 'My God! You look awful. Have you been ill?'

'No, I have not been ill. I've been busy. I am busy. What do you want?'

'How long do you intend to persist with this madness?'

'Madness? I don't know what you're talking about.'

'Pushing Russell out into the cold.'

'Did he send you?' said Willy. 'Russell, I mean?'

'Why would he send me when he lives upstairs?'

Willy blinked several times to rid himself of the crop of small black specks that had recently begun to affect his vision, then, going to the door, checked that it was properly closed. When he turned he found that Libby had unbuttoned her overcoat and removed her hat and was studying one of the maps that Willy had pinned to the wall behind his work table. He scuttled across the room, caught her arm and led her hastily away before she could see more than was good for her.

'Is that it, Wilson?' she said. 'The map of the grand new highway?'

'What if it is?' he said. 'Why are you here?'

'Mother insisted.'

'Did she? Why?'

'She insisted that I give you fair warning,' said Libby.

'Of what?' said Willy.

'That I am, or very soon will become, the owner of certain properties in Riverside ward,' Libby informed him. 'Properties that are, I believe, relevant to your future plans.'

Willy barked with laughter. 'If you mean the bloody Harp of Erin, that Irish rat's nest is no more relevant to my plans than – than . . .'

'St Kentigern's?' Libby suggested.

'St Kentigern's? What about St Kentigern's?'

'I've bought out the leases on the ground.'

'What? But the Church . . .'

'The Church, as it happened, was amenable to the proposal that Mr James put to the archbishop on my behalf. The original grant of ground, made by the second Lord Hannan, does not preclude sale of the balance of the lease provided that—'

'Pig in a poke, Libby. You bought a pig in a poke.'

'Fifty-three years to run on the lease, Willy; that's a very fat pig, indeed.'

'What did it cost you? How much did those conniving bastards—'

'That,' said Libby, 'is a private matter between me and the diocese.'

'They pulled the wool over your eyes,' said Willy. 'You can't do anything with it, you know. You'll be bound hand and foot by clauses and sub-clauses.'

'I don't intend to do anything with it,' said Libby. 'No, that isn't strictly accurate. I do intend to have the church building repaired. If you wish, you may tender for the work.'

'Hah!' said Willy. 'Hah, hah!'

'What's more,' Libby went on, 'I'll be making purchase of Russell's four tenements and the stable in the lane.'

'He'll never sell to you.'

'He has already agreed to do so,' said Libby.

'Then he's an idiot,' Willy shouted. 'The Barony won't extend him another penny-piece in credit when those buildings are gone out of his possession. I'll make damned sure of that.'

'Are you sure you have that much influence, Willy?'

'I have – I have – title deeds and leases that . . .'

'That are going nowhere.' Libby moved past him to the map on the wall, plucking a graphite pencil from a rack on the table as she went. 'Look,' she said. 'Here are the buildings in the Riverside that I'll own.' She scratched the wedge of graphite over the paper. 'Here, here, and here.'

'Don't touch that map. Don't touch it. It's mine.'

She ignored his protest. 'What do you have, Wilson? A derelict cotton factory, forty acres of the Crosshill estate that you've already started to build upon, and leases for development of the ground that bounds the extension of the Pointhouse and Dumbarton railway line?'

'More, more than that,' said Willy.

'Then you may build away to your heart's content.'

'You know I can't build on half those sites until the new road is laid,' he said, quite plaintively. 'What do you want from me, Libby?'

'Nothing,' Libby said. 'In a matter of months, by Christmas at the latest, I'll have everything I've ever wanted.'

'What? A slum in the Riverside?'

'Yes.'

'Dear God Almighty!' Willy shouted. 'Why?'

'Because he left me nothing,' said Libby.

'Who left you nothing – Daddy?'

'Not one penny, not one stick or stone, not so much as a word of farewell let alone a blessing. From the day I stepped out with Peter Galloway I was dead to our daddy. From the day I became a Catholic I was no longer his daughter – or your sister, for that matter. Is that not so?'

'You're a woman, Libby. What could you possibly expect?'

'More respect,' said Libby, 'and a little more love. But it was not to be. Truth to tell, I didn't realise how much I was hurt by the rejection until Peter died and I was left alone in the world.'

'You had her, didn't you? You had the Chink?'

'If it hadn't been for Russell . . .' Libby shrugged.

'That fool! That sentimental idiot! He should never have taken you in. Is this how you intend to repay our generosity – by ruining us?'

Libby tossed the pencil on to the table where it spun like the pointer on a gaming board. 'Your generosity, Willy? What sort of generosity is that?'

'You betrayed us,' Willy said. 'You betrayed Daddy and everything we stood for, everything you had been raised to believe was right.'

'And wasn't,' said Libby. 'Well, now I'll make it right, not in your terms, Willy, but in mine.'

'You and your Chink and your priests and your papish plotters may think you're having the last laugh, but you're not. I'm not the one you'll bring down. Oh, no, no. If anyone's going to suffer it isn't me, Libby. I've a host of friends who'll support me simply because they believe in the things I believe in. I'm not done. I've hardly even started.'

'I'm pleased to hear it,' Libby said.

'You liar! You two-faced hypocrite!'

'I'm not the hypocrite,' said Libby. 'I'm just a poor, feeble woman trying to do her best for herself and for the community.'

'A philanthropist, then,' said Willy. 'A two-faced philanthropist.'

'Is that your last word? Is that your blessing on your only sister?'

'Aye, damn it, it is.'

'In that case,' Libby said, 'good-day to you, Willy.'

And Willy, more out of habit than politeness, growled, 'Good-day.'

Frowning, Chiffin said, 'Mr Draper, I think there's somebody in Mr Maizie's office. Should I be goin' over to see who it is?'

'No,' Bob said. 'I know who it is.'

'Who is it then?' said Chiffin.

'None o' your business, lad.'

'It's not Orpin'ton, is it?'

'For God's sake, Chiffin,' Bob said, 'what would Orpington be doin' in Mr Maizie's office at half past ten in the morning?'

Chiffin, not entirely appeased, shrugged.

He had a tin of Brasso in one hand and a huge yellow duster in the other and was diligently polishing the rings on the beer engines. Evie, not long arrived, was behind him, scrubbing the zinc trough with a mixture of fine sand and soda crystals. She knew why Chiffin was puzzled; Mr Maizie was in the snug, eating a second breakfast of fried bread and bacon and drinking hot coffee, and whoever was over in the cottage had been left there alone.

'I'll betcha it's Mrs Galloway,' Chiffin said to Evie in a stage whisper.

'Chiffin, enough,' Bob growled. 'Keep your nose out o'it.'

Chiffin shrugged again and went on with his polishing, one eye on the door of the snug and the other on the door that led out to the yard.

Evie was curious, too, for Paddy Maizie was jealous of his privacy and allowed no one to enter the office without his express permission. She sluiced hot water from a bucket along the bed of the trough and swirled the sediment carefully into the drain. She ran cold water from the swan-necked tap and laved her hands which were red and smarting from the soda solution.

She had a notion who might be in the office at this early hour and was not entirely surprised when, a few minutes later, Mr Russell Blackstock appeared from the yard and, with a nod to Bob, and a smile in Evie's direction, crossed into the snug and closed the door behind him.

After a moment, Bob went off into the kitchen.

Chiffin turned to Evie and said, 'So it's the man his-self, is it? Wonder what he's been up to. Countin' up his money, like as not.'

'Why would he be countin' his money?' said Evie. 'It ain't Friday night.'

Chiffin lifted the smelly yellow duster to cover half his face and sidling up to Evie leaned close into her and, in a muffled whisper, said, 'Don't you know? I thought you'd know since you an' him's so pally.'

'Pally?' said Evie. 'I've spoken to him three times, that's all.'

'Well, true enough, nobody's supposed t' know, but he keeps his money here, his rent money.'

'He told you this, Chiff, did he?' said Evie. 'Told you this big secret 'cause you're so important?'

'I got eyes in my head,' said Chiffin. 'Money comes in Friday nights, never goes out again.'

'I thought Mr Maizie took it to the bank?'

'God knows what he takes to the bank, but it ain't Mr Blackstock's money. It's stored in that safe – to keep from havin' to share it all with his brother, I reckon,' Chiffin went on. 'Belfer an' Orpington get their cut late Friday nights, an' the rest goes into the safe. For all I know, Paddy sorts out an' tallies it an' presents Mr Blackstock with a total, but the cash is left there, most o' it. By this time it must be the best part o' a small fortune.'

Evie hammered the hard rubber bung into the drain and let the trough fill up with clean water for a final rinsing. Chiffin remained at her elbow, the duster held to his face, like a bandit's mask. He was proud of the fact that he was privy to the secrets of the Harp and knew something about the Blackstocks that she did not. She felt a stirring of disappointment at the thought that what Chiffin said was probably true.

She had always taken Russell Blackstock to be an honourable sort of man, above cheating and deception. She had even managed to put to one side the fact that he employed men like Benjamin Belfer and Percival Orpington. She had been impressed by his quiet manner, by his interest in her, by the kindness he had shown her; impressed most of all by the building in which he had his offices. She could not reconcile the scale of his life with ownership of tenements in Riverside, an Irish pub, and a sister who went to chapel, organised picnics for orphans and wagered on horse-races.

'How many folk have you told about the safe, Chiff?' she asked.

'Just you, chucks, just you.'

'How many folk are liable to know about it, then?'

'Paddy an' Bob, I suppose. Mrs Galloway. Belfer an' Orpington, like as not.' He lowered the duster and winked. 'Me – an' you, too, darlin'.'

'I don't believe a word o'it,' Evie said. 'It's another story, another tale.'

'Well, I can hardly show you the money, can I?' Chiffin said, rather irked that she would not take his word at face value. 'I'm not goin' to break in just for to satisfy your curiosity.'

Evie laughed. 'If you did break in, Chiff, sure I think all you'd find in that green safe is Paddy's collection o' wines an' a few boxes o' his rotten cigars.'

'So,' Chiffin said huffily, 'what was Mr Blackstock doin'

here, all alone across the yard in Paddy's office while Paddy keeps out o' the way?'

'How would I be knowin' that?' said Evie. 'What I can tell you is that a man with all Mr Blackstock's assets don't need to hide money in a pub.'

'Unless it's stole,' said Chiffin.

'Stole?' said Evie. 'Stole from who?'

'The other brother,' Chiffin said.

Then, having run out of facts to prove his thesis, Chiffin took his Brasso and duster off to the far end of the bar and began to polish the rail while, puzzled and a little dismayed, Evie lingered at the trough in the hope that Russell Blackstock might soon emerge from the snug and spare her a few moments of his all-too-precious time.

He could not deny that he was pleased to see her. Even with red hands and tousled hair she had an elfin look that, given more favourable circumstances, he would have found irresistible. He tried to imagine what it would be like to have Evie McKenna as an extra wife. There was nothing wrong with the wife he had but in these past few months he had often speculated on what might have been if he had never left the Riverside, and never met and married Jane.

'Are you finished in the office?' Paddy enquired.

'I am,' Russell answered.

'Do you wish to – ah – take anythin' off with you?'

'Everything's fine where it is.'

'Libby should be droppin' in shortly,' Paddy said.

'I won't tarry,' Russell said. 'I've too much to do.'

'Sure an' you have,' said Paddy. 'Clearin' out the cellar can't be easy.'

'Clearing out the cellar?' said Russell, puzzled.

'That's what Libby says you're doing.'

'She's right, though she does have an odd way of putting it.'

'That's Libby for you,' Paddy said. 'Odd as they come.'

He had spent an hour in Paddy's office with the door bolted, an hour counting banknotes from the bulky canvas bag that occupied the bottom compartment in the big green safe. He had Paddy's accounts to guide him and had no doubt at all that he would find the figures accurate, but somehow he needed to touch the money that he had accumulated over the years, if just to make sure it was real. Six thousand, seven hundred and twelve pounds: a fortune for any tenement family, more than a digger could earn in a lifetime; yet to him it was no more than a safety net, a sum that might be swallowed up in a matter of months if his credit was cut off.

'Are you leavin' now?' Paddy said.

'Yes, I'll just have a word with . . .'

Paddy laughed gently. 'Your secret admirer?'

'Is that what she is?'

'Ask her, an' find out,' said Paddy and, nothing if not tactful, took himself off into the kitchen in search of Bob Draper.

'Evie,' Russell said, 'are you well?'

'Well enough, Mr Blackstock. Would you care for a glass of somethin''?'

'No, thanks. Tell me, is your sister settling in to married life with Belfer?

'She seems to be,' said Evie.

'You must miss her.'

'She's not far away, just downstairs.'

He did not know what to say to her, how to make small talk.

'Your brother's a friend of my sister, I believe,' he said.

'A friend o' the Chinese girl, more like.'

'Don't you approve?' Russell said.

'Not up to me to approve,' said Evie, pouting.

He had touched a nerve, a raw nerve. He leaned on the bar and looked at her. Below, to his left, crouching, the potboy

Chiffin buffed away the bar rail, while pretending that he was deaf.

Pressed against the edge of the trough, Evie looked so dainty that he experienced a confused desire to take her in his arms. He found it impossible to separate pity from yearning, though, and wondered if what he really wanted to do was protect her from harm, for there could be no relationship between them that would not involve him in adultery and bring her pain. He wasn't selfish enough to believe that what she felt for him was passion or, by any adult definition, love, or that by making her his mistress he would find anything more enduring than passing satisfaction. And what could he give her in return? Money, clothes, a room in a decent building up west, a few trinkets to compensate not for what she might do with him in bed but for the hours, days, weeks in which she would be without him, waiting and alone?

He said, 'I expect you'll find out soon, Evie, that changes are about to take place in the Riverside.'

'Changes, Mr Blackstock?'

'You'll have a new landlord for one thing.'

'Who will that be?'

'My sister,' Russell said. 'I'm transferring ownership of the tenements in Salamanca Street to my sister, Mrs Galloway.'

'Will she throw us all out for a new road?'

'Not Libby,' Russell said. 'If anything she'll improve things.'

'Are you – are you leavin' us?' said Evie.

'I'm not leaving Glasgow. I'm just making changes, that's all.'

'Sure an' will you not be down this way again?' Evie said.

All sorts of soft answers popped into his head, all sorts of sympathetic compromises that might offer her hope, and leave his options open.

'No,' he said firmly. 'I will not be down this way again.'

'Not for no reason, Mr Blackstock?'

'Not for any reason, Evie,' he said.

He looked at her for a moment longer, at her blue eyes and delicate features and trim figure under the apron, then he turned on his heel and walked away. At the door, however, he paused and, turning, saw that she was weeping and that the ugly red-haired potboy was stroking her hand consolingly, which, Russell Blackstock thought, was just as it should be and all for the best, perhaps.

For several weeks Mr Orpington had been studying *Bradshaw's General Railway and Steam Navigation Guide* and planning a getaway by routes so intricate that they would ensure not only that he avoided detection but that he would probably spend the best part of the winter in transit before he reached London at all.

It had been fifteen years since last he had been on the run. Much had changed in that time. Now there were Pullmans, non-stop expresses, and telegraph offices at almost every wayside halt to contend with. The very thought of a telegraph office raised the spectre of constables in plain clothing looming out of the shadows as soon as he set foot on a platform. Logically, he knew this was nonsense, of course; he would not be strutting through the new terminus at St Enoch's clad in a topper and velvet-lined overcoat. He would be disguised as a day-labourer, the sort of chap who owned greyhounds and scratched to find the rent. He knew only too well what they looked like and how they behaved, right down to the chop-striding little walk they all had, half swagger and half shuffle.

Preparations for his departure occupied most of his spare time; he even nurtured a faint, fond hope that he might, by chance, bump into the treacherous Ida before he quit Scotland and have an opportunity to leave behind not so much a clean slate as a bloody one.

Gunpowder was easily obtained, fuses too. A word to a

builder's labourer in a yard licensed to use explosives and a cash donation to the fellow's personal welfare fund had turned up a ten-pound bag of gritty, grey powder – far more than he would need – and four lengths of fast fuse. Carrying a little of the stuff in a carpenter's tool bag, Mr Orpington had gone out into the country by train one dank afternoon and, making sure that no one was around, had blown up two fence posts on the edge of a field by way of rehearsal, and had returned home well pleased with the result.

He stored the powder and fuses in a mouse-proof metal box in the cupboard furthest from the fire, covered by the carpenter's tool bag, two felt treads and a flannel blanket. The half-gallon jar of domestic kerosene and two bottles of white spirit were hidden on the high shelf of the larder. Now all that remained to be done was to purchase a few second-hand clothes, and devise a satisfactory means of escape.

Night after night, he pored over the *Bradshaw*, hunched at the table in the spartan apartment with a lamp focused on the blindingly small print and a reading glass to help him make out the numerals. He was no ignorant sneak thief. He did not dismiss the police as idiots. He had considerable respect for their persistence and thoroughness. If he hoped to vanish into thin air then his timing must be no less than perfect.

Even carrying a heavy bag, he could walk from Salamanca Street to Yorkhill station in fifteen minutes. There he would catch the early train on the City and District local line and connect with the first train out of St Enoch's at a quarter past five o'clock in the morning. He would buy a ticket to Wigan but would disembark at Preston for a local service to Liverpool. He would lie up in a cheap lodging house there for at least a week and then, only then, would he head up to London. The plan was less elaborate than he had intended. There was a small degree of risk that he might be spotted before he left Glasgow, but he doubted if that would happen. He had planned a diversion, a splendid diversion, that would occupy the forces of law and order and, at the same time, teach the fools in Belfer's tenement a lesson they would never forget.

He noted down the train times, committed them to memory, and burned the note. Now all he had to do was wait for winter to arrive, felt-footed and stealthy, and fog to swaddle the valley of the Clyde.

21

The streetlamps had all but disappeared in a swirling rain mist and the foul taste of coal smoke lay heavy in the air. It had been a quiet mid-week night in the Harp, for which Evie had been grateful because Bob Draper had sent Chiff and her home early.

Shortly after ten she let herself into the kitchen. Nolan was sprawled on the small bed, reading. The remains of his supper lay upon the table. At her husband's suggestion, Clare had brought up a bowl of stew for Nolly and Evie to reheat, along with four boiled potatoes. Nolan's shifts were shorter now, though some essential work was completed by the light of flares. He arrived home around seven o'clock, washed in the tin bath that he had bought from an ironmonger's on Dumbarton Road and by the time Evie got home had finished his supper and was sound asleep in bed.

Evie took off her shawl and draped it on the back of a chair.

Nolan's damp clothes were arranged on chairs, forming a fence around the hearth. She moved the chairs carefully, and placed the stew pot on the stove.

'What's that you're reading?' she asked.

'Book.'

'I can see it's a book,' she said. 'What book?'

'*Travels in Bible Lands*,' he told her, riffling the pages, 'by the Reverend Charles Duperier.'

'What are you reading that for?'

'Pin gave it me. It's very informative.' He rested the book

against his chest and raised himself a little on an elbow. 'The Sunday school kiddies keep askin' me questions for which I ain't got no answers.'

'What sort o' questions?'

'Like, how far is it from Glasgow to Jerusalem.'

'How far is it from Glasgow to Jerusalem?'

'A bloody long way,' said Nolan, with a grin. 'How about this one: when Joseph an' Mary went to Bethlehem why didn't they take the train?'

'An' the Reverend Doo-per,' said Evie, 'has all the answers, does he?'

'Nah,' said Nolan. 'But he does tell us how far it was from Bethany to the Temple, an' what crops grew in Nazareth. Did you know old Joseph wasn't just a carpenter, he was a builder as well?'

'I don't think I did know that,' said Evie.

She splashed her face with cold water, and towelled her hair at the sink. She had not been in the best of spirits all day. Her bleeding had started, which was why the tears had come so readily, perhaps. She had hoped that Mrs Galloway would appear in the bar and might have more information about the tenement sale but neither Libby nor Pin had shown up that day.

'Pin tells me the Holy Land's smaller than Ireland,' said Nolan.

'What else has Pin told you?' Evie said. 'For instance, has she told you her auntie will soon be our landlord?'

'Eh?' Nolan sat up. 'What are you blatherin' about, Evie?'

'There's about to be, a – a transference of ownership,' Evie said. 'Mr Blackstock's sold his buildings to Mrs Galloway.'

'Who told you that?'

'Mr Blackstock. He came into the Harp this mornin' to . . . well, anyroads, he gave me the news. I'm surprised your Chink hasn't said anythin'.'

'She might not know,' said Nolan. 'Here, I wonder if old Belfer knows.'

'If he doesn't,' said Evie, 'he will soon enough.'

Nolan put the book to one side and swung his feet to the floor.

'By Gar,' he said, 'our Benjamin's in for a shock, eh? Mrs Galloway'll pay him off for sure. She's never been able to stand old Belfer, even though he's done such a good job for her brother all them years.'

'What's this?' said Evie. 'Love talk?'

'Eh?' said Nolan again.

'I mean,' said Evie, 'is this the sort of talk you an' your friend Pin whisper to each other when you're walkin' out?'

'Walkin' out?' said Nolan. 'Huh! I walk her home on Sundays, but that's not the same as walkin' out, now is it?'

Evie served herself with stew. She shoved Nolan's dirty dishes to one end of the table and seated herself. She'd had no appetite for lunch but, to her surprise, she was hungry now. The stews that were delivered from downstairs were better than any she'd ever tasted. Clare told her that Benjamin used herbs for flavouring and never bought anything but fresh vegetables and the best cuts of meat. 'Chiffin thinks Russell Blackstock might need money to finish the wall,' Evie said. 'Could that be true?'

'Aye, it could be,' said Nolan. 'It's a big job an' we're not near done.'

'I didn't know Mrs Galloway had money.'

Nolan sat forward, hands draped across his knees, and did not meet his sister's eye.

'Nolan?' Evie said. 'What're you not tellin' me?'

'It's Pin,' Nolan said. 'She's got the money, or will have on her birthday.'

'When's her birthday?'

'Monday, next week,' said Nolan. 'Eighteen, she'll be.'

'Is it Pin who'll be our landlord, do you think?'

Nolan shook his head. 'I doubt it.'

'If you ask her, will she tell you?'

'Aye, she might.'

'Ask her then,' said Evie. 'Find out what's really goin' on.'

'I won't see her till Sunday.'

'What about Wednesday?'

'I can't make Wednesday mass on time,' Nolan said.

'Then we'll just have to ask Cissie, won't we?' Evie said.

'Cissie?'

'She'll get it from Father Fingle.'

'Do you think he knows what's goin' on?'

'He always does,' said Evie. 'It's him downstairs I'm worried about.'

'Belfer?' said Nolan. 'Why should we worry about him?'

' 'Cause he's Clare's husband,' said Evie. 'It's important for Clare's sake that he holds on to his job.'

'For Clare an' the baby, you mean?' Nolan said.

'Clare an' the baby, it is,' said Evie and, rising, put on the kettle for tea.

Nolan had been fed breakfast and packed off to work and Evie was no more than half awake when her sister arrived. The weather had eased not one whit overnight and condensation clouded the windows and the fire in the grate was reluctant to blaze up, there being no draught to encourage it. Late bedding and early rising had taken its toll on Evie's nerves and she was in no mood for small talk. No more, it seems, was Clare.

Clare threw a letter down on the table.

'What do you know about this, Evie?' she demanded.

Evie picked up the letter and glanced at its contents. The heading – Annan, Cattenach & Gloag, Solicitors at Law – told her all she needed to know. She was shocked at the speed with which the Blackstocks had taken action. She stammered, 'I – I – I heard a rumour about it.'

'An' you didn't have the decency to tell us.'

'It was only last night,' said Evie. 'I wasn't even sure it was true.'

'Well, it is true,' said Clare. 'Read it. Read it. Benjamin's been sacked.'

For a lawyer's letter the dismissal notice was direct and to the point: transfer of ownership – services as factor no longer required – notice to quit occupancy on first day of December – one month's wage in lieu of severance.

'Where's Benjamin now?' said Evie.

'Stormed off in a high old state to talk to Paddy Maizie.'

'Paddy? Why has he gone to talk to Paddy?'

'He could hardly go straight to Blackstock, could he?' Clare said. 'Not without knowin' what's behind it. What do you know about it, Evie?'

'Not much,' said Evie.

'Who's the new owner?'

'Libby Galloway.'

'She's a Catholic.'

'I don't see what that has to do with it,' said Evie. 'Is Benjamin cross?'

'Not cross,' said Clare. 'Furious. He's factored the tenements in Salamanca Street for twenty years, an' has never put a foot wrong.'

'Are you sure?' said Evie.

'Aye, I'm sure,' said Clare heatedly. 'He keeps the buildings in order an' the rents comin' in an' never bothers Mr Blackstock unless he has to.'

'Is that what Benjamin told you?'

'It is,' Clare said.

'An' you believe him?'

' 'Course I believe him. He's my husband.'

Clare had thickened about the middle in the past few weeks, which was natural enough, Evie supposed, but she had also become heavier about the neck and the jaw, not so much fat as coarse, as if marriage, or impending motherhood, had robbed her of some of her beauty.

'Just because he's your husband doesn't make him right,' Evie said.

'In my book it does,' said Clare.

'Is he that admirable a husband, then?'

'Better than I'd hoped for,' Clare said. 'He's not what you, or me, supposed him to be, Evie. He's a good man at heart.'

'You'll be takin' tea with Orpington next,' said Evie.

'Sure an' Benjamin has broke with Orpington,' said Clare.

'So what's Orpington doin' lodgin' upstairs?'

Clare gave no answer. She looked around and, for something to do, stripped blankets and sheets from Nolan's bed and tented them over two kitchen chairs. She flung bolster and pillow into the air, caught them, one in each hand, and thumped them together, making a little pale cloud of dust.

There was no evidence of self-pity in Clare now, not one drop. She reminded Evie of Kiernan who, before illness took hold, had been full of confidence and spleen.

'Can you feel the baby yet?' Evie asked. 'Is it kickin'?'

'Aye, you can feel it stirrin',' said Clare.

'Has Benjamin felt it?'

'What sort of a question is that to be askin' me?'

'Is he pleased, I mean?'

Clare stood motionless by the tented bedclothes, head cocked to one side, a lock of black hair falling across her face like a stain. She looked straight at Evie and said, 'It'll be my one an' only child, like as not, so Benjamin will love it as if it were his own.'

'What?' said Evie, bewildered. 'You mean he can't . . .'

'Benjamin's not made right,' Clare said. 'He has all the

desires of a man but an injury to his parts makes it impossible for him to satisfy them. I think that's why he never married – until I came along.'

'I thought he wanted you?'

'He does want me,' Clare said.

'A fault – what?'

'Soon after he was born a doctor damaged him,' said Clare. 'That's all I'm ever goin' to say about it, Evie. Promise me on the Cross you'll never say a word about it to a livin' soul. My Benjamin has his pride, you know.'

'You mean,' said Evie cautiously, 'he can't . . .?'

'He can't,' Clare said. 'Not rightly.'

'Is it enough for you to have a husband who – can't?'

'A man o' my own an' a baby, that'll have to do me,' Clare said. 'Now you know the truth, Evie, an' even if you don't understand I expect you to show my Benjamin more respect. Now, what about this letter? What can you do about this letter?'

'There's nothin' I can do.'

'Your friend Mr Blackstock, can he not make Libby change her mind?'

'Russell Blackstock isn't my friend,' said Evie. 'He has a wife an' family, aye, an' money too. He doesn't need me for – for anythin'.'

'I wouldn't be so sure o' that,' Clare said.

'Anythin' I'm willin' to give,' Evie said. 'It's not just a man I want, Clare, it's a life. What sort o' a life would it be for me with Russell Blackstock? He as good as told me that himself.'

Clare pursed her lips as if she had tasted something sour.

She leaned across her sister and lifted up the lawyer's letter. 'If Libby Galloway can't be made to change her mind,' she said, 'then we'll have to leave Salamanca Street an' stay with that old woman.'

'In Bellingham Place?' said Evie. 'Sure an' it could be worse.'

'Nah, it could not be worse, not for me an' especially not for Benjamin.'

'Clare,' Evie said, 'what *are* you goin' to do?'

'Put up a fight,' said Clare. 'An' if that doesn't work . . .'

'What?'

'There's always charity.'

Paddy reached out with the bottle and poured Belfer a second snifter of brandy, though the first seemed to have had no effect at all on the poor fellow.

Never in a month of Sundays had he imagined that he would ever feel sorry for Benjamin Belfer whose appearances in the Harp on a Friday could clear the bar within seconds; yet here he was in the snug, offering the chap not only brandy but also advice.

'Calm yourself, man,' Paddy said. 'Do try to calm yourself. I realise it's been a shock. God knows, it's been a shock to all of us.'

'Did you not know, Mr Maizie?' Benjamin said. 'Had you no inklin'?'

'An inklin', yes, a tiny bit of an inklin',' said Paddy. 'I hadn't expected the lady to bring matters to completion with such alacrity, however. When did you receive the letter?'

'First post this mornin'.'

'Have you told anyone else about it?'

'Only Clare, only my wife.'

'It'll be common knowledge by dinner time,' said Paddy. 'Not that I wish to imply your wife's a gossip but . . .'

'I know,' Benjamin said. 'I know how bad news spreads.'

'Grapevine,' Paddy said. 'Panic.'

'Is the tenement to be knocked down? Is that it? Are we all out?'

Paddy stroked his moustache and pondered just how much he might reveal of Libby's extravagant plans. It was typical of the bloody woman to announce her intentions in the form of a lawyer's letter.

He said, 'Far as I'm aware, old chap, the tenements are to remain more or less as they are, though I imagine the new owner will want to effect some repairs and improvements.'

'I could be of assistance in that respect,' Benjamin said. 'I could ensure she gets the best terms an' the best service from the best tradesmen.'

'Come now, Belfer,' Paddy said, 'do you think we don't know how you pad the tradesmens' bills?'

'Oh, now that's a calumny, that is.'

'No, it's not,' said Paddy. 'Everybody in Riverside knows what you've been up to. Mrs Galloway's been after her brother for years to get rid of you.'

'Is that why she bought the buildin's,' Benjamin said, 'to get rid o' me?'

'Do not,' Paddy said, 'be ridiculous.'

'Why didn't he tell me?' Benjamin cried. 'If he wasn't satisfied with what I was doin', why didn't Mr Blackstock tell me face to face, man to man?'

'Perhaps he was afraid of what you would do.'

'Afraid of me? Why would he be afraid of me?'

'How long have you worked for Russell Blackstock?' Paddy said.

'Years,' said Benjamin. 'Before him I worked for his father. Now there was a real gentleman. You knew just where you stood with old Mr Blackstock.'

'Did you steal from him, too?' said Paddy.

'I have never stole from anyone in my life.'

'Oh, God!' said Paddy, casting his eyes upward. 'At least be honest with me, Belfer. I never met the old man, but I've heard the tales. Old man Blackstock was a bigger rogue than you are. He employed you to do his dirty work, isn't that the truth of it? If you skinned a few shekels for yourself here an' there, do you think he didn't know about it? He probably approved.'

'Mr Blackstock an' I understood each other.'

'The boys, the sons, did they understand you?'

'They employed me, didn't they?' said Benjamin.

'Because you knew where their money came from,' said Paddy. 'Well, what we have now, Belfer, is a lady who wishes to start with a clean slate.'

'A bloody Roman Catholic!' Benjamin exclaimed.

It was all Paddy could do not to laugh aloud. He said, 'Did you not marry a Roman Catholic right here in this room hardly more than a month ago?'

'That was different,' Benjamin said. 'Look, I'm dependin' on you to tell the lady I'm all right.'

'Problem is, I don't think you are all right.'

'Then tell her,' said Benjamin, 'I know where the bodies are buried an' who buried them in the first place.'

'Do you expect me to threaten Libby on your behalf?' Paddy said. 'I wouldn't go that route if I were you, Belfer. The last thing you want to do is threaten Libby Galloway. If you do, she'll have your balls on toast, believe me.'

'All I want is for to keep my position an' my house,' Benjamin said. 'I'm a married man now, with a kiddie on the way. Surely she wouldn't throw us out on the street to starve?'

'You have property, don't you? Property in Bellingham Place?'

'It's just a little place for my mam an' dad . . .'

'A little place to hide your money, you mean,' said Paddy.

'Like the money in your safe back there?' said Benjamin. 'Mr Blackstock's cash. If I did learn any tricks that was less than straight, you know better than anyone who I learned them from.'

Paddy was suddenly impatient. His sympathy for Belfer had

evaporated at the first sign of threat. There was little that the factor could do to harm the Blackstocks. Once Libby had her hands on the tenements in Salamanca Street, let alone the church leases, then Belfer would have no authority in Riverside and, with luck, would slink away and find work to suit his talents elsewhere.

'I wouldn't go talkin' about my safe, if I were you, Mr Belfer,' Paddy said, 'or what it might contain. You're an employee, a servant; that's all you've ever been. What's in that safe o' mine is none of your concern.'

Benjamin bit his lip. 'Will you not put in a word for me, Mr Maizie?'

'I will – what's the expression? – I'll make your displeasure known.'

'Remind the lady . . .' Benjamin began. 'Remind the lady that she was at my weddin' an' that she's a friend o' my dear wife.'

'Why don't you remind her yourself?' Paddy said.

'Yes,' said Benjamin Belfer. 'Perhaps that's what I'll do.' He was calmer now, a little too calm for Paddy's liking. He held out his hand. 'Thank you for your advice, Mr Maizie.'

'I hope it's been useful.'

'Useful?' Benjamin said. 'Oh aye, very useful. Very useful indeed.' Then, with a handshake and a bow, he let himself out of the snuggery, and headed, Paddy assumed, for home.

Father Fingle had been up most of the night praying for a sick child. Crouched in a reeking tenement room with five other small children curled on filthy straw strewn on the floor about him and the daddy, drunk as a lord, sprawled insensible on the alcove bed, he had offered comfort to the mother as best he could and prayed harder than he had prayed in a very long while; prayed not just for a bit of divine intervention on behalf of the wee one, but also for the state of his own soul which, these past months, had become as withered as an apple that had been too long in store.

There had been no doctor and no money for a doctor. The two half-crowns he had given the woman out of the poor box had found their way into the hands of the publicans on the Wedderburn Road and, like a miracle without the mystery, had transformed themselves into quantities of strong drink that the daddy had poured down his throat.

There was no doctor, then, no medicine, nowhere near at hand where Father Fingle might scrounge a few drops of laudanum or spirit of nitre to ease the child's cough and break her fever. He did what he had done a hundred times before: he prayed and prayed, clasping his worn crucifix in one hand, his eyes wide open, while he wiped away the strings of phlegm that the child expelled and dabbed sweat from her brow. He kept the oil and the candle, the sprinkler and cotton wool out of sight in the big pocket of his cassock, for he was unwilling to yield to the possibility of the kiddie dying unbaptised, or dying at all, and he knew that the mother, who had all but worn out her faith, would wail if he made the signs of the cross, and he had heard enough wailing for one night. He was not confident that his faith was strong enough or that God and Jesus and the Virgin Mother were there in that mean room looking out for one wee sparrow who would surely have a better life in heaven than she ever had on earth.

Then, around five, her cheeks cooled and her coughing eased.

At first he thought she might be slipping into bliss eternal, and put his ear to her chest and found that the raucous sounds inside her ribcage had almost subsided. He nudged the mother awake, and told her to boil water. He bathed the child's face and gave her cool water to drink, sip by sip, while he held her up with his arm. Her eyes opened, tiny darts of blue-grey colour under sticky lids, she murmured something – Pap or

Pappy; he could not be sure – before she turned on her side and, breathing more easily now, fell into a restful sleep.

It was shortly after nine in the morning when Libby discovered him at the table in the kitchen in the house behind the church. He was bent almost double in the chair, brow resting on the cloth, his hair beaded with yolk from the runny egg on the plate by his head, a cup of tea, stone cold and scummy, hardly more than an inch from his nose.

At first she thought he was dead: but then she thought, No, Father Fingle is not the sort of man to die with his face in fried egg, and she gave him a little shake and then another, less gentle, and he opened his eyes and, with a bewildered grunt, sat up.

'You left the door open, Father,' Libby said.

Still dazed, he looked around, blearily.

'Have you been out all night?' Libby asked.

'Uh! Yes, much of it,' he said. 'Did I miss the early mass?'

'No mass this morning,' Libby said. 'Was it a passing?'

He massaged his face with his hands, reached for the cold cup and would have drunk from it had Libby not removed it.

'I'll make you fresh,' she said. 'By the way, you've egg in your hair.'

'Hair in my egg?' Father Fingle said. 'It wouldn't be the first time.'

'Was it a passing?' Libby said again.

'No,' he said, in a surprised voice. 'No, it wasn't a passing after all.'

'Another miracle, Father?'

'Hardly that, Libby, hardly that.'

He leaned back, creakily, rubbed his face again, then got up and, while Libby busied herself at the stove, went off to visit the water closet on the far side of the hall.

'Do you know,' said Cameron James, 'in all my years of practice I do not believe I have ever seen such a document before.'

'Given that you drafted it, Mr James,' said Libby, 'I assume that, however unique it may be, at least it meets all the legal requirements dictated by the Church and demanded by the civil laws of transfer?'

'Absolutely in all respects,' said Cameron James. 'I take it, Mrs Galloway, that you are not under the impression that the signatures upon this unusual document give you any rights at all, apart from those agreed upon in the original missive? The archbishop and the vicar-general wish you to be very, *very* clear upon that point.'

'In other words,' said Libby, 'I'm not buying a church.'

'Nor a priest,' said Cameron James with a quick glance at Father Fingle. 'Not even a priest who looks as if he might fall asleep at any moment.'

Father Fingle blinked and struggled to pay attention. It was warm in the office and the deep leather chair was rather too comfortable. He had been excited at the prospect of being shot of Mrs Galloway's negotiations, for she had taken him, over the years, a little too close for comfort to the rocky shore of profanation. In just a few minutes, though, everything would be out in the open and all the little bits and pieces of cash money that she had given him would officially pass out of his hands and he would be officially poor again.

Cameron James reached out and opened an inkwell topped with a brass golf ball. He selected a pen from a tray on his desk and held it upright between finger and thumb.

'First, Mrs Galloway,' he said, 'the lease transfer document and title deeds, which have already been signed by the necessary authorities. If you sign, Father Fingle may witness. I take it you've had Annan, Cattenach and Gloag scrutinise the paperwork?'

'To the last colon and full stop,' said Libby. 'They were much impressed with the drafting, I might add.'

'As well they might be.' Cameron James watched the

woman sign her name and the priest witness it. 'Now,' he said, replacing one long document with another. 'The establishment of the Building Fund, for which I have received a bankers' draft for the sum of two thousand and four hundred pounds. It occurs to me, Mrs Galloway, that you may have had an accomplice in planning this manoeuvre, but I will not enquire too deeply into that. Naturally, the diocese is grateful to you for personally undertaking to fund work on St Kentigern's. Need I add that permission has been assigned only on the understanding that the vicar-general or one of his *aides-de-camp* approve all but the most minor repairs, and that I am empowered to review the costings.'

'That is understood,' Libby said.

'Father Fingle?'

'Hmm? Yes, understood.'

'And that property deeds and leases will revert into possession of the archdiocese at the end of the stated term without recompense to you or your heirs in respect of any improvements you may undertake in the interim.'

'That is also understood,' said Libby.

'You're not turning it into a pub, then?' said Cameron James.

'No,' Libby answered him, 'a golf course.'

For a moment the lawyer stared at her incredulously then, chuckling, handed over the pen once more.

'If you ask me, Cissie,' Jock Macpherson said, 'it'll make not one blind bit o' difference to us who owns the building. In fact, it might be to our advantage to have a new landlord – or lady, as seems for to be the case.'

'She's a rum one, that woman,' said Cissie. 'An' she's a Blackstock.'

'I wonder,' Jock said, 'just what sort of a family quarrel led to this?'

'It'll be the brothers, those twins. I never liked those twins.'

'Can't say I know them,' said Jock. 'I mean, they've never bothered me.'

'Is she out to sell, though?'

'I doubt it,' Jock said. 'If she was out to sell she'd have given us notice.'

'Mr Belfer's had notice.'

'Aye, so I heard from Evie.'

'Evie? Have you been seein' Evie?' said Cissie.

'Met her on the stairs, that's all.'

'She's not a happy girl these days,' said Cissie.

'She misses her sister, I expect,' said Jock.

'She needs someone to look out for her,' Cissie said, giving the big man a nudge with her elbow. 'You could do worse, you know.'

'Aye, an' Evie could do better,' Jock said, 'a whole lot better,' then, before the widow could embarrass him further, hastened on upstairs.

What shocked Benjamin more than the letter of dismissal was Patrick Maizie's revelation that everyone knew he was a thief. He had never thought of himself as a thief, had never regarded the skimming of a few shillings from the top of a bill or bullying a tradesman into padding an invoice as anything other than a perquisite of the job, a bonus for the hazards that rent-collecting entailed, and money that wealthy Mr Blackstock would never miss.

Most folk in the city were on the fiddle, and from what he knew of the Blackstocks they were the biggest cheats of all. Even so, in the course of that lonely afternoon, when he went about his business more out of habit than conviction, his wrath curdled into guilt and guilt into shame. By the time he trudged home, just as fog was coming down and the lamps were being lit, he could hardly bear to meet his wife's eye and, when she kissed him, it was all he could do not to burst into tears.

'You've been gone a long time,' Clare said. 'Did it not go well?'

He allowed her to remove his overcoat, and take off his shoes while he sat, mute and melancholy, in the chair before the fire and looked at the room, his wonderfully snug, comfortable room, as if he'd never seen it before.

'No,' he said, at length. 'It did not go well, my dear.'

'Did you speak to Mr Blackstock?'

'I didn't go so far as that.'

'To her then, to Mrs Galloway?'

'No, nor to her either. I – I had words with Mr Maizie.'

'To what outcome?'

'To the outcome that my work hasn't been satisfactory.'

'By whose lights?' said Clare indignantly.

She knelt by his feet, sitting back on her heels.

The light from the fire, stoked and burning brightly, made her appear golden, his golden angel, the one perfect thing that he had ever possessed. He reached out and stroked her hair, wondering how he could explain to her that her husband had built his life upon brutal lies and deceptions. The strutting rages that impotence engendered, the humiliations his mother had heaped upon him, had been washed away by this lovely young woman who, it seemed, was determined to stand by him in spite of his infirmities; but would she, a devout Roman Catholic, still stand by him when she found out that he was a thief?

'I haven't been as honest as I might have been,' he said.

'None of us have,' said Clare. 'Is that her excuse for sacking you?'

'She's a new broom,' he said. 'Off with the old, on with the new.'

'What's wrong with you, Benjamin?' Clare said. 'Why

aren't you fightin' her? I mean why aren't you protestin' any more?'

'I've taken bribes,' Benjamin said. 'Money that wasn't mine.'

'Sure an' is that all that's botherin' you?' Clare leaned her forearms on his knees and scowled up at him. 'Did you not get the job done?'

'Well, aye, I suppose I did.'

'Look how you took us in.'

'Took you in? Deceived you, do you mean?'

'There was no deception. You knew what we were an' what you needed to do to keep us in our place. Sure an' were we not the deceivers, pretendin' to be related to Aunt Cissie when we were nothin' but strays?'

'That's true,' Benjamin conceded. 'I was only half took in, though.'

'You kept us, didn't you?'

'Yes, because I – I liked you.'

She lifted herself and stood before him with her hands on her hips. Her pose reminded him of one of the fat wives at the Red Pit, a boss woman who had ruled the roost among the huts, a woman so self-willed and indomitable that no one could stand up to her. In Clare he glimpsed some of those same qualities, that awful, admirable strength of character that had been hidden until now.

'Do you love me, Benjamin?'

'I do,' he said. 'I do. I do.'

'Then,' she said, 'we'll get through this together.'

'How, dearest, how will we do that?'

'One step at a time,' Clare said. 'One wee step at a time.'

They had lingered over supper discussing every aspect of the situation. What had been, it seemed, mattered not a jot to Clare McKenna Belfer. Her face was firmly turned towards the future, not the past. Was it her youth or her Irishness that gave edge to her optimism, Benjamin wondered, and where had the sullen, sulky girl who had slouched into his ken less than a year ago gone? Was it marriage or motherhood that had altered her?

It was after ten before Clare carried a bowl of stew upstairs for her brother and sister, and Benjamin, calmer than he had been all day, went out to visit the water closet.

The cane came down across his shoulders, spinning him round, and Mr Orpington said, 'I hear you've been given the heave-ho, old son, and it's all change for us poor folk in Salamanca Street.'

'Who told you?' Benjamin said.

'Betty Fowler.'

'Who told her?'

'What does it matter?' Mr Orpington said. 'You know how bad news travels and gathers pace in a narrow place like this. Are you out? Are you off?'

'Aye, so it would seem,' said Mr Belfer.

He glanced upstairs, praying that Clare would not come down. Then he peered into the depths of the close, at the outline of the middens in the yard defined by mist. He caught the cane and nudged Orpington backward, following him down two shallow steps into the yard. He turned Orpington against the wall and released his grip on the cane.

'Oh, I see,' Percival Orpington said. 'It's a secret, is it?'

'An open secret, by the smell o' it,' said Benjamin.

'Not told the wife yet?' Orpington said. 'I saw her trip upstairs not more than a minute ago. The brother'll tell her, you know. Your secret will not be safe for long.'

'It isn't my secret,' Benjamin said. 'Anyroads, Clare knows.'

'Have to move in with Mama, won't you?' Orpington said. 'How will that suit your lovely lady wife?'

The November air was raw. Benjamin, in shirt sleeves,

shivered. Orpington wore the black overcoat with the velvet collar, a silk scarf wrapped around his throat; all that was missing was the topper.

'What Clare an' me do an' where we go ain't your business, Perce,' Benjamin said. 'I've a trick or two up my sleeve yet.'

'I'd wager the family silver on it,' Orpington said. 'Is it true Blackstock's sold out an' the sister is takin' over the beat?'

'Yes,' said Benjamin, 'that appears to be the way of it.'

'He's in straits, then, our boss, our Mr Russell?'

'According to Maizie, he needs capital to finish the harbour.'

'What about the capital he has hidden in the Harp?' said Mr Orpington. 'By capital, of course, I mean cash. Is it still intact?'

Benjamin wrapped his arms, like a butcher-boy, across his chest. The windows of the tenements that backed on to Salamanca Street were pale and subterranean behind the ghostly wreaths of mist. He could smell the river distinctly, taste the sludgy tide, as if the Clyde itself was turning into vapour.

'That's not a question I thought to ask,' Benjamin said, 'nor somethin' Maizie saw fit to tell me.'

'You saw the safe, though? The safe's still there, ain't it?'

'I was in the snuggery, not the office.'

With a swift little hop Mr Orpington was suddenly upon him, the cane pressed against his Adam's apple, pinning him to the rain-wet wall.

'You wouldn't be getting naughty ideas now, would you, Benjamin?'

'Ideas – wha' . . .'

'What we talked about once or twice, in a humorous sort of way.'

'Talked – about . . .'

'What a joke it was in those glory days when we had more than enough of the filthy comin' in to satisfy our needs. Ain't much of a joke now, Benjamin,' Orpington hissed in his ear. 'Ain't no laughing matter now we've both been cast aside. Well, you nurse your grievance how you will and do what you see fit to keep that wife of yours in bread and milk, but don't go nurturin' any ideas about helping yourself to restitution.'

'What – are – you . . .'

'Restitution's my game, old son. Restitution, you might say, is my speciality.'

'The thought – never crossed . . .'

'If it does,' said Percival Orpington, 'discard it or that pretty girl you married might wind up being restituted, too.'

Benjamin heaved his belly forward and swung his arms, breaking Orpington's grasp upon the cane. The struggle lasted no more than half a second before a knife blade, thin as a needle, pricked his throat.

'Keep my wife out of it, Orpington,' he said. 'Slice me if you have to, but keep Clare out of it. If you touch a hair o'her head, I'll . . .'

'You'll do what, Belfer? Snitch me to the coppers?' Orpington took the knife from Benjamin's throat and stepped back. 'No, old son, you're safe as the Bank of England, and your wife too, provided there's no slip twixt the cup and the lip, if you take my meanin'.'

'What,' said Benjamin, 'if it's already gone? What if it's not there?'

'Then I'll know who to blame,' said Orpington.

'I'm not interested in Maizie's safe or Blackstock's money,' Benjamin said. 'For the love of God, Perce, just leave us alone.'

'Only too happy to oblige,' said Orpington, and, with a bow and nod and a wag of the cane, slipped into the murk of the close and, in an instant, was gone.

22

By acquiring control of her father's old properties Libby had stopped Willy's march of progress dead in its tracks. She hadn't seen or heard from Wilson in weeks but had no doubt at all that he would be brooding in his eyrie in Kelvinside, plotting devious new strategies.

Common sense told her that her troubles were just beginning now that she had become responsible for the rowdy tenants of Salamanca Street and for ensuring that Pin's investment would provide for the girl's future, whatever that future might hold. She did not subscribe to the myth that love conquered all. Love alone would not bridge the divisions that the bourgeois citizens of Glasgow had erected to protect themselves. However democratic it might seem in principle, it simply would not do for her ward to marry a day-labourer. If Pin's future was to be linked to that of Nolan McKenna then the young man must somehow be incorporated into the scheme of things.

It had been her intention to turn Sunday lunch at Crosshill House into a celebration to mark her ward's eighteenth birthday. All was not sweetness and light in Crosshill, however, for Russell was not yet reconciled to what she had achieved or, rather, how she had achieved it. In addition, it seemed that Pin preferred to spend Sunday afternoon with Nolan at St Kentigern's surrounded by a mob of noisy brats rather than be toasted in champagne by her family.

Libby quietly put her arrangements for a party to one side

which, under the circumstances, turned out to be a blessing in disguise.

On Saturday morning Mr Percival Orpington wrapped up the last of his books and took them into the city to sell. He quibbled with the bookseller over the price and in the end pocketed three guineas before he went down to the dockland pop-shops to hawk his scarves, suede gloves and dressing-gown, plus a few little trinkets that Ida had failed to find. He got very little for the items, of course, but he had expected to be rooked by the sharp-eyed dealers who obviously had him marked as a gentleman down on his luck.

He walked from the docks to the clothes market near Candleriggs and, being rather too distinguished in his overcoat and topper, paid over the odds for a filthy old pilot jacket, a smelly woollen smock, a pair of faded corduroy breeks and, after much searching, a pair of down-at-heel boots that almost fitted. He bought three pieces of greasy brown paper, wrapped his purchases into one big bundle and, though his ankle was aching like billy-oh, headed out of the city and back towards the Riverside. He stopped off at a smoky public house where he was not liable to be recognised, ate a fish tea washed down with a pint of stout, then hobbled on through gathering dusk until he reached Salamanca Street and, after making sure that the coast was clear, slipped into the close and upstairs to his room.

He rested on the top of the bed for an hour until the throbbing in his ankle eased then he got up and went out again, up to the Masonic Hall in Carpenter Street where he stood guard at the door while Mr Morrison collected the week's Penny Savings. He escorted Mr Morrison, his ledger and little bag of cash to the rank at Partick Cross, saw the cashier safely into a cab, then trudged home to Salamanca Street, where he drank a glass of whisky, peeled off his clothes and fell, exhausted, into bed.

It was done, though, everything prepared and ready.

Tomorrow, Sunday, he wouldn't have to put his nose out of the door. He would spend the afternoon manufacturing the fire-bombs and packing the carpenter's tool bag with everything he needed for the job; then, after midnight, he would put on the shabby clothes he had bought that afternoon and that well-known dapper gentleman, Mr Percival Orpington, would vanish – literally – in a puff of smoke.

Father Fingle made no announcements concerning the changes that were about to take place. The church would have to be inspected by experts and permission for improvements sought from representatives of the diocese and burgh planning authorities before work would properly begin. There were other things to occupy the attention of the worshippers that morning, however, including the appearance of a stranger in their midst.

When Cissie spotted him, she nudged Evie, and whispered, 'My God, do you see what I see? There must be a blue moon in the sky.'

Evie glanced over her shoulder and let out a little 'Ow' of surprise.

'Sure an' what's *he* doin' here?'

'Ask him, not me,' said Cissie, though she had a notion that what had lured the coalman to church was not a return to the religion of his fathers but an interest in the girl at her side.

When it came time for Father Fingle to present the sacraments Jock Macpherson did not join the little procession to the table but knelt in the rear pew with head down and his hands over his face as if he were, perhaps, asking forgiveness for the shallow motives that had brought him here.

'Huh!' Cissie seated herself again after her moment of private prayer. 'I always said it'd be the love of a good woman that'd fetch that hairy old devil back to the bosom o' the Church, but I never thought it'd be you.'

'Me?' said Evie, loud enough to extract a frown from Father Fingle. 'Jock Macpherson's got no interest in me. No. None. Whatsoever.'

'Believe that if you like,' said Cissie, bowing her head again. 'We'll see.'

As soon as the service concluded Evie scrambled out of her seat and made a beeline for the coalman before he could slither away. He was almost out of the door when Evie caught him by the sleeve. He had trimmed his beard and eyebrows and slicked down what remained of the hair on his head with a little scented soap. He wore a clean flannel jacket in respectful black and a plum-coloured scarf about his neck. He looked less coarse and shaggy and much younger, Evie thought, and realised that her friend and neighbour was really quite a handsome feller, if you weren't too fussy about ingrained coal dust and broken fingernails.

'Well, this is a surprise,' she said, giving him more of the eye than she had intended. 'Never a word to any of us, neither. What brings you here, Jock, since it isn't Christmas yet?'

His easy manner seemed to have deserted him. He backed against the little brass cup of holy water that was screwed to the rail in the vestibule as Cissie pushed her way through the crowd in the aisle, then, chuckling, Evie hooked his arm and drew him out into the cold morning light.

'Cat got your tongue, Mr Macpherson?'

'Cat? What cat?'

'Aunt Cissie says you're followin' us.'

'Now why would I be daft enough to do that?'

'She says you're followin' me.' Evie reached up on tiptoe and tucked in the straggling ends of his scarf. 'Is that true?'

'Can a man not come to church . . .'

'Is it true?'

'It's those shifts of yours at the Harp,' Jock said, with a

shrug. 'I'm up early an' you're up late. We never have a chance for a – a chat.'

'If you're so all-fired keen to chat to me, come to the bar.'

'I'm not much of a drinker, Evie. Besides . . .'

'Besides what?' For some odd reason, she was beginning to enjoy teasing the coalman. 'You're not frightened o' Mr Maizie, are you?'

'It's too noisy in the Harp,' Jock said.

'Ooooh!' said Evie. 'You want to have me all to yourself, eh, to whisper sweet bits o' Highland nonsense into me innocent wee ear? One would never guess to look at you that there's a masher lurkin' under all that black dust.'

He suddenly seemed willing to play her game.

He said, 'You'd be surprised what's lurkin' under all this black dust.'

'I can see what's been lurkin' under all that hair,' said Evie, 'an', if you don't mind a compliment, Mr Macpherson, it ain't bad, not bad at all.'

'Thank you, my child,' Jock said, grinning.

'Now, tell me,' Evie said, 'what are you really doin' here? Quick, before Cissie catches up with us.'

'I came to have another look at the woman.'

'What woman?'

'Our new landlord, Libby Galloway.'

'Did you think she'd be standin' up an' announcin' a rent increase?'

'Hardly that,' Jock said. 'I just thought it was – well, time.'

'Time?' said Evie. 'Time for what?'

'Changes all round,' the coalman said.

Then Cissie, flushed and breathless, reached them and, thumping Jock's shoulder with her fist, demanded to be told why he was sneaking into church and just how long it would be before he was ready to take confession.

* * *

Libby could not be sure if she had acquired impatience from Pin or whether, flush with capital, she simply could not bear not to be moving forward. Sometimes she wondered if she was suffering from the same dreadful disease as her brothers, if, in fact, she was a woman on the rise who would stop at nothing to get her own way and not, as she had supposed herself to be, just a philanthropic reactionary with too much time on her hands.

For whatever reason she chose that grey, fog-shrouded Sunday morning to put her proposition to young Mr McKenna.

She persuaded Father Fingle to take Pin off on some Sunday school pretext, cornered Nolan in the empty church and told him what she had in mind.

'No, Mrs Galloway,' Nolan said. 'It's not for me.'

'What?' said Libby, astonished. 'Don't you realise, young man, that you are being offered an excellent opportunity for advancement?'

'Aye,' said Nolan. 'An' I know for why.'

'Oh, do you?' said Libby, with a sinking feeling in the pit of her stomach.

'Sure an' it's so Pin can marry me without havin' to hang her head.'

'Pin has nothing to do with it,' said Libby, lying, of course. 'You are a member of a community in which I have new financial interests and you are, I believe, honest and industrious.'

'For a digger, you mean,' said Nolan. 'A digger's what I am, Mrs Galloway, somethin' Pin seems willin' to accept, even if you can't.'

'Do you want to remain a digger all your life, Nolan?' Libby said. 'Are you so stubborn that you won't accept the sort of opportunity that rarely comes to young men of your age?'

'Not if it means puttin' my brother-in-law out of a job.'

'Ah! Ah-hah!' Libby exclaimed. 'So that's it, is it?'

'Blood's thicker than water, Mrs Galloway,' Nolan told her.

'Belfer is not your relative, your blood relative.'

'Nope, but he's me sister's husband, an' that's good enough for me.'

'You're being exceedingly foolish, you know, putting Belfer's interests before your own. I doubt if he would do the same for you.'

'Sure an' I doubt if he would,' Nolan said. 'But since he an' me are family now it's up to us to look out for him.'

'Belfer's already been dismissed,' said Libby, 'for reasons that I have no intention of explaining to you.'

'You're keen to build up this church, ain't you?'

'Yes, and you would be—' Libby began.

Nolan interrupted her. 'Then he's your man, Belfer I mean. He's the man who'll get the work done quick an' ship-shape. I haven't the clout, nor the sway over the tradesmen. Aye, I know that Benjamin takes a taste o' whatever's goin'. While that's not somethin' I'd ever do myself, I don't grudge him his bit o' extra profit. It's a hard world in the streets o' the Riverside an' me sister's man has the measure of it.'

'I cannot believe that you are defending this man, that you'd put loyalty to a fellow like Belfer before your own happiness.'

'Well,' said Nolan with a sigh. 'I am, an' I do, Mrs Galloway.'

'Would you risk losing Pin to protect him?'

'Is that a threat, Mrs Galloway?' Nolan said. 'Is that not the sort o' thing Mr Belfer might say to one o' his tradesmen?'

'Now you're being insolent,' Libby snapped.

'Nah,' said Nolan, 'I'm only tellin' you the truth as I see it.'

Libby looked towards the Stations of the Cross, at the plaster representations that adhered, more by luck than gravity, to the chapel's peeling walls and then, tapping her foot on the flagstones, threw up her hands in a gesture of capitulation.

'Family first?' she said. 'Is that the nub of it, Nolan McKenna, family before all else?'

'It is, Mrs Galloway, sure an' it is.'

'If – and my mind is not made up – if I were to give Belfer his job back, would you come and work for me then?'

'Doin' what?' said Nolan.

'Building supervisor.'

'I ain't no builder,' Nolan said. 'I'm a labourer. I take orders, Mrs Galloway. I've no experience givin' them.'

'That is surely something that can be learned.'

'Aye, maybe, but who's to teach me?'

Libby hadn't expected the young Irishman to be quite so down-to-earth in estimating his present worth or quite so astute in redefining her proposal. She, it seemed, also had a great deal to learn.

She said, 'My brother, Russell.'

'I work for him already,' said Nolan.

'But not in his builder's yard,' said Libby. 'If I can persuade him to take you into the yard to learn the ropes, will you consider it?'

'Who'll pay me wages?'

'I will,' said Libby.

'A builder's apprentice?' Nolan said. 'Will Mr Blackstock agree?'

'If he's given the contract for repairing St Kentigern's, he might.'

Nolan laughed. 'Small beer for Mr Blackstock, compared to buildin' a harbour. Still, it'll keep it in the family, I suppose. If that's what you want, Mrs Galloway, an' if Mr Blackstock buys it then – aye, I'd be willin' to give it a shot.'

'I take it you know why I'm doing this?'

'To stop me runnin' off an' marryin' Pin on the sly.'

'Yes,' Libby said. 'Precisely. As far as Pin is concerned, however, let's just say I'm investing in the future.'

'My future, or hers?' said Nolan.

'That,' said Libby Galloway, 'is something that remains to be seen. Meanwhile, young man, do we have an agreement of sorts?'

'Aye, Mrs Galloway,' Nolan said. 'Sure an' I think we do.'

Match-maker or chaperone, there was no shaking off Mrs Cissie Cassidy, who declared that she wasn't sacrificing her Sunday afternoon pancakes just because Jock Macpherson had found his way back to God. There was little that Jock or Evie could do about it. Cissie monopolised the conversation for most of the afternoon, while the coalman and the barmaid fed their faces, exchanged an occasional glance, and listened, very patiently, to Cissie's tales of her time in the kitchens of the Royal Restaurant and of the grisly night when she had shed the last little Cassidy and her usefulness to anyone, except her Eamon, had effectively come to an end.

Downstairs in the Belfers' kitchen Benjamin plied Nolan with food in quantities that even Nolan couldn't cope with while Clare, her arm about her husband's waist, thanked her brother again and again for the miracle of redemption that he had pulled off that morning in getting Benjamin back his job. When it came time for Nolan to leave for Sunday school, the couple even followed him out into the street to wave him off and then, alone at last, they kissed and hugged and wound up lying, contentedly enough, side by side on top of the big warm bed.

Lunch over, and Pin departed, Libby and Russell retreated to the morning-room of Crosshill House, where they sipped coffee and soberly discussed the arrangements that Libby had made in respect of her ward. It was, in fact, an exercise in hatchet-burying, one in which Russell was more than willing to play his part, for he, like his sister, had no wish for the Blackstocks to remain at loggerheads forever. He would have made his peace with Wilson, too, if such a thing had been possible but Willy, it seemed, had gone his own wild, impetuous way, and had no wish to return to the family fold.

Sunday school attendance was very sparse that winter afternoon, for small children were not as entranced by fog as they were by big winds or falling snow. The sinuous tendrils of moist grey vapour that crept up from the Clyde were just too silent and sinister to tempt the youngsters to abandon their firesides and venture out of doors, as if they feared that their families would be lost forever while they were gathered, praying, in the lonely little church of St Kentigern. No such fears assailed Miss Pin or Mr Nolan, of course. They were only too pleased to escort the few brave souls who did turn up back to their closes before they set off, arm-in-arm, for Crosshill House. Arm-in-arm soon became hand-in-hand and the conversation, serious at first, was soon punctuated by long pauses while the pair kissed, safe from detection in the bank of fog that came rolling in, quite thickly now, from the river and the sea.

Fog was a bonus for busy Mr Orpington, though his room on the second floor of Belfer's tenement was as cold as a tomb. He did not dare light the fire in case a stray spark ruined his preparations and blew him to kingdom come. Kneeling on the floor, he worked by the light of a single shaded lamp set high on the mantelshelf. He filled four empty ginger beer bottles with a mixture of white spirit and kerosene. He ripped up a sheet to make fuses and placed the bottles, very carefully, along the wall by the door where he would not trip over them. That done, he fashioned two small, tight packets of gunpowder out of brown paper, cut two short lengths of cordite fuse, fed them into the packets and sealed them with soft lumps of beeswax. He put the rest of the gunpowder back into the tin box and, for safety's sake, tucked it back under the sink. He fished out the carpenter's bag, lined it with the flannel blanket and two felt treads and placed the little packets of gunpowder snugly on top. He washed his hands and forearms at the sink, ate a ham sandwich, drank a glass of whisky and then, frozen to the bone and still fully clothed, crawled into bed to snatch a few hours' sleep.

23

It was Evie who wakened at the splitting of the hammer on the lock. Humped under the bedclothes in the big bed, Nolan did not so much as stir. It was, at first, almost pitch dark with only the outline of the window, pale with fog, to lend dimension to the kitchen. She rolled over, sleepily groping for Clare, then sat upright as the first bottle flared across her vision and shattered against the table leg, scattering flames and fiery liquid in all directions.

She let out a piercing shriek and leaped out of bed as a second bottle arched through the door and smeared flame across the wall.

'*Nolan*,' she screamed. '*Nolan. Fire! Fire!*'

Dragging bedclothes with him, Nolan was on his feet and beating with a blanket at the flames that sprinkled the floor, beating too at the modesty curtain that had caught a smattering of liquid fire. Borne inward on the draught from the broken door, the stench of kerosene was sickeningly strong. Smoke rapidly began to accumulate around the globs of fire that sprang up in several parts of the room and from varnished and painted surfaces that had already begun to melt and bubble.

Evie danced this way and that, stamping at the fiery pustules with her bare feet, crying with pain as well as fear while the room filled with clouds of pungent smoke that stung her eyes and gripped her throat. Her bed was patched with burning pieces and the flimsy cotton curtain sent charred fragments, rimmed with flame, floating into the air. There was no inferno, no searing heat or blast, only thickening, choking smoke. She ran through it towards the window, twisted the tap at the sink, grabbed the pail on the draining board and thrust it under the trickle of brown water. Then Nolan caught her by the waist, swept her off her feet and threw a blanket over her head. She felt herself being carried along, legs kicking, her screams muffled, bumping into furniture, then cold air about her, a drumming sound in her head, and she was flung, roughly, out into the street and the blanket was whipped away.

Dazed, she sprawled on the pavement until Nolan yanked her to her feet, and yelled, 'Stay here, Stay away,' and she saw that the close-mouth was filled with black smoke and thin, shivering sheets of flame coloured like a peacock's tail. 'Clare?' she said. 'Where's our Clare?'

But Nolan had already plunged through the smoke back into Belfer's tenement to raise the alarm and rescue as many of the little children as God was willing to steer his way.

If Clare had not been squatting on the chamber pot when the door burst open there's no saying what might have happened. It was her third visit to 'china' that night and she was weary of it, weary too of the awkward weight in her belly, and more than a little bit annoyed at Benjamin, who'd had the gall to grumble when she'd crawled over him again.

There was still light from the grate and the room was warm. She was crouched, half asleep, with the fire at her back, when, without warning, the door shuddered and, with an almighty crack, swung inward on its hinges and someone, she could not make out who, pitched an object into the room. The object, a bottle, did not break. It trundled past her, leaking trickles of flaming liquid, all quite soft and delicate, then the cloth stopper fell out and a sudden soft flash ignited the tassel of the table cover.

'Benjamin?' said Clare enquiringly, and, standing, tossed the contents of the china chamber pot upon the burning cloth, extinguishing it at once. 'Benjamin, get up.'

By then a second object, another bottle, had struck a corner of the grate and splintered, spraying the fireplace with broken glass and, just as Benjamin's feet touched the floor, the fire in the grate roared up furiously, lighting the room with a bluish glare. Clare felt the heat upon her back, sudden and searing, and before her nightgown could catch fire hopped around the table and headed for the door. Benjamin chose a different route, clambering over the armchair. He reached the open door before her, roaring louder than the fire, 'Orpington, Orpington, Orpington,' almost like a battle cry. He was on the point of running out into the close when the man in the close, Orpington or another, swept a great oily wave of liquid into the room, drenching Benjamin's nightshirt in the process, and, to her horror, Clare watched her husband catch fire.

She wasted not one breath crying out for help. She caught the folds of the heavy cover, wrenched it from the table and, using her arms, breasts and belly as a shield, flung the cloth over him and hugged him tightly. He was grunting now, not yelling, and, as flames took hold on the waxy linoleum and clawed into the wooden mantelpiece, he reached behind him, clasped Clare's buttocks and, still draped in the folds of the tablecloth, lugged her piggy-back out of the kitchen into the smoke-filled close.

Nolan loomed out of the gloom.

'Do you have her?' he shouted. 'Is she safe?'

'I have her,' Benjamin said.

'Who did this, man?'

'Orpington,' Benjamin said hoarsely.

'Did you see him?'

'Aye.'

'Take her out,' said Nolan, and, shoving Benjamin towards the close-mouth, dashed off upstairs with a blanket thrown over his head.

Back in the old days Mr Tam McLean had been a carter for the Riverside Fire Brigade and nailed to the wall above the stable doors you could still make out a faded sign that read *Fire. Butt. Carter*. With the advent of a steam fire-engine, half a dozen fire plugs tapped into the water supply and a rudimentary system of electrical alarms, Tam had been taken off the burgh council's books. It had been some years now since he had bounded out of bed with the smell of smoke in his nostrils and cries of 'Fire, Fire, the house is on fire,' ringing, albeit faintly, in his ears. He threw open the window, leaned out and peered down the line of the lane towards Salamanca Street.

Being a wee bit past his prime, with his eyesight fading, at first he could not determine what was fog and what was smoke. The stench, though, was unmistakable. Wakening his wife, he flung on a shirt, breeks and boots and ran downstairs to unhitch the lightest of his mares. Leading her out into the lane, he clambered up on to her back and rode her, without a saddle, out into the street. A crowd had gathered already and more folk were appearing every minute from closes further up the street. He could tell by the layering of the fog that there was no wind, however, and that whatever careless spark or gobbet of hot ash had started a blaze in Belfer's tenement, it was not liable to spread to the stables or any other building in the street.

Hanging on with his knees, he looked with an experienced eye at the tenement windows; a glimmer, a glow of sorts in the first-floor apartment, bright, dancing flames behind the window of Belfer's apartment on the ground floor, and great billows of black smoke pouring from the close-mouth, smoke, he knew, that could kill.

Having little or no faith in electrical apparatus, which had been known to fail before now, Tam brought the mare round and, digging in with his heels, rode off at the gallop to summon the burgh fire brigade from the station next to the police office at the bottom of North Carpenter Street hill.

By the time Mrs McLean threw a shawl over her nightgown and came waddling down the lane with an armful of blankets, Nolan, Jock and Benjamin between them had managed to lead everyone out of the building. Brave men, they were called, all three, but at the time there had been nothing brave about it, only the application of common sense added to desperation.

The tenement, though old, was built of stone and at first the fire was confined to one room on the first floor and the apartment at ground level. What nagged the rescuers was the thought of what might happen if flames were sucked back into the gas main. No one, not even Benjamin, knew where the stop-cock valve to the main pipe was situated. For this reason Benjamin, clad only in a charred nightshirt, ran out to persuade the onlookers to retreat to safety.

Inside the burning building there was no panic, apart from Betty Fowler whose fit of hysteria was soon cured by a hard slap from her sister. With children in every pocket, and a baby cradled in his arms, Nolan guided the tenants down from the upper floors. Jardines, Fowlers and their kiddies, with sheets over their heads and smarting eyes, were then handed over to Jock who manned the half-landing.

The fire in the McKennas' kitchen had not taken firm hold but blistering varnish and smouldering cloth created volumes of smoke that made the last few steps of the descent difficult and dangerous. With a scarf over his face and his Sunday best jacket over his head, Jock steered the weeping tenants through the murk and, turning them as a dog does sheep, chased them safe away across the back court behind the water tank.

'Nolan,' he shouted. 'Nolan, are you there?'

Covering his mouth with cupped hands, he shouted upstairs again and, to his vast relief, saw the big Irishman come leaping downstairs and almost catapult into him. Crouched down, coughing violently, they ducked out through the back close and ran to the shelter of the water tank.

'Did – did you get everyone?' Jock gasped. 'Is everyone accounted for?'

'Everyone,' Nolan said, 'except Orpington.'

'Dear God!' said Jock. 'Is he still in there?'

'Nah,' Nolan said. 'That bastard started it, so he's probably long gone.'

'Gone?' Jock said. 'Gone where?'

'Back to hell for all I care,' Nolan said, then, taking the coalman by the arm, scuttled across the yards to find a safe exit into the street.

It had only been a matter of months since the council had seen fit to establish a permanent force to fight fires and had purchased a magnificent new steam engine. They had also splurged on a stud of fresh horses, a ladder carriage, new hose reels and had even gone so far as to provide every man in the crew with uniform clothing, boots, helmet and a tool belt. The station was controlled by the Police Board and all the crew members were lodged in the immediate vicinity of North Carpenter Street which meant that within fifteen minutes of Tam McLean raising the alarm the engines were clattering through the fog, brass bells clanging, and charging across Wedderburn Road into Salamanca Street.

Mr Orpington checked his pocket watch and grinned.

The training that the fire-fighters had undergone in recent months was obviously paying dividends, he thought; he hadn't expected the engines to pass the Harp for at least another ten minutes. No matter: he was well on schedule. So far, everything had gone like clockwork and his concerns over the effectiveness of gunpowder as an explosive agent had proved groundless.

The door of Paddy Maizie's safe had blown off its hinges neat as ninepence, leaving the big canvas sack full of banknotes inside undamaged. He had dragged the sack over to the ottoman and was busily engaged in packing banknotes into the carpenter's tool bag when the engines came past.

He eased the last of the notes into the bag, tamped them down, and strapped the bag carefully. The haul was larger than he had anticipated and not all the notes were large denomination. There was silver in the safe, too, but he decided not to be greedy and burden himself with more than he could comfortably carry and left it there.

He checked his watch again, then, kicking open a small cabinet, found a bottle of nice French brandy and several glasses. He pulled out the cork with his teeth, poured himself a generous libation and toasted the smoking safe and the carpenter's bag, then, ever cautious, tossed glass and bottle away before elation got the better of him.

It occurred to him to torch Maizie's office but that would only draw attention to the fact that the safe had been rifled and might shorten the time he needed to get out of Glasgow before the peelers came looking for him. As it was, he had twenty-six minutes to reach the railway halt at Yorkhill before the early train pulled in. Ample time, he thought, ample time. Kneeling, he carefully extinguished the oil lamp, then, slinging the carpenter's bag across his shoulder, he slipped out of Paddy Maizie's office and walked, quite jauntily, across the yard, down the dark alley into Salamanca Street and turned left to cross over to the church and the lane by the burial ground, through which he would make good the first leg of his escape.

* * *

'My house, my lovely wee house,' Cissie wailed. 'What're they doin' squirtin' water through the window?'

'They're makin' sure the fire's out, Cissie,' Jock told her.

'I wasn't on fire, though,' Cissie said. 'You tell them mannies to stop.'

'No, no, Mrs Cassidy,' Benjamin said. 'Best to let them get on with it. At least they've got the gas main safely cocked, thank God.'

'All very well for you, Mr Belfer,' Cissie said. 'You still have a place to go to an' a roof over your head. I've nothin' but the rags I stand up in.'

Jock put an arm about Cissie's shoulder and let her weep into his nightshirt, stained though it was with smeary black soot. It was on the tip of his tongue to remind her that she at least had some money tucked away and that this was a rainy day if ever he saw one. But he was too weary now, too deflated to offer much consolation. He was more concerned about Evie than Cissie. Evie was clearly in a state of shock. Even with two of Mrs McLean's horse blankets wrapped about her she was still shivering. He would have carried her in to the stables to join Clare in the feed loft where the Fowler sisters' and the Jardines' children were being washed and settled, but Evie refused to leave the street. She stood with the other homeless tenants in a little area that the firemen had roped off, removed from the crowd of spectators who, defying the cold, had come out to watch the new Riverside Fire Brigade in action.

Within minutes of the arrival of the shiny engines, hoses had been run through the close to the tank and, soon after, water had poured down the steps and gushed through the windows of the ground- and first-floor apartments and clouds of smoke and steam merged with the fog. The tenement's façade had a dreary appearance, with broken windows and great loops of blackened stonework and water, filthy water, swirling out of the close into the gutters.

At first there had been no sign of Nolan, then Evie spotted him talking intimately to the chief fire officer and, some minutes later, no less intimately with a superintendent of the Police Board. Like the others who had fled the building, Nolan was clad in a nightshirt and a blanket and, tall as he was, looked quite pathetic next to the uniformed officers.

Eventually he came splashing through the puddles towards them, the police superintendent hard on his heels.

'Oh, dear!' Benjamin murmured. 'Oh, dear God, it's me they're after.'

The superintendent, almost as tall as Nolan, sported a flowing beard that in density as well as length made Jock's whiskers seem quite sparse.

'Are you Mr Belfer?' the officer asked.

Benjamin tucked the blanket between his thighs and held it there. 'I am, sir, I am.'

'Are you the factor of this building?'

'Yes.'

'Where were you when the conflagration started?'

'In bed, sir, with – with my wife.'

'Someone broke down the door and threw a bottle of inflammable liquid into your kitchen; is that a fair statement?' the officer said.

'Two bottles,' Benjamin said.

'Did you see the perpetrator of the attack?'

'I did,' said Benjamin.

'One of your tenants, so I'm informed?'

'Aye, sir. Mr Orpington. Percival Orpington.'

'Are you quite sure, Mr Belfer?'

'I saw him as clear as I see you,' said Benjamin.

'This man, this Orpington, have you any idea where he might be now, where, in a word, he might be found?'

'I think, an' this is just a guess, just conjecture, sir, I think . . .'

'What?' the superintendent said. 'What d'you think?'

'I think you'll find him at Paddy Maizie's.'

'The pub!' The officer glanced, dubiously, at Nolan. 'Now what would he be doin' in a pub at this hour of the morning?'

'Robbing the safe,' said Benjamin.

Even the greatest of criminal masterminds cannot take into account every quirk of fate or the vagaries of coincidence. What chance, therefore, did Percival Orpington have against a lurcher with a shady past and a gambler with insomnia?

Insomnia was not quite the word to describe the condition that drove Tommy Knox out into the streets in dead of night: overcrowding might be closer to the truth of it. Sharing sleeping accommodation in a single-end with a wife, her mother, five children and two dogs left no place for Tommy to lay his head comfortably and now the children were all at school, he had fallen into the habit of going out at night and sleeping during the day. When his wife and mother-in-law sloped off for a half shift packing boxes in Campbell's Waterproof Warehouse in Commerce Street he had the bed all to himself, if you didn't count the terrier and the lurcher, that is, which Tommy, being very partial to the smell of dogs, did not.

The lurcher Dandy's shady past was more difficult to define. Tommy had bought him at the dog market a year ago when Dandy was, in theory, not much more than a pup. It hadn't taken Tommy long to realise that Dandy was a deal older than the poacher who had sold him claimed and that Dandy had some history behind him, a history that may have included ring-fighting and ratting as well as pursuing gallant hares across private land and ripping the poor beasts limb from limb.

Tommy was also of the opinion that Dandy was not quite a pure-bred cross between a greyhound and a collie, which is what every self-respecting lurcher was supposed to be, but had somewhere in his ancestry a touch of bull mastiff and, just possibly, a trace of Alsatian too. He was certainly a queer-looking creature with a brindled ruff, a broad muzzle filled with strong white teeth, and a placid eye that regarded small mischievous children with great benevolence but that turned instantly red at the mere sniff of a cat, a rat or, worst of all, anything resembling another dog, apart, that is, from the greyhound, now deceased, and the terrier with whom he shared a hearth.

For all his affectionate ways at home, Dandy had brought poor Tommy a heap of trouble over the past twelve months and many a family pet in the neighbourhood had mysteriously gone missing and many another had wound up in pieces in the gutter, until Tommy had taken to roping the brute and walking him only at night when the coast was relatively clear of diversions.

Tommy had heard the fire bell and was well aware that there was some sort of commotion at the bottom end of Salamanca Street. He expected it to be nothing much more than a sparky chimney or a breakfast frying pan that had caught alight; another false alarm. Even if there was a proper blaze, he wasn't drawn to it, not with Dandy on the rope, for Dandy, he knew, would go mad with excitement and try to bite the horses. He chose then to get off the street for a bit and walk about the burial ground which was as quiet as – well – the grave.

There was just enough light from the streetlamps to show him the line of the path around the perimeter, but Dandy had a good nose and, snuffling and sniffing, jerked him along at no great pace through the pale layers of fog.

It was Dandy who heard the man first. Dandy who let out the low warning growl that more often than not preceded chaos.

Tommy tightened his grip on the rope and cocked his head.

He caught the crunch of boots on the ashy gravel of the lane and, curiosity tweaked, let the lurcher lead him to the little iron gate at the rear of the burial ground where, crouched down with a hand over the dog's muzzle, he watched a workman in a pilot jacket come out of the lane and into the shifting light from the streetlamp at the end of Chapelton Road.

There was no black overcoat, no top hat, silk scarf or suede gloves to give Tommy a clue as to the man's identity. He saw the man's face clearly for only a second when he paused to heft up the carpenter's tool bag and adjust his balance. But a second was quite enough for Tommy. His first impulse was to scuttle away, to hide among the gravestones and hope that the fog would protect him, to put as much distance between Mr Orpington and himself as he could, for the mere sight of the Englishman brought an acid rush to his throat and caused his heart to bound about in his chest.

He kept his hand on Dandy's muzzle, and held his breath.

Orpington? Orpington in shabby clothes, carrying a heavy tool bag?

Orpington, though, without the shadow of a doubt, still with that sleek, striding walk of his, not much marred by the hint of a limp. Orpington heading out of the Riverside in the dead of night?

Orpington up to no good.

He watched the debt-collector move on through the moist haze and swing up the long hill that was Chapelton Road. At that moment, Tommy's inquisitiveness overcame his fear and, safe in the knowledge that Dandy and he could outrun the Englishman, he opened the iron gate and, holding the lurcher on a tight leash, let the dog follow the trail.

The railway halt at Yorkhill had been opened for less than a month. It carried heavy traffic later into the morning and again at the end of the day when the city factories let out. The halt was manned only by a ticket-seller in a booth by the gate at the top of the steps that led up from Chapelton Road. A single gas lamp hung at each end of the narrow platform, and a ramp sloped down to a piece of waste ground that was earmarked for a goods yard.

In daylight and better weather, the signal box at the Partick junction was visible and, if you leaned out a little over the rails, the arch of the tunnel that burrowed away under the top of Chapelton Road. When Mr Orpington climbed the steps that November night, however, the signal box and tunnel mouth were lost not so much in darkness as in fog.

He went, boldly enough, to the ticket booth, but found it still shuttered. Slightly discombobulated by the empty booth, he swung the bag round on his shoulder and stared down the line towards the Partick junction from which direction the early morning train would appear.

His elation had dwindled during his walk to the station and he was anxious now, teased by a vague surreal sensation that he was not alone, that someone, or something, had attached itself to him far down the road, someone or something that remained just out of sight in the fog.

There were sounds, though, strange, half-strangled pantings that drifted into and out of earshot. He had stopped once, looked round, and saw nothing. He stopped again halfway up the steps to the platform and looked back down at the patch of broken cobbles below, and saw nothing. And when he stopped, the sound stopped too, and the feeling that he was being followed would not go away.

He had supposed that his confidence would return when he reached the platform but the absence of a collector in the little booth was unexpectedly upsetting. He walked around the booth and then back to the platform's edge, trying to calm himself. Perhaps, he thought, the collector comes up from Partick on the very early train: yes, he told himself, that must be it – or else the fog has held the fellow up and the fog will delay the train and I'll be stranded here in the middle of nowhere and my plan, my perfect plan will founder.

He paced up and down, still with the bag on his shoulder.

He dug out his watch and, squinting, saw that the train was not late yet, that he still had time. When he glanced up from looking at his watch he found that there *was* someone on the steps, a man, a man with a dog on a lead.

The man did not approach the ticket booth but remained at the far end of the platform. He appeared to have no interest at all in Mr Orpington, though the dog panted and pulled against the leash, which at least explained the sounds.

'Hah!' Mr Orpington said to himself. 'Night shift.' Then, moving a step or two towards the man, he called out, 'Will it be on time tonight, do you think?'

The man did not reply, though the dog barked once, sharply.

He was on the point of calling out again when, muffled by fog, he heard the clack of the signal and, thankfully, the shrill hoot of a locomotive's whistle. Blowing out his breath, he gripped the tool bag tightly and, leaning out a little, peered into the swirling mist in search of the locomotive's headlamp.

When he looked up again, the man had moved closer.

He wore a heavy black oilskin jacket and a billed cap hid his face.

The dog was growling now, not whining. It strained at the rope so forcefully that the man had to dig in his heels to hang on to it.

The signal clacked once more.

The rails vibrated with the locomotive's approach. Mr Orpington did not look in that direction, did not look down the line at all. He stared, frowning, at the man in the oilskin, who, as fog was sucked off by the approaching train, tipped back his cap and nodded a greeting.

'You,' Mr Orpington said. 'It's you?'

'Aye, Mr Orpington, sir,' Tommy told him. 'It's me.'

Then, kneeling, he slipped off the rope, and let his doggie go.

24

Christmas was Father Fingle's favourite time of the year. Easter, of course, was the glorious mystery when the priest's faith in redemption in the Lord Jesus was strongest. There were few doubts in Father Fingle's mind now that he had shed the burden of Libby Galloway's money, even if it had been in his possession only temporarily. He had returned to a state of poverty and, with restoration on the cards, had no doubt that the mission of St Kentigern would flourish and more poor souls would be brought to God because of it.

Days of devotion, fasting and abstinence were dutifully observed throughout the month and, to the father's gratification, the scattered flock from Belfer's tenement still turned up for mass.

The girl, Evie, shared a room with Cissie Cassidy in a boarding house on Dumbarton Road, a mile away. Nolan and the coal-heaver, Macpherson, newly returned to the fold, had beds in a working man's hostel not far from the builder's yard where Nolan was employed. The priest had also heard that the other tenants of Belfer's tenement had been temporarily accommodated and would all return to Salamanca Street just as soon as repairs had been carried out and the building passed by the health inspectors.

Mrs Galloway was much occupied with insurance claims and in organising repair work, and the annual concert party in the Our Lady orphanage had suffered from the absence of her guiding hand.

The father, as always, was busy visiting the sick and dying. He had presided over four burials in the first two weeks of Advent, for fog wreaked havoc with the aged.

Even so, Father Fingle took pleasure in the season and often thought of his mother, who had been dead for many years, though her face remained vivid in his memory. He had been the youngest of five, her only son, her favourite, her bonnie wee man who would take on the challenge of the priesthood as soon as he became old enough. She had died, alas, before he had been appointed to his first ministry, and his sisters were scattered far and wide. He wrote to them at Christmas and to each of his nephews and nieces, whom he had never met. He sent them all blessings and good wishes for the year that was to come and, to his delight, would receive back from each of them a little card or greeting assuring him that he was not forgotten in their hearts, or in their prayers.

It was quite late in the evening, and the father was seated at the table in his kitchen with notepaper, pen and ink bottle, happily writing to Tina, his sister Anna's youngest, when a knock upon the door at the end of the hall disturbed him. He could not help but utter a little groan as he blotted the note, cleaned the pen, and got up to see what the caller wanted at this hour.

He opened the door and peeped out.

'Belfer?' he said. 'Mr Belfer?'

'Yes – ah – Father, will you spare me a minute or two, please?'

Father Fingle ushered the factor into the parlour. He lit the gas lamp over the mantle, stirred up the few coals that remained in the grate and invited Benjamin to be seated. He watched the factor lower himself nervously into the chair, as if fearing that it might crack under his weight, though Mr Blackstock's agent was not nearly as plump as he had once been and, indeed, had a gaunt look to him that did not bode well.

'Is someone ill?' Father Fingle said. 'Is your wife – is Clare sick?'

'No, nothin' like that – ah – Father,' Benjamin Belfer replied. 'Clare's in bloomin' good health, though her temper, like mine, is a bit on the short side, somewhat inclined to fray, you might say.'

'Where are you staying?' The priest already knew the answer.

'In my – in Mother's apartment in Bellingham Place.'

'Are you not comfortable there?'

'I'm not comfortable anywhere,' Benjamin said. 'I won't be comfortable till I'm back in my own house here in Salamanca Street.'

'In preference to Bellingham Place? My, my!' said Father Fingle. 'When will the tenement be ready for occupancy?'

'Early in the New Year – if the health inspectors ever get off their tails.'

'What's really troubling you, Benjamin?' Father Fingle said.

'I'm lost,' Benjamin said.

'Lost? In what way are you lost?'

'I don't know who I am, or where I'm goin' now.'

'Are you not still employed by the Blackstocks?'

'Aye, I'm still at it, still collectin' rents an' seein' to repairs for Mrs Galloway, not Mr Russell now. I'm grateful for that, Father Fingle, believe me. I'm grateful for so many things, too many things, things that I – I don't deserve.'

'Did Clare send you to see me?'

'She doesn't know I'm here.'

He looked up and for the first time met the father's eye.

He might be a bully and a coward, Father Fingle thought, but at least he was courageous enough to come here tonight, to take a step in the right direction no matter how it stung his pride to do so.

'Is it, by any chance, what happened to Orpington that's troubling you?'

'Aye, that as much as anythin', I suppose,' Benjamin blurted out. 'Orpington an' me, we were two of a kind. It could have been me there on that platform, alone in the fog. It could've been me that fell under that train.'

'Are you afraid of dying?'

'Yes, I'm afraid of dyin',' Benjamin said. 'I've a wife to look after, an' my mother – well, my mother . . . an' I'll be a father soon.' He hesitated, then, in a rush, went on, 'I've a feeling that Orpington wanted me to go with him to rob Maizie's safe an' run off leavin' everything behind.'

'But you didn't.'

'No, Father Fingle, I didn't.'

'Why not?'

'Because I was afraid.'

'Is that the true reason, Benjamin?'

'I couldn't abandon Clare. I couldn't let her down, her an' our baby.'

Father Fingle sat back, hands folded in his lap. He knew more about the Orpington affair than Belfer gave him credit for and how close the two men had been before the McKennas had wandered into Salamanca Street. He could well imagine how affected Belfer had been by the death of a man who had once been his only friend – and how difficult it must be for Benjamin Belfer to admit that God, not chance, had brought Clare McKenna to him and had changed him, not through fear, but by love.

The fatal accident at Yorkhill railway halt had been thoroughly investigated. The Procurator Fiscal had concluded that Percival Orpington had died by misadventure pursuant upon the commission of the crimes of wilful arson and safe-breaking and had apparently fallen under the wheels of a train while attempting to effect an escape on a night of thick fog. According to the *Glasgow Herald* over six thousand pounds had been retrieved from close to the body, a sum proved to have been stolen from the offices of Patrick Maizie, proprietor of the Harp of Erin public house. The money had subsequently been returned to Paddy Maizie who when asked why he kept such a very large sum on the premises had answered that 'he did not trust banks' an explanation that, while not entirely satisfactory, was impossible to disprove.

Being without known kin the body of Percival Orpington had been buried at council expense in a pauper's grave. No one, not even Benjamin Belfer, had turned up to bid the Englishman farewell.

'Tell me what to do,' Benjamin said. 'I want our baby brought up right.'

'Clare will see to that, never fear,' said Father Fingle. 'It's what will become of you that bothers me.'

'Then give me instruction,' Benjamin said. 'Isn't that the first step?'

'Becoming a Catholic is not a simple matter,' the father said.

'I didn't expect it would be,' said Benjamin. 'But I'm ready.'

Are you? Father Fingle thought: I wonder if you are, Benjamin Belfer.

'Why are you doing this, Benjamin?' he asked.

'For Clare,' Benjamin answered.

'To bring you closer to Clare,' Father Fingle said, 'not to God?'

'Same thing, Father,' Benjamin Belfer said, and although Father Fingle did not entirely agree, he knew that it was at least a start and part of a new beginning not just for Mr Belfer but, perhaps, for all of them.

They met by arrangement on Sunday afternoon after they had broken their fast. There was no pancake treat to look forward to but a couple of hours or so after mass ended they met outside the church and strolled the length of Salamanca Street to inspect progress on the tenement that had been and soon would again be their home.

The soot stains had been buffed off and cracked facing stones above Benjamin's apartment replaced. Wooden scaffolding still clung to the façade, however, for Libby Blackstock had insisted on putting in new windows in all the rooms and Nolan, with a good deal of help from Pin, had managed to obtain a very decent price not only on glass but on sills, sashes and frames, too. Norma, Pin's school friend, had been persuaded to talk sweetly to her father, and her father had written to the manager of the glass manufactory and, after that, Nolan and the manager had settled terms amicably between them at a price that Libby could afford.

It was Nolan's first foray into 'managing' a building contract and he was inordinately proud of himself. For much of the time, however, he was little more than an extra hand, helping erect scaffolds and haul up buckets of mortar to the bricklayers on the first floor. He had even tried his hand at distempering, though Russell Blackstock's painters were a clannish lot and did not make him welcome. Plumbers, gas-fitters and carpenters had done their work and the old tenement was already beginning to take on a fresh new appearance that gladdened the hearts of Mrs Galloway's tenants and made them impatient to be home again.

'It'll have to be new curtains, I'm thinkin',' Cissie Cassidy said.

'New everythin' for us,' said Evie. 'We lost most of what we owned, though it wasn't much to start with.'

'The Galloway woman will furnish it for you, won't she?' said Jock.

'Sure an' that's the plan.'

Evie stepped back from the scaffolding and stared up at the boarded window of the apartment on the first floor.

In six months or a year, after Nolan had married Pin which, without doubt, he would do, she would be here alone. She had never lived alone before, never been without a man to look after her. She had thought at one time, not so long since, that coming to Glasgow would change everything and, in a way, it had. But life, she realised now, was a river that never stopped flowing; you might build harbours, erect quays or dredge out new channels but the river had a mind of its own and would carry you on, willy-nilly, in any direction it chose.

She felt him behind her, his big rough hand on her shoulder.

'Penny for them, Evie?' he said quietly.

How could she tell him that she had been thinking of Russell Blackstock, of the infatuation that she had supposed was love and that had not been love at all. She'd had no experience of men, no experience of what love meant or how it took you, not with a swirl and a swoop but gradually, swelling and receding and swelling again just like the tide until, almost before you knew it, you were caught in it and being carried along whether you liked it or not. She had learned a great deal in the last half year and was too much the realist to stand against it, to wait for another ship that might pass in the night.

'I'm thinking,' she said, 'that it'll be grand for us to be together.'

'Us?' Jock said.

'All of us: Aunt Cissie, Clare, even old Belfer.'

'An' me?' Jock said.

She swung round suddenly and put her arms around him. He, like her brother, was a rock of a man, though thicker about the middle with the weight of the years upon him. But he was no fly-by-night, no fancy-dan. He would keep her in her place without being cruel, for he loved her, of that she was sure, and he would be patient with her because she was young.

'An' you, Jock,' Evie said. 'You especially.'

Then, going up on tiptoe, she kissed him.